LEAVING TIME

LEAVING
TIME

a novel

JODI
PICOULT

RANDOM HOUSE CANADA

PUBLISHED BY RANDOM HOUSE CANADA

www.penguinrandomhouse.ca

Random House Canada and colophon are registered trademarks.

Library and Archives Canada Cataloguing in Publication

Picoult, Jodi –, author
Leaving time / Jodi Picoult.

Issued in print and electronic formats.

ISBN 978-0-345-81335-0
eBook ISBN 978-0-345-81337-4

I. Title.

PS3566.I372L42 2014   813'.54   C2014-901529-1

Jacket design: Gabrielle Bordwin
Jacket photograph: © David Jordan Williams
Book design by Susan Turner

Printed and bound in the United States of America

10 9 8 7 6 5 4 3 2 1

Penguin
Random House
RANDOM HOUSE CANADA

FOR JOAN COLLISON

A true friend will walk hundreds of miles with you,
in rain, snow, sleet, and hail.

PROLOGUE

JENNA

Some people used to believe that there was an elephant grave-yard—a place that sick and old elephants would travel to to die. They'd slip away from their herds and would lumber across the dusty landscape, like the titans we read about in seventh grade in Greek Mythology. Legend said the spot was in Saudi Arabia; that it was the source of a supernatural force; that it contained a book of spells to bring about world peace.

Explorers who went in search of the graveyard would follow dying elephants for weeks, only to realize they'd been led in circles. Some of these voyagers disappeared completely. Some could not remember what they had seen, and not a single explorer who claimed to have found the graveyard could ever locate it again.

Here's why: The elephant graveyard is a myth.

True, researchers have found groups of elephants that died in the same vicinity, many over a short period of time. My mother, Alice, would have said there's a perfectly logical reason for a mass burial site: a group of elephants who died all at once due to lack of food or water; a slaughter by ivory hunters. It's even possible that the strong winds in Africa could blow a scattering of bones into a concentrated pile. *Jenna,* she would have told me, *there's an explanation for everything you see.*

There is plenty of information about elephants and death that is not fable but instead cold, hard science. My mother would have been able to tell me that, too. We would have sat, shoulder to shoulder, beneath the massive oak where Maura liked to shade herself, watching the elephant pick up acorns with her trunk and pitch them. My mother would rate each toss like an Olympic judge. *8.5 . . . 7.9. Ooh! A perfect 10.*

Maybe I would have listened. But maybe, too, I would have just closed my eyes. Maybe I would have tried to memorize the smell of bug spray on my mother's skin, or the way she absentmindedly braided my hair, tying it off on the end with a stalk of green grass.

Maybe the whole time I would have been wishing there really *was* an elephant graveyard, except not just for elephants. Because then I'd be able to find her.

ALICE

When I was nine—before I grew up and became a scientist—I thought I knew everything, or at least I wanted to know everything, and in my mind there was no difference between the two. At that age, I was obsessed with animals. I knew that a group of tigers was called a streak. I knew that dolphins were carnivores. I knew that giraffes had four stomachs and that the leg muscles of a locust were a thousand times more powerful than the same weight of human muscle. I knew that white polar bears had black skin beneath their fur, and that jellyfish had no brains. I knew all these facts from the Time-Life monthly animal fact cards that I had received as a birthday gift from my pseudo-stepfather, who had moved out a year ago and now lived in San Francisco with his best friend, Frank, who my mother called "the other woman" when she thought I wasn't listening.

Every month new cards arrived in the mail, and then one day, in October 1977, the best card of all arrived: the one about elephants. I cannot tell you why they were my favorite animals. Maybe it was my bedroom, with its green shag jungle carpet and the wallpaper border of cartoon pachyderms dancing across the walls. Maybe it was the fact that the first movie I'd ever seen, as a toddler, was *Dumbo*. Maybe it was because the silk lining inside my mother's fur coat, the one she had inherited from her own mother, was made from an Indian sari and printed with elephants.

From that Time-Life card, I learned the basics about elephants. They were the largest land animals on the planet, sometimes weighing more than six tons. They ate three to four hundred pounds of food each day. They had the longest pregnancy of any land mammal— twenty-two months. They lived in breeding herds, led by a female matriarch, often the oldest member of the group. She was the one who decided where the group went every day, when they took a rest, where they ate, and where they drank. Babies were raised and protected by all the female relatives in the herd, and traveled with them, but when males were about thirteen years old, they left—sometimes preferring to wander on their own and sometimes gathering with other males in a bull group.

But those were facts that *everyone* knew. I, on the other hand, became obsessed and dug a little deeper, trying to find out everything I could at the school library and from my teachers and books. So I also could tell you that elephants got sunburned, which is why they would toss dirt on their backs and roll in the mud. Their closest living relative was the rock hyrax, a tiny, furry thing that looked like a guinea pig. I knew that just like a human baby sucks its thumb to calm itself down, an elephant calf might sometimes suck its trunk. I knew that in 1916, in Erwin, Tennessee, an elephant named Mary was tried and hanged for murder.

In retrospect I am sure my mother got tired of hearing about elephants. Maybe that is why, one Saturday morning, she woke me before the sun came up and told me we were going on an adventure. There were no zoos near where we lived in Connecticut, but the Forest Park Zoo in Springfield, Massachusetts, had a real, live elephant— and we were going to see her.

To say I was excited would be an understatement. I peppered my mother with elephant jokes for hours:

What's beautiful, gray, and wears glass slippers? Cinderelephant.

Why are elephants wrinkled? They don't fit on the ironing board.

How do you get down from an elephant? You don't. You get down from a goose.

Why do elephants have trunks? Because they'd look funny with glove compartments.

When we got to the zoo, I raced along the paths until I found myself standing in front of Morganetta the elephant.

Who looked nothing like what I had imagined.

This was not the majestic animal featured on my Time-Life card, or in the books I had studied. For one thing, she was chained to a giant concrete block in the center of her enclosure, so that she couldn't walk very far in any direction. There were sores on her hind legs from the shackles. She was missing one eye, and she wouldn't look at me with the other. I was just another person who had come to stare at her, in her prison.

My mother was stunned by her condition, too. She flagged down a zookeeper, who said that Morganetta had once been in local parades, and had done stunts like competing against undergrads in a tug-o'-war at a nearby school, but that she had gotten unpredictable and violent in her old age. She'd lashed out at visitors with her trunk if they came too close to her cage. She had broken a caregiver's wrist.

I started to cry.

My mother bundled me back to the car for the four-hour drive home, although we had only been at the zoo for ten minutes.

"Can't we help her?" I asked.

This is how, at age nine, I became an elephant advocate. After a trip to the library, I sat down at my kitchen table, and I wrote to the mayor of Springfield, Massachusetts, asking him to give Morganetta more space, and more freedom.

He didn't just write me back. He sent his response to *The Boston Globe*, which published it, and then a reporter called to do a story on the nine-year-old who had convinced the mayor to move Morganetta into the much larger buffalo enclosure at the zoo. I was given a special Concerned Citizen award at my elementary school assembly. I was invited back to the zoo for the grand opening to cut the red ribbon with the mayor. Flashbulbs went off in my face, blinding me, as Morganetta roamed behind us. This time, she looked at me with her good eye. And I knew, I just *knew*, she was still miserable. The things that had happened to her—the chains and the shackles, the cage and the beatings, maybe even the memory of the moment she was taken out of Africa—all that was still with her in that buffalo enclosure, and it took up all the extra space.

For the record, Mayor Dimauro did continue to try to make life better for Morganetta. In 1979, after the demise of Forest Park's resident polar bear, the facility closed and Morganetta was moved to the Los Angeles Zoo. Her home there was much bigger. It had a pool, and toys, and two older elephants.

If I knew back then what I know now, I could have told the mayor that just sticking elephants in proximity with others does not mean they will form friendships. Elephants are as unique in their personalities as humans are, and just as you would not assume that two random humans would become close friends, you should not assume that two elephants will bond simply because they are both elephants. Morganetta continued to spiral deeper into depression, losing weight and deteriorating. Approximately one year after she arrived in L.A., she was found dead in the bottom of the enclosure's pool.

The moral of this story is that sometimes, you can attempt to make all the difference in the world, and it still is like trying to stem the tide with a sieve.

The moral of this story is that no matter how much we try, no matter how much we want it . . . some stories just don't have a happy ending.

PART I

How to explain my heroic courtesy? I feel
    that my body was inflated by a mischievous boy.

Once I was the size of a falcon, the size of a lion,
    once I was not the elephant I find I am.

My pelt sags, and my master scolds me for a botched
    trick. I practiced it all night in my tent, so I was

somewhat sleepy. People connect me with sadness
    and, often, rationality. Randall Jarrell compared me

to Wallace Stevens, the American poet. I can see it
    in the lumbering tercets, but in my mind

I am more like Eliot, a man of Europe, a man
    of cultivation. Anyone so ceremonious suffers

breakdowns. I do not like the spectacular experiments
    with balance, the high-wire act and cones.

We elephants are images of humility, as when we
    undertake our melancholy migrations to die.

Did you know, though, that elephants were taught
    to write the Greek alphabet with their hooves?

Worn out by suffering, we lie on our great backs,
    tossing grass up to heaven—as a distraction, not a prayer.

That's not humility you see on our long final journeys:
    it's procrastination. It hurts my heavy body to lie down.

—DAN CHIASSON, "The Elephant"

JENNA

When it comes to memory, I'm kind of a pro. I may only be thirteen, but I've studied it the way other kids my age devour fashion magazines. There's the kind of memory you have about the world, like knowing that stoves are hot and that if you don't wear shoes outside in the winter you'll get frostbite. There's the kind you get from your senses—that staring at the sun makes you squint and that worms aren't the best choice of meal. There are the dates you can recall from history class and spew back on your final exam, because they matter (or so I'm told) in the grand scheme of the universe. And there are personal details you remember, like the high spikes on a graph of your own life, which matter to nobody but yourself. Last year at school, my science teacher let me do a whole independent study on memory. Most of my teachers let me do independent studies, because they know I get bored in class and, frankly, I think they're a little scared that I know more than they do and they don't want to have to admit it.

My first memory is white at the edges, like a photo taken with too bright a flash. My mother is holding spun sugar on a cone, cotton candy. She raises her finger to her lips—*This is our secret*—and then tears off a tiny piece. When she touches it to my lips, the sugar dissolves. My tongue curls around her finger and sucks hard. *Iswidi*, she tells me. *Sweet*. This is not my bottle; it's not a taste I know, but it's a good one. Then she leans down and kisses my forehead. *Uswidi*, she says. *Sweetheart*.

I can't be more than nine months old.

This is pretty amazing, really, because most kids trace their first memories to somewhere between the ages of two and five. That doesn't mean that babies are little amnesiacs—they have memories long before they have language but, weirdly, can't access them once they start talking. Maybe the reason I remember the cotton candy episode is because my mother was speaking Xhosa, which isn't our language but one she picked up when she was working on her doctorate in South Africa. Or maybe the reason I have this random memory is as a trade-off my brain made—because I *can't* remember what I desperately wish I could: details of the night my mother disappeared.

My mother was a scientist, and for a span of time, she even studied memory. It was part of her work on post-traumatic stress and elephants. You know the old adage that elephants never forget? Well, it's fact. I could give you all my mother's data, if you want the proof. I've practically got it memorized, no pun intended. Her official published findings were that memory is linked to strong emotion, and that negative moments are like scribbling with permanent marker on the wall of the brain. But there's a fine line between a negative moment and a traumatic one. Negative moments get remembered. Traumatic ones get forgotten, or so warped that they are unrecognizable, or else they turn into the big, bleak, white *nothing* I get in my head when I try to focus on that night.

Here's what I know:

1. I was three.
2. My mother was found on the sanctuary property, unconscious, about a mile south of a dead body. This was in the police reports. She was taken to the hospital.
3. I am not mentioned in the police reports. Afterward, my grandmother took me to stay at her place, because my father was frantically dealing with a dead elephant caregiver and a wife who had been knocked out cold.

4. Sometime before dawn, my mother regained consciousness and vanished from the hospital without any staff seeing
her go.
5. I never saw her again.

Sometimes I think of my life as two train cars hitched together at
the moment of my mom's disappearance—but when I try to see how
they connect there's a jarring on the track that jerks my head back
around. I know that I used to be a girl whose hair was strawberry
blond, who ran around like a wild thing while my mother took endless
notes about the elephants. Now I'm a kid who is too serious for her
age and too smart for her own good. And yet as impressive as I am
with scientific statistics, I fail miserably when it comes to real-life
facts, like knowing that Wanelo is a website and not a hot new band.
If eighth grade is a microcosm of the social hierarchy of the human
adolescent (and to my mother, it certainly would have been), then
reciting fifty named elephant herds in the Tuli Block of Botswana
cannot compete with identifying all the members of One Direction.

It's not like I don't fit in at school because I'm the only kid without
a mother. There are lots of kids missing parents, or kids who don't
talk about their parents, or kids whose parents are now living with
new spouses and new kids. Still, I don't really have friends at school. I
sit at the lunch table on the far end, eating whatever my grandmother's packed me, while the cool girls—who, I swear to God, call themselves the Icicles—chatter about how they are going to grow up and
work for OPI and make up nail-polish color names based on famous
movies: Magent-lemen Prefer Blondes; A Fuchsia Good Men. Maybe
I've tried to join the conversation once or twice, but when I do, they
usually look at me as if they've smelled something bad coming from
my direction, their little button noses wrinkled, and then go back to
whatever they were talking about. I can't say I'm devastated by the
way I'm ignored. I guess I have more important things on my mind.

The memories on the other side of my mother's disappearance
are just as spotty. I can tell you about my new bedroom at my grandma's place, which had a big-girl bed—my first. There was a little

woven basket on the nightstand, which was inexplicably filled with pink packets of Sweet'N Low, although there was no coffeemaker around. Every night, even before I could count, I'd peek inside to make sure they were still there. I still do.

I can tell you about visiting my father, at the beginning. The halls at Hartwick House smelled like ammonia and pee, and even when my grandma urged me to talk to him and I climbed up on the bed, shivering at the thought of being so close to someone I recognized and didn't know at all, he didn't speak or move. I can describe how tears leaked out of his eyes as if it were a natural and expected phenomenon, the way a cold can of soda sweats on a summer day.

I remember the nightmares I had, which weren't really nightmares, but just me being awakened from a dead sleep by Maura's loud trumpeting. Even after my grandma came running into my room and explained to me that the matriarch elephant lived hundreds of miles away now, in a new sanctuary in Tennessee, I had this nagging sense that Maura was trying to tell me something, and that if I only spoke her language as well as my mother had, I'd understand.

All I have left of my mother is her research. I pore over her journals, because I know one day the words will rearrange themselves on a page and point me toward her. She taught me, even in absentia, that all good science starts with a hypothesis, which is just a hunch dressed up in fancy vocabulary. And my hunch is this: She would never have left me behind, not willingly.

If it's the last thing I do, I'm going to prove it.

When I wake up, Gertie is draped over my feet, a giant dog rug. She twitches, running after something she can only see in her dreams.

I know what *that* feels like.

I try to get out of bed without waking her, but she jumps up and barks at the closed door of my bedroom.

"Relax," I say, sinking my fingers into the thick fur at the ruff of her neck. She licks my cheek but doesn't relax at all. She keeps her eyes fixed on the bedroom door, as if she can see what's on the other side.

Which, given what I have planned for the day, is pretty ironic.

Gertie leaps off the bed, her wagging tail pounding the wall. I open the door and let her scramble downstairs, where my grandmother will let her out and feed her and start to cook breakfast for me.

Gertie came to my grandmother's house a year after I did. Before that, she had lived at the sanctuary and she was best friends with an elephant named Syrah. She'd spend every day at Syrah's side; and when Gertie got sick Syrah even stood guard over her, gently rubbing her with her trunk. It was not the first story of a dog and an elephant bonding, but it was a legendary one, written up in children's books and featured on the news. A famous photographer even shot a calendar of unlikely animal friendships and made Gertie Ms. July. So when Syrah was sent away after the sanctuary closed, Gertie was just as abandoned as I was. For months, no one knew what had happened to her. And then one day, when my grandmother answered the doorbell, there was an animal rescue officer asking if we knew this dog, which had been found in our neighborhood. She still had her collar, with her name embroidered on it. Gertie was skinny and flea-bitten, but she started licking my face. My grandmother let Gertie stay, probably because she thought it would help me adjust.

If we're going to be honest here—I have to tell you it didn't work. I've always been a loner, and I've never really felt like I belong here. I'm like one of those women who read Jane Austen obsessively and still hope that Mr. Darcy might show up at the door. Or the Civil War reenactors, who growl at each other on battlefields now spotted with baseball fields and park benches. I'm the princess in an ivory tower, except every brick is made of history, and I built this prison myself.

I did have *one* friend at school, once, who sort of understood. Chatham Clarke was the only person I ever told about my mother and how I was going to find her. Chatham lived with her aunt, because her mother was a drug addict and in jail; and she had never met her father. "It's noble," Chatham told me. "How much you want to see your mother." When I asked her what that meant, she told me about how once her aunt had taken her to the prison where her mom was serving her term; how she'd dressed up in a frilly skirt and those shoes that look like black mirrors. But her mother was gray and lifeless, her eyes dead and her teeth rotted out from the meth, and Chatham said that even though her mother said she wished she could give her a hug, she had never been so happy for something as she was for that wall of plastic between them in the visiting booth. She'd never gone back again.

Chatham was useful in a lot of ways—she took me to buy my first bra, because my grandmother hadn't thought to cover up a nonexistent bosom and (as Chatham said) no one over the age of ten who has to change in a school locker room should let the girls go free. She passed me notes in English class, crude stick-figure drawings of our teacher, who used too much self-tanner and smelled like cats. She linked arms with me as we walked down the hall, and every wildlife researcher will tell you that when it comes to survival in a hostile environment, a pack of two is infinitely safer than a pack of one.

One morning Chatham stopped coming to school. When I called her house no one answered. I biked over there to find a For Sale sign. I didn't believe that she'd leave without any word, especially since she knew that was what had freaked me out so much about my mom's disappearance, but it got harder and harder to defend her to myself as a week went by, and then two. When I started skipping homework assignments and failing tests, which wasn't my style at all, I was summoned to the school counselor's office. Ms. Sugarman was a thousand years old and had puppets in her office, so that kids who were too traumatized to say the word *vagina* could, I guess, put on a Punch and Judy show about where they'd been inappropriately touched. Anyway, I didn't think Ms. Sugarman could guide me out of a paper bag, much less through a broken friendship. When she asked me what I thought had happened to Chatham, I said I assumed she had been raptured. That I was Left Behind.

Wouldn't be the first time.

Ms. Sugarman didn't call me back into her office again, and if I was considered the oddball in school before, I was completely off-the-charts weird now.

My grandmother was puzzled by Chatham's vanishing act. "Without telling you?" she said at dinner. "That's not how you treat a friend." I didn't know how to explain to her that the whole time Chatham was my partner in crime, I was anticipating this. When someone leaves you once, you expect it to happen again. Eventually you stop getting close enough to people to let them become important to you, because then you don't notice when they drop out of your world. I know that sounds incredibly depressing for a thirteen-year-old, but it beats being forced to accept that the common denominator must be *you*.

I may not be able to change my future, but I'm sure as hell going to try to figure out my past.

So I have a morning ritual. Some people have coffee and read the paper; some people check Facebook; others straight-iron their hair or do a hundred sit-ups. Me, I pull on my clothes and then go to my computer. I spend a lot of time on the Internet, mostly at www.NamUs.gov, the official Department of Justice website for missing and unidentified persons. I check the Unidentified Persons database quickly, to make sure that no medical examiners have entered new information about a deceased woman Jane Doe. Then I check the Unclaimed Persons database, running through any additions to the list of people who have died but have no next of kin. Finally, I log in to the Missing Persons database and go right to my mom's entry.

Status: Missing
First name: Alice
Middle name: Kingston
Last name: Metcalf
Nickname/Alias: None
Date LKA: July 16, 2004, 11:45 P.M.
Age LKA: 36
Age now: 46
Race: White
Sex: Female
Height: 65 inches

Weight: 125
City: Boone
State: NH
Circumstances: Alice Metcalf was a naturalist and researcher at the New England Elephant Sanctuary. She was found unconscious the evening of July 16, 2004, at approximately 10:00 P.M., one mile south of the body of a female sanctuary employee who had been trampled by an elephant. After being admitted to Mercy United Hospital in Boone Heights, NH, Alice regained consciousness at approximately 11:00 P.M. She was last seen by a nurse checking her vitals at 11:45 P.M.

Nothing's changed on the profile. I know, because I am the one who wrote it.

There's another page about my mother's hair color (red) and eye color (green); about whether she had any scars or deformities or tattoos or artificial limbs that could be used to identify her (no). There's a page that lists the clothing she was wearing when she disappeared, but I had to leave that blank, because I don't know. There's an empty page about possible transportation methods and another about dental records and one for her DNA sample. There's a picture of her, too, that I scanned from the only photo in the house my grandma hasn't squirreled away in the attic—a close-up of my mother holding me in her arms, in front of Maura the elephant.

Then there's a page for the police contacts. One of them, Donny Boylan, retired and moved to Florida and has Alzheimer's (you'd be amazed at what you can learn from Google). The other, Virgil Stanhope, was last listed in a police newsletter for being promoted to detective at a ceremony on October 13, 2004. I know, from my digital sleuthing, that he is no longer employed by the Boone Police Department. Aside from that, it appears he has disappeared off the face of the earth.

It's not nearly as uncommon as you think.

There are entire families whose homes were abandoned with television sets blaring, kettles boiling, toys strewn across the floor; families whose vans were found in empty parking lots or sunk in local ponds, and yet no bodies were ever located. There are college girls who went missing after they wrote their numbers down on napkins for men at bars. There are grandfathers who wandered into the woods and were never heard from again. There are babies who were kissed good night in their cribs, and gone before the light of morning. There are mothers who wrote out grocery lists, got in their cars, but never came home from the Stop & Shop.

"Jenna!" My grandmother's voice interrupts me. "I'm not running a restaurant!"

I shut down my computer and head out of my bedroom. On second thought, I reach into my lingerie drawer and pull a delicate blue scarf out of its recesses. It doesn't work at all with my jean shorts and tank top, but I loop it around my neck, hurry downstairs, and climb onto one of the counter stools.

"It's not like I have nothing better to do than wait on you hand and foot," my grandmother says, her back to me as she flips a pancake in the skillet.

My grandmother is not the TV grandmother, a cuddly, white-haired cherub. She works as a meter maid for the local parking enforcement office, and I can count on one hand the number of times I've seen her smile.

I wish I could talk to her about my mom. I mean, she has all the memories I don't—because she lived with my mother for eighteen years, while I, on the other hand, had a measly three. I wish I had the kind of grandmother who showed me pictures of my missing mom when I was little, or baked a cake on her birthday, instead of just encouraging me to seal my feelings inside a little box.

Don't get me wrong—I love my grandmother. She comes to hear me sing in school chorus concerts, and she cooks vegetarian for me even though she likes meat; she lets me watch R-rated movies because (as she says) there's nothing in them I won't see in the halls between classes. I love my grandmother. She just isn't my mom.

The lie I've told my grandma today is that I'm babysitting for the son of one of my favorite teachers—Mr. Allen, who taught me seventh-grade math. The kid's name is Carter, but I call him Birth Control, because he's the best argument ever against procreation.

He's the least attractive infant I've ever met. His head is enormous, and when he looks at me, I'm pretty sure he can read my mind.

My grandmother pivots, pancakes balanced on a spatula, and freezes when she sees the scarf around my neck. True, it doesn't match, but that's not why her mouth pinches tight. She shakes her head in silent judgment and smacks the spatula against my plate as she sets down the food.

"I felt like accessorizing," I lie.

My grandmother doesn't talk about my mother. If I'm empty inside because she vanished, then Grandma's full to bursting with anger. She can't forgive my mother for leaving—if that's what happened—and she can't accept the alternative—that my mother can't come back, because she's dead.

"Carter," my grandmother says, smoothly peeling back the conversation one layer. "Is that the baby who looks like an eggplant?"

"Not all of him. Just his forehead," I clarify. "Last time I sat for him, he screamed for three hours straight."

"Bring earplugs," my grandmother suggests. "Will you be home for dinner?"

"I'm not sure. But I'll see you later."

I tell her that every time she leaves. I tell her, because it's what we both need to hear. My grandmother puts the frying pan in the sink and picks up her purse. "Make sure you let Gertie out before you go," she instructs, and she's careful not to look at me or my mother's scarf as she passes.

I started actively searching for my mother when I was eleven. Before that, I missed her, but I didn't know what to do about it. My grandmother didn't want to go there, and my father—as far as I knew—had never reported my mother missing, because he was catatonic in a psychiatric hospital when it happened. I bugged him about it a few times, but since that usually triggered new meltdowns, I stopped bringing it up.

Then, one day at the dentist's office, I read an article in *People* magazine about a kid who was sixteen who got his mother's unsolved murder case reopened, and how the killer was brought to justice. I started to think that what I lacked in money and resources I could make up for in sheer determination, and that very afternoon, I decided to try. True, it could be a dead end, but no one else had succeeded in finding my mom. Then again, no one had looked as hard as I planned to look, either.

Mostly, I was dismissed or pitied by the people I approached. The Boone Police Department refused to help me, because (a) I was a minor working without my guardian's consent; (b) my mother's trail was stone cold ten years later; and (c) as far as they were convinced, the related murder case had been solved—it had been ruled an accidental death. The New England Elephant Sanctuary, of course, was completely disbanded, and the one person who could tell me more about what had happened to that caregiver who died—namely, my dad—wasn't even able to accurately give his own name or the day of the week, much less details about the incident that caused his psychotic break.

So I decided that I would take matters into my own hands. I tried to hire a private detective but learned quickly they don't do work pro bono, like some lawyers. That was when I started babysitting teachers' kids, with a plan to have enough money saved by the end of this summer to at least get someone interested. Then I started the process of becoming my own best investigator.

Almost every online search engine to find missing people costs money and requires a credit card, neither of which I had. But I did manage to find a how-to book, *So You Want to Be a PI?*, at a church rummage sale, and I spent several days memorizing the information in one chapter: "Finding Those Who Are Lost."

According to the book, there are three types of Missing People:

1. People who are not really missing but have lives and friends that don't include you. Old boyfriends and the college roommate you lost touch with—they're in this category.
2. People who are not really missing but don't want to be found. Deadbeat dads and mob witnesses, for example.

3. Everyone else. Like runaways and the kids on milk cartons who are stolen away by psychos in white vans with no windows.

The whole reason PIs can find someone is that lots of people know exactly where the Missing Person is. You just aren't one of them. You need to find someone who *is*.

People who disappear have their reasons. They might have committed insurance fraud or be hiding from the cops. They might have decided to start over. They might be up to their eyeballs in debt. They might have a secret they want no one to find out. According to *So You Want to Be a PI?*, the first question you need to ask yourself is: Does this person want to be found?

I have to admit, I don't know if I want to hear the answer to that. If my mother walked away willingly, then maybe all it would take is knowing I'm still searching—knowing that, after a decade, I haven't forgotten her—to make her come back to me. I sometimes think it would be easier for me to learn that my mother died ten years ago than to hear that she lived and chose not to return.

The book said that finding those who are lost is like doing a word jumble. You have all the clues, and you're trying to unscramble them to make an address. Data collection is the weapon of the private investigator, and facts are your friends. Name, birth date, social security number. Schools attended. Military service dates, employment history, known friends and relatives. The farther you cast your net, the more likely you are to catch someone who has had a conversation with the Missing Person about where he wished they could go on vacation, or what his dream job might be.

What do you do with these facts? Well, you start by using them to rule things out. The very first Web search I did, at age eleven, was to go to the Social Security Death Index database and search its index for my mother's name.

She was not listed as deceased, but that doesn't tell me enough. She could be alive, or she could be living under a different identity. She could be dead and unidentified, a Jane Doe.

She was not on Facebook or Twitter, or Classmates.com, or the alumni network of Vassar, her college. Then again, my mother was always so absorbed in her work and her elephants, I don't imagine she would have had much time for those distractions.

There were 367 Alice Metcalfs in online phone directories. I called two or three a week, so my grandmother wouldn't freak out when she saw the long-distance charges on the phone bill. I left a lot of messages. There was one very sweet old lady in Montana who wanted to pray for my mom, and another woman who worked as a producer at an L.A. news station who promised to bring the story to her boss as a human-interest piece, but none of the people I called were my mother.

The book had other suggestions, too: searching prison databases, trademark applications, even the genealogy records of the Church of Jesus Christ of Latter-day Saints. When I tried those, I didn't get any results. When I Googled "Alice Metcalf," I got too many—more than 1.6 million. So I narrowed it down by searching for "Alice Kingston Metcalf Elephant Grief," and got a listing of all her scholarly research, most of it done prior to 2004.

On the sixteenth page of the Google search, however, was an article in an online psychology blog about the grieving process of animals. Three paragraphs into it, Alice Metcalf was quoted as saying, "It's egotistical to think that humans have a monopoly on grief. There is considerable evidence that elephants mourn the loss of those they love." This was a tiny sound bite, unremarkable in many ways, something she'd said a hundred times before in other journals and scholarly papers.

But this blog entry was dated 2006.

Two years after she disappeared.

Although I've searched the Internet for a year, I have not found any other proof of my mother's existence. I don't know if the date on the online article was a typo, if they were quoting my mother from years earlier, or if my mother—apparently alive and well in 2006—is still alive and well.

I just know I found it, and that's a start.

. . .

In the spirit of leaving no stone unturned, I haven't limited my search to the suggestions in *So You Want to Be a PI?* I posted on missing persons Listservs. I once volunteered at a carnival to be a hypnotist's subject in front of a crowd of people eating corn dogs and blooming onions, hoping he'd release the memories jammed inside me, but all he told me was that, in a past life, I was a scullery maid at a duke's palace. I went to a free seminar on dream lucidity at the library, figuring I could transfer some of those skills to my stubborn locked mind, yet it turned out to be all about journaling and not much else.

Today, for the first time, I'm going to a psychic.

There are a few reasons I haven't been before. First, I didn't have enough money. Second, I didn't have any idea where to find a reputable one. Third, it wasn't very scientific, and if my mother, in absentia, had taught me anything, it was to believe cold, hard facts and data. But then two days ago, when I was restacking my mother's notebooks, a bookmark fell out of one.

It wasn't a bookmark, really. It was a dollar, origami-folded in the shape of an elephant.

All of a sudden, I could remember my mother with her hands flying over a bill, creasing and folding, flipping and reversing, until I stopped my toddler crying and stared, riveted, by the tiny toy she had made me.

I had touched the little elephant as if I expected it to disappear in a puff of smoke. And then my eye fell on the open page of the journal, a paragraph that suddenly stuck out like it was written in neon:

> I always get the funniest expressions from colleagues when I tell them that the best scientists understand that 2–3 percent of whatever it is they are studying is simply not quantifiable—it may be magic or aliens or random variance, none of which can be truly ruled out. If we are to be honest as scientists . . . we must admit there may be a few things that we are not supposed to know.

I took that as a sign.

Everyone else on the planet would rather look at a folded master-piece than the original flat piece of paper, but not me. Me, I had to start from the beginning. So I spent hours gingerly unfolding my mother's handiwork, pretending I could still feel the heat of her fingertips on the bill. I went step by step, as if I were performing surgery, until I could refold the dollar the way she had; until I had a small herd of six new tiny green elephants marching across my desk. I kept testing myself all day, too, to make sure I had not forgotten, and every time I succeeded I flushed with pride. I fell asleep that night picturing a dramatic, movie-of-the-week moment when I finally found my missing mother and she didn't know it was me, until I fashioned a dollar bill into an elephant in front of her eyes. And then she hugged me. And did not let go.

You'd be surprised at how many psychics are listed in the local yellow pages. New Age Spirit Guides, Psychic Advice from Laurel, Pagan Priestess Tarot Readings, Readings by Kate Kimmel, The Phoenix Rising—Advice on Love, Wealth, Prosperity.

Second Sight by Serenity, Cumberland Street, Boone.

Serenity didn't have a big ad or a 1-800 number or a last name, but she was within biking distance of my house, and she was the only one who promised to do a reading for the bargain price of ten dollars.

Cumberland Street is in a part of town that my grandmother always tells me to stay away from. It's basically an alley with a bankrupt convenience store that's been boarded up, and a hole-in-the-wall bar. Two wooden placards sit on the sidewalk, one advertising two-dollar shots before 5:00 P.M. and another, which reads: TAROT, $10, 14R.

What is 14R? An age requirement? A bra size?

I'm nervous about leaving my bike on the street, since I don't have a lock for it—I never have to lock it up at school or on Main Street or anywhere else I normally go—so I haul it into the corridor to the left of the bar entrance and drag it up the stairs, which smell like beer and sweat. At the top is a small foyer. One door is labeled 14R and has a sign on the front: READINGS BY SERENITY.

The foyer walls are covered with peeling velveteen wallpaper. Yellow stains bloom on the ceiling, and it smells like too much potpourri. There's a rickety side table propped up on a phone book for balance. On it is a china dish filled with business cards: SERENITY JONES, PSYCHIC.

There's not much room for me and a bike in the little foyer. I jostle it in a stilted half circle, trying to lean it against the wall.

I can hear the muffled voices of two women on the other side of the interior door. I'm not sure if I'm supposed to knock, to tell Serenity I'm here. Then I realize that if she is any good at her job, she must already know.

Just in case, though, I cough. Loudly.

With the bike frame balanced against my hip, I press my ear against the door.

You're troubled by a very big decision.

There is a gasp, a second voice. *How did you know?*

You have serious doubts that what you decide is going to be the right path.

The other voice, again: *It's been so hard, without Bert.*

He's here now. And he wants you to know that you can trust your heart.

There is a pause. *That doesn't sound like Bert.*

Of course not. That was someone else *who's watching over you.*

Auntie Louise?

Yes! She says you were always her favorite.

I can't help it; I snort. *Way to recover, Serenity,* I think.

Maybe she's heard me laugh, because there's no more conversation coming from the other side of the door. I lean closer to listen more carefully, and knock the bike off balance. Stumbling to keep my footing, I trip over my mother's scarf, which has unraveled. The bicycle—and I—crash into the little table, and the bowl falls off and shatters.

The door is yanked open, and I look up from where I'm crouched in the pretzel of bike frame, trying to gather the pieces. "What's going on out here?"

Serenity Jones is tall, with a swirl of pink cotton-candy hair piled high on her head. Her lipstick matches her coiffure. I have this weird feeling that I've met her before. "Are you Serenity?"

"Who's asking?"

"Shouldn't you *know*?"

"I'm prescient, not omniscient. If I were omniscient this would be Park Avenue and I'd be squirreling my dividends away in the Caymans." Her voice sounds overused, like a couch with its springs busted. Then she notices the broken bits of china in my hand. "Are you *kidding* me? That was my grandmother's scrying bowl!"

I have no idea what a scrying bowl is. I just know I'm in deep trouble. "I'm sorry. It was an accident . . ."

"Do you have any idea how old this is? It's a family heirloom! Thank Baby Jesus my mother isn't alive to see this." She grabs for the pieces, fitting the edges together as if they might magically stick.

"I could try to fix it—"

"Unless you're a magician, I don't see that happening. My mother *and* my granny are both rolling in their graves, all because you don't have the sense God gave a weasel."

"If it was so precious, why did you just leave it sitting around in your entryway?"

"Why did *you* bring a bicycle into a room the size of a closet?"

"I thought it would get stolen if I left it in the hall," I say, getting to my feet. "Look, I'll pay for your bowl."

"Sugar, your Girl Scout cookie money can't cover the cost of an antique from 1858."

"I'm not selling Girl Scout cookies," I tell her. "I'm here for a reading."

That stops her in her tracks. "I don't do kids."

Don't or *won't*? "I'm older than I look." This is a fact. Everyone assumes I'm still in fifth grade, instead of eighth.

The woman who was inside having a reading suddenly is framed in the doorway, too. "Serenity? Are you all right?"

Serenity stumbles, tripping over the frame of my bike. "I'm fine." She smiles tightly at me. "I can't help you."

"I beg your pardon?" the client says.

"Not you, Mrs. Langham," Serenity answers, and then she mutters to me: "If you don't leave right now, I'll call the cops and press charges."

Maybe Mrs. Langham doesn't want a psychic who's mean to kids; maybe she just doesn't want to be around when the police come. For whatever reason, she looks at Serenity as if she is about to say something, but then edges past us both and bolts down the flight of stairs.

"Oh great," Serenity mutters. "Now you owe me for a priceless heirloom *and* the ten bucks I just lost."

"I'll pay double," I blurt out. I have sixty-eight dollars. It's every penny I've made this year from babysitting, and I'm saving it for a private eye. I'm not convinced Serenity is the real deal. But I'd be willing to part with twenty dollars to find out.

Her eyes glint when she hears that. "For you," she says, "I'll make an age exception." She opens the door wider, revealing a normal living room, with a couch and a coffee table and a television set. It looks like my grandmother's house, which is a little disappointing. Nothing about this screams *psychic*. "You got a *problem*?" she asks.

"I guess I was kind of expecting a crystal ball and a beaded curtain."

"You have to pay extra for those."

I look at her, because I'm not sure if she's kidding. She sits down heavily on the couch and gestures at a chair. "What's your name?"

"Jenna Metcalf."

"All right, Jenna," she says and sighs. "Let's get this over with." She hands me a ledger and asks me to put down my name, address, and phone number.

"How come?"

"Just in case I need to communicate with you afterward. If a spirit has a message, or whatnot."

I bet more likely it's to send me emails advertising 20 percent off my next reading, but I take the leather-bound book and sign in. My palms are sweating. Now that the moment's here, I'm having second thoughts. The worst-case scenario is that Serenity Jones turns out to be a hack, another dead end when it comes to the mystery of my mother.

No. The worst-case scenario is that Serenity Jones turns out to be a talented psychic, and I learn one of two things: that my mother willingly abandoned me, or that my mother's dead.

She takes the tarot deck and begins to shuffle it. "What I'm about to tell you during this reading might not make sense right now. But remember the information, because one day, you might hear something and realize what the spirits were trying to tell you today." She says this the same way flight attendants tell you how to buckle and release the latch on your seat belt. Then she hands the deck to me, to cut into three piles. "So what do you want to know? Who's got a crush on you? If you're going to get an A in English? Where you should apply to college?"

"I don't care about any of that." I hand the deck back, unbroken. "My mother disappeared ten years ago," I say, "and I want you to help me find her."

There is one passage in my mother's field research journals that I know by heart. Sometimes, when I am bored in class, I even write it in my own notebook, trying to replicate the loops of her handwriting.

It's from her time in Botswana, when she was a postdoc studying elephant grief in the Tuli Block, and she recorded the death of an elephant in the wild. This happened to be the calf of a fifteen-year-old female named Kagiso. Kagiso had given birth just after dawn, and the calf was either born dead or died very shortly afterward. This was not, according to my mother's notes, unusual for an elephant having her first calf. What was strange was how Kagiso reacted.

TUESDAY
0945 Kagiso standing beside calf in broad sunlight, in open clearing. Strokes its head and lifts its trunk. No movement from calf since 0635.
1152 Kagiso threatens Aviwe and Cokisa when the other females come to investigate body of calf.

1515 Kagiso continues to stand over body. Touches calf with her trunk. Tries to lift it.

WEDNESDAY
0636 Worried about Kagiso, who has not been to watering hole.
1042 Kagiso kicks brush over body of calf. Breaks off branches to use as cover.
1546 Brutally hot. Kagiso goes to watering hole and returns to remain in vicinity of calf.

THURSDAY
0656 Three lionesses approach; begin to drag off calf's carcass. Kagiso charges; they run east. Kagiso stands over body of calf, bellowing.
0820 Still bellowing.
1113 Kagiso remains standing over dead calf.
2102 Three lions feed on calf carcass. Kagiso nowhere in sight.

At the bottom of the page, my mother had written this:

Kagiso abandons body of her calf after keeping vigil for three days.
There is much documented research about how an elephant calf under the age of two will not survive if it's orphaned.
There's nothing written, yet, about what happens to the mother who loses her baby.

My mother did not know at the time she wrote this that she was already pregnant with me.

"I don't do missing people," Serenity says, in a voice that doesn't allow even a sliver of *but*.

"You don't do kids," I say, ticking one of my fingers. "You don't do missing people. What exactly *do* you do?"

She narrows her eyes. "You want energy alignment? No problem. Tarot? Step right up. Communicating with someone who's passed?

I'm your girl." She leans forward, so I understand, in no uncertain terms, that I've hit a brick wall. "But I do *not* do missing people."

"You're a psychic."

"Different psychics have different gifts," she says. "Precognition, aura reading, channeling spirits, telepathy. Just because I've been given a taste doesn't mean I get the whole smorgasbord."

"She vanished ten years ago," I continue, as if Serenity hasn't spoken. I wonder if I should tell her about the trampling, or the fact that my mother was brought to the hospital, and decide not to. I don't want to feed her the answers. "I was only three."

"Most missing people disappear because they want to," Serenity says.

"But not all," I reply. "She didn't leave me. I know it." I hesitate, unwinding my mother's scarf and pushing it toward her. "This belonged to her. Maybe that would help . . . ?"

Serenity doesn't touch it. "I never said I *couldn't* find her. I said I *wouldn't*."

In all the ways I've imagined this meeting going down, this was not one of them. "Why?" I ask, stunned. "Why wouldn't you want to help me, if you can?"

"Because I am not Mother Freaking Teresa!" she snaps. Her face turns tomato red; I wonder if she's seen her own imminent death by high blood pressure. "Excuse me," she says, and she disappears down a hallway. A moment later, I hear a faucet running.

She's gone for five minutes. Ten. I get up and start wandering around the living room. Arranged on the fireplace mantel are pictures of Serenity with George and Barbara Bush, with Cher, with the guy from *Zoolander*. It makes no sense to me. Why would someone who hobnobs with celebrities be hawking ten-dollar tarot readings in East Nowhere, New Hampshire?

When I hear the toilet flush I race back to the couch and sit down again, as if I've been there the whole time. Serenity returns, composed. Her pink bangs are damp, as if she's splashed water on her face. "I'm not going to charge you for my time today," she says, and I snort.

"I'm truly sorry to hear about your mother. Maybe someone else can tell you what you want to hear."

"Like who?"

"I have no idea. It's not like we all hang out at the Paranormal Café on Wednesday nights." She moves to the door, holding it wide open, my cue to leave. "If I hear of anyone who does that sort of thing, I'll be in touch."

I suspect this is a flat-out lie, spoken to get me the hell out of her living room. I step into the foyer and wrangle my bike upright. "If you won't find her for me," I say, "can you at least tell me if she's dead?"

I can't believe I've asked that until the words are hanging between us, like curtains that keep us from seeing each other clearly. For a second I think about grabbing my bike and running out the door before I have to hear the answer.

Serenity shudders as if I've hit her with a Taser. "She's not."

As she closes the door in my face, I wonder if this is a flat-out lie, too.

Instead of going back home, I bike past the outskirts of Boone, three miles down a dirt road, to the entrance of the Stark Nature Preserve, named after the Revolutionary War general who coined the state motto, "Live Free or Die." But ten years ago, before it was the Stark Nature Preserve, it was the New England Elephant Sanctuary, which had been founded by my father, Thomas Metcalf. Back then, it sprawled over two thousand acres, with a two-hundred-acre perimeter between the sanctuary and the nearest residential home. Now, more than half the acreage has become a strip mall, a Costco, and a housing development. The rest is kept in conservation by the state.

I park my bike and walk for twenty minutes, passing the birch forest and the lake, overgrown and weedy now, where the elephants would come daily for water. Finally, I reach my favorite spot, under a massive oak with arms twisted like a witch. Although most of the woodlands are blanketed with moss and ferns this time of the year, the ground under this tree has always been carpeted with bright purple mushrooms. It looks like the kind of place fairies would live, if they were real.

They're called *Laccaria amethystina*. I looked them up online. It seemed like something my mother would have done, if she'd seen them.

I sit down in the middle of the mushrooms. You'd think I'd crush the heads, but they give way to my weight. I stroke the underside of one, with its ridged accordion pleats. It feels like velvet and muscle at the same time, just like the tip of an elephant's trunk.

This was the spot where Maura had buried her calf, the only elephant ever born at the sanctuary. I was too young to remember it, but I've read about it in my mother's journals. Maura arrived at the sanctuary already pregnant, although the zoo that had shipped her off didn't know it at the time. She delivered nearly fifteen months after her arrival, and the calf was stillborn. Maura carried him to the spot beneath the oak and covered him with pine needles and branches. The next spring, the most beautiful violet mushrooms exploded there, where the calf's remains had eventually been formally buried by the sanctuary staff.

I take my cell phone out of my pocket. The only good thing about selling off half the sanctuary property is that now there is a huge cellular tower not too far away, and service is probably better here than in all the rest of New Hampshire. I open a browser and type: "Serenity Jones Psychic."

The first thing I read is her Wikipedia entry. *Serenity Jones (b. November 1, 1966) is an American psychic and medium. She appeared multiple times on* Good Morning America, *and had her own television show,* Serenity!, *where she did cold readings of the audience and also one-on-one readings with individuals, but specialized in missing persons cases.*

Missing persons cases? Are you *kidding* me?

She worked with various police departments and the FBI and claimed a success rate of 88 percent. However, her failed prediction about the kidnapped son of Senator John McCoy was widely reported in the media and led the family to press charges. Jones has not been in the public eye since 2007.

Is it possible that a famous medium—even a disgraced one—had dropped off the face of the earth and resurfaced a decade later near Boone, New Hampshire? Absolutely. If anyone was ever looking for a place to keep a low profile, it was in my hometown, where the most exciting thing to happen all year is the July Fourth Cow Plop Bingo tournament.

I scan a list of her public predictions.

In 1999, Jones told Thea Katanopoulis that her son Adam, who had been missing for seven years, was alive. In 2001 Adam was located, working on a merchant marine ship off the coast of Africa.

Jones accurately predicted the acquittal of O. J. Simpson and the great quake of 1989.

In 1998, Jones said the next presidential election would be postponed. Although the election itself in 2000 was not delayed, the official results were not reported for 36 days.

In 1998, Jones told the mother of missing college student Kerry Rashid that her daughter had been stabbed and DNA evidence would exonerate the man eventually convicted of the crime. In 2004, Orlando Ickes was freed as a result of the Innocence Project and his former roommate indicted for the crime instead.

In 2001, Jones told police that Chandra Levy's body would be found in a heavily wooded area on a slope. It was located the following year in Rock Creek Park, Maryland, on a steep incline. She also predicted that Thomas Quintanos IV, a NYC firefighter presumed dead after 9/11, was alive, and he was indeed pulled from the rubble five days after the attack on the World Trade Center.

On her television show in 2001, Jones led police on camera to the Pensacola, Florida, home of mail carrier Earlen O'Doule, locating a secret locked room in his basement and the presumed-dead Justine Fawker, who had been abducted eight years earlier at age 11.

On her television show in November 2003, Jones told Senator John McCoy and his wife that their abducted son was still alive and could be found at a bus terminal in Ocala, Florida. The boy's remains were located there, decomposing.

From there on, things had gone downhill for Serenity Jones.

In December 2003, Jones told the widow of a Navy SEAL she would give birth to a healthy boy. The woman miscarried fourteen days later.

In January 2004, Jones told Yolanda Rawls of Orem, Utah, that her missing five-year-old daughter, Velvet, had been brainwashed and was being raised by a Mormon family, touching off a wave of protests in Salt Lake City. Six months later Yolanda's boyfriend confessed to the girl's murder and led police to a shallow grave near the local dump.

In February 2004, Jones predicted that Jimmy Hoffa's remains would be discovered in the cement walls of a bomb cellar built by the Rockefeller family in Woodstock, Vermont. This proved incorrect.

In March 2004, Jones stated that Audrey Seiler, a University of Wisconsin–Madison student who went missing, was the victim of a serial killer and that a knife would be found with evidence on it. Seiler was found to have staged her own kidnapping in an attempt to get her boyfriend's attention.

In May 2007, she predicted that Madeleine McCann, who had disappeared while on vacation with her parents in Portugal, would be found by August. The case remains unsolved.

She hasn't made any public psychic predictions since that. From what I can see, *she* went missing.

No wonder she doesn't *do kids.*

Okay, she made one colossal public mistake in the McCoy case, but in her defense, she had been half right: They *did* find the missing boy. He just wasn't alive. It was bad luck that, after having a string of successes, her first failure involved a superfamous politician.

There are pictures of Serenity at the Grammys with Snoop Dogg and at the White House Correspondents' Dinner with George W. Bush. There's another photo of her in *US Weekly*'s Fashion Police section wearing a dress with two giant silk rosettes sewn over her boobs.

I click on my YouTube app and type in Serenity's name and the senator's. A video loads, showing Serenity on a television show set, with her ice cream swirl of hair, wearing a pink pantsuit just a few shades darker. Across from her on a purple couch is Senator McCoy, a guy with a jaw that could be used to measure right angles and a perfect glint of silver at his temples. His wife sits beside him, clutching his hand.

I'm not really into politics, but we studied Senator McCoy in school as an example of political failure. He'd been groomed for a presidential run, hanging out with the Kennedys in Hyannisport and giving a keynote speech at the Democratic National Convention. But then his seven-year-old son was abducted from his private school's playground.

In the clip, Serenity leans toward the politician. "Senator McCoy," she says, "I have had a *vision*."

Cut to a gospel choir on the set. "A vision!" they sing out, like musical punctuation.

"A vision of your little boy . . ." Serenity pauses. "Alive and well."

The senator's wife collapses into her husband's arms and sobs.

I wonder if she picked Senator McCoy on purpose; if she really had a vision of the kid, or just wanted the media hype to surround her, too.

The video jumps to the bus terminal in Ocala. There is Serenity, accompanying the McCoys into the building, heading in a zombie trance to a bunch of lockers near the men's room. There's Senator McCoy's wife, crying, *"Henry?"* as Serenity tells a policeman to open locker number 341. There's the stained suitcase, which is hauled out by the cop, as everyone else reels backward from the stench of the body inside.

For a moment, the camera tumbles and the video goes sideways. Then the cameraman pulls his shit together, in time to catch Serenity throwing up, Ginny McCoy fainting dead away, and Senator McCoy, the Democratic Party golden boy, yelling at him to stop filming, and punching him when he doesn't.

Serenity Jones hadn't just fallen from grace—she'd crashed and burned. The McCoys sued Serenity, who eventually settled. Senator McCoy was subsequently arrested twice on DUI convictions, re-signed from the Senate, and went somewhere to treat his "exhaustion." His wife died a year later from an overdose of sleeping pills. And Serenity quietly, quickly, became invisible.

The woman who'd royally screwed up with the McCoys was the same woman who'd also found dozens of kids who had disappeared. She was also the Serenity Jones who now resided in the seediest part of town and who was starved for cash. But had she lost her ability to find missing people . . . or had she always been faking it? Was she once *actually* psychic—or just lucky?

For all I know, paranormal talent is like riding a bike. For all I know, it comes back, if you just give it a try.

So in spite of the fact that I am pretty sure Serenity Jones does not ever want to see me on her doorstep again, I also know that finding my mother is exactly the sort of training wheels she needs.

ALICE

We've all heard the phrase before: *He's got a memory like an elephant.* As it turns out, this is not cliché but science.

I once saw an Asian elephant in Thailand who had been trained to do a trick. All the schoolchildren brought to meet him at the reserve where he was kept in captivity were told to sit in a line. Then they were asked to take off their shoes, and these shoes were jumbled into a pile. The mahout who worked with the elephant then instructed her to give the shoes back to the children. The elephant did, carefully weeding through the pile with her trunk and dropping the shoes that belonged to each child in his or her lap.

In Botswana, I saw a female elephant charge a helicopter three times; it held a vet who was going to dart her for a study. At the sanctuary, we had to request a no-fly zone, because medical helicopters passing overhead caused the elephants to bunch, pulling themselves into close proximity. The only helicopters some of these elephants had ever seen were the ones from which park rangers had shot their families with scoline fifty years earlier, during the culling.

There are anecdotes of elephants that have witnessed the death of a herd member at the hands of an ivory poacher, and then charged through a village at night, seeking out the individual who had been wielding the gun.

In the Amboseli ecosystem in Kenya, there are two tribes that have historically come into contact with the elephants: the Masai, who dress in red garments and use spears to hunt them; and the Kamba, who are farmers and have never hunted elephants. One study suggested elephants showed greater fear when they detected the scent of clothes worn previously by the Masai rather than the Kamba. They bunched, moved farther from the scent faster, and took longer to relax after identifying the scent of the Masai.

Mind you, in this study, the elephants never saw the cloth. They relied solely on olfactory clues, which could be attributed to each tribe's diet and pheromonal secretions (the Masai consume more animal products than the Kamba; the Kamba villages are known to have a strong smell of cattle). What is interesting is that elephants can accurately and reliably figure out who is friend and who is foe. Compare this to us humans, who still walk down dark alleys at night, fall for Ponzi schemes, and buy lemons from used-car salesmen.

I'd think, given all those examples, the question isn't whether elephants can remember. Maybe we need to ask: *What won't they forget?*

SERENITY

I was eight years old when I realized the world was full of people no one else could see. There was the boy who crawled beneath the jungle gym at my school, staring up my skirt when I swung on the monkey bars. There was the old black woman who smelled like lilies, who sat on the edge of my bed and sang me to sleep. Sometimes, when my mother and I were walking down a street, I felt like a salmon swimming upstream: It was that hard to keep myself from bumping into the hundreds of people coming at me.

My mama's great-grandmother was a full-blooded Iroquois shaman, and my father's mother read tea leaves for her coworkers on cigarette breaks at the cracker factory where she used to work. None of that talent filtered through the blood to my own parents, but my mama has all sorts of stories about me as a toddler, having the Gift. I'd tell her that Aunt Jeannie was on the phone. Five seconds later, the phone would ring. Or I'd insist on wearing my rain boots to preschool, even though it was a perfectly sunny day, and, sure enough, the heavens would open up in an unexpected downpour. My imaginary friends were not always children but also Civil War soldiers and Victorian dowagers and, once, a runaway slave named Spider with rope burns around his neck. Other kids at school found me strange and steered clear of me, so much so that my parents decided to move from New York to New Hampshire. They sat me down before my first day of second grade and said, "Serenity, if you don't want to get hurt, you're going to have to hide your Gift."

So I did. When I went into class and took a seat beside a girl, I didn't speak to her unless another student did first, so that I knew I wasn't the only one who could see her. When my teacher, Ms. De-Camp, picked up a pen that I knew was going to explode with ink all over her white blouse, I bit my lip and watched it happen instead of warning her. When the class gerbil escaped and I had a vision of it running across the principal's desk, I pushed the thought out of my head until I heard the shrieks coming from the main office.

I made friends, just like my parents said I would. One was a girl named Maureen, who invited me to her house to play with her Polly Pocket collection and who told me secrets, like that her older brother hid *Playboys* under his mattress and that her mother stored a shoe box full of cash behind a loose panel in her closet. So you can imagine how I felt the day that Maureen and I were on the playground swings and she challenged me to see who could jump off the swings the farthest, and I had a quick flash of her lying on the ground with ambulance lights in the background.

I wanted to tell her we shouldn't jump, but I also wanted to keep my best friend, who knew nothing about my Gift. So I stayed silent, and when Maureen counted to three and went sailing through the air, I stayed put on my swing and closed my eyes so that I wouldn't have to see her fall with her leg pinned beneath her, snapping clean in two.

My parents had said that, if I didn't hide my second sight, I'd get hurt. But it was better that I get hurt than someone else. After that, I promised myself that I'd always speak up if my Gift helped me see something coming, no matter what it cost me.

In this case, it was Maureen, who called me a freak and started hanging with the popular girls.

As I got older I got better at figuring out that not everyone who spoke to me was alive. I'd be talking to someone and would, peripherally, see a spirit cross behind. I got used to not paying attention, the same way most of you register the faces of the hundreds of people who cross your path daily, without actually looking at their features. I told my mother she needed to get her brakes checked before the light went on in the dashboard signaling something was wrong; I congratulated our neighbor on her pregnancy a week before the doctor told her she was expecting. I reported whatever information came to me without editing it or making a judgment call about whether or not I should speak up.

My Gift, however, was not all-encompassing. When I was twelve, the auto parts dealership my father owned burned to the ground. Two months later, he committed suicide, leaving my mother a rambling apology note, a picture of himself in an evening gown, and a mountain of gambling debts. I hadn't predicted any of these things, and I cannot tell you how many times since I've been asked why not. Let me tell you, no one wants to know the answer to that more than I do. But then again, I can't guess the Powerball numbers or tell you which stocks to follow. I didn't know about my father, and years later, I didn't foresee my mother's stroke, either. I'm a psychic, not the Wizard of Freaking Oz. I've replayed things in my head, wondering if I missed a sign, or if somebody on the other side didn't get through to me, or if I'd been too distracted by my French homework to notice. But over the years I've come to realize that maybe there are things I'm not supposed to know, and besides—I don't really *want* to see the whole landscape of the future. I mean, if I *could*, what's the point of living?

My mother and I resettled in Connecticut, where she got a job as a maid at a hotel and I dressed in black and dabbled in Wicca and survived high school. It was not until college that I started to really celebrate my Gift. I taught myself to read tarot and did readings for my sorority sisters. I subscribed to *Fate* magazine. Instead of my schoolbooks, I read about Nostradamus and Edgar Cayce. I wore Guatemalan scarves and gauzy skirts and burned incense in my dorm room. I met another student, Shanae, who was interested in the occult. Unlike me, she couldn't communicate with those who had passed, but she was an empath and would get sympathy stomachaches every time her roommate had her period. Together, we attempted scrying. We would set candles in front of us, sit down before a mirror, and gaze into it long enough to see our past lives. Shanae came from a long line of psychics, and it was she who told me that I should ask my spirit guides to introduce themselves; that her aunties and her grandma, who were both mediums, had spirit guides on the other side. And so I formally met Lucinda, the elderly black woman who used to sing me to sleep; and Desmond, a sassy gay man. They were with me all the time, pets sleeping at my feet that would wake up, attentive, when I called their names. From then on, I spoke to my spirit guides constantly, relying on them to help me navigate the next world, either by leading me or by leading others to me.

Desmond and Lucinda were the best of babysitters, letting me—a virtual toddler—explore the paranormal plane without getting hurt. They made sure I didn't encounter demons—spirits that had never been human. They steered me away from asking questions with answers I was not yet meant to know. They taught me to control my Gift, instead of letting it control *me*, by setting boundaries. Imagine what it would be like if the telephone woke you up every five minutes, all night long. That's what happens with spirits, if you don't set up parameters. They also explained that it was one thing to want to share my predictions as they came, but another to read someone unbidden. I've had it done to me by other psychics, and let me tell you, it's like having someone go through your underwear drawer when you're not home, or being in an elevator, unable to get away when someone invades your personal space.

I did readings for five dollars during the summer up at Old Orchard Beach in Maine. Then, after I graduated, I found clients through word of mouth, while supporting myself at various odd jobs. I was twenty-eight, working as a waitress at a local diner, when the Maine gubernatorial candidate came in for a photo op with his family. While the cameras were flashing on him and his wife with plates full of our signature blueberry pancakes, his little girl hopped up on one of the counter stools. "Boring, huh?" I said, and she nodded. She couldn't have been more than seven. "How about some hot chocolate?" As her hand brushed mine to take the mug, I felt the strongest jolt of *black* I'd ever felt; that's the only way I can describe it.

Now, this little girl didn't give permission to be read, and my spirit guides were broadcasting that loud and clear, telling me I had no right to intervene. But across the diner, her mother was smiling and waving for the cameras, and she didn't know what I did. When the candidate's wife ducked into the ladies' room, I followed. She held out her hand to shake, thinking I was another voter to charm. "This is going to sound crazy," I said, "but you need to get your daughter tested for leukemia."

The woman's smile froze. "Did Annie tell you about her growing pains? I'm sorry she bothered you, and I appreciate your concern, but her pediatrician said it's nothing to worry about." Then she walked away.

I told you so, Desmond sneered silently as, moments later, the candidate left with his entourage and his family. For a long moment, I stared down at the half-empty mug the little girl had left behind, before I dumped its contents into a bus tray. *That's the hard part, honey*, Lucinda told me. *Knowing what you know, and not being able to do a damn thing about it.*

A week later, the candidate's wife came back to the diner—alone, dressed in jeans instead of a pricey red wool suit. She made a beeline for me, where I was wiping down a table in a booth. "They found cancer," she whispered. "It wasn't even in Annie's blood yet. I made them do a bone marrow test. But because it's so early"—here she started to sob—"she has a good chance of surviving." She grabbed my arm. "How did you know?"

That might have been the end of it—a good psychic deed, a way for me to tell the ever-snarky Desmond *I told you so*—but the candidate's wife happened to be the sister of the producer of the *Cleo!* show. America loved Cleo, a talk-show host who had grown up in the projects of Washington Heights and was now one of the most recognizable women on the planet. When Cleo read a book, so did every woman in America. When she said she was giving away fuzzy bamboo bathrobes for Christmas gifts, the company's website crashed. When she asked a candidate for an interview, he won his election. And when she invited me onto the show to do a reading for her, my life changed overnight.

I told Cleo things that any idiot could have guessed: that she would become more successful, that *Forbes* would list her as the richest woman in the world that year, that her new production company would launch an Oscar winner. But then something crept into my head, and because she had given me permission, I blurted it out—even though I should have thought twice. "Your daughter is looking for you."

Cleo's best friend, who was part of the show that day, said, "Cleo doesn't have a daughter."

This was true; she was a single woman who'd never been linked to anyone in Hollywood. But tears welled in Cleo's eyes. "Actually, I do," she confessed.

It was one of the biggest news stories of the year: Cleo admitted to being date-raped as a sixteen-year-old, and sent to a convent in Puerto Rico, where the baby was born and put up for adoption. She launched a public search for the girl, who was now thirty-one, and they had a tearful television reunion. Cleo's ratings skyrocketed; she won an Emmy. And as a reward, her production company transformed me from diner waitress to celebrity psychic, and gave me my own syndicated show.

I had a special connection when it came to kids. Police departments invited me to go into the woods where the bodies of children had been found, to see if I could read anything about the murderer. I went into homes where children had been abducted, and tried to sense a trail for law enforcement to follow. I'd walk through crime scenes with blood spatter staining the protective booties I had to wear, and try to visualize what had happened. I'd ask Desmond and Lucinda if a missing child had crossed over yet. Unlike faux psychics who'd call in hotline tips as a way of garnering fame for themselves, I always waited for the cops to come to *me*. Sometimes the cases I pursued on my show were recent ones; sometimes they were cold. I had a remarkable accuracy rate, but then again, I could have told you when I was seven that I wasn't faking. At the same time, I started sleeping with a .38 under my pillow, and I invested in a complicated alarm system for my house. I hired a bodyguard named Felix, who was a cross between a Sub-Zero refrigerator and a pit bull. Using my Gift to help those who had lost loved ones put a target on my back; perps who knew I could point a finger at them could find me easily.

Mind you, I had my critics. The skeptics called me a fraud who bilked people out of money. Well, there *are* psychics who bilk people out of money. I call them the swamp witches, the faux psychics along the side of the road. Just like there are good lawyers and ambulance chasers, good doctors and quacks, there are good psychics and charlatans. The other, odder complaint came from those who berated me for taking a God-given talent and charging money for it. To them, I apologize for not wanting to break a couple of my favorite habits—namely, eating and living indoors. No one ever bitches to Serena Williams or Adele for capitalizing on *their* talent, do they? Mostly, I ignored what people said about me in the press. Engaging with haters is like rearranging pictures on the *Titanic*. What's the point?

So yes, I had detractors, but I also had fans. Thanks to them, I got to appreciate the finer things in life: Frette linens, a bungalow in Malibu, Moët & Chandon, Jennifer Aniston's cell number on speed dial. All of a sudden I wasn't just doing readings; I was scrutinizing Nielsen ratings. I stopped listening to Desmond when he told me I was being a media whore. The way I saw it, I was still helping people. Didn't I deserve a little something in return?

When Senator McCoy's boy was kidnapped during fall sweeps, I knew I had a once-in-a-lifetime chance to become *the* greatest psychic of all time. After all, what better endorsement for my Gift than a politician who was probably going to be president? I had visions of him creating a Department of Paranormal Affairs, with me at the head; of the cute little town house I'd buy in Georgetown. I just had to convince him—a man who lived every moment in the public eye—that he could gain something from me, too, other than the ridicule of his constituents.

He had already used every connection at his disposal to mount a nationwide search for his son, but nothing had turned up. I knew that the odds of the senator coming onto my TV show and letting me do a live reading were slim at best. So I used the weapons in my *own* arsenal: I contacted the wife of the Maine governor, whose daughter was now in remission. Whatever she said to Senator McCoy's wife worked, because his people called my people; and the rest, as they say, is history.

When I was little, and I couldn't trust myself to tell the difference between a spirit and a living being, I just assumed that anyone and everyone had something to say to me. When I was famous, I knew very well how to tell the difference between the two worlds, but I was too distracted to listen.

I should not have gotten so cocky. I should not have assumed that my spirit guides would come whenever I called. That day on the show, when I told the McCoys that I had a vision of their little boy alive and well, I lied.

I didn't have a vision of their boy. The only thing I was seeing was another Emmy.

I was used to Lucinda and Desmond covering my ass, and so when the McCoys sat across from me as the cameras rolled, I waited for them to tell me something about the kidnapping. Lucinda was the one who pushed Ocala into my head. Desmond, though, told her to keep her mouth shut, and after that, they said nothing. So I improvised, and told the McCoys what they—and America—wanted to hear.

And we all know how that turned out.

In the aftermath, I secluded myself. I did not turn on the TV or radio, where my critics were having a field day. I did not want to talk to my producers or to Cleo. I was humiliated, and worse, I had hurt a couple that was already devastated. I had given them the possibility of hope, and ripped it away.

I blamed Desmond. And when he finally showed his sorry spirit ass to me again, I told him to take Lucinda and go away, because I never wanted to speak to them again.

Be careful what you wish for.

Eventually, some other scandal took the place of the one I had created, and I went back to my TV show. But my spirit guides had done exactly what I'd asked, and I found myself on my own. I made psychic predictions, but they were overwhelmingly wrong. I lost confidence, and eventually I lost everything.

Aside from being a diner waitress, though, I was completely unqualified to do anything but be a psychic. And so I found myself in the position of those I'd once sneered at. I became a swamp witch, setting up tables at country fairs and posting flyers on local bulletin boards, hoping to attract the occasional desperate client.

It's been over a decade since I had a true, electrifying psychic thought, but I've still been able to scrape by, thanks to people like Mrs. Langham, who comes every week to try to connect with her dead husband, Bert. The reason she keeps returning is that, it turns out, I have a skill for faking readings just as much as I once had a skill for legitimately performing them. It's called cold reading, and it's all about body language, visual cues, and some good old-fashioned fishing. The basic premise is this: People who want a psychic reading are highly motivated to have it be successful, particularly if they're trying to connect with someone who's passed. They crave information as much as I want to be able to provide it. This is why a good cold reading says way more about the client than about the swamp witch performing it. I can throw out a whole stream of non sequiturs: *Aunt, the Spring, water-related, an S sound, Sarah or maybe Sally, and there's something about education? Books? Writing?* Chances are my client will react to at least one item in that list, trying desperately to make it significant to herself. The only supernatural power at work here is the ability of the average person to find meaning in random details. We are a race that sees the Virgin Mary in the cut stump of a tree, that can find God in the twist of a rainbow, that hears *Paulisdead* when a Beatles song is played backward. The same intricate human mind that makes sense of the nonsensical is the human mind that can believe a fake psychic.

So how do I play the game? Good swamp witches are good detectives. I pay attention to how the things I say affect the client—a dilation of pupils, an intake of breath. I plant clues with the words I choose. For example, I might say to Mrs. Langham, "Today I'm going to present a memory you're thinking of . . . ," and then I start talking about a holiday, and lo and behold, that turns out to be *exactly* what she's thinking about. The word *present* is already lurking in the back of her mind, so whether or not she realizes it, I've just cued her to think about a time she received a gift, which means she's remembering a birthday, or maybe Christmas. Just like that, it looks like I've read her mind.

I take note of flickers of disappointment when I say something that doesn't make sense to her, so I know to back off and head in another direction. I look at how she is dressed and how she speaks, and I make assumptions about her upbringing. I ask questions, and half the time, the client gives me the answer I'm looking for:

I'm getting a B . . . Did your grandfather's name begin with that letter?

No . . . Could it be a P? My grandfather's name was Paul.

And bingo.

If I don't get enough information from the client, I have two options. Either I can Go Positive—create a message from someone dead that anyone in their right mind would want to hear, such as *Your grandfather wants you to know that he's at peace, and he wants you to be at peace, too.* Or I can "Barnum" the client, with a comment that would apply to 99 percent of the population but that she is bound to interpret personally: *Your grandfather knows you like to make decisions carefully, but feels that occasionally you rush to judgment.* Then I sit back and let the client feed me more rope I can run with. You'd be surprised how people feel the need to fill in all the gaps in the conversation.

Does this make me a con man? I guess that's one way to look at it. I prefer to think of myself as Darwinian: I'm adapting, so that I can survive.

Today, however, has been an absolute disaster. I lost a good client, my grandmother's scrying bowl, and my composure—all within the past hour—thanks to a scrawny kid and her rusty bicycle. Jenna Metcalf was not, as she said, older than she looked—Christ, she probably still believed in the tooth fairy—but she was as powerful as a giant black hole, sucking me back into the nightmare of the McCoy scandal. *I don't do missing people,* I told her, and I meant it. It's one thing to fake a message from a deceased husband; it's another thing entirely to give false hope to someone who needs closure. You know where that kind of behavior gets you? Living above a bar in Crapville, NH, and spending every Thursday collecting unemployment benefits.

I like being a fraud. It's safer to make up what clients want to hear. That way they don't get hurt, and neither do I, when I find myself reaching into the next world and getting no response, just crushing frustration. In a way, I think it would have been easier if I'd never had a Gift. That way, I wouldn't know what I am missing.

And then along came someone who couldn't remember what she'd lost.

I don't know what it was about Jenna Metcalf that rattled me so badly. Maybe her eyes, which were a pale sea green under the shaggy red fringe of her hair—supernatural, arresting. Maybe the way her cuticles had been bitten down to the quick. Or maybe how she seemed to shrink, like Alice in Wonderland, when I told her I wouldn't help her. That's the only explanation I can offer as to why I answered when she asked if her mother was dead.

I wanted my psychic abilities back so badly in that moment that I tried; I tried in a way I'd given up trying years ago, because disappointment feels like slamming into a brick wall.

I closed my eyes and attempted to rebuild the bridge between me and my spirit guides, to hear anything—a whisper, a sneer, a hitch of breath.

Instead, there was utter silence.

And so, for Jenna Metcalf, I did exactly what I swore never to do again: I opened up that door of possibility, knowing damn well she'd step into the slice of sunshine it provided. I told her that her mother wasn't dead.

When what I *really* meant was: I have no idea.

When Jenna Metcalf leaves, I take a Xanax. If anything qualifies as a reason to break out the antianxiety medication, it's this—a girl who hasn't just made me think of the past but has cracked it over my head like a two-by-four. By three o'clock, I am blissfully unconscious on the couch.

I should tell you that I haven't dreamed in years. Dreaming is the closest the average human gets to the paranormal plane; it's the time when the mind lets down its guard and the walls get thin enough for there to be glimpses to the other side. That's why, after sleeping, so many people report a visit from someone who's passed. But not me, not since Desmond and Lucinda left.

Today, though, when I fall asleep, my mind is a kaleidoscope of color. I see a flag, whipping across my field of vision, but then realize it's not a flag—it's a blue scarf, wound around the neck of a woman whose face I can't see. She is lying on her back near a sugar maple, immobile, being trampled by an elephant. At second glance I realize maybe she *isn't* being trampled; the elephant is going out of its way to *not* step on her, lifting one of its back feet and moving it over the woman's body without touching it. As the elephant reaches out its trunk and tugs at the scarf, the woman doesn't move. The elephant's trunk strokes her cheek, her throat, her forehead, before slipping the scarf free and lifting it, so that the wind carries it off like a rumor.

The elephant reaches down for something leather-bound I cannot quite make out, which is tucked beneath the woman's hip—a book? An ID badge holder? I'm amazed at the dexterity the animal has, flipping it open. Then it places its trunk on the woman's chest again, almost like a stethoscope, before slipping silently into the forest.

I wake up with a start, disoriented and surprised to be thinking of elephants, wondering at the storm that still seems to be filling my head. But it's not thunder, it's someone banging on the front door.

I already know who it's going to be as I get up to open it.

"Before you freak out, I'm not here to try to convince you to find my mother," Jenna Metcalf announces, pushing past me into my apartment. "It's just that I left something behind. Something really important . . ."

I close the front door, rolling my eyes when I see that ridiculous bicycle parked in my foyer again. Jenna starts looking around the space where we had been sitting a few hours ago, ducking beneath the coffee table and poking around under the chairs.

"If I'd found something I would have contacted you—"

"I doubt it," she says. She starts opening up drawers where I keep my stamps, my secret stash of Oreos, and my take-out menus.

"Do you *mind*?" I say.

But Jenna is ignoring me, her hand stuck between the cushions of the couch. "I *knew* it was here," she says with obvious relief, and like floss, she pulls out the blue scarf from my dream and winds it around her neck.

Seeing it, three-dimensional and close enough to touch, makes me feel a little less crazy—I had only been incorporating a scarf this kid had been wearing into my subconscious. But there's other information in that dream that makes no sense: the onion-skin wrinkles of an elephant's hide, the ballet of its trunk. Plus something else that I had not realized until this moment: The elephant had been checking to see if the woman was inhaling and exhaling. The animal had left— not because the woman had *stopped* breathing but because she still *was*.

I don't know how I know this, I just do.

My whole life, this is how I've defined the paranormal: can't understand it, can't explain it, can't deny it.

You cannot be a born psychic and not believe in the power of signs. Sometimes it's the traffic that makes you miss your flight, which winds up crashing into the Atlantic. Sometimes it's the single rose that blooms in a garden full of weeds. Or sometimes it's the girl you dismissed, who haunts your sleep.

"Sorry I bothered you," Jenna says. "Or whatever."

She is already halfway out the door when I hear my voice calling her name. "Jenna. This is probably crazy. But," I say, "was your mother in the circus or something? A zookeeper? I . . . I don't know why, but there's something important about elephants?"

I haven't had a true psychic thought in seven years. *Seven* years. I tell myself this one is coincidence, luck, or the aftereffects of the burrito I had for lunch.

When she turns around, her face is washed with an expression that's equal parts shock and wonder.

I know, in that moment, that she was meant to find me.

And that I am going to find her mother.

ALICE

There is no question that elephants understand death. They may not plan for it the way we do; they may not imagine elaborate afterlives like those in our religious doctrines. For them, grief is simpler, cleaner. It's all about loss.

Elephants are not particularly interested in the bones of other dead animals, just other elephants. Even if elephants come across the body of another elephant that has been long dead, its remains picked apart by hyenas and its skeleton scattered, they bunch and get tense. They approach the carcass as a group, and caress the bones with what can only be described as reverence. They stroke the dead elephant, touching it all over with their trunks and their back feet. They will smell it. They might pick up a tusk or a bone and carry it for a while. They will place even the tiniest bit of ivory under their feet and gently rock back and forth.

The naturalist George Adamson wrote of how, in the 1940s, he had to shoot a bull elephant that was breaking into government gardens in Kenya. He gave the meat to locals and moved the rest of the carcass a half mile from the village. That night, elephants discovered the carcass. They took the shoulder blade and the femur and brought the bones back to the spot where the elephant had been shot. In fact, all of the great elephant researchers have documented death rituals: Iain Douglas-Hamilton, Joyce Poole, Karen McComb, Lucy Baker, Cynthia Moss, Anthony Hall-Martin.

And me.

I once saw a herd of elephants walking in the reserve in Botswana when Bontle, their matriarch, went down. When the other elephants realized she was in distress, they attempted to lift her with their tusks, trying to get her to stand. When that didn't work, some of the young males mounted Bontle, again seeking to bring her back to consciousness. Her calf, Kgosi, who was about four at the time, put his trunk in her mouth, the way young elephants greet their mothers. The herd rumbled and the calf was making sounds that seemed like screams, but then they all got very quiet. At this point I realized she had died.

A few of the elephants moved toward the tree line, collecting leaves and branches, which they brought to cover Bontle. Others tossed dirt onto her body. The herd stood solemnly with Bontle's body for two and a half days, leaving only to get water or food, and then returning. Even years later, when her bones had been bleached and scattered, her massive skull caught in the crook of a dry riverbank, the herd would stop when passing by, standing in silence for a few minutes. Recently, I saw Kgosi—now a big young male of eight years—approach the skull and stick his trunk in the spot where Bontle's mouth would have been. Clearly these bones had general significance to him. But if you had seen it, I think you'd believe what I do: that he recognized that these particular bones had once been his mother.

JENNA

"Tell me again," I demand.

Serenity rolls her eyes. We've been sitting in her living room for an hour while she goes over the details of a ten-second dream she had about my mother. I know it's my mother because of the blue scarf, the elephant, and . . . well, because when you desperately want to believe something's true, you can convince yourself of just about anything.

True, Serenity might have Googled me the minute I walked out the door, and concocted some crazy trance with a pachyderm. But if you Google "Jenna Metcalf," it takes three pages before you get to any mention of my mother, and even then, it's an article that only references me as her three-year-old daughter. There are too many other Jenna Metcalfs who have done too much with their lives, and my mother's disappearance was too long ago. Also, Serenity didn't know I was coming back for the scarf I left behind.

Unless she *did*, which proves she's the real deal, right?

"Listen," Serenity says, "I can't tell you any more than what I already have."

"But my mother was breathing."

"*The woman* I dreamed about was breathing."

"Did she, like, gasp? Make any sounds?"

"No. She was just lying there. It's just . . . a sense I had."

"She's not dead," I murmur, more to myself than to Serenity, because I like the way the words fill me up with bubbles, like my blood has been carbonated. I know I should be angry or upset getting even this loose proof that my mother might still be alive—and that she's abandoned me for the past decade—but I'm too happy about the thought that if I play my cards right, I will see her again.

Then I can choose to hate her or I can ask her myself why she didn't come for me.

Or I can just crawl into her arms and suggest we start from scratch.

All of a sudden, my eyes widen. "Your dream. It's new evidence. If you tell the police what you told me, they'll reopen my mother's case."

"Honey, there isn't a detective in this country that's going to take the dream of a psychic and write it up as formal evidence. It's like asking the DA to call the Easter Bunny as a witness."

"But what if it actually happened? What if what you dreamed was just a piece of the past, looping itself into your head?"

"That's not how psychic information works. I once had a client come to me whose grandmother had passed. Her grandmother was a very strong presence, showing me the Great Wall, Tiananmen Square, Chairman Mao, fortune cookies. It was like she was doing everything in her power to get me to say China. So I asked if her grandma had visited China, or been into feng shui or something like that, and the client said that didn't sound like her grandma, it didn't make sense. Then Grandma showed me a rose. I told the client, and she said, *Gram was more of a wildflower girl.* So I'm thinking, China . . . rose. China . . . rose. And the client looks up and says to me, *Well, when she died, I inherited her whole set of china, and it's got a rose pattern.* Now, I have no idea why Grandma was showing me egg rolls instead of a gravy bowl with a rose on it. But that's what I mean—an elephant might not really be an elephant. It could be standing in for something else."

I look at her, confused. "But you've told me twice now that she's not dead."

Serenity hesitates. "Look, you should know that I don't exactly have a perfect track record."

I shrug. "Just because you screwed up once doesn't mean you'll screw up again."

She opens her mouth, but then snaps it shut.

"Back when you used to find missing people," I ask, "how did you do it?"

"I'd take a piece of clothing or a toy that belonged to the child. Then I'd go for a walk with the cops, trying to retrace the last few minutes where he was seen," Serenity says. "And sometimes I'd get . . . something."

"Like?"

"A flash in my head—of a street sign or type of landscape, or a make of car, or even once a goldfish bowl that turned out to be in the room where the kid was being locked up. But . . ." She shifts uneasily. "My psychic arteries may have hardened a little bit."

I don't know how a psychic could ever lose, if—as Serenity says—the information she gets might be a direct hit or might actually mean the exact opposite. It seems to me like the biggest career safety net *ever*. And yeah, maybe the elephant Serenity pictured is some metaphor for a huge obstacle my mother's faced; but as Freud would probably say, maybe it's really an elephant. There's only one way to find out. "You have a car, right?"

"Yeah . . . what? Why?"

I walk across the living room, wrapping my mother's scarf around my neck. Then I reach into one of the drawers I'd searched through when I first arrived, in which I'd seen a jangle of car keys. I toss them to Serenity and walk out the door of her apartment. I may not be psychic, but I know this much: She's too curious about what that dream means not to follow.

Serenity drives a yellow VW Bug from the 1980s that has rusted through in a lacy pattern behind the passenger door. My bike is pretzeled into the backseat. I direct her on back roads and state highways, getting lost only twice, because you can cut through alleyways on a bike that you can't cut through with a car. When we get to the Stark

Nature Preserve, we are the only car parked in the lot. "Now are you going to tell me why you dragged me here?" she asks.

"This used to be an elephant sanctuary," I tell her.

She looks out the window, as if she expects to still see one. "Here? In New Hampshire?"

I nod. "My dad was an animal behaviorist. He started the place, before he met my mom. Everyone thinks about elephants living in superhot places like Thailand and Africa, but they can adapt really well to cold, and even snow. When I was born he had seven elephants here that he'd rescued from zoos and circuses."

"Where are they now?"

"The Elephant Sanctuary in Tennessee took them all, when this place shut down." I look at the chain gate across the trailhead. "The land was sold back to the state. I was too little to remember when it happened." I open the passenger door and get out of the car, glancing back to make sure that Serenity is following me. "We have to walk the rest of the way."

Serenity looks down at her leopard-print flip-flops and then at the overgrown trail. "Where?"

"You tell me."

It takes Serenity a moment to understand what I'm asking her to do. "Oh no," she says. "*Hell* no." She pivots on her heel and starts back to the car.

I grab her arm. "You told me you haven't had a dream in years. But you dreamed about my mom. It's not going to hurt to see if you get a flash of something, is it?"

"Ten years isn't a cold case, it's an ice trail. There's nothing still here now that existed back when your mother disappeared."

"*I'm* here," I say.

Serenity's nostrils flare.

"I know the last thing you want is to prove that your dream didn't really mean anything at all," I say. "But it's kind of like winning the lottery, right? If you don't buy a ticket, you never even have a chance."

"I buy a goddamn ticket every week, and I've never won the

Powerball," Serenity mutters, but she steps over the chain and starts bushwhacking through the overgrown trail.

We walk in silence for a while, as insects zip past our heads and summer hums around us. Serenity walks with her hand brushing the browse; at one point she breaks off a leaf and sniffs it before moving on. "What are we looking for?" I whisper.

"I'll tell you when I know."

"It's just that we're practically off the grounds of the old sanctuary—"

"Do you or do you not want me to concentrate?" Serenity interrupts.

So I'm quiet for a few more minutes. But there's something that's been nagging at me for the whole car ride; it feels like a bone caught at the back of my throat. "Serenity?" I ask. "If my mother *wasn't* alive and you knew that . . . would you lie to me and tell me she was?"

She stops and turns, hands on her hips. "Sugar, I don't know you well enough to like you, much less protect your tender little teenage heart. I don't know why your mother isn't coming through to me. It could be because she's alive, not dead. Or it could be, like I said, because I'm rusty. But I promise you . . . if I get any sense that your mother's a spirit or even a ghost, I'll tell you the truth."

"A spirit *or* a ghost?"

"They're two different things. You can thank Hollywood for making everyone think they're one and the same." She looks over her shoulder at me. "When the body expires, it's over. Done. Elvis has left the building. But the soul is still intact. If you've led a decent life and you don't have a lot of regrets, you may hang around for a bit, but sooner or later you'll finish the transition."

"Transition?"

"Cross over. Go to Heaven. Whatever you want to call it. If you go through that process, you become a spirit. But let's say you've been a jerk in this lifetime and St. Peter or Jesus or Allah is going to judge your sorry ass and you'll probably go to Hell or some other bad real estate in the afterlife. Or maybe you're angry that you died young, or hell, maybe you don't even realize you're dead at all. For any one of those reasons, you might decide you aren't quite ready to leave this world, or be dead yet. The problem is—you *are* dead. There's no way around that. So you stay here, in limbo, as a ghost."

We are walking again, side by side, through the thick brush. "So if my mother's a spirit, she's gone . . . somewhere else?"

"That's right."

"And if she's a ghost, where is she?"

"Here. She's part of this world, but not the same part you're in." Serenity shakes her head. "How do I explain this . . ." she mutters, then snaps her fingers. "I once saw a documentary about Disney animators. There are all these transparent layers with different lines and colors that stack on top of each other to make a single Donald Duck or Goofy. I think it's like that, for ghosts. They're another layer, laid over our own world."

"How do you know all this?" I ask.

"It's just what I've been told," Serenity says. "It's the tip of the iceberg, from what I can tell."

I glance around, trying to see all these ghosts that must be hovering at the edges of my peripheral vision. Trying to feel my mother. Maybe it wouldn't be all that bad, if she was dead but still somewhere close by. "Would I know it? If she was a ghost and she tried to talk to me?"

"You ever hear the phone ring, and pick it up, and just get dead air? That could be a spirit, trying to tell you something. They're energy, so the easiest way for them to try to get your attention is by manipulating energy. Phone lines, computer glitches, turning lights on and off."

"Is that how they communicate with you?"

She hesitates. "For me, it's more like when I first tried contact lenses. I could never adjust, because I could tell there was something foreign in my eye that didn't belong. It wasn't uncomfortable—it just wasn't part of me. That's how it feels when I get information from the other side. Like an afterthought, except I'm not the one who's thought it."

"Kind of like you can't help but hear it?" I ask. "Like a song you can't stop humming?"

"I guess so."

"I used to think I saw my mom all the time," I say softly. "I'd be in a crowded place and I'd let go of my grandma's hand and start running toward her, but I was never able to catch up."

Serenity is staring at me with a strange look on her face. "Maybe you *are* psychic."

"Or maybe missing someone and finding someone have the same symptoms," I say.

Suddenly, she stops walking. "I'm feeling something," she says dramatically.

I look around, but all I see is a small hummock of tall grass, a few trees, and a delicate mobile of monarch butterflies turning slowly overhead. "We're nowhere near a sugar maple," I point out.

"Visions are like metaphors," Serenity explains.

"Which is pretty ironic, because that's a simile," I say.

"What?"

"Never mind." I pull the blue scarf off my neck. "Wouldn't it help if you held this?"

I pass it to her, but she rears away like it's going to give her the plague. The thing is, I've already let go of it, and a gust of wind carries it skyward, a tiny tornado spiraling further and further away.

"No!" I scream, and like a shot, I run after it. It dips and rises, teasing me, caught on air currents, but never coming close enough for me to catch. After a few minutes, the scarf gets tangled in the branches of a tree, about twenty feet up. I find a foothold and try to shimmy up the tree, but there are no knots on the bark for toeholds. Frustrated, I fall down hard on the ground, tears stinging my eyes.

There's so little I have of her.

"Here."

I find Serenity crouched beside me, her hands laced together to give me a leg up.

I scratch my cheek and my arms as I climb; my fingernails break as I dig them into the bark. But I manage to get high enough to reach the first notch made by a branch. I scrabble around with my hand and feel dirt and twigs, the abandoned nest of an enterprising bird.

The scarf is caught on something. I pull, finally tugging it free. Leaves and sticks rain down on me, on Serenity. And something more substantial smacks me on the forehead as it falls to the ground.

"What the hell is that?" I ask, as I wrap my mother's scarf around my neck again, and tie it tightly.

Serenity stares down at her palms, astounded. She hands me the thing that fell.

It's a cracked black leather wallet with its contents still intact: thirty-three dollars. An old-style MasterCard with those Venn diagram circles. And a New Hampshire driver's license, issued to Alice K. Metcalf.

It is evidence, real, honest to God evidence, and it's burning a hole in the pocket of my shorts. With this, I can prove that my mother's disappearance might not have been of her own free will. How far could she have gone without any money or credit cards?

"Do you know what this means?" I ask Serenity, who has gotten very quiet now that we've hiked back to her car and started driving into town. "The police can try to find her."

Serenity glances at me. "It's been ten years. It's not as easy as that."

"Yes, it is. New evidence equals a reopened case. Bam."

"You think that's what you want," she says. "But you may be surprised."

"Are you kidding me? This is what I've dreamed of for . . . well, as long as I can remember."

She purses her lips. "Every time I used to ask my spirit guides questions about what it was like in their world, they'd make it clear there were some things I wasn't supposed to know. I thought it was to protect some big cosmic secret about the afterlife . . . but eventually I realized it was to protect *me*."

"If I *don't* try to find her," I tell her, "then I'll spend my whole life wondering what would have happened if I did."

She stops at a red light. "And if you find her—"

"*When*," I correct.

"*When* you find her," Serenity says, "are you going to ask her why she didn't come looking for you all these years?" I don't answer, and she turns away. "All I'm saying is if you want answers, you better be ready to hear them."

I realize that she's driving right past the police station. "Hey, stop," I cry out, and she slams on the brakes. "We have to go in there and tell them what we found."

Serenity pulls over to the curb. "*We* don't have to do anything. I reported my vision to you. I even drove you all the way to that state park. And I'm happy you got what you wanted. But I personally do not need or want to become involved with the police."

"So that's it?" I say, stunned. "You throw information into someone else's life like a grenade and you walk away before it explodes?"

"Don't shoot the messenger."

I don't know why I'm surprised. I don't know Serenity Jones at all, and I shouldn't expect her to help me. But I'm sick and tired of people in my life abandoning me, and she will be just one more. So I do what is easiest, when I feel like I'm in danger of being left behind. I make sure I'm the one to walk away first. "No wonder people hated you," I say.

At that, her head snaps up.

"Thanks for the *vision*." I get out of the car, untangling my bike from the backseat. "Have a nice life."

I slam the door shut, park my bike, and walk up the granite steps of the police station. I approach the dispatcher inside the glass booth. She is maybe a few years older than me, a recent high school grad, and she is wearing a shapeless polo shirt with a police logo on the chest, and too much black eyeliner. On the computer screen behind her, I can see that she's been checking her Facebook page.

I clear my throat, which I know she can hear since there's a little grid in the glass that separates us. "Hello?" I say, but she keeps typing.

I knock on the glass, and her eyes flicker toward mine. I wave to get her attention.

The phone rings, and she turns away from me as if I don't matter at all and takes the call instead.

I swear—it's kids like her who are giving my generation a really bad reputation.

A second dispatcher walks toward me. She is a squat older woman, shaped like an apple, with a frizzy blond perm. She has a name tag, POLLY. "Can I help you?"

"Yes," I say, offering my most mature smile, because really, what adult is going to take a thirteen-year-old girl seriously when she says she wants to report a disappearance that happened a decade ago? "I'd like to talk to a detective."

"What's this about?"

"It's kind of complicated," I say. "Ten years ago an employee was killed at the old elephant sanctuary, and Virgil Stanhope was investigating it . . . and I . . . I really need to talk to him directly."

Polly purses her lips. "What's your name, sweetheart?"

"Jenna. Jenna Metcalf."

She takes off her head mike and walks into a back room I cannot see.

I scour the wall of missing people and deadbeat dads. If my mother's face had been plastered up there ten years ago, would I even be standing here now?

Polly reappears on my side of the glass wall, entering through a doorway that has a push-button combination lock on its knob. She leads me to a bank of chairs and sits me down. "I remember that case," she says to me.

"So you know Detective Stanhope? I realize he's not working here anymore, but I thought you might be able to tell me where he is now . . ."

"I'm not sure how you're going to get in touch with him." Polly puts her hand gently on my arm. "Virgil Stanhope is dead."

The residential facility where my father has lived since Everything Happened is only three miles from my grandmother's home, but I don't go there very often. It's depressing, because it (a) always smells like pee and (b) has cutouts of snowflakes or fireworks or jack-o'-lanterns taped to the windows as if the building houses kindergartners rather than the mentally ill.

The facility is called Hartwick House, which makes me think of a PBS drama and not the sad reality of superdrugged zombies watching the Food Network in the main lounge as aides bring around tiny cups of pills to keep them placid, or sandbag patients draped slack over the arms of wheelchairs as they sleep off ECT treatments. Most of the time when I go there, I don't feel scared—just hideously depressed to think that my dad, who used to be seen in conservation circles as something of a savior, couldn't manage to save himself.

Only once have I been really freaked out at Hartwick House. I was playing checkers with my dad in the lounge when a teenage girl with greasy ropes of hair burst through the double doors holding a kitchen knife. I have no idea where she got it; anything that could be considered a weapon—even shoelaces—is forbidden at Hartwick House or kept in cabinets with more security than Rikers Island. But anyway, she outsmarted the system, and she came through the double doors with her crazy gaze locked right on my face. Then she pulled back her arm, and the knife went flying through the air toward me.

I ducked. I slid, boneless, under the table. I covered my head with my arms and tried to make myself disappear while the burly aides tackled and sedated her, before carrying her back to her room.

You'd think a nurse or two would have come by to make sure I was okay, but they were occupied with the other residents, who were screaming and panicking in the aftermath. I was still shaking when I got enough courage to poke my head out and crawl into my seat again.

My father was not screaming or panicking. He was making his move. "King me," he said, as if nothing at all had happened.

It took me a while to realize that in his world—wherever that was—nothing *had* happened. And that I couldn't be mad at him for not caring if I had been carved up like a Thanksgiving turkey by a psycho teenager. You can't blame someone if they honestly don't understand that their reality isn't the same as yours.

Today, when I get to Hartwick House, my father isn't in the lounge. I find him sitting in his room, in front of the window. In his hands is a bright rainbow of embroidery floss, twisted into knots—and not for the first time I think that someone's enterprising idea of therapy is another person's frustrated hell. He glances up at me when I walk in, and he doesn't go ballistic—which is a good sign that today, he's not too agitated. I decide to use this to my advantage, and broach the topic of my mother.

I kneel in front of him, stilling his hands as they tug at the floss, tangling it even worse. "Dad," I say, as I draw the orange thread through the loops of the other colors and drape it over his left knee. "What do you think would happen, if we found her?"

He doesn't answer me.

I tug free the candy-apple-red thread. "I mean, what if she's the only reason we're broken?"

I let my hands grasp his, where they are clasped around two more strands of floss. "Why did you let her go?" I whisper, holding his gaze. "Why didn't you ever tell the police she was missing?"

My father had a breakdown, sure, but he's had moments of lucidity in the past ten years. Maybe no one would have taken him seriously if he said my mother was lost. But then again, maybe they *would* have.

Then, maybe, there would be a missing persons case to reopen. Then I wouldn't have to start from scratch, trying to get the police to investigate a disappearance that they didn't even know was a disappearance ten years ago, when it happened.

Suddenly the expression on my father's face changes. The frustration melts like foam where the ocean hits sand, and his eyes light up. They are the same color as mine, a too-green that makes people uneasy. "Alice?" he says. "Do you know how to do this?" He lifts the handful of thread.

"I'm not Alice," I tell him.

He shakes his head, confused.

I bite my lip, untangle the strands, and weave them to make a bracelet, a simple series of knots any day camper would know by heart. His hands flutter over mine like hummingbirds as I work. When I'm done, I unclip it from the safety pin that is fastened to his pants and tie it around his wrist, a bright bangle.

My father admires it. "You were always so good at this kind of thing," he says, smiling up at me.

That's when I realize why my father did not report my mother as a missing person. Maybe she wasn't missing, not to him. He's always been able to find her, in my face and my voice and my presence.

I wish it were that easy for me.

When I get home, my grandmother is watching *Wheel of Fortune* on television, calling out the answers before the contestants, and giving Vanna White fashion advice. "That belt makes you look like a tramp," she tells Vanna, and then she sees me in the doorway. "How did it go today?"

I falter a moment before realizing she is talking about babysitting, which of course I didn't really do. "It was okay," I lie.

"There are stuffed shells in the fridge if you want to reheat them," she says, and her gaze flits back to the screen. "Try an *F*, you stupid cow," she shouts.

I take advantage of this distraction and run upstairs with Gertie at my heels. She makes herself a nest on my bed out of pillows and turns in circles to get comfortable.

I don't know what to do. I've got information, and nowhere to go with it.

Reaching into my pocket, I take out the wad of bills I brought and peel one of the dollars off. I start folding it mindlessly, seamlessly, into an elephant, but I keep screwing up and finally crumple it into a ball and throw it on the floor. I keep seeing my father's hands making angry knots in the embroidery floss.

One of the original detectives who investigated the elephant sanctuary has Alzheimer's. The other is dead. But maybe it's not the end of the road. I'll just have to find a way to get the current detectives in the department to see that the department screwed up ten years ago, and should have considered my mother a missing person.

That should go over really well.

I turn on my laptop, and with a buzzy chord, it comes alive. I type in my password and open a search engine. "Virgil Stanhope," I type. "Death."

The first article that pops up is a notice about the ceremony where he was going to be made detective. There is a picture of him, too—sandy hair swept to the side, a big, fat, toothy grin, an Adam's apple that looks like the knob on a door. He looks goofy, young, but I guess ten years ago, that's just what he was.

I open a new window, log in to a public records database (which costs me $49.95 a year, FYI), and find the death notice of Virgil Stanhope. Tragically, it's dated the same day as his detective ceremony. I wonder if he got his badge and crashed in a car accident on the way home or, worse, on the way there. A life interrupted.

Well. I can relate to that.

I click on the link, but it won't open. Instead, I get a page stating there's a server error.

So I go back to my first search and rummage through the article descriptions until I find one that makes all the hair stand up on the back of my neck.

"Stanhope Investigations," I read. *Find the future in the past.*

It's a crappy slogan. But I still click to open the page in a new window.

Licensed. Domestic and marital relationship investigations. Surveillance services. Bail recovery agent. People searches. Child custody investigations. Accidental death investigations. Missing persons.

There is another button at the top: About Us.

Vic Stanhope is a licensed private investigator and former law enforcement officer and detective. He holds degrees in criminal justice and forensic science from the University of New Haven. He belongs to the International Association of Arson Investigators, the National Association of Bail Enforcement Agents, the National Association of Certified Investigators.

It could be a coincidence . . . if not for the tiny thumbnail photograph of Mr. Stanhope.

True, he looks older. And true, he has that buzz cut guys get when they're losing their hair and they try to channel Bruce Willis to look supertough. Yet his Adam's apple is still front and center in the photo, unmistakable.

I suppose Vic and Virgil could be twins. But still. I grab my cell phone and punch in the number on the screen.

Three rings later, I hear someone grab the receiver on the other end. It sounds like it falls to the floor with a run of static and curses, and then is recovered. "What."

"Is this Mr. Stanhope?" I whisper.

"Yeah," the voice growls.

"*Virgil* Stanhope?"

There is a pause. "Not anymore," the voice slurs, and he hangs up.

My pulse is racing. Either Virgil Stanhope is back from the dead or he never *was* dead.

Maybe he just wanted people to think that, so he could disappear.

And if this is the case—he's the perfect person to find my mother.

ALICE

Anyone who has ever seen elephants come across the bones of another individual would recognize the calling card of grief: the intense silence, the droop of the trunk and ears, the hesitant caresses, the sadness that seems to wrap the herd like a shroud when they encounter the remains of one of their own. But there's been some question as to whether elephants distinguish between the bones of elephants they knew well and those of elephants they did not.

Some of the research that has been coming out from my colleagues at Amboseli up in Kenya, where they have more than twenty-two hundred elephants that are recognized individually, has been intriguing. Taking one herd at a time, the researchers revealed several key items: a small bit of ivory, an elephant skull, and a block of wood. They did this experiment as one would have in a lab, carefully maintaining the presentation of the objects and recording the responses of the elephants to see how long they lingered at each item. Without a doubt, the tiny piece of ivory was the most intriguing to the elephants, followed by the skull and then the wood. They stroked the ivory, picked it up, carried it, rolled it beneath their hind feet.

Then the researchers presented the families with the skull of an elephant, the skull of a rhino, and the skull of a water buffalo. In this set of objects, the elephant skull was the item that interested the herd the most.

Finally, the researchers focused on three herds that had, in the past few years, suffered the death of their leader. The families were presented with the skulls of those three matriarchs.

You'd think that the elephants would have been most interested in the skull that belonged to the matriarch who had led their own herd. After all, the other parts of the controlled experiment clearly show that the elephants were capable of showing preference, instead of randomly examining the items out of general curiosity.

You'd think that, given the examples I had personally witnessed in Botswana of elephants who seemed deeply moved by the death of one of their own, and capable of remembering that death years later, they would have paid tribute to their own leader.

But that's not what happened. Instead, the Amboseli elephants were equally attracted to the three skulls. They may have known and lived with and even deeply mourned an individual elephant, but that behavior was not reflected in these results.

Although the study proves that elephants are fascinated by the bones of other elephants, some might say it also proves that an elephant experiencing grief for an individual must be a fiction. Some might say if the elephants did not distinguish between the skulls, the fact that one of those skulls was their own mother wasn't important.

But maybe it means that *all* mothers are.

VIRGIL

Every cop has one that got away.

For some, it becomes the stuff of legend, the story they tell at every department Christmas bash and when they have a few too many beers with the guys. It's the clue they didn't see that was right in front of their eyes, the file they couldn't bear to throw away, the case that was never closed. It's the nightmare they still have every now and then, from which they wake up sweaty and startled.

For the rest of us, it's the nightmare we're still living.

It's the face we see over our shoulder in the mirror. It's the person on the other end of the phone, when we hear that mysterious dead air. It's always having someone with us, even when we're alone.

It's knowing, every second of every day, that we failed.

Donny Boylan, the detective I was working with back then, told me once that *his* case was a domestic dispute call. He didn't slap cuffs on the husband, because the guy was a reputable business owner everyone knew and liked. He figured a warning was enough. Three hours after Donny left the house, the guy's wife was dead. Single gunshot wound to the head. Her name was Amanda, and she was six months pregnant at the time.

Donny used to call her his ghost, the case that haunted him for years. My ghost is named Alice Metcalf. She didn't die, like Amanda, as far as I know. She just disappeared, along with the truth about what happened ten years ago.

Sometimes, when I wake up after a bender, I have to squint because I'm pretty sure Alice is on the other side of my desk, in the spot where clients sit when they are asking me to take pictures of their wives in the act of cheating, or track down a deadbeat dad. I work alone, unless you count Jack Daniel's as an employee. My office is the size of a closet and smells of take-out Chinese and rug-cleaning fluid. I sleep on the couch here more often than I do at my apartment, but to my clients, I am Vic Stanhope, professional private investigator.

Until I wake up with my head throbbing and a tongue too thick for my mouth, an empty bottle next to me, and Alice staring me down. *Like hell you are*, she says to me.

"This," Donny Boylan said to me, ten years ago, as he popped another antacid tablet into his mouth. "This couldn't have happened two weeks from now?"

Donny was counting the days until his retirement. As I sat with him, he gave me a litany of all the things he did not need: paperwork from the chief, red lights, a rookie like me to train, the heat wave that was aggravating his eczema. He also did not need a call at 7:00 A.M. from the New England Elephant Sanctuary, reporting the death of one of their caregivers.

The victim was a forty-four-year-old long-term employee. "You have any idea what kind of shitstorm this is going to cause?" he asked. "You remember what it was like three years ago when the place opened?"

I did. I had just joined the force then. There were townspeople protesting the arrival of "bad" elephants—the ones who'd gotten kicked out of their zoos and circuses for acting out violently. Editorials every day chastised the planning board, which had allowed Thomas Metcalf to build his sanctuary, albeit with two concentric fences to keep the citizens safe from the animals.

Or vice versa.

Every day for the first three months of the sanctuary's existence a few of us were sent over to keep the peace at the sanctuary gates, where the protests were centered. It turned out to be a nonissue. The animals adapted quietly and the townspeople got used to having a sanctuary nearby, and there were no complications. Until that 7:00 A.M. phone call, anyway.

We were waiting inside a small office. There were seven shelves, each filled with binders labeled with the names of the elephants— Maura, Wanda, Syrah, Lilly, Olive, Dionne, Hester. There was a mess of papers on the desk, a stack of ledgers, three half-finished cups of coffee, and a paperweight shaped like a human heart. There were invoices for medication, and squash, and apples. I whistled, looking at the sum total of a bill for hay. "Holy crap," I said. "That could buy me a car."

Donny wasn't happy, but then, Donny was never happy. "What's taking so goddamn long?" he asked. We had been waiting now for almost two hours, while the staff tried to corral the seven elephants into the barn. Until then, our major crimes unit could not collect evidence inside the enclosure.

"You ever seen someone who's been trampled by an elephant?" I asked.

"You ever shut up?" Donny replied.

I was investigating a strange series of marks stretched along the wall, like hieroglyphs or something, when a man crashed into the office. He was skittish, nervous, his eyes frantic behind his glasses. "I can't believe this happened," he said. "This is a nightmare."

Donny stood up. "You must be Thomas Metcalf."

"Yes," the man said, distracted. "I'm sorry to keep you here so long. It's been crazy, trying to get the elephants secure. They're quite agitated. We've got six of them in the barn, and the seventh won't come close enough for us to entice her with food. But we've put up some temporary hot wire so that you can still get into the other side of the enclosure . . ." He led us out of the small building into sunshine so bright the world looked overexposed.

"Do you have any idea how the victim might have gotten into the enclosure?" Donny asked.

Metcalf blinked at him. "Nevvie? She's worked here since we opened. She's handled elephants for more than twenty years. She does our books, and she's also the night caregiver." He hesitated. "Was. She *was* the night caregiver." Suddenly he stopped walking and covered his face with his hands. "Oh God. This is all my fault."

Donny looked at me. "How so?" he asked.

"Elephants can sense tension. They must have been agitated."

"By the caregiver?"

Before he could respond, there was suddenly a bellow so loud that I jumped. It came from somewhere on the other side of the fence. The leaves of the trees rustled.

"Isn't it a little far-fetched to think that an animal the size of an elephant could sneak up on someone?" I asked.

Metcalf turned. "Have you ever seen an elephant stampede?" When I shook my head, he smiled grimly. "Hope that you never do."

We led a crew of major crimes unit investigators, walking for five minutes before we came to a small hill. As we crested it, I saw a man seated next to the body. He was a giant, with shoulders broad as a banquet table, strong enough to commit murder. His eyes were red-rimmed, puffy. He was black, and the victim was white. He was well over six feet tall, and certainly strong enough to overpower someone smaller. These were the sorts of things I noticed then, as an apprentice detective. He was cradling the victim's head in his lap.

The woman's skull had been crushed. Her shirt had been torn away from her, but for modesty she was draped with a sweatshirt. Her left leg was bent at an impossible angle, and bruises mottled her skin.

I walked a few feet away as the medical examiner crouched down to do his job. I didn't need a doc to tell me she was definitely dead.

"This is Gideon Cartwright," Metcalf said. "He's the one who found his mother-in-law . . ." He let his voice trail off.

I couldn't peg the man's age, but it couldn't have been more than ten years younger than the victim. Which meant the victim's daughter—his wife—had to be considerably younger than he was.

"I'm Detective Boylan." Donny knelt beside the man. "Were you here when this happened?"

"No. She was the night caregiver; she was out here alone last night," he said, his voice breaking. "It should have been me."

"You work here, too?" Donny asked.

The MCU drones had blanketed the area like a swarm of bees. They were photographing the body and trying to limit the area of their investigation. The problem was, this was an outdoor crime scene with no solid boundaries. Who knew how far the woman had been chased by the elephant that ran her down? Who knew if there were any clues that could point to the moment of death? There was a deep hole about twenty yards away, and I could see human footprints on the edge. There may have been shreds of trace evidence caught in the trees. But mostly there were leaves and grass and dirt and elephant dung and flies and nature. God only knew how much of that was important to the crime scene, and how much of it was business as usual.

The medical examiner directed two of his agents to put the body in a bag and approached us. "Let me guess," Donny said. "Cause of death: trampling?"

"Well, there was certainly trampling. But I don't know if that was the cause of death. Skull's split in half. Could have happened before the trampling, or as a result of it."

I realized, too late, that Gideon was listening to every word.

"No no no," Metcalf was suddenly shouting. "You can't put that there. It's a hazard for the elephants." He pointed to the crime scene tape being staked out over a vast square by the MCU guys.

Donny squinted. "The elephants aren't getting back in here anytime soon."

"I beg your pardon? I never said that you could take over the property. This is a natural protected habitat—"

"And a woman was killed in it."

"It was an accident," Metcalf said. "I will not let you affect the daily routine of the elephants here—"

"Unfortunately, Dr. Metcalf, you don't get to make that choice."

A muscle ticked in his jaw. "How long will it take?"

I could see Donny losing patience. "I can't really say. But in the meantime Lieutenant Stanhope and I will need to speak to everyone who interacts with the elephants."

"There are four of us. Gideon, Nevvie, me, and Alice. My wife." Those last words were directed right at Gideon.

"Where's Alice?" Donny asked.

Metcalf stared at Gideon. "I assumed she was with you."

His face was twisted with grief. "I haven't seen her since last night."

"Well, neither have I." The blood drained from Metcalf's face. "If Alice is gone, who has my daughter?"

I am pretty certain that my current landlady, Abigail Chivers, is two hundred years old, give or take a few months. Seriously, you'd think so, too, if you met her. I've never seen her wearing anything but a black dress with a brooch at her throat, her white hair scraped into a bun, and her pinched mouth shrinking even tighter whenever she pokes her head into my office and starts opening and slamming shut cabinets. She raps her cane on the desk six inches from my head. "Victor," she says. "I can smell the work of the devil."

"Really?" I lift my head off the desk and run my tongue over my teeth, which feel furry. "All I can smell is cheap booze."

"I will not condone something illegal—"

"Hasn't been illegal in a century, Abby." I sigh. We've had this fight dozens of times. Have I mentioned that in addition to being a teetotaler, Abigail is also apparently in the throes of dementia, and she is just as likely to call me President Lincoln as she is to call me Victor? Of course, this works to my advantage, too. Like when she tells me I'm late on the rent and I lie and say I've already paid for the month.

For an old gal, she's awfully spry. She whacks her cane on the cushions of the couch and even looks in the microwave. "Where is it?"

"Where's what?" I ask, playing dumb.

"Satan's tears. Barley vinegar. Joy juice. I know you're hiding it somewhere."

I offer her my most innocent smile. "Would I do something like that?"

"Victor," she says, "do not lie to me."

I cross my heart. "Swear to God, there is no booze in this room." I get to my feet and stagger to the tiny bathroom attached to my office space. It is big enough for a toilet, a sink, and a vacuum cleaner. I close the door behind me, take a piss, and then open the lid of the toilet tank. Fishing out the bottle I started last night, I take a long, healthy swig of whiskey, and just like that, the dull throb of my head starts to fade.

I put the bottle back in its hiding place, flush, and open the door. Abby is still hovering. I haven't lied to her, just massaged the truth. It's what I was taught to do a lifetime ago, when I was training to be a detective. "Now, where were we?" I ask, and just then, the telephone rings.

"Drinking," she accuses.

"Abby, I'm shocked," I say smoothly. "I didn't think you indulged." I steer her toward the door, the phone still ringing. "How about we finish this later? Over a nightcap, maybe?" I push her outside as she protests, then grab for the phone and fumble it. "What?" I snap into the receiver.

"Is this Mr. Stanhope?"

In spite of the quick swig of whiskey, my temples feel like they're in a vise again. "Yeah."

"*Virgil* Stanhope?"

When a year passed, and then two, and then five, I started to realize what Donny had told me was true: Once a cop has a ghost, that ghost is there to stay. I couldn't get rid of Alice Metcalf. So instead, I got rid of Virgil Stanhope. I thought, stupidly, that if I started over, I could start fresh—free from guilt and questions. My dad had been a veteran, a small-town mayor, an all-around upstanding man. I borrowed his name, thinking some of his traits might rub off on me. I figured maybe I could become the kind of guy people trusted, instead of the one who'd fucked up royally.

Until this moment, no one had questioned me.

"Not anymore," I mutter, and I slam down the receiver. I stand in the middle of my office, pressing my hands to my aching head, but I can still hear her. I can hear her even when I go back into the bathroom and pull the bottle of whiskey out of the toilet tank again, even when I drink it down to its last drop.

I never actually heard Alice Metcalf speak. She was unconscious when I found her, unconscious when I went to the hospital to see her, and then she was gone. But in my imagination, when she's sitting across from me passing judgment, she sounds exactly like the voice that was just on the other end of the phone.

We had been sent to the sanctuary for a reported death that wasn't suspicious at the time of the initial call to the police. And in fact, there was no reason on that morning ten years ago to assume that Alice Metcalf or her child was missing. They could have been out grocery shopping, blissfully unaware of the goings-on at the sanctuary. They could have been in the local park. Alice's cell phone had been called, but by Thomas's own admission she never remembered to carry it anywhere. And the nature of her work, studying the cognition of elephants, meant that she often disappeared into the far reaches of the property for hours at a time to do observation, often—to her husband's chagrin—taking her three-year-old with her.

I was hoping she'd turn up with a cup of coffee, back from an early morning Dunkin' Donuts jaunt, the baby gumming a bagel. The last place I wanted them to be was in the sanctuary, with that seventh elephant still running loose.

I didn't want to let myself think of what might have already happened to them.

Four hours into the investigation, MCU had collected ten boxes of evidence: husks of squash and tufts of dried grass, leaves black with what might have been dried dung and might have been dried blood.

While they worked the scene, we accompanied Nevvie's body to the main gate of the sanctuary with Gideon. He moved slowly; his voice was as hollow as a drum. As a cop, I'd seen enough tragedy to know he was either truly affected by the death of his mother-in-law or else worthy of an Oscar. "My condolences," Donny said. "I imagine this is very hard for you."

Gideon nodded, wiping his eyes. He looked like a man who'd been through hell.

"How long have you worked here?" Donny asked.

"Since the sanctuary opened. And before that, with a circus down South. It's where I met my wife. Nevvie was the one who got me my first job." His voice broke on the dead woman's name.

"Have you ever seen elephants display aggressive behavior?"

"Have I seen it?" Gideon asked. "Sure, at the circus. Here, not a lot. A swat, if a keeper surprises them in a bad way. Once, one of our girls freaked when she heard a cell phone ring that sounded like calliope music. You know how they say elephants never forget? Well, it's true. But not always in a good way."

"So it's possible that something upset one of the . . . girls . . . and she knocked down your mother-in-law?"

Gideon looked at the ground. "I guess."

"You don't sound very convinced," I said.

"Nevvie knew her way around an elephant," Gideon said. "She wasn't some stupid rookie. This was just . . . bad timing."

"What about Alice?" I asked.

"What about her?"

"Does she know her way around an elephant?"

"Alice knows elephants better than anyone I've ever met."

"Did you see her last night?"

He looked at Donny, and then at me. "Off the record?" he said. "She came to me for help."

"Because the sanctuary was having problems?"

"No, because of Thomas. When the sanctuary started hemorrhaging money, he changed. His mood swings, they're wild. He's been spending all his time locked in his study, and last night, he really scared Alice."

Scared. The word was a red flag.

I got the sense he was holding something back. I wasn't surprised; he wouldn't talk out of turn about his boss's domestic troubles if he wanted to keep his job. "Did she say anything else?" Donny asked.

"She mentioned something about taking Jenna somewhere so she'd be safe."

"Sounds like she trusts you," Donny said. "How does that play out with your wife?"

"My wife is gone," Gideon answered. "Nevvie is all the family I have—*had*—left."

I stopped walking as we approached the massive barn. Five elephants milled in the enclosure behind it, shifting beside each other like storm clouds, their quiet rumbles shaking the ground beneath our feet. I had the uncanny sense that they understood every single word we'd been saying.

It made me think of Thomas Metcalf.

Donny faced Gideon. "Is there anyone you can think of who'd want to hurt Nevvie? Anyone human, that is?"

"Elephants, they're wild animals. They're not our pets. Anything could have happened." Gideon reached a hand toward the metal bars of the fence as one of the elephants stuck her trunk through it. She sniffed at his fingers, then picked up a rock and chucked it at my head.

Donny laughed. "Look at that, Virg. She doesn't like you."

"They need to be fed." Gideon slipped inside, and the elephants began to trumpet, knowing what was coming.

Donny shrugged and kept walking. I wondered if I was the only one who noticed that Gideon had not really answered his question.

"Go away, Abby," I shout; at least I think I'm shouting, because my tongue feels about ten sizes too big for my mouth. "I told you, I'm not drinking."

This is, technically, true. I'm *not* drinking. I'm drunk.

But my landlady is still knocking, or maybe that's a jackhammer. At any rate, it won't stop, so I haul myself up from the floor, where I guess I passed out, and yank open the door of my office.

I'm having a hard time focusing, but the person in front of me definitely isn't Abby. She is only five feet tall, and she's wearing a backpack and a blue scarf around her neck that makes her look like Isadora Duncan or Frosty the Snowman or something. "Mr. Stanhope," she says. "*Virgil* Stanhope?"

Spread across Thomas Metcalf's desk were reams of paper covered with tiny symbols and numbers, like some kind of code. There was a diagram on it, too, one that looked like an octagonal spider made with jointed arms and legs. I'd practically failed the course in high school, but it looked like chemistry to me. As soon as we entered, Metcalf scrambled to roll the paper up. He was sweating, although it wasn't really all that hot outside. "They're missing," he said, frantic.

"We're going to do everything in our power to find them—"

"No, no. My *notes*."

I may not have been to a lot of crime scenes at that point in my career, but I still thought it was strange that a guy whose wife and kid were missing seemed to care less about them than about some pieces of paper.

Donny looked at the piles on the desk. "Aren't they right there?"

"Obviously not," Metcalf snapped. "Obviously I'm talking about the pages that *aren't* here."

The papers were some weird sequence of numbers and letters. It could have been a computer program; it could have been a satanic code. It was the same kind of writing I had seen earlier on the wall. Donny glanced at me and raised his brow. "Most guys would be pretty concerned about their missing family, considering that an elephant killed someone here last night."

Metcalf continued to sift through the stacks of paper and books, moving them from left to right as he cataloged them mentally.

"Which is why I've told her a thousand times not to bring Jenna into the enclosures—"

"Jenna?" Donny repeated.

"My daughter."

He hesitated. "You and your wife have been fighting a lot, haven't you?"

"Who told you that?" he scoffed.

"Gideon. He said you upset Alice last night."

"*I* upset *her*?" Thomas replied.

I stepped forward, as Donny and I had discussed. "Mind if I use the bathroom?"

Metcalf waved me to a small room down the hall. Inside was a newspaper article, yellowed and curling in a broken frame, about the sanctuary. There was a picture of Thomas and a pregnant woman, smiling at the camera with an elephant lurking behind them.

I opened the medicine cabinet and sorted through Band-Aids, Neosporin, Bactine, Advil. There were three prescription bottles, all recent refills, with Thomas's name on them: Prozac, Abilify, Zoloft. Antidepressants.

If what Gideon said about the mood swings was true, it would make sense for Thomas to be on medication.

I flushed the toilet for good measure, and by the time I came back into the office, Metcalf was pacing around the perimeter of the room like a caged tiger. "I don't mean to tell you how to do your job, Detective," he said, "but I'm the injured party, not the one who did the injuring. She ran off with my daughter *and* my life's work. Shouldn't you be looking for her, instead of grilling me?"

I stepped forward. "Why would she steal your research?"

He sank down in his desk chair. "Because she's done it before. Multiple times. She's broken into my office to get my notes." He unrolled the long scroll on his desk. "This does not leave this room, gentlemen . . . but I am on the verge of a major breakthrough in the field of memory. It's well established that memories are elastic before they're encoded by the amygdala, but my research proves that each time the memory is recalled, it returns to that mutable state. That suggests memory loss can indeed happen after memory retrieval, if there's a pharmacological roadblock that disrupts protein synthesis in the amygdala . . . Imagine if you could erase traumatic memories with chemical agents years after the fact. It would completely change the way we treat post-traumatic stress. And it would make Alice's behavioral work on grief look like conjecture instead of science."

Donny looked over his shoulder at me. *Wacko*, he mouthed. "And your daughter, Dr. Metcalf? Where was she when you walked in on your wife?"

"Asleep," he said, his voice breaking. Turning away from us, Metcalf cleared his throat. "It's blatantly clear that the one place my wife is *not* is in this study . . . which begs the question—why are you still here?"

"Officer Stanhope," Donny said pleasantly, "why don't you go tell MCU to wrap it up, while I ask Dr. Metcalf just a few more questions?"

I nodded, deciding that Donny Boylan was the unluckiest son-of-a-bitch on the police force. Somehow, we'd come to certify a reported death caused by elephant trampling and instead had uncovered a domestic dispute between a nut job and his wife—one which may or may not have resulted in two missing persons and maybe even a homicide. I started walking toward the area where the crime scene investigators were still cataloging useless crap when suddenly all the hair stood up on the back of my neck.

When I turned around, the seventh elephant was staring me down from the other side of a very flimsy portable electric fence.

She was huge, this close. Her ears were pinned back against her head, and her trunk dragged on the ground. Sparse hair sprouted from the bony ridge of her brow. Her eyes, they were soulful and brown. She bellowed, and I fell back, even though there was a fence between us.

She trumpeted again, louder this time, and moved away. Then she stopped, after a few steps, and turned to look at me. She did the same thing two more times.

It was almost as if she was waiting for me to follow.

When I didn't move, the elephant returned and reached delicately between the electric lines of the fencing. I could feel hot breath huffing from the end of her trunk; I could smell hay and dust. I held my breath, and she touched my cheek, as gently as a whisper.

This time, when she started to move, I followed, keeping the fence between us, until the elephant made a sharp turn and started to walk away from me. She moved into a valley, and the moment before she disappeared from view, she glanced back at me again.

In high school, we used to cut across cow pastures as shortcuts. They were protected by electric fences. We'd leap, then grab the wire and soar over. As long as we let go before our feet touched the ground, we wouldn't get a shock.

I started to run, hurdling the wire. At the last moment my shoe dragged on the dirt and my hand was shocked numb. I fell, rolling in the dust, and then scrambled upright, racing toward the spot where the elephant had disappeared.

About four hundred yards away, I found the elephant standing over the body of a woman.

"Holy fuck," I whispered, and the elephant rumbled. When I took a step forward, her trunk shot out, whacking me on the shoulder and knocking me down. I had no doubt that was a warning; she could have swatted me halfway across the sanctuary if she'd really wanted.

"Hey, girl," I said softly, making eye contact. "I can tell you want to take care of her. I want to take care of her, too. You just have to let me get a little closer. I promise, she'll be okay."

As I kept talking, the elephant's posture relaxed. The ears pinned against her head fluttered forward; her trunk curled over the woman's chest. With a delicacy I would never have imagined in an animal so big, she lifted her massive feet and stepped away from the body.

In that moment I really got it; I understood why the Metcalfs had started this sanctuary and why Gideon wouldn't blame one of these creatures for killing his relative. I understood why Thomas would try to understand the brains of these animals. There was something I could not put my finger on—not just a complexity, or a connection, but an *equality*, as if we both knew we were on the same side here.

I nodded at the elephant, and I swear to God, she nodded back at me.

Maybe I was naïve; maybe I was just an idiot—but I knelt beside that elephant, close enough for her to crush me if she wanted to, and felt for the woman's pulse. She had dried blood matting her scalp and her face; her features were purple and swollen. She was totally unresponsive . . . and she was alive.

"Thank you," I said to the elephant, because it was clear to me, anyway, that she had been protecting this woman. I looked up, but the animal had disappeared, slipping silently into the fringe of trees beyond this little valley.

I hauled the body into my arms and started to sprint toward the MCU investigators. In spite of what Thomas Metcalf had said, Alice hadn't run away with his daughter, or his precious research. She was right here.

Once, when I went on a bender, I had a hallucination that I was playing poker with Santa Claus and a unicorn that kept cheating. Suddenly the Russian mafia burst into the room and started beating on St. Nick. I ran away, climbing up the fire escape before they could get me, too. The unicorn was right beside me, and when we got to the roof of the building, he told me to jump off and fly. I came to at that moment because my cell phone rang, and I had one leg over the edge, as if I was freaking Peter Pan. There but for the grace of God, I thought. I poured all the booze in my place down the sink drain that morning.

I was sober for three days.

During that time a new client asked me to get pictures of her husband, who she thought was cheating on her with another woman. He disappeared for hours at a time on weekends, saying he was going to the hardware store, and never returned with a single purchased item. He had started to erase messages on his cell phone. He seemed, she said, like he wasn't the man she had married.

I tracked the guy one Saturday to—of all places—a zoo. He was with a woman, all right—one who happened to be about four years old. The girl ran up to the fence at the elephant enclosure. Immediately, I thought of the animals I'd seen at the sanctuary, roaming free through the vast acreage, not cooped up in a little concrete pen. The elephant was rocking back and forth as if it were moving to music none of us could hear. "Daddy," the little girl said. "It's dancing!"

"I once saw an elephant peel an orange," I said casually, remembering a visit to the sanctuary after the caregiver's death. It had been one of Olive's behaviors; she rolled the tiny fruit under her massive front foot until it split, then delicately unraveled the peel with her trunk. I nodded at the man—my client's husband. I happened to know they didn't have any children. "Cute kid," I said.

"Yeah," he replied, and I could hear the wonder in his voice that comes when you find out you're having a baby, not when your child is four. Unless, of course, you have only just discovered that you're her dad.

I had to go home and tell my client that her husband wasn't two-timing her with another woman but that he had a whole life she had not known about.

Was it any wonder that night I dreamed of finding Alice Metcalf's unconscious body, and of the vow I'd made that elephant, which I never did keep: *I promise, she'll be okay.*

And that was when my run of sobriety ended.

I can't remember all the details about the eight hours or so after I found Alice Metcalf, because so much happened in such a short amount of time. She was brought by ambulance to the local hospital, still unconscious. I gave instructions to the paramedics who accompanied her to call us the minute she came to. We asked cops from neighboring towns to help complete a sweep of the elephant sanctuary, because we didn't know if Alice Metcalf's daughter was still out there. At about 9:00 P.M., we swung by the hospital, only to be told that Alice Metcalf was still out cold.

I thought we should arrest Thomas as a person of interest. Donny said that wasn't possible, since we didn't know if any crime had been committed. He said that we'd have to wait for Alice to wake up and tell us herself what had happened, and if Thomas had anything to do with her head injury or the kid's disappearance or Nevvie's death.

We were still at the hospital waiting for her to regain consciousness when Gideon called, panicked. Twenty minutes later, we accompanied him to the sanctuary enclosure, shining flashlights into the dark, where Thomas Metcalf was standing in his bare feet and bathrobe, trying to secure chains around the front legs of an elephant. She kept trying to rip away from her restraints; a dog was barking and nipping at him, attempting to stop him. Metcalf kicked the dog in the ribs, and it whimpered away on its belly. "It'll only take a few minutes to get the U0126 into her system—"

"I don't know what the hell he's doing," Gideon said, "but we do *not* chain elephants here."

The elephants were rumbling, an unholy earthquake that shuddered across the ground and up my legs.

"You've got to get him out of there," Gideon muttered, "before the elephant gets hurt."

Or vice versa, I thought.

It took an hour to talk Thomas out of the enclosure. It took another thirty minutes for Gideon to get close enough to the terrified animal to remove the shackles. We handcuffed Metcalf, which seemed awfully fitting, and brought him to a psychiatric hospital sixty miles south of Boone. For a while, during the drive, we were out of the range of cell phone coverage, which is why it wasn't until an hour later I got the message that Alice Metcalf was awake.

By then, we had been on the job for sixteen hours.

"Tomorrow," Donny pronounced. "We'll interview her first thing. Neither one of us is going to be any good right now."

And so began the biggest mistake of my life.

Sometime between midnight and 6:00 A.M., Alice signed herself out of Mercy hospital and disappeared off the face of the earth.

• • •

"Mr. Stanhope," she says. "*Virgil* Stanhope?"

When I open the door, the kid speaks the word like an accusation, as if being named Virgil is equivalent to having an STD. Immediately all my defenses kick in. I'm not Virgil and haven't been for a long time. "You've got the wrong person."

"Didn't you ever wonder what happened to Alice Metcalf?"

I peer more closely at her face, which is still kind of blurry, thanks to the amount I've drunk. Then I squint. This must be another hallucination. "Go away," I slur.

"Not until you admit that you're the guy who dropped my mother off, unconscious, at a hospital ten years ago."

Just like that, I'm stone-cold sober, and I know who this is standing before me. Not Alice, and not just a hallucination. "Jenna. You're her daughter."

The light that washes over that girl's face looks like the kind of thing you see in paintings in cathedrals, the sort of art that breaks your heart even as you stare at it. "She told you about me?"

Alice Metcalf had not told me anything, of course. She wasn't at the hospital when I went back there the morning after the trampling to take her statement. All the nurse could tell me was that she'd signed her own paperwork for discharge, and that she mentioned someone named Jenna.

Donny took that as proof that Gideon's story had been the legitimate one, that Alice Metcalf had run off with her daughter as she'd been hoping to. Given the fact that her husband was a whack job, that seemed like a happy ending. At the time, Donny had been two weeks shy of retirement, and I knew he wanted to clear out the paperwork on his desk—including the caregiver's death at the New England Elephant Sanctuary. *It was an accident, Virgil,* he said emphatically, when I pushed him to dig deeper. *Alice Metcalf is not a suspect. She's not even a missing person, until someone reports it.*

But nobody ever did. And when I tried to, I was stonewalled by Donny, who told me that if I knew what was good for me, I'd just let this one go. When I argued that he was making the wrong call here,

Donny lowered his voice. "I'm not the one making it," he said cryptically.

For a decade, there were things about that case that didn't sit right with me.

Yet now, ten years later, here is the proof that Donny Boylan was right all along.

"Holy shit," I say, rubbing my temples. "I can't believe this." I let the door fall back so that Jenna walks in, wrinkling her nose at the crumpled fast-food wrappers on the floor and the smell of stale smoke. With a shaking hand, I pull a cigarette from my shirt pocket and light up.

"Those things will kill you."

"Not fast enough," I mutter, drawing in for that kick of nicotine. I swear, sometimes that's the only thing that keeps me alive another day.

Jenna slaps down a twenty-dollar bill. "Well, try to pull it together for just a little bit longer," she says. "At least long enough for me to hire you."

I laugh. "Sweetheart, save your piggy-bank change. If your dog's missing, put up flyers. If a guy dumped you for a hotter girl, stuff your bra and make him jealous. That advice, it's all free, by the way, 'cause that's how I roll."

She doesn't blink. "I'm hiring you to finish your job."

"What?"

"You have to find my mother," she says.

There is something I never told anyone about that case.

The days after the death at the New England sanctuary were, as you can imagine, a freaking PR nightmare—with Thomas Metcalf in a drugged stupor at a residential psychiatric treatment facility and his wife AWOL, the only caregiver left was Gideon. The sanctuary itself was bankrupt and in default, all the cracks in its foundation now laid bare to the public. No food was coming in for the elephants, no more hay. The property was going to be seized by the bank, but in order for that to happen its residents—all thirty-five thousand pounds of them—needed to be relocated.

It's not easy to find a home for seven elephants, but Gideon had grown up in Tennessee and knew about a place in Hohenwald called The Elephant Sanctuary. They recognized this as an emergency and were willing to do whatever they could for the New Hampshire animals. They agreed to house the elephants in their quarantine barn until a new one could be built for them specifically.

That week a new case got thrown onto my desk—a babysitter, seventeen years old, who was responsible for a six-month-old's brain damage. I immersed myself in trying to get the girl—a cheerleader with blond hair and a perfect white smile—to admit to shaking the infant. Which is why, on the day of Donny's retirement party, I was still at my desk when the medical examiner's report on Nevvie Ruehl came through.

I knew what it said already—that the caregiver's death was accidental, caused by the trampling of an elephant. But I found myself scrolling through the text, reading the weight of the victim's heart, brain, liver. On the last page was a list of the articles found with the body.

One of those items was a single strand of red hair.

I grabbed the report and ran downstairs, where Donny was wearing a party hat and blowing out the candles on a cake shaped like an eighteenth hole. "Donny," I murmured, "we have to talk."

"Now?"

I pulled him into the hallway. "Look."

I shoved the ME's report into his hand and watched him scan the results. "You dragged me out of my own going-away party to tell me what I already know? I've already told you, Virg. Put it to rest."

"That hair," I said. "The red one. That's not the victim's. She was blond. Which means that there could have been a struggle."

"Or that someone reused a body bag."

"I'm pretty sure that Alice Metcalf has red hair."

"So do six million other people in the United States. And even if it does happen to belong to Alice Metcalf, so what? The two women knew each other; trace evidence would transfer due to their interactions. This would only prove that at some point, they were in proximity. That's Forensics 101."

He narrowed his eyes. "I'm going to give you a little advice. No detective wants to be in charge of a town that's on edge. Two days ago most of Boone was shitting bricks about crazy rogue elephants that could kill them in their sleep. Now everyone's finally settling down again, since the elephants are leaving. Alice Metcalf is probably in Miami, enrolling her kid in preschool under a fake name. If you start saying this case might not have been accidental but actually a murder, you're going to create a fresh panic. When you hear hoofbeats, Virgil, chances are it's a horse, not a zebra. People want cops who keep them safe from trouble—not cops who go looking for it where it doesn't exist. You want to make detective? Stop being Superman, and be Mary Fucking Poppins instead."

He patted me on the back and headed toward the room full of revelers.

"What did you mean?" I yelled after him. "When you said it wasn't your call?"

Donny stopped in his tracks, looked into the crowd of celebrating coworkers, and then grabbed my arm and pulled me in the opposite direction, where there would be no chance of us being overheard. "Did you ever wonder why the press didn't go apeshit over this? It's New Fucking Hampshire. Nothing ever happens here. Anything that smells like potential homicide is usually as irresistible as crack. Unless," he said quietly, "people far more powerful than you or me inform them to stop digging."

Back then, I still believed in justice, in the system. "You're telling me the chief's okay with that?"

"It's an election year, Virg. The governor can't win a second term on a zero-crime platform if the public thinks there's still a murderer wandering around Boone." He sighed. "That governor is the same guy who increased the budget for public safety so you could get hired in the first place. So you could protect the community without having to choose between a cost-of-living raise and a Kevlar vest." He looked directly at me. "Suddenly, doing the right thing isn't so black and white, is it?"

I watched Donny walk away, but I never joined him at the party. Instead, I returned to my desk and worked the last page of the ME's report free from its staple. Folding it into quarters, I slipped the page into the pocket of my jacket.

I put the rest of the ME's report in the closed case file of Nevvie Ruehl and instead pored over the evidence I had for the shaken baby. Two days later, Donny officially retired, and I got the teenage cheer-leader to confess.

The elephants, I heard, adapted well in Tennessee. The sanctuary land was sold—half to the state in conservation, and half to a devel-oper. After all the debts were paid, the remaining funds were managed by a lawyer to pay for the residential care of Thomas Metcalf. His wife never came back to claim any of it.

Six months afterward, I was promoted to detective. The morning of the ceremony, I dressed in my one good suit and took, from my nightstand drawer, the folded page of the ME's report. I tucked this into my breast pocket.

I needed to remind myself that I was no hero.

"She's missing again?" I ask.

"What do you mean *again*?" Jenna answers. She sits down in the chair across from my desk and folds her legs, Indian-style.

That, at least, cuts through the fog in my brain. I stub my ciga-rette out in a stale cup of coffee. "Didn't she run off with you?"

"I'm going to say no," Jenna says, "since I haven't seen her in ten years."

"Wait." I shake my head. "What?"

"You were one of the last people to see my mother alive," Jenna explains. "You dropped her off at the hospital, and then when she disappeared you didn't even do what any policeman with half a brain would do—go after her."

"I had no reason to go after her. She signed herself out of the hospital. Adults do that every day—"

"She had a *head* injury—"

"The hospital wouldn't have flagged it as long as they felt she was safe to be checking out, or else it would have been a HIPAA violation. Since they didn't seem to have a problem with her leaving, and since we never heard otherwise, we assumed that she was okay and that she was running off with you."

"Then how come you never charged her with kidnapping?"

I shrug. "Your father never officially reported her missing."

"I guess he was too busy being electrocuted as part of his therapy."

"If you weren't with your mother, who's been taking care of you all this time?"

"My grandmother."

So that was where Alice had stashed the baby. "And why didn't *she* report your mother's disappearance?"

The girl's cheeks flush. "I was too young to remember, but she says she went to the police station the week after my mom disappeared. I guess nothing ever came of it."

Was that true? I couldn't remember anyone formally lodging a missing persons complaint about Alice Metcalf. But then maybe the woman hadn't seen me. Maybe she'd seen Donny instead. It wouldn't have surprised me if Alice Metcalf's mother had been dismissed when she asked for help, or if Donny had tossed the paperwork intentionally so that I wouldn't stumble across it, because he knew I'd want to follow up and drag out the case.

"The point is," Jenna says. "You should have tried to find her. And you didn't. So you owe me now."

"What makes you so sure she can be found?"

"She's not dead." Jenna looks me in the eye. "I think I'd know it. *Feel* it."

If I had a Ben Franklin for every time I'd heard that from someone who was hoping for good news in a missing persons case only to have the remains turn up—well, I'd be drinking Macallan whiskey, not JD. But instead I say, "Is it possible she didn't come back because she didn't want to? A lot of people reinvent themselves."

"Like you?" she asks, staring right at me. *"Victor?"*

"Okay, yeah," I admit. "If your life sucks completely, sometimes it's easier to start over."

"My mom *did not* just decide to become someone else," she insists. "She liked who she was. And she wouldn't have left me behind."

I did not know Alice Metcalf. But I know there are two ways to live: Jenna's way, where you hang on to what you have in a death grip so you don't lose it; or my way, where you walk away from everything and everyone that matters before they can leave you behind. Either way, you're bound to be disappointed.

It's possible that Alice knew her marriage was a mess, that it was only a matter of time before she screwed up her kid, too. Maybe, like me, she cut bait before her life got even worse.

I spear a hand through my hair. "Look, no one wants to hear that maybe she's the reason her mother flew the coop. But my advice to you is to put this behind you. File it away in the drawer that's saved for all the other crap that isn't fair, like how the Kardashians are famous and how good-looking people get served faster at restaurants and how a kid who can't skate to save his life winds up on the varsity hockey team because his dad is the coach."

Jenna nods but says, "What if I told you I had proof that she didn't leave of her own free will?"

You can give the detective shield back, but you can't always get rid of the instincts. All the hair on my forearms stands up. "What do you mean?"

The kid reaches into her backpack and pulls out a wallet. A muddy, faded, cracked leather wallet that she hands to me. "I hired a psychic, and we found this."

"You've gotta be kidding," I say, my hangover roaring back full force. "A psychic?"

"Well, before you say she's a hack—she found something that *your* whole team of crime scene investigators never managed to find." She watches me open the clasp of the wallet and sort through the credit cards and driver's license. "It was up in a tree, on the sanctuary property," Jenna says. "Close to where my mom was found unconscious—"

"How do you know where she was found unconscious?" I ask sharply.

"Serenity told me. The psychic?"

"Oh, well, good, because I thought maybe you had a less reliable source."

"Anyway," she continues, ignoring me, "it was buried under a lot of stuff—birds had been making nests up in there for a while." She takes it out of my hands and slips from the cracked plastic photo insert the only picture still even remotely visible. It's bleached and faded and wrinkled, but even I can see the gummy mouth of a smiling baby.

"That's me," Jenna says. "If you were going to run away from a child forever . . . wouldn't you at least keep a picture?"

"I stopped trying to figure out why humans do what they do a long time ago. As for the wallet—it doesn't prove anything. She could have dropped it while she was running."

"And it magically flew up fifteen feet into a tree?" Jenna shakes her head. "Who put it up there? And why?"

Immediately I think: *Gideon Cartwright.*

I don't have any reason to suspect the man; I have no idea why his name pops into my head. As far as I know he went to Tennessee with those elephants and lived there happily ever after.

Then again, it was Gideon who Alice allegedly confided in about her failed marriage. And it was Gideon whose mother-in-law was killed.

Which brings me to my next thought.

What if the death of Nevvie Ruehl had not been an accident, as Donny Boylan had pushed me to believe? What if Alice had been the one to kill Nevvie, had stashed her own wallet in the tree to make it look like she was the victim of foul play—and then run away before she could be named as a suspect?

I look across my desk at Jenna. *Be careful what you wish for, sweetheart.*

If I still had a conscience, I might feel a twinge about agreeing to help a kid find her mother, considering that it might involve pinning a homicide on the woman. But then again, I can play my cards close to my chest, and let the girl believe this is just about finding a missing person, not a possible murderer. Besides, maybe I'm doing her a favor. I know what loose ends can do to a soul. The sooner she knows the truth, whatever it is, the sooner she can get on with her future.

I hold out my hand. "Ms. Metcalf," I say. "You've got yourself a private eye."

ALICE

I have studied memory extensively, and the best analogy I've found to explain its mechanics is this: Think of the brain as the central office of your body. Every experience you have on any given day, then, is a folder being dropped on a desk to be filed away for future reference. The administrative assistant who comes in at night, while you're asleep, to clear that logjam in her in-box is the part of the brain called the hippocampus.

The hippocampus takes all these folders and files them in places that make sense. This experience is a fight with your husband? Great, let's put it with a few more of those from last year. This experience is a memory of a fireworks display? Cross-reference it with a Fourth of July party you attended a while back. She tries to place each memory where there are as many related incidents as possible, because that is what makes them easier to retrieve.

Sometimes, though, you simply cannot remember an experience. Let's say you go to a baseball game, and someone tells you later that two rows behind you there was a woman sobbing in a yellow dress—but you have absolutely no recollection of her. There are only two scenarios in which this is possible. Either the incident was never dropped off for filing: You were focused instead on the batter and didn't pay attention to the crying woman. Or the hippocampus screwed up and coded that memory in a place it should not be: That sad woman gets linked to your nursery school teacher, who also used to wear a yellow dress, which is a place you'd never find it.

You know how sometimes you have a dream about someone from your past who you barely remember and whose name you couldn't recall if your life depended on it? It means that you accessed that path serendipitously, and found a bit of buried treasure.

Things you do routinely—things that get consolidated repeatedly by that hippocampus—form nice big connections. Taxi drivers in London have been proven to have very large hippocampi, because they have to process so much spatial information. We don't know, however, if they are born with naturally large hippocampi, or if the organ grows as it is put to the test, like a muscle being exercised.

There are also some people who cannot forget. People with PTSD may have smaller hippocampi than ordinary people. Some scientists believe that corticoids—stress hormones—can atrophy the hippocampus and cause memory disruptions.

Elephants, on the other hand, have enlarged hippocampi. You hear, anecdotally, that an elephant never forgets, and I do believe this is true. Up in Kenya, at Amboseli, researchers have done playbacks of long-distance contact calls in an experiment that suggests adult female elephants can recognize more than a hundred individuals. When the calls were from a herd with which they had associated, the elephants being tested responded with their own contact calls. When the vocalizations were from an unfamiliar herd, they bunched and backed away.

There was one unusual response in this experiment. During its course, one of the older female elephants that had been recorded died. They played back her contact call three months after her death, and again at twenty-three months postmortem. In both instances, her family responded with their own contact calls and approached the speaker—which suggests not just processing or memory but abstract thought. Not only did the family of the lost elephant remember her voice, but for just a moment as they approached that speaker, I bet they hoped to find her.

As a female elephant gets older, her memory improves. After all, her family relies on her for information—she is the walking archive that makes the decisions for the herd: Is it dangerous here? Where are we going to eat? Where are we going to drink? How are we going to find water? A matriarch might know migratory routes that have gone unused for the life span of the entire herd—including herself—yet somehow have been passed down and encoded into a recollection.

But my favorite story about elephant memory comes from Pilanesberg, where I did some of my doctoral work. In the nineties, to control the South African elephant population, there had been massive culling, in which park rangers shot adults within the herds and translocated the babies to places where there was a need for elephants. Unfortunately, the juveniles were traumatized and didn't behave the way they were supposed to. In Pilanesberg, a group of translocated young elephants didn't know how to function as a legitimate herd. They needed matriarchs, someone to guide them. And so an American trainer named Randall Moore brought to Pilanesberg two adult female elephants that, years ago, had been sent to the United States after being orphaned during a cull in the Kruger National Park.

The young elephants immediately took to Notch and Felicia—the names we gave these surrogate mothers. Two herds formed, and twelve years passed. And then, in a tragic accident, Felicia was bitten by a hippo. The bush vet needed to clean and dress the wound repeatedly while it healed, but he couldn't anesthetize Felicia each time. You can only dart an elephant three times a month or the M99 drug builds up too much in its system. Felicia's health was at risk, and if she died, her herd would find itself in jeopardy once again.

That's when we thought about elephant memory.

The trainer who'd worked with these two females more than a decade ago had not seen them since they were released into the reserve. Randall was happy to come to Pilanesberg to help. We tracked the two herds, which at this point had merged because of the injury of the older female.

"There are my girls," Randall said, delighted, as the jeep shuddered to a halt in front of the herd. "Owala," he called. "Durga!"

To us, these elephants were Felicia and Notch. But both of the stately ladies turned at the sound of Randall's voice, and he did what *no one* did with the fragile, skittish Pilanesberg herd: He got out of the jeep and started walking toward them.

Now, look, I've worked in the wild with elephants for twelve years. There are some herds you can approach on foot, because they're used to researchers and their vehicles and they trust us; and even so, it's not something I would do without carefully thinking it through. But this was not a herd that was familiar with humans; this was not even a stable herd. In fact, the younger elephants immediately stampeded away from Randall, identifying him as one of those two-legged beasts that had killed their own mothers. The two matriarchs, however, came closer. Durga—Notch—approached Randall. She stuck her trunk out and gently snaked it around his arm. Then she glanced back at her nervous young adoptive charges, still snorting and huffing on the ridge of the hill. She turned to Randall again, trumpeted once, and ran off with her babies.

Randall let her go, then turned to the other matriarch and said softly, "Owala . . . kneel."

The elephant we called Felicia walked forward, knelt down, and let Randall climb on her back. Although she'd had no direct contact with people in twelve years, she remembered not only this individual man as her trainer but all the commands he had taught her. Without being given any anesthetic, she allowed Randall to direct her to stay, lift her leg, turn—commands that made it possible for the bush vet to scrape away the pus from the infected area, clean the wound, and give her an injection of antibiotics.

Long after her infection healed, long after Randall had returned to training circus animals, Felicia went back to leading her patchwork family in Pilanesberg. To any researcher, to anyone at all, she was a wild elephant.

But somewhere, somehow, she remembered who she used to be, too.

JENNA

There is another recollection I have of my mother that ties to a conversation scrawled in her journal. It's a single handwritten page, scraps of dialogue that for some reason she didn't ever want to forget. Maybe that's why I remember it so clearly, too, why I can flesh out what she has written as if it is a movie playing out before me.

She is lying on the ground, her head in my father's lap. They are talking as I yank the heads off wild daisies. I'm not paying attention, but part of my brain must be, recording everything, so that even now I can hear the gossip of mosquitoes and the words my parents toss back and forth. Their voices rise and fall and swoop like the tail of a kite.

Him: You have to admit, Alice, there are certain animals that know there's one perfect mate.
Her: Crap. Complete and utter crap. Prove to me that monogamy exists in the natural world, without an environmental influence.
Him: Swans.
Her: Too easy. And not true! A quarter of black swans cheat on their mates.
Him: Wolves.
Her: They've been known to mate with another wolf if their mate

is kicked out of the pack or isn't able to breed. That's circumstance, not true love.

HIM: I should have known better than to fall for a scientist. Your idea of a Valentine's heart probably has an aorta.

HER: Is it a crime to be biologically relevant?

She sits up and pins him onto the ground, so that now he is lying beneath her and her hair swings over his face. It looks like they're fighting, but they are both smiling.

HER: Do you know a vulture caught cheating on his mate will be attacked by others?

HIM: Is that supposed to scare me?

HER: I'm just saying.

HIM: Gibbons.

HER: Oh, come on. *Everyone* knows gibbons are unfaithful.

He rolls, so that now he is on top, looking down at her.

HIM: Prairie voles.

HER: Only because of the oxytocin and vasopressin released in their brains. It's not love. It's chemical commitment.

Slowly, she grins.

HER: You know, now that I think about it . . . there *is* one species that's completely monogamous. The male anglerfish, which is a tenth the size of the girl of his dreams, follows her scent, bites her, and hangs on until his skin fuses into hers and her body absorbs his. They mate for life. But it's a really short life, if you're the guy in the relationship.

HIM: I'd fuse to you.

He kisses her.

HIM: Right at the lips.

When they laugh, it sounds like confetti.

HER: Fine. If it shuts you up about this once and for all.

They stop talking for a little while. I hold my palm over the ground. I have seen Maura lift her rear foot inches above the dirt, moving it slowly back and forth like she is rolling it over an invisible stone. My mother says that she can hear the other elephants when she does that; that they talk even when we don't hear them. I wonder if that's what my parents are doing now: speaking without sound.

When my father's voice comes again, it sounds like the string on a guitar that is pulled so tight, you can't tell if it is music or crying.

HIM: Do you know how a penguin picks his mate? He finds a perfect pebble, and gives it to the female he has his eye on.

He hands my mother a small stone. Her hand closes around it.

Most of my mother's journals from her time in Botswana are stuffed chock-full of data: the names and movements of elephant families trekking across the Tuli Block; dates when males came into musth and females calved; hourly logs of the behavior of animals who do not care or do not know they are being watched. I read each entry, but instead of seeing elephants, I picture the hand that wrote the notes. Was there a cramp in her fingers? A callus where the pencil pressed too hard against the skin? I put together the clues of my mother the same way she shuffled and reshuffled the observations of her elephants, trying to make a bigger picture from the smallest details. I wonder if it was just as frustrating for her, to get glimpses but never the whole mystery revealed. I guess a scientist's job is to fill in the gaps. Me, though, I look at a puzzle and can only see the single missing piece.

I am starting to think Virgil feels the same way, and I have to admit, I don't exactly know what that says about either of us.

When he says he'll take the job, I don't quite trust him. It's hard to believe a guy who is so hungover that he looks like he's having a stroke when he tries to put on his jacket. I figure my best bet is to make sure that he remembers this conversation, which means getting him out of his office and sober. "Why don't we talk over some coffee?" I suggest. "I passed a diner on my way here."

He grabs his car keys, but *that's* not happening. "You're drunk," I say. "I'm driving."

He shrugs, going along with it until we walk out the entryway of the building, and he sees me unlock my bike.

"What the fuck is that?"

"If you don't know, you're drunker than I thought," I say, and I climb on the seat.

"When you said you'd drive," Virgil mutters, "I assumed you had a car."

"I'm *thirteen*," I point out and gesture at the handlebars.

"Are you kidding? What is this, 1972?"

"You can run alongside instead if you want," I say, "but with the headache I'm guessing you have, I'd take Door Number One instead."

Which is how we wind up arriving at the diner with Virgil Stanhope sitting on my mountain bike, his legs spread, while I stand up between them and pedal.

We seat ourselves at a booth. "How come there weren't any flyers?" I say.

"Huh?"

"Flyers. With my mom's face on them. How come no one set up a command center at a crappy Holiday Inn conference room and manned a telephone bank for tips?"

"I told you already," Virgil replies. "She was never a missing person."

I just stare at him.

"Okay, correction: If your grandmother actually filed a missing persons report, it got lost in the shuffle."

"You're saying I grew up without a mother because of human error?"

"I'm saying I did my job. Someone else didn't do *theirs*." He looks at me over the edge of his mug. "I was called in to the elephant sanctuary because there was a dead body there. It was ruled an accident. Case closed. When you're a cop, you don't try to make messes. You just clean up the spills."

"So you're basically admitting you were too lazy to care that one of your witnesses for the case had disappeared."

He scowls. "No, I was making the assumption that your mother left of her own free will, or else I would have heard otherwise. I assumed she was with *you*." Virgil narrows his eyes. "Where were you when your mother was found by the cops?"

"I don't know. Sometimes she left me with Nevvie during the day, but not at night. I just remember eventually being with my grandma, at her place."

"Well, I should start by talking to *her*."

I shake my head immediately. "No way. She'd kill me if she knew I was doing this."

"Doesn't she want to know what happened to her daughter?"

"It's complicated," I say. "I think maybe it hurts her too much to keep dragging it up. She's from that generation that just puts on a stiff upper lip or whatever and soldiers through the bad stuff and pretends it never happened. Whenever I used to cry for my mom, my grandma tried to distract me—with food, or a toy, or with Gertie, my dog. And then one day when I asked she said, *She's gone.* But the way she said it, it sounded like a knife. So I learned pretty fast to stop asking."

"What took you so long to come forward? Ten years isn't just a cold case. It's a freaking Arctic wasteland."

A waitress walks by, and I signal to her, trying to get her attention, since Virgil needs coffee if he's going to be of any use to me. She doesn't see me at all.

"That's what it's like to be a kid," I say. "No one takes you seriously. People look right through you. Even if I'd been able to figure out where to go when I was eight or ten . . . even if I'd managed to get myself to the police station . . . even if you hadn't left your job and the sergeant at the front desk told you a kid wanted to get you to reopen a closed case . . . what would you have done? Would you have let me stand in front of your desk talking while you smiled and nodded and didn't pay attention? Or told your cop buddies about the girl who showed up and wanted to play detective?"

Another waitress bustles out of the kitchen, and a wedge of noises—frying, banging, clattering—squawks through the swinging door. This one, at least, comes right toward us. "What can I get you?" she asks.

"Coffee," I say. "A whole pot." She looks at Virgil, snorts, and retreats. "It's like that old saying," I tell him. "If no one hears you, are you even talking?"

The waitress brings us two cups of coffee. Virgil hands me the sugar even though I haven't asked for it. I meet his gaze, and for a moment, I can see through the haze of the booze, and I am not sure if I'm comforted by what I see, or a little scared. "I'm listening now," he says.

The list of what I remember about my mother is embarrassingly short.

There's that moment where she fed me cotton candy: *Uswidi. Iswidi.*

There's the conversation about mating for life.

There's a glimpse I have of her laughing as Maura reaches her trunk over a fence and pulls her hair free from its ponytail. My mother's hair is red. Not strawberry-blond and not orange, but the color of someone who's burning up inside.

(Okay, so, maybe the reason I remember this incident is because I've seen a photo someone snapped at that very moment. But the smell of her hair—like cinnamon sugar—that's a real memory that has nothing to do with a picture. Sometimes, when I really miss her, I eat French toast, just so that I can close my eyes and breathe in.)

My mother's voice, when she was upset, wobbled like a heat mirage of asphalt in the summer. And she would hug me and tell me it was going to be all right, even though she had been the one to cry.

Sometimes I would wake up in the middle of the night and find her watching me sleep.

She never wore rings. But she had a necklace that she never took off.

She used to sing in the shower.

She took me out on the ATV with her to watch the elephants, even though my father thought it was too dangerous for me to be in the enclosures. I rode on her lap, and she would lean down and whisper in my ear, *This can be our secret.*

We had matching pink sneakers.

She knew how to fold a dollar bill into an elephant.

Instead of reading me books at night, she told me stories: how she had seen an elephant free a baby rhino stuck in the mud; how a little girl whose best friend was an orphaned elephant left her family home to go to university and returned years later, to have that now fully grown elephant wrap a trunk around her and pull her close.

I remember my mother sketching, drawing the giant G clefs of elephant ears, which she would then mark with notches or tears to help her identify the individual. She would list behaviors: *Syrah reaches for and removes plastic bag from Lilly's tusk; given that vegetation is routinely carried in tusks, this suggests awareness of foreign object and subsequent cooperative removal* . . . Even something as soft as empathy would be given the most academic treatment. It was part of being taken seriously in her field: not to anthropomorphize elephants, but to study their behavior clinically and, from that, to extrapolate the facts.

Me, I look at the facts I remember about my mother, and I guess at her behavior. I do the opposite of what a scientist should do.

I can't help but think: If my mother met me now, would she be disappointed?

Virgil turns my mother's wallet over in his hands. It is so fragile that the leather starts to crumble beneath his fingers. I see that, and I feel a stab in my chest, as if I'm losing her all over again. "This doesn't necessarily mean that your mother was a victim of foul play," Virgil says. "She could have lost the wallet the night she wound up unconscious."

I fold my hands on the table. "Look, I know what you think—that she's the one who put the wallet up in the tree, so she could disappear. But it's pretty hard to climb a tree and hide a wallet when you're knocked out cold."

"If that's what she was doing, why didn't she leave it someplace it might actually be found?"

"And then what? Smash herself in the head with a rock? If she really wanted to disappear, why wouldn't she have just run?"

Virgil hesitates. "There might have been extenuating circumstances."

"Like?"

"Your mother wasn't the only one injured that night, you know."

Suddenly I understand what he's saying: My mother may have been trying to make herself look like she was a victim when, in reality, she was the perp. My mouth goes dry. Of all the potential personas I've given my mother over the past decade, *murderer* wasn't one of them. "If you *really* thought my mother was a killer, why didn't you go after her when she disappeared?"

His mouth opens and closes around empty air. *Bam*, I think. "The death was ruled an accident," he says. "But we did find a red hair at the scene."

"That's like saying you found a bimbo on *The Bachelor.* My mom wasn't the only redhead in Boone, New Hampshire."

"We found the hair *inside* the body bag of the deceased."

"So, (a) that's gross, and (b) big deal. I watch *Law & Order: SVU.* It just means that they had contact with each other. That probably happened ten times a day."

"Or it could mean that hair got transferred during a physical altercation."

"How did Nevvie Ruehl die?" I demand. "Did the medical examiner say the cause of death was homicide?"

He shakes his head. "He ruled it an accident, caused by blunt force trauma due to trampling."

"I may not remember a lot about my mom, but I know she wasn't five thousand pounds," I say. "So let me toss out a different scenario. What if *Nevvie* went after *her*? And one of the elephants saw the whole thing and retaliated?"

"They *do* that?"

I wasn't sure. But I remembered reading in my mother's journals about elephants that held grudges, that might wait years to even the score against someone who'd harmed them or someone they cared about.

"Besides," Virgil said, "you just told me that your mother left you in Nevvie Ruehl's care. I doubt she would have let Nevvie babysit if she thought the woman was dangerous."

"I doubt my mom would have let Nevvie babysit if she also wanted to murder her," I point out. "My mom didn't kill her. It just doesn't add up. There were a dozen cops swarming around that night; based on pure probability, chances are one of *them* was a redhead. You don't know if that hair belongs to my mother."

Virgil nods. "But I know how to find out."

Here's one more thing I remember: Inside, my parents are fighting. *How can you do that?* my father accuses. *Make this all about you.*

I am sitting on the floor, crying, but no one seems to hear me. I won't move, because moving is what led to all the shouting. Instead of staying on the blanket and playing with the toys my mother had brought into the elephant enclosure, I had chased a yellow butterfly as it flew a dotted line across the sky. My mother had had her back to me; she was recording her observations. And just then, my father had driven by, and had seen me heading downhill, where the butterfly went . . . and where elephants happened to be standing.

This is the sanctuary, not the wild, my mother says. *It's not like she got between a mother and a calf. They're used to people.*

My father yells back: *They are* not *used to toddlers!*

Suddenly a pair of warm arms closes around me. She smells of powder and limes, and her lap is the softest place I know. "They're mad," I whisper.

"They're scared," she corrects. "It sounds the same."

Then she starts to sing, close to my ear, so that her voice is the only one I hear.

Virgil has a plan, but the place he wants to go is too far away for me to bike, and I'm still not getting in a car with him. As we walk out of the diner, I agree to meet him at his office the next morning. The sun's swinging low, using a cloud as a hammock. "How do I know you won't be blitzed tomorrow, too?" I ask.

"Bring a Breathalyzer," Virgil suggests drily. "I'll see you at eleven."

"Eleven's not the morning."

"It is for me," he replies, and he starts walking down the road toward his office.

By the time I get back home, my grandmother is draining carrots in a colander. Gertie, curled up in front of the refrigerator, beats her tail twice on the floor, but that's all the hello I'm getting. When I was little, my dog used to practically knock me down if I came back after a trip to the bathroom; *that's* how happy she was to see me again. I wonder if, as you get older, you stop missing people so fiercely. Maybe growing up is just focusing on what you've got, instead of what you don't.

There's a sound like footsteps overhead. When I was little I was sure my grandmother's house was haunted; I was always hearing stuff like that. My grandmother assured me it was rusty pipes or the house settling. I used to wonder how something made of brick and mortar could settle, when I seemed incapable of doing just that.

"So," my grandmother says, "how was he?"

For a second I freeze, wondering if she's been having me followed. How ironic would *that* be—my grandma tracking me as I'm tracking down my mom with a private investigator? "Um," I reply. "A little under the weather."

"I hope you don't catch whatever he has."

Unlikely, I think, unless being a drunk is contagious.

"I know you think the sun rises and sets on Chad Allen, but even if he's a good teacher, he's an irresponsible parent. Who leaves their baby alone for two days?" my grandmother mutters.

Who leaves their baby alone for ten years?

I'm so wrapped up in thinking about my mom that it takes me an extra beat to remember that my grandmother still believes I have been sitting for Carter, Mr. Allen's freaky, alien-headed kid, who she now thinks has a cold. And he's going to be my excuse tomorrow, too, when I go back to see Virgil. "Well, he wasn't alone. He had *me*."

I follow my grandmother into the dining room, taking the time to snag two clean glasses and the carton of orange juice from the refrigerator. I force down a few bites of fish sticks, chewing methodically, before I hide the rest of my meal under the mashed potatoes. I'm just not hungry.

"What's wrong?" my grandmother asks.

"Nothing."

"I've spent an hour making this dinner for you; the least you can do is eat it," she says.

"How come there wasn't a search for her?" I blurt out and then cover my mouth with my napkin, as if I can stuff the words back inside.

Neither of us wants to pretend she doesn't know who I'm talking about. My grandmother goes very still. "Just because you don't remember, Jenna, doesn't mean it didn't happen."

"*Nothing* happened," I say. "Not for ten years. Don't you even care? She's your *daughter*!"

She gets up and dumps her plate—which is still mostly full—into the kitchen trash.

All of a sudden I feel the way I felt that day when I was tiny, and chased that butterfly down a hill toward the elephants, and realized I had made a colossal tactical error.

All these years I thought my grandmother didn't talk about what had happened to my mother because it was too hard for *her*. Now, I wonder if she didn't talk about what had happened because it would be too hard for *me*.

I know, before she speaks, what she is going to say. And I don't want to hear it. I run upstairs with Gertie at my heels and slam my bedroom door, then bury my face in the fur at my dog's neck.

It takes about two minutes before the door opens. I don't glance up, but I can feel her there, all the same. "Just say it," I whisper. "She's dead, isn't she?"

My grandmother sits down on the mattress. "It's not that simple."

"Yes, it is." Suddenly I am crying even though I don't want to be. "Either she is, or she isn't."

But even as I challenge my grandmother, I understand it's *not* that simple. Logic says that if I have been right—if my mother never would have willingly left me—then she would have come for me. Which, obviously, she didn't.

It doesn't take a rocket scientist to figure that one out.

And yet. If she were dead, wouldn't I know it? I mean, don't you hear those stories all the time? Wouldn't I feel like a piece of me was gone?

A little voice inside me says, *Don't you?*

"When your mother was little, whatever I told her to do, she would choose the opposite," my grandmother says. "I asked her to wear a dress to her high school graduation, she showed up in cutoff shorts. She'd point to two haircuts in a magazine and ask which I liked better; then she'd choose the one I didn't. I suggested she study primates at Harvard; she picked elephants in Africa." My grandmother looks down at me. "She was also the smartest person I have ever met. Smart enough to outwit any policeman, if she wanted to. So if she was alive, and had run away, I knew I couldn't trap her into coming home. If I started putting her face on milk cartons and setting up a hotline, she would only run farther away, faster."

I wonder if this is true. If my mother has only been playing a game. Or if it's my grandmother who's been fooling herself.

"You said you filed a missing persons report. What happened?"

She takes my mother's scarf from the back of my desk chair, runs it through the sieve of her fist. "I said I *went* to file a missing persons report," my grandmother says. "I went three times, in fact. But I never stepped inside the front door."

I stare at her, stunned. "What? You never told me that!"

"You're older now. You deserve to know what happened." She sighs. "I wanted answers. At least I thought I did. And I knew *you* would, when you were older. But I couldn't bring myself to go inside. I was afraid to hear what the police might find." She looks at me. "I don't know what would have been worse. Learning Alice was dead and couldn't come home, or learning she was alive and didn't *want* to. Nothing they told me was going to be good news. There wasn't going to be a happily ever after here. There was just going to be you and me; and I thought the sooner we moved on, the sooner we could both start over."

I think of what Virgil had hinted at this afternoon—the third option that my grandmother hasn't considered: that perhaps my mother had run away not from us but from a murder charge. I guess that's not exactly something you want to hear about your daughter, either.

I don't think of my grandmother as old, really, but when she gets up off the bed, she looks her age. She moves slowly, like all of her is aching, and stands silhouetted in the doorway. "I know what you look up on your computer. I know you never stopped asking what happened." Her voice is as thin as the seam of light that surrounds her body. "Maybe you're braver than I am."

There is one entry in my mother's journals that feels like a hairpin turn, a moment where, if she hadn't reversed direction, she would have become someone entirely different.

Maybe even someone *here*.

She was thirty-one, working in Botswana on her postdoc. There is a vague reference to some bad news from home, and how she had taken a leave of absence. When she returned, she threw herself into her work, documenting the effects of traumatic memory on elephants. Then one day, she came across a young male that had gotten its trunk caught in snare wire.

This was not uncommon, I guess. From what I've read in her journals, bush meat was a staple for some villagers, and every now and then that necessity was ratcheted up into a business. But traps meant for impala sometimes wound up entangling other animals: zebra, hyena, and, one day, a thirteen-year-old bull named Kenosi.

At his age, Kenosi wasn't part of his mother's breeding herd anymore. Although his mother, Lorato, was still the matriarch, Kenosi had gone off with the other young bulls, a roving teenage bachelor gang. He'd play-fight with his buddies when he came into musth, like the stupid boys in my school who shove each other in front of girls to try to get noticed. But like with teenage humans, these were just practice runs of hormones, and other males could upstage them simply by showing up and being older and cooler. This happened in the elephant community, too, when older males knocked the young ones out of musth, which was biologically perfect, since they wouldn't actually be ready to breed until about age thirty, anyway.

Except Kenosi wasn't ever going to get it on with a lucky female, because the snare had practically severed his trunk, and an elephant without a trunk cannot survive.

My mother saw Kenosi's injury in the field and knew immediately he was going to die a slow and painful death. So she put aside her work for the day and went back to camp to call the Department of Wildlife, which was the government agency allowed to put the elephant out of its misery. But Roger Wilkins, the official assigned to that game reserve, was new there. "I have a lot on my plate," he told her. "Just let nature take its course."

The job of a researcher is to do just that: to respect nature, not to manage it. But even if these were wild animals, they were also *her* elephants. My mother would not stand by idly and let an elephant suffer.

There's a break in the journal. She changes from pencil to black pen, and there is an entire page filled with blank lines. Here's what I've imagined happening in that gap:

I walk into the main office at camp, where my boss is sitting with a tiny box fan blowing stale air. Alice, *he says.* Welcome back. If you need more time off—

I cut him off. That isn't why I'm here. I tell him about Kenosi, and about that asshole Wilkins.

It's an imperfect system, *my boss admits, and because he doesn't know me very well, he thinks I will just go away.*

If you don't pick up that phone, *I threaten,* then I will. But I'm going to call *The New York Times,* and the BBC, and *National Geographic.* I'm going to call the World Wildlife Fund and Joyce Poole and Cynthia Moss and Dame Daphne Sheldrick. I am going to unleash a swell of bleeding hearts and animal lovers on Botswana. And as for you: I'm going to bring so much shit raining down on this camp that this elephant research study funding is going to dry up before the sun sets. So you can pick up that phone, *I say.* Or else I will.

Anyway, that's what I imagine she *would* have said. But when my mother actually starts writing again, it is a detailed account of how Wilkins arrived holding on to a knapsack and a grudge. How he sourly rode beside her in the jeep, clutching his rifle, as she located Kenosi and his homeys. I knew from reading my mother's journals that the Land Rovers did not get closer than forty feet to bull herds—they were too unpredictable. But before my mother could explain this, Wilkins raised his gun and cocked the trigger.

Don't! my mother screamed, grabbing the barrel of the rifle and pointing it at the sky. She threw the Land Rover into gear, driving forward to push the other young bulls out of the way first. Then she pulled off to the side, looked at him, and said, *Now. Shoot.*

He did. Through the jaw.

The skull of an elephant is a mass of honeycombed bone, made to protect the brain, which sits in a cavity behind all this infrastructure.

You cannot kill an elephant by shooting it in the jaw or the forehead, because although the bullet will do damage, it will not hit the brain. If you want to humanely kill an elephant, you have to shoot it cleanly behind the ear.

My mother wrote that Kenosi was bellowing his heart out, in pain, worse off than he had been before. She used curse words she had never used in her life, in multiple languages. She was contemplating grabbing that gun and turning it on Wilkins. And then something remarkable happened.

Lorato, the matriarch—the mother of Kenosi—came charging down the hill toward where her son was stumbling around, bleeding. The only obstacle in her way was my mother's vehicle.

My mother knew not to get between an elephant and her calf, even if that calf was thirteen years old. She threw the Land Rover into reverse and zoomed backward, leaving a clear path between Kenosi and Lorato.

Before the matriarch could get there, however, Wilkins took a second shot, and this one hit its mark.

Lorato stopped on a dime. This is what my mother wrote:

She reached out to Kenosi, stroking his body from tail to trunk, paying special attention to the spot where the snare wire had cut into his hide. She stepped over his massive bulk, standing above him the way a mother would protect her calf. She was secreting from her temporal glands, dark streaks marking the sides of her head. Even as the bull herd moved away, even as Lorato's breeding herd joined her and reached out to touch Kenosi, she refused to move. The sun fell, the moon rose, and still she stood, unable or unwilling to leave him.

How do you say good-bye?

That night, there were meteor showers. It seemed to me that even the sky was weeping.

Two pages later in the journal, my mother had composed herself enough to write about what had happened with the objectivity of a scientist:

Today I saw two things I never thought I would see.

First, the good: Because of Wilkins's behavior, the researchers in the reserve have now been given the right to euthanize an elephant on our own, if necessary.

Second, the devastating: A female elephant whose baby wasn't a baby anymore by any means still returned with a fury when he was in distress.

Once a mother, always a mother.

That's what my mom scrawled at the bottom of the page.

What she didn't write was that this was the day she narrowed her study on trauma and elephants to the effects of grief instead.

Unlike my mother, I don't think what happened to Kenosi was tragic. When I read it, actually, it makes me feel like I'm filled with sparks from those meteor showers she talks about.

After all, the last thing Kenosi saw, before he closed his eyes forever, was his mother coming back to him.

The next morning, I wonder if it's time to tell my grandmother about Virgil.

"What do you think?" I ask Gertie. Certainly it would be easier to get a lift to his office, instead of having to bike all the way across town. So far all I have to show for my search are calf muscles that rival a ballerina's.

My dog thumps her tail against the wooden floor. "Once for yes, twice for no," I say, and Gertie cocks her head. I hear my grandmother call for me—it's the second time—and I clatter down the stairs to find her standing at the counter, shaking cereal into a bowl for my breakfast.

"I overslept. No time for anything hot today. Although why you can't feed yourself at the age of thirteen, I have no idea," she huffs. "I've seen goldfish with better survival skills than you." She hands me a milk carton and unplugs her cell phone from its charger. "Take the recycling out before you leave for your sitting job. And for God's sake brush your hair before you go. It looks like there's a woodland creature nesting inside."

This is not the same woman who came into my room last night with all her defenses down. This is not the same woman who admitted to me that she, too, is still consumed by thoughts of my mother.

She digs in her purse. "Where are the car keys? I swear I have the first three signs of Alzheimer's . . ."

"Grandma . . . what you said last night . . ." I clear my throat. "About me being brave enough to search for my mom?"

She shakes her head, so slightly that if I weren't staring so hard at her, I might have missed it. "Dinner's at six," she announces, in a voice that lets me know this conversation is over, before I really ever had a chance to get it started.

To my surprise, Virgil looks as comfortable in the police station as a vegetarian at a barbecue festival. He doesn't want to use the front door; we have to sneak in the back after an officer has buzzed himself in. He doesn't want to chat up the desk sergeant or the dispatchers. There's no grand tour: *This is where my locker was; this is where we kept the donuts.* I'd been under the impression that Virgil left this job because he wanted to, but I'm beginning to wonder if maybe he did something to get fired. This much I know: There's something he's not telling me.

"See that guy?" Virgil says, pulling me around the bend of a hallway so that I can peek at the man sitting at the desk of the evidence room. "That's Ralph."

"Um, Ralph looks like he's a thousand years old."

"He looked like he was a thousand years old back when I was still working here," Virgil says. "We used to say he'd become just as fossilized as the stuff he watches over."

He takes a deep breath and walks down the corridor. The evidence room has a half door, with the top open. "Hey, Ralph! Long time no see."

Ralph moves as if he's underwater. His waist pivots, then his shoulders, and finally his head. Up close, he has as many wrinkles as the elephants in the photos clipped to my mother's journal entries. His eyes are as pale as apple jelly, and look to be about the same consistency. "Well," Ralph says, so slowly that it sounds like *whaaaaale*. "Rumor has it that you walked into the cold case evidence room one day and never came out."

"What is it Mark Twain said? Reports of my death have been greatly exaggerated."

"Guess if I ask you where you've been, you're not gonna tell me, anyway," Ralph replies.

"Nope. And I'd be awfully grateful if you didn't mention me being here, either. I get itchy when people ask too many questions." Virgil takes a slightly mashed Twinkie from his pocket and sets this on the counter between us and Ralph.

"How old is that?" I murmur.

"These things have enough preservatives in them to keep them on the shelves until 2050," Virgil whispers. "And besides, Ralph can't read the tiny print of the expiration date."

Sure enough, Ralph's entire face lights up. His mouth creases in a smile, and it has ripple effects that remind me of a YouTube video I once saw of a building implosion. "You remember my weakness, Virgil," he says, and he glances at me. "Who's your sidekick?"

"My tennis partner." Virgil leans through the opening in the door. "Look, Ralphie. I need to check out one of my old cases."

"You're not on payroll anymore—"

"I was barely on payroll when I was on payroll. Come on, bud. It's not like I'm asking to mess with any active investigation. I'm just freeing up a little space for you."

Ralph shrugs. "I guess it can't hurt, as long as the case is closed . . ."

Virgil unlatches the door and pushes past him. "No need to get up. I know the way."

I follow him down a long, narrow hallway. Metal shelving lines both walls from floor to ceiling, and there are cardboard boxes neatly jammed into every available space. Virgil's lips move as he reads the labels of the banker's boxes, arranged by case number and date. "Next aisle," he mutters. "This one only goes back to 2006."

After a few more minutes he stops, and starts to monkey-climb the shelving. He pulls one of the boxes free and tosses it into my arms. It's lighter than I was expecting. I set it on the floor so that he can pass down three more boxes.

"That's it?" I say. "I thought you told me there was a ton of evidence taken from the sanctuary."

"There was. But the case was solved. We only kept the items that were connected to people—things like soil and trampled plants and debris that turned out to not be consequential were destroyed."

"If someone's already gone through it all, why are we going back to it?"

"Because you can look at a mess twelve times and see nothing. And then you look the thirteenth time, and whatever you were searching for is staring out at you, clear as day." He opens the lid of the top box. Inside are paper storage bags, sealed with tape. On the tape, and on the bags, it says NO.

"No?" I read. "What's in that bag?"

Virgil shakes his head. "That stands for Nigel O'Neill. He was a cop who was searching for evidence that night. Protocol means that the officer has to put his initials and the date collected on the bag and the tape, to make the chain of evidence hold up in court." He points to the other markings on the bag: a property number, with a list of items: SHOELACE, RECEIPT. Another: VICTIM'S CLOTHING—SHIRT, SHORTS.

"Open that one," I direct.

"Why?"

"You know how sometimes a specific item can jog a memory? I want to see if that's true."

"The victim here wasn't your mother," Virgil reminds me.

As far as I'm concerned, that remains to be seen. But he opens the paper bag, snaps on a pair of gloves from a box on the shelf, and pulls out a pair of khaki shorts and a shredded, stiff polo shirt with the New England Elephant Sanctuary logo embroidered on the left breast.

"Well?" he prompts.

"Is that *blood*?" I ask.

"No, it's dried Kool-Aid. If you want to be a detective, be a detective," he says.

Still, it kind of freaks me out. "It looks like the same uniform *everyone* wore."

Virgil keeps rummaging. "Here we go," he says, pulling out a bag that is so flat there can't possibly be anything in it. The evidence tag says #859, LOOSE HAIR INSIDE BODY BAG. He takes the bag and slips it into his pocket. Then he picks up two of the boxes and carries them toward the entrance, glancing over his shoulder. "Make yourself useful."

I follow him, the other boxes stacked in my arms. I'm pretty sure he took the lighter ones on purpose. These feel like they're full of rocks. At the entrance, Ralph glances up from the nap he's been taking. "Good to catch up, Virgil."

Virgil points his finger. "You never saw me."

"Saw what?" Ralph says.

We duck out the same back entrance of the police station and carry the boxes to Virgil's truck. He manages to stuff them into the backseat, which is already jammed with food wrappers and old CD cases and paper towels and sweatshirts and empty bottles. I climb into the passenger seat. "Now what?"

"Now we have to go sweet-talk a lab into doing a mitochondrial DNA test."

I don't know what that is, but it sounds like something that would be part of a thorough investigation. I'm impressed. I glance at Virgil, who, I should say, has cleaned up pretty nicely now that he's not completely drunk. He's showered and shaved, so he smells like a pine forest instead of stale gin. "Why did you leave?"

He glances at me. "Because we got what we came for."

"I meant the police department. Didn't you *want* to be a detective?"

"Apparently not as much as you do," Virgil murmurs.

"I think I deserve to know what I'm getting for my money."

He snorts. "A bargain."

He backs up too fast, and one of the boxes tumbles over. The storage bags inside spill out, so I unbuckle my seat belt and twist around, trying to right the mess. "It's hard to tell what's evidence and what's your trash," I say. The tape has peeled off one of the brown paper bags, and the evidence inside has fallen into a nest of McDonald's fish fillet wrappers. "This is gross. Who eats fifteen fish fillets?"

"It wasn't all at once," Virgil says.

But I'm barely listening, because my hand has closed around the evidence that was dislodged. I pivot forward, still holding the tiny pink Converse sneaker.

Then I look down at my feet.

I've had pink Converse high-tops for as long as I can remember. Longer. They're my one indulgence, the only items of clothing I ever ask my grandmother for.

I'm wearing them in every photograph of me as an infant: propped up against a clan of teddy bears, sitting on a blanket with a pair of huge sunglasses balanced on my nose; brushing my teeth at the sink, naked except for those shoes. My mother had a pair, too—old, beaten ones that she had kept from her college days. We did not wear identical dresses or have the same haircut; we didn't practice putting on makeup. But in this one small thing, we matched.

I still wear my sneakers, practically every day. They're kind of like a good-luck charm, or maybe a superstition. If I haven't taken mine off, then maybe . . . well. You get it.

The roof of my mouth feels like a desert. "This was mine."

Virgil looks at me. "You're sure?"

I nod.

"Did you ever run around barefoot when you were in the sanctuary with your mother?"

I shake my head. That was a rule; no one went inside without footwear. "It wasn't like a golf course," I said. "There were knobs of grass and thicket and bush. You could trip in the holes that the elephants dug." I turn the tiny shoe over in my hand. "I was there, that night. And I *still* don't know what happened."

Had I gotten out of bed and wandered into the enclosures? Had my mom been looking for me?

Am I the reason she's gone?

My mother's research comes thundering into my head. *Negative moments get remembered. Traumatic ones get forgotten.*

Virgil's face is unreadable. "Your father told us you were asleep," he says.

"Well, I didn't go to sleep wearing shoes. Someone must have put them on me and tied the laces."

"Someone," Virgil repeats.

Last night, I dreamed about my father. He was creeping through the tall grass near the pond in the sanctuary enclosure, calling my name. *Jenna! Come out, come out, wherever you are!*

We were safe out here, because the two African elephants were inside the barn having their feet examined. I knew that home base in this game was the wide wall of the barn. I knew that my father always won, because he could run faster than me. But this time, I was not going to let him.

Bean, he said, his name for me. *I can see you.*

I knew he was lying, because he started walking *away* from my hiding spot.

I had dug myself into the banks of the pond the way the elephants did when my mother and I watched them playing, spraying each other with the hoses of their trunks or rolling like wrestlers in the mud to cool their hot skin.

I waited for my father to pass the big tree where Nevvie and Gideon would set dinner for the animals—cubes of hay and Blue Hubbard squash and entire watermelons. Enough to feed a small family, or a single elephant. As soon as he was in its shadow, I scrambled up from the bank where I'd been wallowing and ran forward.

It wasn't easy. My clothes were caked with dirt; my hair was knotted in a rope down my back. My pink sneakers had been sucked into the muck of the pond. But I knew I was going to win, and a giggle slipped from my lips, like the squeal of helium from the neck of a balloon.

It was all that my father needed. Hearing me, he spun and raced toward me, hoping to cut me off before I could flatten my muddy handprints against the corrugated metal wall of that barn.

Maybe he would have reached me, too, if Maura hadn't thundered from the tree cover, trumpeting so loudly that I froze. She swung her trunk and knocked my father across his face. He fell to the ground, clutching his right eye, which swelled within seconds. She danced nervously between us, so that my father had to roll out of the way or risk being crushed.

"Maura," he panted. "It's all right. Easy, girl—"

The elephant bellowed again, an air horn that left my ears ringing.

"Jenna," my father said quietly, "don't move." And under his breath: "Who the hell let that elephant out of the barn?"

I started crying. I didn't know if I was scared for me or for my father. But in all the times my mother and I had observed Maura, I'd never seen her act violent.

Suddenly the door of the barn slid open on its thick cable track, and my mother was standing in the massive doorframe. She took one look at my father, Maura, and me. "What did you do to her?" she asked him.

"Are you kidding? We were playing hide-and-seek."

"You and the elephant?" As she spoke, my mother slowly moved between Maura and my father, so that he could safely get up.

"No, for Christ's sake. Me and Jenna. Until Maura came out of nowhere and smacked me." He rubbed his face.

"She must have thought you were trying to hurt Jenna." My mother frowned. "Why on earth were you playing hide-and-seek in Maura's enclosure?"

"Because she was supposed to be in the barn having foot care done."

"No, just Hester."

"Not according to the information that Gideon posted on the whiteboard—"

"Maura didn't feel like coming in."

"And I was supposed to know that how?"

My mother kept cooing to Maura, until the animal lumbered a distance away, still watching my father warily.

"That elephant hates everyone but you," he muttered.

"Not true. Apparently, she likes Jenna." Maura rumbled a response, approaching the tree line to graze, and my mother scooped me into her arms. She smelled of cantaloupe, the treat she must have been feeding Hester in the barn while the pads of the elephant's feet were being soaked and scraped and treated for cracks. "For someone who screams at me for taking Jenna into the enclosures, you picked an interesting place to play games."

"There weren't supposed to be any elephants in this— Oh, for God's sake. Never mind. I can't win." My father touched his hand to his head and winced.

"Let me take a look at that," my mother said.

"I have a meeting with an investor in a half hour. I'm supposed to be explaining to him how safe it is to have a sanctuary in a populated area. And now I'll be giving that speech with a black eye that was given to me by an elephant."

My mother shifted me to one hip and touched his face, prodding gently. These moments, when we seemed like a pie before any of the pieces are eaten, were the best ones for me. They almost could erase the other moments.

"It could be worse," my mother said, leaning against him.

I could see him, *feel* him, soften. It was the sort of observation my mother always tried to point out to me in the field: just the shift of body, the slide of the shoulders, that let you know there was no longer an invisible wall of fear. "Oh, really," my father murmured. "How so?"

My mother smiled up at him. "I could have been the one to deck you," she said.

. . .

For the past ten minutes, I've been sitting on an examination table observing the mating behavior of the Fundamentally Alcoholic, Washed-Up Male and the Oversexed, Overblown Cougar.

Here are my scientific field notes:

The Male is uneasy, caged. He sits and taps his foot incessantly, then gets up and paces. He has put a little effort into grooming today, in anticipation of seeing the Cougar, who enters the room.

She wears a white laboratory coat and too much makeup. She smells like the perfume inserts in magazines that are so overwhelming you are tempted to lob the whole issue across the room, even if it means you'll never find out the *Ten Things Guys Want in Bed* or *What Makes Jennifer Lawrence Mad!* She is a blond with dark roots, and someone needs to tell her that pencil skirts are not doing her ass any favors.

The Male makes the first move. He uses dimples as a weapon. He says, *Wow, Lulu, long time no see.*

The Cougar rebuffs his advances. *Whose fault is that, Victor?*

I know, I know. You can beat me up all you want.

A subtle but measurable change in the atmospheric pressure. *Is that a promise?*

Teeth. Lots of them.

Careful now. Don't start something you can't finish, the Male says.

I don't recall that ever being a problem for us. Do you?

From where I am sitting making my observations, I roll my eyes. Either this is the best argument for contraception since the Octomom . . . or this crap really works between men and women, and I will probably not have a date until I'm menopausal.

The Cougar's senses are better than the Male's; she radars my snark all the way across the room. She touches the Male on his shoulder and flicks her eyes toward me. *Didn't know you had kids.*

Kids? Virgil looks at me as if I'm the bug he's squashed on the sole of his shoe. *Oh, she's not mine. She's actually the reason I'm here.*

Duh, even *I* know that's the wrong thing to say. The Cougar's painted mouth pinches tight. *Don't let me keep you from getting down to business.*

Virgil grins, superslow, and I can practically see the Cougar start to drool. *Why, Tallulah*, he says, *I'd like to do just that with you. But you know I have to take care of my client first.*

The Cougar's cell phone rings, and she looks at the number flashing on the screen. "Jesus on a cracker," she says and sighs. "Give me five minutes."

She slams out of the examination room, and Virgil hops on the metal table beside me, running one hand down his face. "You have no idea how much you owe me."

This surprises me. "You mean you don't really like her?"

"Tallulah? God, no. She used to be my dental hygienist, and then she quit and became a DNA squint. Every time I see her I think about her scraping plaque off my teeth. I'd rather date a sea cucumber."

"They throw up their own stomachs when they eat," I say.

He considers this. "I've taken Tallulah out to dinner. Like I said, I'd go for the sea cucumber."

"Then why are you acting like you want her to plug and play?"

His eyes widen. "You did *not* just say that."

"Ride the baloney pony." I grin. "Storm the trenches . . ."

"What the hell is wrong with kids these days?" Virgil mutters.

"Blame it on my upbringing. I had a profound lack of parental guidance."

"And you think *I'm* disgusting because I have a drink every now and then."

"(A) I think you drink all the time, and (b) if you want to get specific, what makes you disgusting is that you're totally playing Tallulah, who thinks you're planning to ask for her number."

"I'm taking one for the team, for Christ's sake," Virgil says. "You want to find out if your mother was the person who left that hair behind on Nevvie Ruehl's body? Then we have two choices. We can either try to sweet-talk someone at the police department to order up a test through the state lab, which they won't do because the case is closed and because the backlog is over a year's wait . . . or we can try to get the test done at a private lab." He looks up at me. "For free."

"Wow. You *are* taking one for the team," I say, all fake wide-eyed innocence. "You can bill me for condoms. I feel bad enough, you know, without having to worry about her trying to trap you in a pregnancy."

He scowls. "I'm not going to sleep with Tallulah. I'm not even going to ask her out. I'm just going to let her *think* I am. And because of that, she's going to do your buccal swab and fast-track it, as a favor."

I stare at him, impressed by his plan. Maybe he *is* going to turn out to be a decent private investigator, if he's this wily. "This is what you should say when she comes back," I instruct: " 'I may not be Fred Flintstone, but I can make your Bed Rock.' "

Virgil smirks. "Thanks. If I need any help, I'll ask."

As the door opens again, Virgil jumps off the table, and I bury my face in my hands and start to sob. Well, I pretend to, anyway.

"My God," the Cougar says. "What happened?"

Virgil looks just as baffled as she is. "What the fuck?" he mouths.

I hiccup, louder, "I just want to find my m-mother." Through damp eyes, I look at Tallulah. "I don't know where else to go."

Virgil gets into character, slinging an arm around my shoulders. "Her mom disappeared years ago. Cold case. We don't have much to work with."

Tallulah's face softens. I have to admit, it makes her look less like Boba Fett. "You poor kid," she says and then she turns her adoring eyes on Virgil. "And you—helping her out like this? You're one of a kind, Vic."

"We need a buccal swab. I've got a hair that may or may not have been her mother's, and I want to try to match the mitochondrial DNA. At least it would be a starting point for us." He glances up. "Please, Lulu. Help an old . . . friend?"

"You're not so old," she purrs. "And you're the only person I ever let call me Lulu. You got the hair with you?"

He hands her the bag he found at the evidence room.

"Great. We'll get started on the kid's sequencing right away." She pivots, rummaging in a cabinet for a paper-wrapped packet. I am sure it's going to be a needle, and that terrifies me because I hate needles, so I start shaking. Virgil catches my eye. *You're overacting*, he whispers.

But he figures out pretty quick that I'm seriously terrified, because my teeth start chattering. I can't tear my eyes away from Tallulah's fingers as she rips the sterile packaging away.

Virgil reaches for my hand and holds on tight.

I can't remember the last time I held someone's hand. My grandmother's, maybe, to cross the street a thousand years ago. But that was duty, not compassion. This is different.

I stop shivering.

"Relax," Tallulah says. "It's only a big Q-tip." She snaps on a pair of rubber gloves and a mask, and instructs me to open my mouth. "I'm just going to rub this on the side of your cheek. It won't hurt."

After about ten seconds, she removes the swab and sticks it into a little vial, which she labels. Then she does the whole thing again.

"How long?" Virgil asks.

"A few days, if I move heaven and earth."

"I don't know how to thank you."

"*I* do." She walks her fingers up the crook of his arm. "I'm free for lunch."

"Virgil isn't," I blurt out. "You told me you have a doctor's appointment, remember?"

Tallulah leans in to whisper, although—unfortunately—I hear every word. "I still have my hygienist scrubs if you want to play doctor."

"If you're late, *Victor*," I interrupt, "you won't be able to get a refill on your Viagra." I hop off the table, grab Virgil's arm, and pull him out of the room.

We are laughing so hard as we round the corner of the hallway that I think we might collapse before we make it outside. In the sunshine, we lean against the brick wall of Genzymatron Labs, trying to catch our breath. "I don't know whether I should kill you or thank you," Virgil says.

I look at him sideways and put on my huskiest Tallulah voice. "Well . . . I'm free for lunch."

That just makes us laugh harder.

And then, when we stop laughing, we both remember at the same time why we're here, and that neither of us really has something to laugh about. "Now what?"

"We wait."

"For a whole week? There has to be something else you can do."

Virgil looks at me. "You said your mother kept journals."

"Yeah. So?"

"Could be something relevant in there."

"I've read them a million times," I say. "They're research about elephants."

"Then maybe she mentioned her coworkers. Or any conflicts with them."

I slide down along the brick wall, so that I am sitting on the cement walkway. "You still think my mother is a murderer."

Virgil crouches down. "It's my job to be suspicious."

"Actually," I say, "it *used* to be your job. Your job right now is to find a missing person."

"And then what?" Virgil replies.

I stare at him. "You would do that? You would find her for me, and then take her away again?"

"Look," Virgil says and sighs. "It's not too late. You can fire me and leave and I swear to you, I'll forget about your mother and what crimes she may or may not have committed."

"You're not a cop anymore," I remind him. And that gets me thinking about how skittish he was at the police department, how we had to sneak around, instead of walking in the front door and saying hello to his colleagues. "Why *aren't* you a cop anymore?"

He shakes his head, and suddenly he's closed off, sealed shut. "None of your damn business."

Just like that, everything changes. It seems impossible that we were laughing a few minutes ago. He's six inches away from me and he might as well be on Mars.

Well. I should have expected it. Virgil doesn't really care about me; he cares about solving this case. Suddenly uncomfortable, I walk in silence toward his truck. Just because I've hired Virgil to figure out my mother's secrets doesn't give me the liberty to know all of *his*.

"Look, Jenna—"

"I get it," I interrupt. "This is strictly business."

Virgil hesitates. "Do you like raisins?"

"Not really."

"Then how about a date?"

I blink at him. "I'm a little young for you, creeper."

"I'm not hitting on you. I'm telling you the pickup line I used on Tallulah, when she was cleaning my teeth and I asked her out." Virgil pauses. "In my defense, I was completely trashed at the time."

"That's a defense?"

"You got anything better I can use as an excuse?"

Virgil grins, and just like that, he's *back*, and whatever I said to upset him doesn't crackle between us anymore. "I see your point," I reply, trying to sound nonchalant. "That is possibly the worst pickup line I have ever heard in my life."

"Coming from you, that's really saying something."

I look up at Virgil and smile. "Thanks for that," I reply.

I will admit to you that my memory is sometimes fuzzy. Things that I chalk up to nightmares might actually have happened. Things that I think I know for sure may change, over time.

Take the dream I had last night about my father playing hide-and-seek, which I am pretty sure was not a dream but a reality.

Or that memory I have of my mother and father, talking about animals that mate for life. Although it's true I can recall every single word, the actual voices are less clear.

It's my mom, definitely. And it must be my dad.

Except sometimes, when I see his face, it's not.

ALICE

Grandmothers in Botswana tell their children that if you want to go quickly, go alone. If you want to go far, you must go together. Certainly this is true of the villagers I have met. But it might surprise you to know that it is also true of elephants.

Elephants are often seen checking in with others in their herd by rubbing against an individual, stroking with a trunk, putting that trunk in a friend's mouth after that individual has suffered a stressful experience. But in Amboseli, researchers Bates, Lee, Njiraini, Poole, et al. decided to scientifically prove that elephants are capable of empathy. They categorized moments when elephants seemed to recognize suffering in or threat to another elephant and took action to change that: by working cooperatively with other elephants, or protecting a young calf that couldn't take care of itself; by babysitting another's calf or comforting it by allowing it to suckle; by assisting an elephant that had become stuck or had fallen down, or that needed a foreign object, like a spear or snare wire, removed.

I did not get a chance to conduct a study on the scale of the one at Amboseli, but I have my own anecdotal evidence of elephant empathy. There was a bull in the game reserve that we nicknamed Stumpy because, as a youngster, he had lost a large part of his trunk in a noose-shaped wire snare. He didn't have the ability to break off branches or twirl the grass with his trunk like spaghetti, cutting it off with his toenails to put in his mouth. For most of his life, even when he was an adolescent, his herd would feed him. I've seen elephants create a definitive plan to get a calf up the steep bank of a riverbed—a series of coordinated behaviors that includes some of the herd breaking down the bank to make less of a grade, and others guiding the baby from the water, and more still helping to pull her out. But you could argue that there's an evolutionary advantage to keeping Stumpy or that calf alive.

It gets more interesting, though, when there is not an evolutionary advantage to empathetic behavior. When I was in Pilanesberg, I watched an elephant come across a rhino calf that was stuck in the mud of a watering hole. The rhinos were distressed, and that in turn upset the elephant, which stood around trumpeting and rumbling. Somehow, she managed to convince the rhinos that she had practice doing this, and to just get out of the way and let her take over. Now, in the great ecological sphere of things, it was not beneficial to the elephant to rescue a rhino baby. And yet she went in and lifted the baby with her trunk, even though the rhino mother charged her each time she tried. She risked her own life for the offspring of a different species. Likewise, in Botswana, I saw a matriarch come upon a lioness that was stretched out beside an elephant path while her cubs played in the middle of it. Normally, if an elephant sees a lion it will charge— it recognizes the animal as a threat. But this matriarch waited very patiently for the lioness to collect her cubs and move away. True, the cubs were no threat to this elephant, but one day they would be. Right then, however, they were just someone's babies.

And yet, empathy has its limits. Although elephant calves are allomothered by all females in the herd, if the biological mother dies, her baby usually will, too. An orphaned calf that is still milk-fed will not move away from its mother's fallen body. Eventually, the herd will have to make a decision: stay with the grieving baby, and run the risk of not feeding their own calves or getting to water . . . or leave, and consider the certain death collateral damage. It's quite disturbing to watch, actually. I've witnessed what looks like a good-bye ceremony, where the herd touches the calf, where they rumble their distress. And then they move away, and the baby dies of starvation.

Yet once in the wild I saw something different. I came across an isolated calf that had been left behind at a watering hole. Now, I don't know the circumstances—if its mother had died or if the calf had gotten disoriented and wandered off. At any rate, an unrelated herd came by at the same time a hyena trotted in from a different direction. The calf was fair game for the hyena—unprotected, luscious. However, the matriarch of that passing herd had a calf of her own, maybe a tiny bit older. She saw the hyena scoping out the abandoned calf and chased the hyena off. The calf ran over to her and tried to nurse, but she pushed him away and started to move on.

For the record, this is normal behavior. Why, from a Darwinian standpoint, would she limit the resources of a calf with her own genetic makeup by nursing an unrelated baby? Although there *are* records of adoption within herds, the majority of allomothers will not nurse an orphaned calf; there just is not enough milk to go around without compromising their own biological offspring. Moreover, this elephant was not related; the matriarch had no biological ties to the orphaned calf.

That baby, however, let out the most desperate, lonely cry.

The matriarch was a good hundred feet ahead of him at this point. She froze, spun, and charged the calf. It was shocking and terrifying, and yet that baby stood his ground.

The matriarch grabbed him with her trunk and tucked him fiercely between the playpen of her massive legs, walking off with him. For the next five years, every time I saw that calf, he was still part of this new family.

I would argue that there is a special empathy elephants have for mothers and children—either their own species's or another's. That relationship seems to hold a precious significance and a bittersweet knowledge: An elephant seems to understand that if you lose a baby, you suffer.

SERENITY

My mother, who had not wanted me to showcase my Gift, lived long enough for the world to hail me as a successful psychic. I brought her to my set in L.A. to meet her favorite soap star, from the original *Dark Shadows*, who came on my show for a reading. I bought her a little bungalow near my Malibu home, with enough room for her to have a vegetable garden and orange trees. I took her to film premieres and award shows and shopping on Rodeo Drive. Jewelry, cars, vacations—I could give her anything she wanted—but I couldn't predict the cancer that eventually consumed her.

I watched my mother shrink away, until she finally passed. When she did she weighed seventy-five pounds and looked like she would break in a strong wind. I had lost my father years ago, but this was different. I was the best actress in the world—fooling the public into thinking that I was happy and rich and successful, when in reality I knew that a fundamental piece of me was gone.

My mother's passing made me a better psychic. I understood viscerally, now, how people would grasp at the threads I could give them, in an attempt to sew shut the gap where a loved one had been ripped away. In my dressing room at the studio, I would look in the mirror and pray for my mother to come to me. I bargained with Desmond and Lucinda to show me *something*. I was a psychic, dammit. I deserved a sign, to know that wherever she was on the other side, she was all right.

For three years, I got messages from hundreds of spirits trying to contact loved ones here on earth . . . but not a single syllable came through from my own mom.

Then one day, I got into my Mercedes to drive home and went to toss my purse on the passenger seat and it landed in my mother's lap.

My first thought was: *I am having a stroke.*

I stuck out my tongue. There was something I'd read once in a viral email about diagnosing a stroke and not being able to stick out your tongue, or maybe it was having it flop to one side. I couldn't remember.

I felt for my mouth, to see if it was drooping.

"Can I say a simple sentence?" I said out loud. *Yes, fool,* I thought. *You just did.*

I swear on all that's holy, I was a practicing, celebrated psychic, but when I saw my mother sitting there, I was certain I was dying.

My mother was just looking at me, smiling, not saying a word.

Heatstroke, I thought, still not taking my eyes off her, but it wasn't all that hot.

Then I blinked. And she was gone.

In the aftermath, I thought of a lot of things. That if I'd been on the 101, I probably would have caused a multicar pileup. That I would have traded everything I owned to hear her speak one more time.

That she did not look the way she had when she died, feeble and brittle and birdlike. She was the mother I remembered from my childhood, the one strong enough to carry me when I was sick and scold me when I was being a pain in the ass.

I have never seen my mother again, although it's not for lack of trying. But I learned something that day. I believe we've lived many times and have been reincarnated many times, and a spirit is the amalgam of all the lifetimes in which that soul existed. But when a spirit approaches a medium, it comes back with one particular personality, one particular form. I used to think spirits manifested in a certain way so that the living person could recognize them. Yet after my mother came to me, I realized that they come back in the way they want to be remembered.

You may hear this and feel skeptical. You'd be right to feel that way. Skeptics keep the swamp witches at bay; or so I thought, before I became one myself. If you haven't had a personal experience with the paranormal, you *should* question what you're being told.

This is what I would have said to a skeptic, had they approached me the day I saw my mother in the passenger seat: She was not translucent or shimmering or milky white. She was as solid to me as the guy who took my parking ticket minutes later when I pulled out of the garage. It was as if I'd Photoshopped a memory of my mother into the here-and-now, a trick of mechanics, like those videos where the dead Nat King Cole sings with his daughter. No question about it— my mother was as real as the steering wheel under my shaking hands.

But doubt has a way of blooming like fireweed. Once it takes hold, it's nearly impossible to eradicate. It's been years since a spirit has come to me for help. If a skeptic said to me right now, *Who do you think you're kidding?* I suppose I'd say, *Not you. And certainly not me.*

The kid at the Genius Bar who is supposed to be helping me has the people skills of Marie Antoinette. She grunts as she turns on my ancient MacBook and lets her fingers tickle the keyboard. She doesn't make eye contact. "What's wrong?" she asks.

For starters? I'm a professional psychic with no connection to the spirit world; I missed my last two rent payments; I stayed up till 3:00 A.M. last night watching a *Dance Moms* marathon; and the only way I could get into these pants today was by wearing Spanx.

Oh, and my computer's broken.

"When I try to print something," I say, "nothing happens."

"What do you mean, *nothing happens?*"

I stare at her. "What do people usually mean when they say that?"

"Does your screen turn black? Does anything come out of the printer? Do you get an error message? Did you document *anything*?"

I have a theory about Gen Y, these narcissistic twenty-somethings. They don't want to wait their turn. They don't want to work their way up the ladder. They want what they want *now*—in fact, they're sure they deserve it. Young people like this, I believe, are soldiers who died in Vietnam, and have been reincarnated. The timing's right, if you do the math. These kids are still pissed about getting killed in a war they didn't believe in. Being rude is just another way of saying: *Kiss my twenty-five-year-old ass.*

"Hey, hey, LBJ," I say under my breath. "How many kids have you killed today?"

She doesn't glance up.

"Make love, not war," I add.

The techie looks at me like I've lost my mind. "Do you have Tourette's?"

"I'm a psychic. I know who you used to be."

"Oh, Jesus Christ."

"No, not him," I correct.

Chances are, if she was killed in Vietnam in her past life, she was male. Spirit is genderless. (In fact, some of the best mediums I've ever met are gay, and I think it's because they have that balance of masculine and feminine in them. But I digress.) I once had a very famous client—a female R & B singer—who had died in a concentration camp in a previous existence. Her current ex was the SS soldier who had shot her back then, and her job in this life was to survive him. Unfortunately, in this existence, he was beating her up every time he got drunk—and I will bet you anything that, after she dies, she'll return in some other incarnation that crosses with his. That's all a human life is, really—a do-over, a chance to get it right . . . or you'll be brought back to try again.

The techie opens a new menu with a few keystrokes. "You have a backlog of print jobs," she says, and I wonder if she will judge me for printing out the *Entertainment Weekly* recap of *The Real Housewives of*

New Jersey. "That could be the problem." She pushes some buttons, and suddenly the screen goes black. "Huh," she murmurs, frowning.

Even *I* know it is not good when your computer technician frowns.

Suddenly the store printer, on a table adjacent to us, hums to life. It starts spitting out pages at breakneck speed, covered from top to bottom with Xs. The papers pile up, overflowing onto the floor, as I rush to pick them up. I scan them, but they are gibberish, unintelligible. I count ten pages, twenty, fifty.

The techie's supervisor approaches her as she tries furiously to stop my computer from printing. "What's the problem?"

One of the pages flies right from the paper feed into my hands. This page is covered with nonsense, too, except for one small rectangle in the center, where the Xs give way to hearts.

The techie looks like she is going to burst into tears. "I don't know how to fix it."

In the middle of the string of hearts is the only recognizable word on the page: JENNA.

Holy Hell.

"*I* do," I say.

There is nothing more frustrating than being given a sign and not knowing which way it points. That's how it feels when I go home, open myself up to the universe, and get served up a steaming hot bowl of Nothing. In the past, Desmond or Lucinda or both of my spirit guides would have helped me interpret how the name of that kid glitching up my computer is connected to the spirit world. Paranormal experiences are just energy manifesting itself in some way: a flashlight flickering on when you haven't pressed the button; a vision during an electrical storm; your cell phone ringing, and no one on the other end of the line. A surge of energy pulsed through networks to give me a message—I just can't tell who's sent it.

I'm not too thrilled about contacting Jenna, since I'm pretty sure she hasn't forgiven me for leaving her at the steps of the police department. But I can't deny that there's something about that kid that makes me feel more genuinely psychic than I've felt in seven years. What if Desmond and Lucinda sent me this as a test, to see how I'd react, before they committed to being my spirit guides again?

At any rate, I can't risk pissing off whoever's sent me this sign, just in case my whole future depends on it.

Fortunately, I have Jenna's contact information. That ledger I make new clients fill out when they come for a reading? I tell them it's in case a spirit comes to me with an urgent message, but in reality, it's so I can invite them to like my Facebook page.

She has written down a cell phone number, so I call her.

"If this is supposed to be some kind of customer service survey with one being total crap and five being the Ritz-Carlton of psychic experiences, I'll give you a two, but only because you managed to find my mother's wallet. Without that, it's a negative four. What kind of person abandons a thirteen-year-old alone in front of a police department?"

"Honestly, if you think about it," I say, "what *better* place to leave a thirteen-year-old? But then again, you're not the average thirteen-year-old, are you?"

"Flattery will get you nowhere," Jenna says. "What do you want, anyway?"

"Someone on the other side seems to think I'm not done helping you."

She is quiet for a second, letting this sink in. "Who?"

"Well," I admit. "That part's a little fuzzy."

"You lied to me," Jenna accuses. "My mother's dead?"

"I didn't lie to you. I don't know that it's your mother. I don't even know that it's a woman. I just feel like I'm supposed to get in touch with you."

"How?"

I could tell her about the printer, but I don't want her to freak out. "When a spirit wants to talk, it's like a hiccup. You can't *not* hiccup, even if you try. You can get rid of the hiccups, but that doesn't prevent them in the first place. You understand?" What I don't tell her is that

I used to get these messages so often, I got jaded. Bored. I didn't know why people made a big deal out of it; it was just part of me, the same way I had pink hair and all my wisdom teeth. But that's the attitude you have when you don't realize that at any moment, you might lose it. I'd kill for those psychic hiccups now.

"Okay," Jenna says. "What do we do now?"

"I don't know. I was thinking that maybe we should go back to that place where we found the wallet."

"You think there's more evidence?"

All of a sudden in the background I hear another voice. A male voice. "Evidence?" he repeats. "Who *is* that?"

"Serenity," Jenna says to me, "there's someone I think you should meet."

I may have lost my mojo, but that doesn't keep me from seeing, in a single glance, that Virgil Stanhope is going to be as useful to Jenna as screen doors on a submarine. He is distracted and dissipated, like a former high school football star who's spent the past twenty years pickling his organs. "Serenity," Jenna says. "This is Virgil. He was the detective on duty the day my mother disappeared."

He looks at my hand, extended, and shakes it perfunctorily. "Jenna," he says, "c'mon. This is a waste of time—"

"No stone left unturned," she insists.

I plant myself squarely in front of Virgil. "Mr. Stanhope, in my career I've been called in to dozens of crime scenes. I've been in places where I had to wear booties because there was brain matter on the floor. I've gone to homes where kids were abducted and led law enforcement officers to the woods where they were found."

He raises a brow. "Ever testified in court?"

My cheeks pinken. "No."

"*Big* surprise."

Jenna steps in front of him. "If you two can't play together, there's going to be a time-out," she says, and she turns to me. "So what's the plan?"

Plan? I don't have a plan. I am hoping that if I walk around this wasteland long enough, I'll have a flash of recognition. My first in seven years.

Suddenly a man walks by, holding a cell phone. "Did you see him?" I whisper.

Jenna and Virgil lock eyes and then look at me. "Yes."

"Oh." I watch the guy get into his Honda and drive away, still talking on his cell. I'm a little deflated to find out he's a living person. In a crowded hotel lobby, I used to see maybe fifty people, and half of them would be spirits. They weren't rattling chains or holding their severed heads but rather talking on their cell phones, or trying to hail a cab, or taking a mint from the jar at the front of the restaurant. Ordinary stuff.

Virgil rolls his eyes, and Jenna elbows him in the gut.

"Are spirits here right now?" she asks.

I glance around, as if I might still see them. "Probably. They can attach themselves to people, places, things. And they can move around, too. Free range."

"Like chickens," Virgil says. "Don't you think it's weird that with all the homicides I saw as a cop, never once did I see a ghost hanging around a dead body?"

"Not at all," I say. "Why would they want to reveal themselves to you, when you were fighting so hard not to see them? That would be like going into a gay bar if you're straight, and hoping to get lucky."

"What? I'm not gay."

"I didn't say— Oh, never mind."

In spite of the fact that this man is a Neanderthal, Jenna herself seems fascinated. "So let's say there's a ghost attached to me. Would it watch me when I shower?"

"I doubt it. They were alive once; they understand privacy."

"Then what's the fun in being a ghost?" Virgil says under his breath. We step over the chain at the gate, moving with unspoken agreement into the sanctuary.

"I didn't say it was fun. Most of the ghosts I've met haven't been too happy. They feel like they've left something unfinished. Or they were so busy looking into glory holes in their last life they have to get their act together before they move on to whatever comes next."

"You're telling me the Peeping Tom I arrested in the gas station bathroom automatically develops a conscience in the afterlife? Seems a little convenient."

I look back over my shoulder. "There's a conflict between body and soul, sometimes. That friction is free will. Your guy probably didn't come to earth to spy on folks in a gas station bathroom, but somehow ego or narcissism or some other garbage happened to him in his life while he was here. So even though his soul might have been telling him *not* to look through that hole, his body was saying *Tough luck*." I push through some tall grass, untangling a reed that has gotten snared in the fringe of my poncho. "It's like that for drug addicts, too. Or alcoholics."

Virgil abruptly turns. "I'm going this way."

"Actually," I say, pointing in the opposite direction, "I'm getting the feeling we should go *this* way." I am not really getting that feeling at all. It's just that Virgil seems like such an ass that if he says *black* I'm determined to say *white* right now. He's already judged and hanged me, which leads me to believe he knows exactly who I am and can remember Senator McCoy's boy. In fact, if I weren't so completely convinced that there is a reason I have to be with Jenna at this moment, I would bushwhack back to my car and drive the hell home.

"Serenity?" Jenna asks, because she's had the good sense to follow me. "What you said about the body and the soul back there? Is that true for anyone who does bad things?"

I glance at Jenna. "Something tells me that isn't a philosophical question."

"Virgil thinks the reason my mother disappeared was because she was the one who killed the caregiver at the sanctuary."

"I thought it was an accident."

"That's what the police said back then, anyway. But I guess there were some questions Virgil never got answered—and my mother up and left before he got the chance to ask them." Jenna shakes her head. "The medical report said blunt force trauma from trampling was the cause of death, but, I mean, what if it was just blunt force trauma caused by a person? And then the elephant trampled the body once it was dead? Can you even tell the difference?"

I didn't know; that was a question for Virgil, if we ever found each other in the woods again. But it didn't surprise me that a woman who loved elephants as much as Jenna's mother had might have one of her animals trying to cover up for her. That Rainbow Bridge pet lovers always talk about? It's there. I'd occasionally been told by those who'd crossed over that the person waiting for them on the other side was not a person at all but a dog, a horse, once even a pet tarantula.

Assuming that the death of the caregiver at this sanctuary wasn't an accident—that Alice might still be alive and on the run—it would explain why I hadn't gotten the clear sense that she was a spirit trying to contact her daughter. On the other hand, that wasn't the *only* reason why.

"You still want to find your mother if it means learning she committed murder?"

"Yeah. Because then at least I'd know that she's still alive." Jenna sinks down into the grass; it's nearly as high as the crown of her head. "You said you'd tell me if you knew she had passed. And you still haven't said she's dead."

"Well, I certainly haven't heard from her spirit yet," I agree. I don't clarify that the reason might be not because she's alive but rather because I'm a hack.

Jenna starts plucking tufts of grass and sprinkling them over her bare knees. "Does it get to you?" she asks. "People like Virgil thinking you're crazy?"

"I've been called worse. And besides, neither one of us is going to know who's right until we're both dead."

She considers this. "I have this math teacher, Mr. Allen. He said that when you're a point, all you see is the point. When you're a line, all you see is the line and the point. When you're in three dimensions, you see three dimensions and lines and points. Just because we can't see a fourth dimension doesn't mean it doesn't exist. It just means we haven't reached it yet."

"You," I say, "are wise beyond your years, girl."

Jenna ducks her head. "Those ghosts you met, before. How long do they stick around?"

"It varies. Once they get their closure, they usually move on."

I know what she's asking, and why. It's the one myth about the afterlife that I hate debunking. People always think they're going to be reunited with their loved ones for eternity, once they die. Let me tell you: It doesn't work that way. The afterlife isn't just a continuation of this one. You and your beloved dead husband don't pick up where you left off, doing the crossword at the kitchen table or arguing over who finished the milk. Maybe in some cases, it's possible. But just as often as not, your husband might have moved on, graduating to a different level of soul. Or maybe you're the one who's more spiritually evolved, and you'll bypass him while he's still figuring out how to leave this life behind.

When my clients used to come to me, all they wanted to hear from a loved one who had passed was *I will be waiting when you get here.*

Nine times out of ten, what they got instead was *You won't be seeing me again.*

The girl looks sunken, small. "Jenna," I lie, "if your mother was dead, I would know."

I had thought I was going to Hell because I was making a living by scamming clients who thought I still had a Gift. But clearly today I am guaranteeing myself a front-row seat at Lucifer's one-man show, by making this child believe in me when I cannot even believe in myself.

"Oh hey, are you two done with your picnic, or should I keep traipsing around here looking for a needle in a haystack? No, correction," Virgil says. "Not a needle. A needle's *useful.*"

He towers over us with his hands on his hips, scowling.

Maybe I'm not supposed to just be here for Jenna. Maybe I'm supposed to be here for Virgil Stanhope, too.

I get to my feet and try to push away the tsunami of negativity rolling off him. "Maybe if you opened yourself up to the possibility, you'd find something unexpected."

"Thanks, Gandhi, but I prefer to deal in legitimate facts, not woo-woo mumbo jumbo."

"That woo-woo mumbo jumbo won me three Emmys," I point out. "And don't you think we're *all* a little psychic? Haven't you ever thought about a friend you haven't seen in forever, and then he calls? Out of the blue?"

"No," Virgil says flatly.

"Of course. You don't *have* any friends. What about when you're driving down the road with your GPS on and you think, *I'm gonna take a left*, and sure enough, that's what the GPS tells you to do next."

He laughs. "So being psychic is a matter of probability. You have a fifty-fifty chance of being right."

"You've never had an inner voice? A gut reaction? Intuition?"

Virgil grins. "Want to guess what my intuition's telling me right now?"

I throw up my hands. "I quit," I say to Jenna. "I don't know why you thought I'd be the right person to—"

"I recognize this." Virgil starts striking through the reeds with purpose, and Jenna and I both follow. "There used to be a really big tree, but see how it got split by lightning? And there's a pond over there," he says, gesturing. He tries to orient himself by pivoting a few times, before walking about a hundred yards to the north. There, he moves in concentric widening circles, stepping gingerly until the ground sinks beneath his shoe. Triumphantly, Virgil leans down and starts pulling away fallen branches and spongy moss, revealing a deep hole. "This is where we found the body."

"Who was *trampled*," Jenna says pointedly.

I take a step back, not wanting to get in the middle of this drama, and that's when I see something winking at me, half buried in the thicket of moss that Virgil overturned. I lean down and pull out a chain, its clasp intact, with a tiny pendant still dangling: a pebble, polished to the highest gloss.

Another sign. *I hear you*, I think, to whoever is beyond that wall of silence, and let the necklace pool in the valley of my palm. "Look at this. Maybe it belonged to the victim?"

Jenna's face drains of color. "That was my mom's. And she never, ever took it off."

When I meet a nonbeliever—and, sugar, let me tell you, they seem to be attracted to me like bees to nectar—I bring up Thomas Edison. There isn't a person on this planet who wouldn't say he was the epitome of a scientist; that his mathematical mind allowed him to create the phonograph, the lightbulb, the motion picture camera and projector. We know he was a freethinker who said there was no supreme being. We know he held 1,093 patents. We also know that before he passed, he was in the process of inventing a machine to talk to the dead.

The height of the Industrial Revolution was also the height of the Spiritualist movement. The fact that Edison was a supporter of the mechanical breakthroughs in the physical world doesn't mean he wasn't equally entranced by the metaphysical. If mediums could do it via séance, he reasoned, surely a machine calibrated with great care could communicate with those on the other side.

He didn't talk much about this intended invention. Maybe he was afraid of his concept being stolen; maybe he had not come up with a specific design. He told *Scientific American* magazine that the machine would be "in the nature of a valve"—meaning that, with the slightest effort from the other side, some wire might be tripped, some bell might be rung, some proof might be had.

Can I tell you that Edison believed in the afterlife? Well, although he was quoted as saying that life wasn't destructible, he never came back to tell me so personally.

Can I tell you he wasn't trying to debunk Spiritualism? Not entirely.

But it is equally possible that he wanted to apply a scientist's brain to a field that was hard to quantify. It is equally possible that he was trying to justify what I used to do for a living, by giving cold, hard evidence.

I also know that Edison believed the moment between being awake and being asleep was a veil, and it was in that moment that we were most connected to our higher selves. He would set pie tins out on the floor beside each arm of his easy chair and take a nap. Holding a big ball bearing in each hand, he'd nod off—until the metal struck metal. He'd write down whatever he was seeing, thinking, imagining at that moment. He became pretty proficient at maintaining that in-between state.

Maybe he was trying to channel his creativity. Or maybe he was trying to channel . . . well . . . spirits.

After Edison's death, no prototypes or papers were found that suggested he'd started work on his machine to talk to the dead. I suppose that means the folks in charge of his estate were embarrassed by his Spiritualist leanings, or they didn't want that to be the memory left behind of a great scientist.

Seems to me, though, that Thomas Edison got the last laugh. Because at his home in Fort Myers, Florida, there's a life-size statue of him in the parking lot. And in his hand, he's holding that ball bearing.

I am having the sense of a male presence.

Although, if I'm going to be honest, that might just be a sinus headache coming on.

"Of course you're sensing a guy," Virgil says, balling up the aluminum foil that housed his chili dog. I have never seen a human being eat the way this man eats. The terms that come to mind are *giant squid* and *wet vac.* "Who else would give a chick a necklace?"

"Are you always this rude?"

He picks off one of my French fries. "For you, I'm making a special exception."

"You still hungry?" I ask. "How about I serve up a steaming platter of *I told you so?*"

Virgil scowls. "Why? Because you tripped over a piece of jewelry?"

"Well, what did *you* find?" The pimply boy in the corrugated metal trailer who served up our hot dogs is watching this exchange. "What?" I bark at him. "Have you never seen people argue?"

"He's probably never seen someone with pink hair," Virgil murmurs.

"At least I still *have* hair," I point out.

That, at least, hits him where it hurts. He runs a hand over his nearly buzzed cut. "This is badass," he says.

"You just keep telling yourself that." I glimpse the teen hot dog vendor from the corner of my eye again, staring. Part of me wants to believe that he's drawn to the spectacle of the Human Hoover polishing off the rest of my lunch, but there's a niggling thought in my head that maybe he recognizes me as the celebrity I used to be. "Don't you have some ketchup bottles to fill?" I snap, and he shrinks back from the window.

We are sitting outside in a park, eating the hot dogs I bought after Virgil realized he didn't have a dime on him.

"It's my father," Jenna says, over a mouthful of her tofu dog. She is wearing the necklace now. It dangles over her T-shirt. "That's who gave it to my mother. I was there. I remember."

"Great. You remember your mother getting a rock on a chain, but not what happened the night she vanished," Virgil says.

"Try holding it, Jenna," I suggest. "When I used to get called in for kidnappings, the way I got my best leads was to touch something that had belonged to the missing child."

"Spoken like a bitch," Virgil says.

"I beg your pardon?"

He looks up, all innocence. "Female dog, right? Isn't that how bloodhounds track, too?"

Ignoring him, I watch Jenna curl the necklace into her fist, squeeze her eyes shut. "Nothing," she says after a moment.

"It'll come," I promise. "When you least expect it. You've got a lot of natural ability, I can tell. I bet you'll remember something important when you're brushing your teeth tonight."

This is not necessarily true, of course. I've been waiting for years now, and I'm as dry as a bar in Salt Lake City.

"She's not the only one who could use that to jog a memory," Virgil says, thinking out loud. "Maybe the guy who gave it to Alice could tell us something."

Jenna's head snaps up. "My father? He can't even remember *my* name half the time."

I pat her arm. "No need to be embarrassed about the sins of the fathers. My daddy was a drag queen."

"What's wrong with that?" Jenna asks.

"Nothing. But he happened to be a very *bad* drag queen."

"Well, my father's in an institution," Jenna says.

I look at Virgil over her head. "Ah."

"Far as I know," Virgil says, "no one ever went back to talk to your father, after your mom disappeared. Maybe it's worth a try."

I've done enough cold reading to be able to tell when a person is not being transparent. And right now, Virgil Stanhope is lying like a rug. I don't know what his game is, or what he hopes to get out of Thomas Metcalf, but I'm not letting Jenna go with him alone.

Even if I swore I'd never go back into a psychiatric facility.

After the incident with the senator, I had a run of dark days. There was a lot of vodka involved, and some prescription medication. My manager at the time was the one who suggested I take a vacation, and by *vacation*, she meant a little sojourn at a psych ward. It was incredibly discreet—the kind of place that celebrities go to to *refresh*, which is Hollywoodspeak for *get your stomach pumped, dry out,* or *have ECT.* I was there for thirty days, long enough to know I would never let myself get that low again if it meant returning.

My roommate was a pretty little thing who was the daughter of a famous hip-hop artist. Gita had shaved off all her hair and had a line of piercings down the curve of her spine, linked by a thin platinum chain, which made me wonder how she slept on her back. She talked to an invisible posse that was absolutely real to her. When one of those imaginary people apparently came after her with a knife, she had run into traffic and gotten hit by a taxi. She was diagnosed as a paranoid schizophrenic. At the time I lived with her, she believed that she was being controlled by aliens through cell phones. Every time someone tried to send a text, Gita went ballistic.

One night, Gita started rocking back and forth in her bed, saying, "I'm gonna get struck by lightning. I'm gonna get struck by lightning."

It was a clear summer night, mind you, but she wouldn't stop. She kept this up, and an hour later, when a thunderstorm cell came sweeping through the area, she started to scream and rip at her own skin. A nurse came in, trying to calm her down. "Honey," she said, "the thunder and the lightning are outside. You're safe in here."

Gita turned to her, and in that one moment I saw nothing but clarity in her eyes. "You know nothing," she whispered.

There was a drumroll of thunder, and suddenly the window shattered. A neon arc of lightning staggered in, seared the rug, and burned a hole the size of a fist into the mattress beside Gita, who started rocking harder. "I told you I was gonna get struck by lightning," she said. "I told you I was gonna get struck by lightning."

I tell you this story by way of explanation: The people we define as crazy just might be more sane than you and me.

"My father's not going to be helpful," Jenna insists. "We shouldn't even bother."

Again, my cold reading skills shine: The way she cuts her eyes to the left like that, the way she is now chewing on her fingernail—Jenna's lying, too. Why?

"Jenna," I ask, "can you run to the car and see if I left my sunglasses in there?"

She gets up, more than happy to escape this conversation.

"All right." I wait for Virgil to meet my gaze. "I don't know what you're up to, but I don't trust you."

"Excellent. Then we feel exactly the same way about each other."

"What are you not telling her?"

He hesitates, deciding whether or not to trust me, I'm sure. "The night the caregiver was found dead, Thomas Metcalf was nervous.

Antsy. It could have been because his wife and daughter were missing at the time. And it could have been because he was already showing signs of a breakdown. But it also could have been a guilty conscience."

I lean back, crossing my arms. "You think Thomas is a suspect. You think Alice is a suspect. Seems to me you think everyone's to blame except yourself, for saying in the first place that the death was an accident."

Virgil looks up at me. "I think Thomas Metcalf might have been abusing his wife."

"That's a damn good reason to run away," I say, thinking out loud. "So you want to meet with him and try to get a reaction out of him."

When Virgil shrugs, I know I'm right.

"Did you ever consider what that might do to Jenna? She already thinks her mother abandoned her. You're going to take off her rose-colored glasses and show her that her father was a bastard, too?"

He shifts. "She should have thought of that before she hired me."

"You're really an ass."

"That's what I get paid for."

"Then for all intents and purposes, you ought to be in a different tax bracket." I narrow my gaze. "You and I know you're not getting rich off this case. So what do you get out of it?"

"The truth."

"For Jenna?" I ask. "Or for you, because you were too lazy to find it out ten years ago?"

A muscle tics in his jaw. For a second I think I've crossed the line, that he is going to get up and storm off. Before he can, though, Jenna reappears. "No sunglasses," she says. She is still holding the stone, still fastened around her neck.

I know that some neurologists think that autistic kids have brain synapses so close together and firing in such quick succession that they cause hyperawareness; that one of the reasons children on the spectrum rock or stim is to help them focus instead of having all sensations bombard them at once. I think clairvoyance isn't really all that much different. In all probability, neither is mental illness. I asked Gita, once, about her imaginary friends. *Imaginary?* she repeated, as if

I were the one who was crazy, for not seeing them. And here's the kicker—I understood what she was talking about, because I'd *been* there. If you notice someone talking to a person you can't see, she may be a paranoid schizophrenic. But she may also just be psychic. The fact that *you* can't see the other half of the conversation doesn't mean it's not truly happening.

That's the other reason I don't particularly want to visit Thomas Metcalf in a psychiatric facility: I just may be coming face-to-face with people who can't control a natural gift I'd kill to have once again.

"You know how to get to the institution?" Virgil asks.

"Really," Jenna says, "it's really not such a great idea to visit my dad. He doesn't always react well to people he doesn't know."

"I thought you said he doesn't even recognize *you* sometimes. So who's to say we're not just old friends he's forgotten?"

I see Jenna trying to work through Virgil's logic, deciding if she should be protecting her father or trying to take advantage of his weak defenses.

"He's right," I say.

Virgil and Jenna are both shocked by my statement. "You *agree* with him?" Jenna asks.

I nod. "If your dad has anything to contribute about why your mother left that night, it might point us in the right direction."

"It's up to you," Virgil says, noncommittal.

After a long moment, Jenna says, "The truth is, my mother's all he ever talks about. How they met. What she looked like. When he knew he was going to ask her to get married." She bites her lower lip. "The reason I said I didn't want you to go to the institution is because I didn't want to share that with you. With *anyone*. It's, like, the only connection I have with my dad. He's the one person who misses her as much as I do."

When the universe calls, you don't place it on hold. There is a reason I keep circling back to this girl. It's either because of her gravitational pull or because she's a drain I'm bound to be sucked down.

I offer my brightest smile. "Sugar," I say, "I'm a sucker for a good love story."

ALICE

The matriarch had died.

It was Mmaabo, who had slipped to the back of her herd yesterday, her movements laborious and jerky, before she sank down on her front knees and then toppled over. I had been up for thirty-six straight hours, observing. I noted how Mmaabo's herd—her daughter Onalenna, who was her closest companion—had tried to lift her mother with her tusks and had managed to prop her on her feet, only to have Mmaabo fall over for good. How her trunk had reached toward Onalenna one last time before unfurling on the ground, like a skein of ribbon. How Onalenna and the others in the herd had made sounds of distress, had tried to prod their leader with their trunks and their bodies, pushing and pulling at Mmaabo's corpse.

After six hours, the herd left the body. But almost immediately, another elephant approached. I thought it was a trailing member of Mmaabo's herd but recognized the notched triangle on the left ear and the freckled feet of Sethunya, the matriarch of a different, smaller herd. Sethunya and Mmaabo were not related, but as Sethunya approached, she, too, got quieter, softer in her movements. Her head bowed, her ears drooped. She touched Mmaabo's body with her trunk. She lifted her left rear foot and held it above Mmaabo's body. Then she stepped over Mmaabo, so that her front legs and back legs straddled the fallen elephant. She began to sway back and forth. I timed this for six minutes. It felt like a dance, though there was no music. A silent dirge.

What did it mean? Why was an elephant not related to Mmaabo so profoundly affected by her death?

It had been two months since the death of Kenosi, the young bull who'd been caught in the snare, two months since I'd officially narrowed the focus of my postdoctoral work. While other colleagues working at the game reserve were studying the migration patterns of Tuli Block elephants and how they affected the ecosystem; or the effects of drought on the reproductive rate of elephants; or musth and male seasonality, my science was cognitive. It could not be measured with a geographic tracking device; it was not in the DNA. No matter how many times I recorded instances of elephants touching another elephant's skull, or returning to the site where a former herd member died, the moment I interpreted that as grief, I was crossing a line animal researchers were not supposed to cross. I was attributing emotion to a nonhuman creature.

If anyone had ever asked me to defend my work, here's what I would have said: The more complex a behavior is, the more rigorous and complicated the science behind it. Math, chemistry, that's the easy stuff—closed models with discrete answers. To understand behavior—human or elephant—the systems are far more complex, which is why the science behind them must be *that* much more intricate.

But no one ever asked. I'm pretty sure my boss, Grant, thought this was a phase I was going through, and that sooner or later, I'd get back to science, instead of elephant cognition.

I had seen elephants die before, but this was the first time since I'd changed my research focus. I wanted every last detail to be noted. I wanted to make sure I didn't overlook anything as too mundane; any action that I might learn later was critical to the way elephants mourn. To that end, I stayed there, sacrificing sleep. I marked down which elephants came to visit, identifying them by their tusks, their tail hair, the marks on their bodies, and sometimes even the veins on their ears, which had patterns as unique as our own thumbprints. I cataloged how much time they spent touching Mmaabo, where they explored. I wrote down when they left the body, and if they returned. I cataloged the other animals—impala, and one giraffe—that passed through the vicinity, unaware that a matriarch had fallen. But mostly, I stayed because I wanted to know if Onalenna would come back.

It took her nearly ten hours to return, and when she did, it was twilight and her herd was off in the distance. She stood quietly beside her mother's corpse as night fell, immediate as a guillotine. Every now and then she would vocalize, to be answered by rumbles from the northeast—as if she needed to check in with her sisters, and to remind them she was still here.

Onalenna hadn't moved in the past hour, which is probably why I was so startled by the arrival of a Land Rover, the headlights slicing through the dark. It startled Onalenna, too, and she backed away from her dead mother, her ears flapping in threat. "There you are," Anya said, as she pulled her vehicle closer. She was another elephant researcher, who was studying how migratory routes had changed because of poaching. "You didn't answer your walkie-talkie."

"I turned the volume down. I didn't want to disturb her," I said, nodding toward the nervous elephant.

"Well, Grant needs you to do something."

"Now?" My boss had been less than encouraging when I told him about shifting my focus to elephant grief. He hardly talked to me at all now. Did this mean he was coming around?

Anya looked at Mmaabo's body. "When did it happen?"

"Almost twenty-four hours ago."

"Have you told the rangers yet?"

I shook my head. I would, of course. They'd come down and cut the tusks off Mmaabo, to discourage poachers. But I thought, for a few more hours at least, her herd deserved to have time to grieve.

"When should I tell Grant to expect you?" Anya asked.

"Soon," I said.

Anya's vehicle slipped into the bush, becoming a tiny pinprick of light in the inky distance, like a firefly. Onalenna blew out, a huffing sound. She slipped her trunk into her mother's mouth.

Before I could even record that behavior, a hyena trotted into the space in front of Mmaabo. The spotlight I had on the scene caught the bright white incisors as he opened his jaws. Onalenna rumbled. She reached out her trunk, which seemed too far from the hyena to do damage. But African elephants have an extra foot or so of trunk length that, like an accordion, can punch out at you when you least expect it. She popped that hyena so hard it went rolling away from Mmaabo's corpse, whimpering.

Onalenna turned her heavy head toward me. She was secreting from her temporal glands, deep gray streaks.

"You're going to have to let her go," I said out loud, but I am not sure which one of us I was trying to convince.

I woke with a start when I felt the sun on my face, the first shards of daylight. My first thought was that Grant was going to kill me. My second thought was that Onalenna was gone. In her place were two lionesses, tearing at Mmaabo's hindquarters. Above, a vulture swam through the sky in a figure eight, awaiting its turn.

I didn't want to go back to camp; I wanted to sit by Mmaabo's corpse to see if any other elephants would continue to pay their respects.

I wanted to find Onalenna and see what she was doing now, how the herd was behaving, who was the new de facto matriarch.

I wanted to know if she could turn grief off like a faucet, or if she still missed her mother. How long it took for that feeling to pass.

Grant was punishing me, plain and simple.

Out of all the colleagues that my boss could have picked to babysit some New England asshole that was coming here for a week's visit, he chose me. "Grant," I said. "It's not every day we lose a matriarch. You have to recognize how critical this is to my research."

He looked up from his desk. "The elephant's still going to be dead a week from now."

If my research wouldn't sway Grant, maybe my schedule would. "But I'm already supposed to take Owen out today," I told him. Owen was the bush vet; we were collaring a matriarch for a new study that was being done by a research team from the University of KwaZulu-Natal. Or in other words: *I am busy*.

Grant looked up at me. "Fantastic!" he said. "I'm sure this fellow would love to see you do the collaring." And so, I found myself sitting at the entrance of the game reserve, waiting for Thomas Metcalf of Boone, New Hampshire, to arrive.

It was always a hassle when visitors came. Sometimes they were the fat cats who sponsored a collar for GPS monitoring, and wanted to come with their wives and their business buddies to play the politically correct version of the Great White Hunter game—instead of killing elephants, they watched a vet dart one so it could be collared, and then toasted their magnanimousness with G & T sundowners. Sometimes it was a trainer from a zoo or a circus, and when that was the case, they were almost always idiots. The last guy I'd had to squire around in my Land Rover for two days was a keeper at the Philadelphia Zoo, and when we saw a six-year-old bull secreting from its temporal glands, he insisted the baby was coming into musth. No matter how I argued with him (I mean, *really*? A six-year-old male just cannot come into musth!), he assured me that he was right.

I'll admit, when Thomas Metcalf pried himself out of the African taxi (which is an experience in and of itself, if you haven't been in one before), he did not look the way I expected. He was about my age, with small, round glasses that steamed up when he stepped into the humidity, so that he fumbled to grab the handle of his suitcase. He looked me over, from my messy ponytail to my pink Converse sneakers. "Are you George?" he said.

"Do I *look* like a George?" George was one of my colleagues, a student none of us ever thought would finish his PhD. In other words, the butt of all the jokes—that is, until I started studying elephant grief.

"No. I mean, I'm sorry. I was expecting someone else."

"Sorry to disappoint you," I said. "I'm Alice. Welcome to the Northern Tuli Block."

I led him to the Land Rover, and we started winding along the unmarked, dusty paths that looped through the reserve. As we rolled along, I recited the spiel we give visitors. "The first elephants were recorded here in roughly A.D. 700. In the late eighteen hundreds, when guns were supplied to local chiefs, it affected the elephant population dramatically. By the time the Great White Hunters arrived, the elephants were almost gone. It wasn't until the game reserve was founded that the numbers increased. Our research staff is in the field seven days a week," I said. "Although we are all involved in different research projects, we also take care of core monitoring—observing the breeding herds and their associations, identifying the individuals in each, tracking their activity and their habitat, determining home range, doing census once a month, recording births and deaths, estrus and musth; collecting data on bull elephants, recording rainfall—"

"How many elephants do you have here?"

"About fourteen hundred," I said. "Not to mention leopard, lion, cheetah—"

"I can't imagine. I have six elephants, and it's hard enough to figure out who's who if you haven't been with them day in and day out."

I had grown up in New England, and I knew that the odds of there being wild elephants there were about as high as me spontaneously growing another arm. Which meant this guy ran either a zoo or a circus—neither of which I endorsed. When trainers tell you that the behaviors taught to elephants are things they'd do in the wild, they're lying. In the wild, elephants do not stand on their hind legs or walk grabbing each other's tails or skip around in a ring. In the wild, elephants are always only a few yards away from another elephant. They are constantly stroking and rubbing and checking in with each other. The whole relationship between humans and elephants in captivity is about exploitation.

As if I didn't already dislike Thomas Metcalf for being my punishment, I now disliked him on principle.

"So," he said, "what do you do here?"

God save me from tourists. "I'm the local Mary Kay cosmetics salesgirl."

"I meant, what *research* do you do?"

I glanced at him from the corner of my eye. There was no reason for me to feel defensive toward a man I had met a minute ago—a man whose knowledge of elephants was far less comprehensive than mine. And yet I was so used to the raised eyebrows when I talked about my new research that I had become accustomed to not talking about it.

I was saved from replying by a waterfall of horns and hooves bolting across the path. I grabbed the steering wheel and braked at the last moment. "You'd better hang on," I suggested.

"They're amazing!" Thomas gasped, and I tried not to roll my eyes. When you live here, you get jaded. To tourists, everything is new, worth slowing down for, an adventure. Yes, that's a giraffe. Yes, it's extraordinary. But not after you've seen one for the seven hundredth time. "Are they antelope?"

"They're impala. But we call them McDonald's."

Thomas pointed to the rump of one animal, now grazing. "Because of the markings?"

Impala have two black lines running down each hind leg, and another line streaking their stub tail, which does look a little like the Golden Arches. But their nickname comes from being the most prevalent meal in the bush for predators. "Because over one billion have been served," I said.

There is a difference between the romance of Africa and the reality of it. Tourists who come on safari excited to see a kill, who are then lucky enough to witness a lioness taking down its prey, often become quiet and queasy. I watched Thomas's face go pale. "Well, Toto," I said. "Guess you're not in New Hampshire anymore."

As we waited at the main camp for Owen, the bush vet, I told Thomas the rules of safari. "Don't get out of the vehicle. Don't stand up in the vehicle. The animals see us as one big entity, and if you separate yourself from that profile, you're in trouble."

"Sorry to keep you. There was a rhino relocation that didn't go as smoothly as I hoped." Owen Dunkirk came hurrying out, carrying a bag and his rifle. Owen was a bear of a man who preferred to dart from a vehicle rather than a helicopter. We used to be on good terms, until I switched my focus of fieldwork. Owen was old school; he believed in evidence and statistics. I might as well have said I was using a research grant to study voodoo or prove the existence of unicorns. "Thomas," I said. "This is Owen, our vet. Owen, this is Thomas Metcalf. He's visiting for a few days."

"You sure you're still up to this, Alice?" Owen said. "Maybe you've forgotten how to collar, since you've been writing elephant eulogies and whatnot."

I ignored his jab, and the strange look Thomas Metcalf gave me. "I'm pretty sure I can do this with my eyes closed," I told Owen. "Which is more than I can say for you. Aren't you the guy who missed your shot last time? A target as big as . . . well . . . an elephant?"

Anya joined us in the Land Rover. When we went out to collar an elephant, we needed two researchers and three vehicles, so that the herd could be managed while we did our work. The other two Land Rovers were being driven by rangers, one of whom had already been tracking Tebogo's herd today.

Collaring is an art, not a science. I don't like to collar during droughts, or in the summer, when the temperature's too high. Elephants overheat so quickly that you need to monitor their temperature when they go down. The idea is to get the vet about twenty meters from the elephant, so that he can safely shoot the dart. Once that matriarch drops, panic ensues, which is why you ideally want experienced rangers around you who know how to push a herd, and you *don't* want novices like Thomas Metcalf, who might do something stupid.

When we reached Bashi's vehicle, I glanced around, pleased. The landscape was perfect for a darting—flat and wide, so that the elephant, if she ran, wouldn't hurt herself. "Owen," I said, "you ready?"

He nodded, loading the M99 into his dart gun.

"Anya? You take the rear and I'll take the head. Bashi? Elvis? We want to push the herd to the south," I said. "Okay, on three."

"Wait." Thomas put his hand on my arm. "What do *I* do?"

"Stay in the Rover and try not to get yourself killed."

After that, I forgot about Thomas Metcalf. Owen shot the dart, which landed square in Tebogo's bottom. She startled and squealed, whipping her head around. She didn't pull out the little flag, and neither did another elephant, although sometimes I'd seen that happen.

Her distress was contagious, though. The herd bunched, some facing backward around her for protection, some trying to touch her. There was rumbling that rattled the ground, and every elephant began to secrete, the oily residue streaking their cheeks. Tebogo walked a few steps, nodded, and then the M99 kicked in. Her trunk went limp, her head drooped, her body swayed, and she started to go down.

That was when we had to act, and fast. If the herd wasn't moved away from the fallen matriarch, they could injure her trying to get her upright again—spearing her with a tusk—or make it impossible for us to get close enough to Tebogo to revive her with an antidote. She could have fallen on a branch; she could have fallen on her trunk. The trick was to never show fear. If the herd came after us now and we backed off, we'd lose everything—including this matriarch.

"Now," I yelled, and Bashi and Elvis revved their engines. They clapped, howled, and chased the herd with the vehicles, scattering the elephants so that we could pull closer to the matriarch. As soon as there was a good gap between us and the other elephants, Owen and Anya and I leaped out of our vehicle, leaving the rangers to manage the flustered herd.

We only had about ten minutes. Immediately I made sure Tebogo was fully on her side, and that the ground beneath her was clear. I folded her ear over her eye to protect her from dirt and direct sunlight. She stared at me, and I could see the terror in her gaze.

"Shh," I soothed. I wanted to stroke her, but knew I couldn't. Tebogo was not asleep, she was conscious of every noise and touch and smell. For this reason, I would touch her as minimally as possible.

I put a small stick between the two fingers of her trunk, so that it would remain open; an elephant can't breathe through its mouth and will suffocate if the opening of the trunk is blocked. Tebogo snored lightly as I poured water on her ear and over her body, cooling her down for comfort. Then I slipped the collar around her thick neck, settling the receiver of the unit on the top of the elephant, and tied it down under her chin. I tightened the ratchet of the bolt, leaving a space of two hands between her chin and the counterweight, and filed down the metal edges. Anya worked madly, taking blood and a tiny skin clipping from Tebogo's ear and plucking tail hair for DNA, measuring her feet and her temperature, her tusks and the height from foot to scapula. Owen did a once-over, cataloging the elephant for injury, checking her breathing. Finally, we inspected the collar to make sure the GPS system was working, beeping properly.

The whole thing had taken nine minutes, thirty-four seconds.

"We're good," I said, and Anya and I collected all the equipment we'd brought out to the elephant and carried it back to the vehicle.

Bashi and Elvis both drove off as Owen leaned down beside Tebogo once more. "Here, pretty girl," he cooed, and he injected the antidote into her ear, right into the bloodstream.

We wouldn't leave until we knew the elephant was up. Three minutes later, Tebogo rolled to her feet, shaking her massive head, trumpeting at her herd. The collar seemed to fit all right as she meandered closer, rejoining them in a flurry of rumbles and bellows, touching and urinating.

I was hot, sweaty, a mess. I had dirt on my face and elephant drool on my shirt. And I had completely forgotten Thomas Metcalf was still there until I heard his voice.

"Owen," he said. "What's in the dart? M99?"

"That's right," the vet replied.

"I've read that a pinprick is enough to kill a human."

"True."

"So the elephant you just darted, she wasn't asleep. She was only paralyzed?"

The vet nodded. "Briefly. But as you can see, no harm done."

"Back at the sanctuary," Thomas said, "we have an Asian elephant named Wanda. She was at the zoo in Gainesville in 1981, when there were floods in Texas. Most of the animals were lost, but after twenty-four hours someone saw her trunk sticking up in a flooded area. She was submerged for two days, pretty much, before the water receded enough for her to be rescued. Afterward, she was terrified of thunderstorms. She wouldn't let any keepers give her a bath. She wouldn't step in a puddle. And this went on for years."

"I don't know that I'd equate a ten-minute darting with forty-eight hours of trauma," Owen said, bristling.

Thomas shrugged. "Then again," he pointed out, "you're not an elephant."

As Anya bounced the Land Rover back to camp, I sneaked glances at Thomas Metcalf. It was almost as if he were implying that elephants had the capacity to think, to feel, to hold a grudge, to forgive. All of which came dangerously close to my beliefs—the same beliefs that I was ridiculed for, here.

I listened to him telling Owen about the New England Elephant Sanctuary as we traveled the twenty minutes back to the main camp. In spite of what I'd assumed, Metcalf was *not* a circus trainer or a zookeeper. He talked about his elephants like they were his family. He talked about them the way . . . well, the way I talked about mine. He ran a facility that took elephants once kept in captivity and let them live out the rest of their years in peace. He had come here to see if there was any way of making that experience more like their lives in the wild, short of bringing them back to Africa and Asia.

I'd never met anyone like him.

When we arrived at camp, Owen and Anya walked toward the research facility to log Tebogo's data. Thomas stood, his hands in his pockets. "Listen. You're off the hook," he said.

"Excuse me?"

"I get it. You don't want to be saddled with me. You don't want to have to do the dog and pony show for some visitor. You've made that patently clear."

My rudeness had caught up to me, and now my cheeks burned. "I'm sorry," I said. "You're not who I thought you were."

Thomas stared at me for a long moment, long enough to change the direction of the wind for the rest of my life. Then, slowly, he grinned. "You were expecting George?"

"What happened to her?" I later asked Thomas, as we drove out into the reserve by ourselves in a Land Rover. "Wanda?"

"It took two years, and I spent a lot of time getting my clothes soaked, but now she swims in the sanctuary pond all the time."

When he said that, I knew where I was going to take him. I put the Rover into low gear, surfing through the deep sand of a dry river-bed until I found what I was looking for. Elephant tracks look like Venn diagrams, the print of the front foot overlapping the back. These were fresh—flat, shiny circles that hadn't had time to be covered with dust. I could probably figure out the individual whose track I was seeing if I really wanted to, by paying attention to the crack marks of the imprint. Multiplying the back foot's circumference by 5.5 would give me her height. And I knew it was a female, because this was a breeding herd—there were multiple tracks, instead of the solitary line of a bull.

It was not all that far from Mmaabo's body. I wondered if this herd had come across her, what they had done.

Pushing the thought out of my head, I put the truck in gear and followed the trail. "I've never met anyone who ran an elephant sanctuary."

"And I've never met anyone who's ever collared an elephant. I guess we're even."

"What made you want to start a sanctuary?"

"In 1903 there was this elephant at Coney Island named Topsy. She helped build the theme park, and gave rides, and performed in shows. One day, her handler threw his lit cigarette in her mouth. She killed him, big surprise, and was labeled a dangerous elephant. Topsy's owners wanted her killed, so they turned to Thomas Edison, who was trying to show the dangers of AC current. He rigged up the elephant, and she died within seconds." He looked at me. "Fifteen hundred people watched, including my great-grandfather."

"So the sanctuary is some kind of legacy?"

"No, I didn't really remember the story until I was in college and worked one summer at a zoo. They had just gotten an elephant, Lucille. This was big news because elephants are always a draw. They were hoping she would pull the revenue of the zoo back into the black. I was hired as an assistant to the head keeper, who had extensive experience with circus elephants." He glanced out at the bush. "Did you know that you don't even have to touch an elephant with a bull hook to get it to do what you want? You just put it near the ear, and they'll move away from the threat of the pain, because they know what to expect. Needless to say, I made the grave mistake of saying that elephants were conscious of how badly we were treating them. I was fired."

"I just changed the focus of my fieldwork to how elephants grieve."

He glanced at me. "They're better at it than people."

I put my foot on the brake, so we rolled to a stop. "My colleagues would argue with you. No, actually, they'd *laugh* at you. Like they laugh at me."

"Why?"

"For their work, they can use collars, and measurements, and experimental data. What looks like cognition to one scientist looks like conditioning to another—and there's no conscious thought necessary for *that*." I turned to him. "But let's say I *could* prove it. Can you imagine the implications for wildlife management? Like you said to Owen—is it ethical to dart an elephant with M99 if she's fully aware of what we're doing? Especially if it's a precursor to a shot in the head, like when we cull a herd? And if we shouldn't be doing that, how *do* we manage elephant populations?"

He glanced at me, fascinated. "That collar you put on the elephant—does it measure hormones? Stress levels? Is she sick? How do you predict a death, so you know which elephant to collar?"

"Oh, we can't predict death. That collar's for someone else's project. They're trying to find out the turning radius of an elephant."

"Whatever the elephant needs it to be," Thomas said with a laugh. "That's the punch line, right?"

"I'm not kidding."

"Really? How could anyone possibly think that research matters more than what *you're* doing?" He shook his head. "Wanda? The elephant that nearly drowned? She has a partially paralyzed trunk, and she needed a security blanket of sorts when she came to the sanctuary. She got into the habit of dragging a tire around with her. Eventually, she bonded with Lilly and didn't need the tire all the time anymore because she had a friend. But when Lilly died, Wanda was pretty devastated. After Lilly was buried, Wanda brought her tire to the grave site and laid it down on top of the dirt. It was almost like she was paying tribute. Or maybe she thought Lilly needed a little comfort now."

I had never heard anything so moving in my life. I wanted to ask him if sanctuary elephants stayed with the bodies of those they'd considered family. I wanted to ask if Wanda's behavior was the anomaly or the norm. "Can I show you something?"

Making a decision on the spot, I took a detour, driving in a widening circle, until we reached Mmaabo's body. I knew that Grant would have a fit if he learned I had taken a visitor to see an elephant corpse; one of the reasons we told the rangers of deaths was so that they could avoid taking tourists near a decaying body. By now, scavengers had picked apart the elephant; flies buzzed in a cloud around the carcass. And yet Onalenna and three other elephants were standing quietly nearby. "This was Mmaabo," I said. "She was the matriarch of a herd of about twenty elephants. She died yesterday."

"Who's in the distance?"

"Her daughter and some of the rest of the herd. They're mourning," I said defensively. "Even if I'm never able to prove it."

"You *could* measure it," Thomas said, mulling. "There are researchers who've worked with baboons in Botswana, to measure stress. I'm pretty sure that fecal samples showed an increase in glucocorticoid stress markers after one of the baboons in the group was killed by a predator—and those markers were more pronounced in baboons that were socially linked to the dead one. So if you can get fecal matter from elephants—which looks to be pretty abundant—and can statistically show a rise in cortisol—"

"Then maybe it works like it does in humans, to trigger oxytocin," I finished. "Which would be a biological reason for elephants to seek out comfort from each other after the death of a member of the herd. A scientific explanation for grief." I stared at him, amazed. "I don't think I've ever met anyone quite as passionate as I am about elephants."

"First time for everything," Thomas murmured.

"You don't just run a sanctuary."

He ducked his head. "My undergraduate degree was in neurobiology."

"Mine, too," I said.

We both stared at each other, further adjusting our expectations. I noticed that Thomas had green eyes, and that there was a ring of orange around each of his irises. When he grinned, I felt as if I'd taken a dart of M99, as if I was caught in the prison of my own body.

We were interrupted by the sounds of rumbling. "Ah," I said, forcing myself to turn away. "Like clockwork."

"What is?"

"You'll see." I put the Land Rover into low gear and started up a steep incline. "When you approach wild elephants," I explained quietly, "you do it the way you'd want your own worst enemy to approach you. Would you feel comfortable if he came in and surprised you from behind? Or cut between you and your child?" I pulled the vehicle in a wide circle at the plateau, and then crested the edge downhill to reveal a breeding herd splashing in a pond. Three calves piled on top of each other in a mud puddle, the one on the bottom rolling out from underneath his cousins and spraying a fountain in the air. But even their mothers were wading and kicking, making waves, wallowing.

"That's the matriarch," I told him, pointing to Boipelo. "And that's Akanyang, with the folded ear. She's Dineo's mother. Dineo's the cheeky one, tripping his brother, over there." I introduced Thomas to each elephant by name, ending with Kagiso. "She's due to deliver in about a month," I told him. "Her first calf."

"Our girls play in the water all the time," Thomas said, delighted.

"I figured they picked that behavior up at the zoos where they used to live, as distraction. I assumed that, in the bush, it's always life or death."

"Well, yeah," I agreed. "But play is part of life. I've seen a matriarch slide down a steep bank on her butt, just for fun." I leaned back, propping my sneakers on the dashboard, letting Thomas watch the antics. One calf threw herself sideways in the mud, displacing her younger sibling, who squealed his distress. Just like that, their mother trumpeted: *Enough, you two.*

"This is exactly what I came here to see," Thomas said softly.

I looked at him. "A watering hole?"

He shook his head. "When an elephant is brought to us at the sanctuary, she's already broken. We do our best to put her back together again. But it's all guesswork, unless you know what she looked like when she was whole." Thomas faced me. "You're lucky, to see this every day."

I didn't tell him that I'd also seen calves orphaned by culling, and droughts so severe that the skin of the elephants stretched over their hip bones like canvas on a frame. I didn't tell him how, in the dry season, herds would split up so that they didn't have to compete with each other for limited resources. I didn't tell him about Kenosi's brutal death.

"I told you my life story," Thomas said, "but you haven't told me what brought you to Botswana."

"They say people who work with animals do it because they're no good around other people."

"Having met you," he said drily, "I'll refrain from commenting."

The elephants were nearly all out of the water by now, trudging up the steep slope to dust their backs with dirt and amble into the distance, wherever the matriarch led. The last female pushed her baby's rump, giving him a boost uphill before scrambling up herself. They moved away in a silent, syncopated rhythm; I've always thought elephants walk as if they have music being piped into their heads that no one else can hear. And from the roll of their hips and their swagger, I'm going to guess that the artist is Barry White.

"I work with elephants because it's like watching people at a café,"

I told Thomas. "They're funny. Heartbreaking. Inventive. Intelligent. God, I could go on and on. There's just so *much* of us in them. You can watch a herd and see babies testing limits, moms taking care, teenage girls coming out of their shells, teenage boys blustering. I can't watch lions all day, but I could watch *this* my whole life."

"I think I could, too," Thomas said, but when I faced him he was not looking at the elephants. He was staring at me.

It was the habit of the camp not to let our guests walk unescorted through the main camp. At dinnertime, rangers or researchers would meet guests at their huts and lead them by flashlight to the dining hall. This wasn't meant to be charming; it was practical. I'd seen more than one tourist run in a panic after a warthog crossed the path unannounced.

When I went to get Thomas for dinner, his door was ajar. I knocked, and then pushed it open. I could smell the soap from his shower hanging in the air. The fan was turning over the bed, but it was still beastly hot. Thomas sat at the desk in his khakis and a white tank, his hair damp, his jaw freshly shaved. His hands were moving with quick efficiency over what looked like a tiny square of paper.

"Just a second," he said, not looking up.

I waited, jamming my thumbs into my belt loops. I rocked back and forth on the heels of my boots.

"Here," Thomas said, turning around. "I made this for you." He reached for my hand and pressed into my palm a tiny origami elephant, crafted out of a U.S. dollar bill.

In the days that followed, I started to see my adopted home through Thomas's eyes: the quartz glittering in the soil like a handful of diamonds that had been tossed outside. The symphony of birds, grouped by voice part on the branches of a mopane tree, being conducted by a distant vervet monkey. Ostriches running like old ladies in high heels, their plumes bobbing.

We talked about everything from poaching in the Tuli Circle to the residual memories of elephants and how they tied in to PTSD. I played him tapes of musth songs and estrus songs, and we wondered if there could be other songs passed down, in low frequencies we could not hear, to teach elephants the history they mysteriously accumulated: which areas were dangerous and which were safe; where to find water; what the most direct route was from one home range to another. He described how an elephant might be transported to the sanctuary from a circus or a zoo after being labeled dangerous, how tuberculosis was a growing problem in captive elephants. He told me about Olive, who had performed on television and at theme parks, who one day broke loose from her chains, and how a zoologist was killed trying to catch her. Of Lilly, whose leg was broken in a circus and never reset. They had an African elephant, too—Hester—who was orphaned as a result of culling in Zimbabwe, and who had performed in a circus for almost twenty years before her trainer decided to retire her. Thomas was in negotiations, now, to bring in another African elephant named Maura, who he hoped would be a companion for Hester.

In return I told him that while wild elephants will kill with their front feet, kneeling to crush their victims, they use their sensitive back feet to stroke the body of a fallen elephant, how the pads of those feet will hover over the skin and circle, as if they are sensing something we can only guess at. I told him how I once brought the jawbone of a bull back to camp to study, and how that night Kefentse, a subadult male, broke into camp, took the bone from my porch, and returned it to the place of his friend's death. I told him how, the first year I came to the reserve, a Japanese tourist who had wandered away from camp was killed by a charging elephant. When we went to retrieve the body, we found the elephant covering the man, standing vigil.

On the evening before Thomas was supposed to fly home, I took him somewhere I'd never taken anyone before. At the top of the hill was a huge baobab tree. The native people believed that when the Creator called the animals together to help plant all the trees, the hyena was late. He was given the baobab, and he was so

angry, he planted it upside down, giving it a topsy-turvy look, as if
its roots were scratching the sky instead of buried beneath the
ground. Elephants liked to eat the bark of the baobab, and used it
for shade. The old bones of an elephant named Mothusi were scattered in its vicinity.

I watched Thomas go still as he realized what he was seeing. The
bones glowed in the boil of the sun. "Are these . . ."

"Yes." I parked the Rover and got out, encouraging him to do the
same. This area was safe, at this time of day. Thomas moved carefully
through Mothusi's remains, picking up the long curve of a rib, touching his fingertips to the honeycomb center of a split hip joint. "Mothusi died in 1998," I told him. "But his herd still visits. They get
quiet and reflective. Kind of like we would, if we went to visit someone's grave." I leaned down, picking up two vertebrae and notching
them together.

Some of the bones had been carried off by scavengers, and we had
Mothusi's skull at the camp. The remaining bones were so white that
they looked like rips in the weave of the earth. Without really thinking about what we were doing, we started gathering them, until they
formed a collection at our feet. I pulled up a long femur, grunting as
I dragged it. We moved in silence, creating a puzzle that was larger
than life.

When it was done, Thomas took a stick and drew an outline
around the elephant's skeleton. "There," he said, stepping back. "We
just did in an hour what it took nature forty million years to do."

There was a peace wrapped around us, like cotton batting. The
sun was setting, simmering through a cloud. "You could come back
with me, you know," Thomas said. "At the sanctuary, you'd be able to
observe plenty of grief. And your family in the States must miss you."

My chest tightened. "I can't."

"Why?"

"I saw a calf get shot, in front of its mother. And not a little calf,
either—a nearly grown one. She wouldn't leave him, not for days.
When I saw that, something just . . . changed in me." I glanced at
Thomas. "There's no biological advantage to grief. In fact, in the

wild, it can be downright dangerous to be moping around or swearing off food. I couldn't look at that matriarch and say I was watching a conditioned behavior. That was sorrow, pure and simple."

"You're still grieving for that calf," Thomas said.

"I guess I am."

"Is his mother?"

I didn't reply. I had seen Lorato in the months since Kenosi's death. She was busy with her younger calves; she had gone back to being a matriarch. She had moved past that moment in a way that I hadn't been able to.

"My father died last year," Thomas said. "I still look for him in crowds."

"I'm sorry."

He shrugged. "I think grief is like a really ugly couch. It never goes away. You can decorate around it; you can slap a doily on top of it; you can push it to the corner of the room—but eventually, you learn to live with it."

Somehow, I thought, elephants had taken it a step further. They didn't grimace every time they entered the room and saw that couch. They said, *Remember how many good memories we had here?* And they sat, for just a little while, before moving elsewhere.

Maybe I started crying; I can't remember. But Thomas was so close now that I could smell the soap on his skin. I could see the sparks of orange in his eyes. "Alice. Who have you lost?"

I froze. This wasn't about me. I wouldn't let him make it that way.

"Is that why you push people away?" he whispered. "So they can't get close enough to hurt you when they're gone?"

This virtual stranger knew me better than anyone else in Africa. He knew me better than I knew myself. What I was really researching was not how elephants deal with loss but how humans can't.

And because I did not want to let go, because I didn't know how, I wrapped my arms around Thomas Metcalf. I kissed him in the shade of the baobab tree, with its upside-down roots in the air, with its bark that could be cut a hundred times and still heal itself.

JENNA

The walls of the institution where my father lives are painted purple. It makes me think of Barney, that giant, creepy dinosaur, but apparently some very renowned psychologist wrote an entire PhD dissertation about which color inspires healing, and this was right at the top of the list.

The nurse on duty looks straight at Serenity when we walk in, which I guess makes sense, because we appear to be a family unit—if a dysfunctional one. "Can I help you?"

"I'm just here to see my dad," I say.

"Thomas Metcalf," Serenity adds.

I know several of the nurses here; this one I haven't met, which is why she doesn't recognize me. She puts a clipboard on the counter so that I can sign us in, but before I do, I hear my father's voice, shouting somewhere down the hall. "Dad?" I call out.

The nurse looks bored. "Name?" she says.

"Sign us in and meet me in Room 124," I tell Serenity, and I start to run. I can feel Virgil falling into step beside me.

"Serenity Jones," I hear her say, and then I throw open the door to my dad's room.

He is fighting against the grip of two burly orderlies. "For the love of God, let me go," he yells, and then he spies me. "Alice! Tell them who I am!"

There's a broken radio that looks like it's been hurled across the room, its wires and transistors draped across the floor like a robot autopsy. The trash can has been overturned, and there are crumpled paper pill cups and tangles of masking tape and the peel of an orange scattered around. In my father's hand is a box of breakfast cereal. He's holding on to it like it's a vital organ.

Virgil stares at my dad. I can only imagine what he's seeing: a man with wild snowy hair and pretty lousy personal grooming habits, who's skinny and fierce and completely off his rocker. "He thinks you're Alice?" Virgil says under his breath.

"Thomas," I soothe, stepping forward. "I'm sure the gentlemen will understand if you calm down."

"How can I calm down when they're trying to steal my research?"

By now, Serenity has come through the doorway, too, stopping dead at the struggle. "What's going on?"

The orderly with a blond buzz cut glances up. "He got a little agitated when we tried to throw out the empty cereal box."

"If you stop fighting, Thomas, I'm sure they'll let you keep your . . . your research," I say.

To my surprise, that's all it takes for my dad to go limp. Immediately the orderlies release him, and he sinks back in the chair, clutching that stupid box to his chest. "I'm all right now," he mutters.

"Cuckoo for Cocoa Puffs," Virgil murmurs.

Serenity shoots him a sharp glare. "Thank you so much," she says pointedly to the orderlies, as they pick up the trash that's all over the floor.

"No problem, ma'am," one replies, as the other pats my dad on the shoulder.

"You take it easy, bro," he says.

My dad waits until they leave and then stands and grabs my arm. "Alice, you cannot imagine what I've just discovered!" His eyes focus suddenly past me, on Virgil and Serenity. "Who are they?"

"Friends of mine," I say.

That seems to be good enough. "Look at this." He points to the box. There is a bright cartoon of something that might be a turtle and might be a cucumber with legs, saying in a thought bubble: DID YOU KNOW . . .

> . . . *that crocodiles can't stick out their tongues?*
>
> . . . *that honeybees have hair on their eyes to help them collect pollen?*
>
> . . . *Anjana, a chimp at a rescue facility in South Carolina, has raised white tiger cubs, leopard, and lion cubs—bottle-feeding and playing with the babies?*
>
> . . . *Koshik, an elephant, can accurately speak six Korean words?*

"Of course he's not *speaking* six words," my father says. "He's imitating the keepers. I Googled the scientific paper this morning after that imbecile Louise finally got off the computer because she'd reached the next level of Candy Crush. What's fascinating is that he apparently learned to communicate for social reasons. He was kept apart from other elephants, and the only interaction he had socially was with human caregivers. You know what this means?"

I glance at Serenity and shrug. "No, what?"

"Well, if there's documented proof that an elephant learned to imitate human speech, can you imagine the implications for how we think about elephants' theory of mind?"

"Speaking of theories," Virgil says.

"What's your field of study?" my father asks him.

"Virgil does . . . retrieval work," I improvise. "Serenity's interested in communication."

He brightens. "Through what medium?"

"Yes," Serenity says.

My father looks baffled for a moment but then forges on. "Theory of mind covers two critical ideas: that you have an awareness of being a unique being, with your own thoughts and feelings and intentions . . . and that this is true for other beings, and that they don't know what you're thinking or vice versa until these things are communicated. The evolutionary benefit, of course, of being able to predict the behavior of others based on that is enormous. For example, you can pretend to be injured, and if someone doesn't know you're faking, they will bring you food and take care of you and you don't have to do any work. Humans aren't born with this ability—we develop it. Now, we know that for theory of mind to exist, humans have to use mirror neurons in the brain. And we know that mirror neurons fire when the task involves understanding others through imitation—and when acquiring language. If Koshik the elephant is doing that, doesn't it also stand to reason that the other things mirror neurons signify in humans—like empathy—are also present in elephants?"

When I hear him talk, I realize how incredibly smart he must have been, before. I realize what made my mother fall in love with him.

That reminds me why we're here.

My father turns to me. "We need to get in touch with the authors of the paper," he muses. "Alice, can you imagine the implications for my research?" He reaches for me—I feel Virgil tense up—and hugs me, swinging me in a circle.

I know he thinks I'm my mother. And I know it's totally creepy. But you know, sometimes it's just nice to be hugged by my dad, even if the reasons are all wrong.

He puts me down, and I have to admit, I haven't seen him look this fired up in a while.

"Dr. Metcalf," Virgil says, "I know this is really important to you, but I wonder if you might have time to answer a few questions about the night your wife disappeared."

My father's jaw tightens. "What are you talking about? She's right here."

"That's not Alice," Virgil replies. "That's your daughter, Jenna."

He shakes his head. "My daughter is a child. Look, I don't know what you're playing at, but—"

"Stop agitating him," Serenity interjects. "You're not going to get anything out of him if he's upset."

"Out of me?" my father's voice rises. "You're here to steal my research, too?" He advances on Virgil, but Virgil grabs my hand and pulls me between them, so that my father cannot help but see me.

"Look at her face," he urges. "*Look* at her."

It takes five seconds for my dad to respond. And let me tell you, five seconds is a really long time. I stand there, watching his nostrils flare with every breath and his Adam's apple climb up and down the ladder of his throat.

"Jenna?" my father whispers.

For just a fraction of a second, when he looks at me, I know that he's not seeing my mother. That I'm—what did he say?—a unique being, with my own thoughts and feelings and intentions. That I *exist*.

And then he's crushing me against him again, but this is different—protective and amazed and tender, as if he could shield me from the rest of the world, which is ironically all I've ever done for him. His hands span my back like wings.

"Dr. Metcalf," Virgil says, "about your wife—"

My father holds me at arm's length and glances in the direction of Virgil's voice. That's all it takes to break whatever glass thread has been spun between us. When he turns to me again, I know he's not seeing me at all. In fact, he's not even looking at my face.

His gaze is fixated on the tiny pebble hanging from a chain around my neck.

Slowly, he lifts the pendant with his fingers. He turns it over so that the mica glitters. "My wife," he repeats.

His fist tightens on the chain, snapping it off my neck. The necklace falls to the floor between us as my father slaps me so hard that I go flying across the room.

"You fucking bitch," he says.

ALICE

I have a story that is not one of my own but was told to me by Owen the bush vet. A few years ago, researchers were darting in a communal area. They had targeted one specific female, and shot the M99 dart from a vehicle. She dropped, as expected. But the herd bunched very tightly around the female, preventing the other rangers from driving them away. They couldn't get to her to put on the collar, so they waited a bit to see what would happen.

Two concentric circles formed around the fallen female. The outer circle stood with their backsides to her, facing out at the vehicles, impassive. But there was an inner circle behind them that the researchers could not quite see, blocked as they were by the bulky bodies on the front line. They could hear rustling, and movement, and the snapping of branches. Suddenly, as if on cue, the herd stepped away. The elephant that had been darted lay on her side, covered with broken branches and a huge pile of soil.

After birth, a calf is dusted by its mother to cover the smell of blood, which is a huge attraction for predators. But there was no blood on this female elephant. I've heard, too, that the reason elephants might cover a corpse is to mask the death smell—but again, I don't believe it. Elephant noses are so incredibly sensitive, there is no way they would have mistaken an elephant that had been darted for one that was no longer alive.

I have of course seen elephants dust and cover dead companions or calves that did not survive. It often seems to be a behavior reserved for deaths that are unexpected or somehow aggressive. And the deceased does not necessarily have to be an elephant. A researcher who came to the reserve via Thailand told a story of an Asian bull that was part of an elephant-back safari company. He had killed the mahout who had trained him and cared for him for fifteen years. Now, the bull was in musth—which in Hindi means "madness." In musth, brainpower takes a backseat to hormones. Yet after the attack the bull got very still and backed away, as if he knew he had done something wrong. Even more interesting were the female elephants, which covered the mahout with dirt and branches.

The week before I left Botswana forever, I had been putting in long hours. I observed Kagiso with her dead calf; I was writing up notes from the death of Mmaabo. One hot day, I got out of the jeep to stretch my legs, and I lay down beneath the baobab tree where I had last been with Thomas.

I am not a light sleeper. I do not do stupid things, like get out of the Land Rover in spots that are heavily trafficked by elephants. I do not even remember closing my eyes. But when I awakened, my pad and pencil were somewhere on the ground and my mouth and eyes were gritty with dirt. There were leaves in my hair and branches piled on top of me.

The elephants that had covered me were nowhere to be found when I awakened, which was probably a good thing. I could just as easily have been killed as partially buried alive. I had no explanation for my deep, comatose nap, for my lapse of judgment, except that I was *not* myself. I was more than myself.

I've always found it ironic that the elephants which found me sleeping assumed I was dead, when in reality I was full of life. Approximately ten weeks along, to be exact.

SERENITY

Once, on my TV show, I had on a doctor who talked about hysterical strength—the life-and-death moments when people do extraordinary things, like lifting a car off a loved one. The common denominator was a high-stress situation that triggered adrenaline, which in turn led to someone transcending the limits of what his or her muscles should be capable of doing.

I had seven guests that day. Angela Cavallo, who had lifted a 1964 Chevy Impala off her son Tony; Lydia Angyiou, who had wrestled a polar bear in Quebec when it was coming after her seven-year-old son during a game of pond hockey; and DeeDee and Dominique Proulx, twelve-year-old twins who had pushed a tractor off their grandfather when it toppled over on a steep slope. "It was, like, crazy," DeeDee told me. "We went back and tried to move the tractor, after. We couldn't budge it an inch."

It's what I'm thinking about when Thomas Metcalf smacks Jenna across the face. One minute, I'm watching like a spectator, and the next, I'm shoving him away and diving against all principles of space and gravity so that Jenna lands in my arms. She looks up at me, as surprised as I am to find herself in my embrace. "I've got you," I tell her fiercely, and I realize I mean it, in every interpretation.

I am not a mother, but maybe that's what I'm supposed to be right now for this girl.

Virgil, for his part, smacks Thomas so hard that he falls back into the chair. A nurse and one of the orderlies burst into the room, having heard the crash. "Grab him," the nurse says, and Virgil moves aside as the orderly restrains Thomas. She glances at us, on the floor. "Are you all right?"

"Fine," I say, as Jenna and I stand.

The truth is, I'm not all right, and neither is she. She's gingerly touching the spot where she was slapped, and me, I feel like I'm going to throw up. Have you ever felt like the air was too heavy or gotten an inexplicable chill? That's somatic intuition. I used to be a pretty good empath—I could walk into a room as if I were dipping my toe into bathwater to test it for energy, and know if it was good or bad, if a murder had gone down there or if there was sadness coating the walls like layers of paint. For whatever it's worth, there's some weird shit swirling around Thomas Metcalf.

Jenna is trying hard to hold it together, but I can see the sheen of tears in her eyes. From across the room, Virgil pushes off the wall, clearly agitated. His jaw is so tight I can tell he's fighting to not unleash a stream of curses at Thomas Metcalf. He blows out of the room, a tornado.

I look at Jenna. She stares at her father as if she has never seen him before; and maybe that's true, in a way. "What do you want to do?" I murmur.

The nurse glances at us. "I think we'll sedate him, for a while. Might be best if you come back later."

I wasn't asking *her*, but that's all right. Maybe it even makes it easier for Jenna to leave her father, who still hasn't apologized. I slip my arm through hers and pull her tight against me, tugging her out of the room. As soon as I cross the threshold, it's easier to breathe.

There's no sign of Virgil in the hallway, or even in the front foyer. I lead Jenna past other patients, who stare at her as we pass. At least their caregivers have the grace to pretend they don't see her fighting back her sobs, her cheek red and swollen.

Virgil paces in front of my car. He looks up when he sees us. "We shouldn't have come here." He grasps Jenna's chin and turns her face so that he can see the damage. "You're going to have a hell of a shiner."

"Great," she says, glum. "Should be fun explaining that to my grandma."

"Tell her the truth," I suggest. "Your dad's not stable. If he decked you, it wouldn't be out of character—"

"I already knew that before we came," Virgil blurts out. "I knew Metcalf was violent."

Jenna and I face him. "What?" she asks. "My dad isn't violent."

Virgil just raises an eyebrow. "*Was,*" he repeats. "Some of the most psychopathic guys I've ever met are domestic abusers. They're charming as all get-out when they're in public; in private, they're animals. There was some indication during the investigation that your dad was abusive to your mother. Another employee mentioned it. Clearly your father thought you were Alice, back there. Which means—"

"That my mom might have run away to protect herself," Jenna says. "She might have had absolutely nothing to do with Nevvie Ruehl's death."

Virgil's cell phone starts to ring. He answers it, hunching forward so that he can hear the call. He nods and walks a few feet away.

Jenna looks up. "But that still doesn't explain where my mom went or why she didn't try to come for me."

Out of the blue, I think: *She's stuck.*

I still don't know if Alice Metcalf is dead, but she is certainly acting the way an earthbound spirit would—like a ghost who's afraid of being judged for her behavior while living.

I'm saved from answering Jenna by the return of Virgil. "My parents were happily married," Jenna tells him.

"You don't call the love of your life a fucking bitch," Virgil says frankly. "That was Tallulah at the lab. The mitochondrial DNA from your cheek swab was a match to the hair from the evidence bag. Your mother was the redhead in close proximity to Nevvie Ruehl before she died."

To my surprise, Jenna seems annoyed by this information, rather than upset. "Look, could you make up your mind? Is it my mother who's the crazed killer, or is it my father? Because I'm getting whiplash bouncing back and forth between your theories."

Virgil looks at Jenna's injured eye. "Maybe Thomas went after Alice, and she ran into the enclosure to escape. Nevvie was there doing whatever she was supposed to be doing that night for her job. She got in the way, and was killed in the process by Thomas. Feeling guilty about a murder is a pretty good trigger to lose your grasp on reality and wind up in an institution . . ."

"Yeah," Jenna says sarcastically. "And then he cued the elephant to come walk back and forth on top of Nevvie so it would *look* like she was trampled. Because, you know, they're trained to do that."

"It was dark. The elephant could have stepped on the body accidentally—"

"Twenty or thirty times? I read the autopsy report, too. Plus, you don't have any evidence of my father being inside those enclosures."

"Yet," Virgil says.

If Thomas Metcalf's room made me queasy, then being between these two makes me feel like my head is going to explode. "Too bad Nevvie's gone," I say cheerfully. "She'd be a great resource."

Jenna takes a step toward Virgil. "You know what I think?"

"Does it matter? Because you and I both know you're going to tell me anyway . . ."

"I think that you're so busy accusing everyone else that night so you don't have to admit that *you're* the one to blame for a crappy investigation."

"And I think *you're* a spoiled little shit who isn't actually brave enough to open Pandora's box and see what's inside."

"You know what?" Jenna yells. "You're fired."

"You know what?" Virgil shouts back. "I quit."

"Good."

"Fine."

She turns on her heel and starts running.

"What am I supposed to do?" he asks me. "I said I'd find her mom. I didn't say she'd like the results. God, that kid drives me up a freaking wall."

"I know."

"Her mother probably stayed away because she's such a pain in the ass." He grimaces. "I don't mean that. Jenna's right. If I'd trusted my instincts ten years ago, we'd never be here."

"The question is, would Alice Metcalf?"

We both think about that for a moment. Then he glances at me. "One of us should go after her. And by *one of us*, I mean *you*."

I take my keys out of my purse and unlock the car. "You know, I used to filter the information I got from spirits. If I thought it was going to be painful to my client, or upsetting, I'd leave the message out of my reading. Just pretend I never heard it. But eventually I realized it wasn't my business to judge the information I was getting. It was just my job to relay it."

Virgil squints. "I can't tell if you're agreeing with me."

I slide into the driver's seat, turn on the ignition, and roll down my window. "I'm just saying that you don't have to be the ventriloquist. You're the dummy."

"You just wanted to be able to say that to my face."

"A little bit," I confess. "But I'm trying to tell you to stop being invested in where this is leading, and stop trying to steer it. Just follow where it goes."

Virgil shades his eyes in the direction Jenna went. "I don't know if Alice is a victim who ran to save her life, or a perp who took someone else's life. But the night we were called to the sanctuary, Thomas was upset about Alice stealing his research. Kind of like he was today."

"You think that's why he tried to kill her?"

"No," Virgil says. "I think *that* was because she was having an affair."

ALICE

I have never seen a better mother than an elephant.

I suppose that if humans were pregnant for two years, the investment might be enough to make us all better mothers. A baby elephant can do no wrong. He can be naughty, he can steal food from his mother's mouth, he can move too slowly or get stuck in mud, and still, his mother is patient beyond belief. Babies are the most precious things in an elephant's life.

The protection of the calves is the responsibility of the entire herd. They cluster, with the babies walking in the middle. If they pass one of our vehicles, the baby is on the far side, with the mother forming a shield. If the mother has another daughter, six to twelve years old, they often sandwich the baby between them. Often, that sibling will come up to the vehicle, shaking her head to threaten you, as if to say, *Don't you dare; that's my little brother.* When it's the height of the day and nap time, babies sleep under the canopies of their mothers' massive bodies, because they are more susceptible to sunburn.

The term given to the way babies are brought up in elephant herds is *allomothering*, a fancy word for "It takes a village." Like everything else, there is a biological reason to allow your sisters and aunts to help you parent: When you have to feed on 150 kilograms of food a day and you have a baby that loves to explore, you can't run after him *and* get all the nutrition you need to make milk for him. Allomothering also allows young cows to learn how to take care of a baby, how to protect a baby, how to give a baby the time and space it needs to explore without putting it in danger.

So theoretically you could say an elephant has many mothers. And yet there is a special and inviolable bond between the calf and its birth mother.

In the wild, a calf under the age of two will not survive without its mother.

In the wild, a mother's job is to teach her daughter everything she will need to know to become a mother herself.

In the wild, a mother and daughter stay together until one of them dies.

JENNA

I'm walking along the state highway when I hear a car crunching on the gravel behind me. It's Serenity, of course. She pulls up and swings open the passenger door. "Let me at least drive you home," she says.

I peer into the car. The good news is that Virgil isn't in it. But that doesn't mean I feel like a heart-to-heart with Serenity, where she tries to convince me that Virgil is just doing his job. Or worse, that he may be right.

"I like walking," I tell her.

There is a run of flashing lights, and a cop car pulls up behind Serenity.

"Great," she says and sighs. And to me: "Get in the goddamn car, Jenna."

The cop is young enough to still have zits, and a flat top as manicured as the eighteenth green at a golf course. "Ma'am," he says. "Is there a problem?"

"Yes," I say, at the same time Serenity says, "No."

"We're fine," I add.

Serenity grits her teeth. "Honey, get in the car."

The cop frowns. "I beg your pardon?"

With a loud sigh, I climb into the VW. "Thanks anyway," Serenity says, and she puts on her left signal and pulls into traffic doing about six miles an hour.

"At this rate I'd get home faster if I *did* walk," I mutter.

I poke through the trash that litters her car: ponytail scrunchies, gum wrappers, Dunkin' Donuts receipts. An ad for a sale at Jo-Ann fabric, even though to my knowledge she is not crafty in the least. A half-eaten granola bar. Sixteen cents and a dollar bill.

Absently, I take the dollar bill and start folding it in the shape of an elephant.

Serenity glances at me as I flip and crease and press. "Where'd you learn how to do that?"

"My mother taught me."

"What were you, a savant?"

"She taught me in absentia." I look at her. "You'd be surprised how much you can learn from someone who's completely disappointed you."

"How's your eye?" Serenity asks, and I almost laugh, it's such a perfect transition.

"Hurts." I take the finished elephant and prop it in the little nook that has the radio controls. Then I shrink down in my seat, pressing my shoes against the dashboard. Serenity has a fuzzy blue steering wheel cover meant to look like a monster, and an ornate cross hanging from her rearview mirror. They seem about as far apart on the belief scale as humanly possible, and it gets me thinking: Can a person hold tightly to two thoughts that look, at first sight, as if they'd cancel each other out?

Could my mother *and* my father both be blamed for what happened ten years ago?

Could my mom leave me behind but still love me?

I glance at Serenity, with her violently pink hair, and the too-tight leopard-print jacket, which makes her look like a human sausage. She is singing a Nicki Minaj song, and getting all the lyrics wrong, and the radio isn't even on. It's easy to make fun of someone like her, but I love that she doesn't apologize for herself: not when she curses in front of me; not when people in elevators stare at her makeup style (which I'd say is pretty much geisha-meets-clown); not even when—it should be noted—she made a colossal mistake that cost her a career. She may not be very happy, but she is happy to *be*. It's more than I can say about myself. "Can I ask you a question?" I say.

"Sure, sugar."

"What's the meaning of life?"

"Well, Christ on a cracker, girl. That's not a question. That's a philosophy. A question is, *Hey, Serenity, can we swing through a McDonald's?*"

I'm not letting her off the hook that easily. I mean, someone who talks to spirits all the time can't just chat about the weather and baseball. "Didn't you ever *ask*?"

She sighs. "Desmond and Lucinda, my spirit guides, said all the universe wants from us is two things: Don't do any intentional harm to yourself or anyone else, and get happy. They told me humans make it more complicated than it needs to be. I thought for sure they were feeding me a line. I mean, there's got to be more to it than *that*. But if there is, I guess I'm not supposed to know it yet."

"What if the meaning of my life is to find out what happened to *hers*?" I ask. "What if that's the only thing that will make me happy?"

"Are you so sure it will?"

Because I don't want to answer, I turn on the radio. By now, we're on the outskirts of town, anyway, and Serenity drops me off at the rack where I've locked up my bike. "You want dinner, Jenna? I make a mean Chinese take-out order."

"Thanks but no thanks," I say. "My grandmother's expecting me."

I wait for her to drive off, so she can't see that I'm not going home.

It takes another half hour to bike to the sanctuary, and twenty minutes to hike through the uneven brush to the spot with the purple mushrooms. My cheekbone is still throbbing as I lie back on the lush grass and listen to the wind play through the branches overhead. It's the hour that's the seam between day and night.

Probably I have a concussion, because I fall asleep for a while. It's dark when I wake up, and I don't have a light on my bike, and I'll probably be grounded for missing dinner. But it's worth it, because I have been dreaming about my mother.

In my dream, I was really little, in nursery school. My mother had insisted that I go because it wasn't normal for a three-year-old to be socialized only with adult animal behaviorists and a bevy of elephants. My class had taken a field trip to meet Maura; afterward, the other kids painted strangely shaped animals that the teachers enthused about no matter how biologically inaccurate they were: *It's so gray! How creative to make* two *trunks! Well done!* My elephant paintings were not only precise but detailed—I put the notch in Maura's ear, the same way my mother did when she sketched the elephant; I made the hair on her tail kinky, when every other kid in my class had completely overlooked its presence. I knew exactly how many toenails she had on each foot (three on the back foot, four on the front). My teachers, Miss Kate and Miss Harriet, said I was like a tiny little Audubon, although I had no idea what that meant at the time.

Other than that, I was a mystery to them: I didn't watch television, so I had no idea who the Wiggles were. I couldn't tell the Disney princesses apart. Most of the time the teachers took the quirks of my upbringing in stride—I mean, this was nursery school, not SAT prep. But one day, in preparation for the holidays, we were given sheets of fancy white paper and told to draw a picture of our family. We were then going to make a macaroni frame, spray it with gold paint, and put this inside as a gift.

Other kids started drawing right away. There were all sorts of families: Logan lived with his mom, alone. Yasmina had two dads. Sly had a baby brother, and then two older brothers, who had a mom that was different from his. There were various permutations of siblings, but it was clear that if there were extra people in the family, they were kids.

Me, I drew myself with five parents.

There was my father, with his glasses. My mother, with her flaming red ponytail. Gideon and Grace and Nevvie, all wearing khaki shorts and the red polo top that was the sanctuary uniform.

Miss Kate sat down next to me. "Who are all these people, Jenna? Are these your grandma and grandpa?"

"No," I told her, pointing. "That's my mommy and that's my daddy."

That led to my mother being pulled aside at pickup. "Dr. Metcalf," Miss Harriet said, "Jenna seems to have a little trouble identifying her immediate family."

She showed my mother the picture. "It looks completely accurate to me," my mother replied. "All five adults take care of Jenna."

"That isn't the concern," Miss Harriet said.

It was then that she pointed out the spider writing, my disastrously spelled attempts to label these people. There was MOM, holding one of my hands, and there was DAD, holding the other. Except DAD wasn't the man I'd drawn with glasses. *He* was in a corner, nearly pushed off the page.

My happy little family unit was either wishful thinking or the uncanny observation of a three-year-old who saw more than anyone expected.

I'm going to find my mother—before Virgil can. Maybe I can save her from being arrested; maybe I can warn her. Maybe the two of us can run off together, this time. True, I'm going up against a private investigator who unravels mysteries for a living. But I know one thing he doesn't.

My dream under the tree was what brought to the surface something I guess I've known all along. I know who gave my mother that necklace. I know why my parents were fighting back then. I know who, all those years ago, I *wished* was my dad.

Now I just have to find Gideon again.

PART II

Children are the anchors of a mother's life.

—Sophocles, *Phaedra*, fragment 612

ALICE

In the wild, we often didn't realize an elephant was pregnant until she was about to deliver. The mammary glands would swell at about twenty-one months, but before that, short of doing a blood test or having witnessed a bull mating with a particular female nearly two years earlier, it was very hard to predict an impending birth.

Kagiso was fifteen, and we had only just recently figured out that she was going to have a calf. Every day, my colleagues would try to spot her, to see if she had delivered yet. For them, it was good field-work. But for me, it became a reason to get out of bed.

I did not yet know I was pregnant. All I knew was that I had been more tired than usual, listless in the heat. Research that had energized me before now seemed to be routine. If I did happen to witness some-thing remarkable in the field, the first thought to cross my mind was *I wonder what Thomas would have made of that.*

I had told myself that my interest in him was due solely to the fact that he was the first colleague who hadn't mocked my research. When Thomas left, it was with the feeling of a summer romance—a trinket that I could take out and examine for the rest of my life, the same way I might save a seashell from a beach vacation or the ticket from my first Broadway musical. Even if I'd wanted to see if this rickety frame of a one-night stand could bear the load of a full-fledged relationship, it wasn't practical. He lived on a different continent; we both had our respective research.

But, as Thomas had pointed out in passing, it wasn't like one of us studied elephants and one of us studied penguins. And due to the trauma of a life spent in captivity, there were often more deaths and grieving rituals to observe at elephant sanctuaries than there were in the wild. The opportunity to continue my research wasn't limited to the Tuli Block.

After Thomas left for New Hampshire, we communicated through the secret code of scholarly articles. I sent him detailed notes about Mmaabo's herd, which was still visiting her bones a month after her death. He sent back a story of the passing of one of his elephants, and how three of her companions stood in the barn stall where she'd collapsed, serenading her body for several hours. What I really meant when I wrote *This might interest you* was *I miss you*. What he really meant when he wrote *Thought of you the other day* was *You are always on my mind*.

It was almost as if there was a tear in the fabric I was made of, and he was the only color thread that would match to stitch it back up.

One morning when I was tracking Kagiso, I realized that she was no longer walking with her herd. I began to search the vicinity, and found her a half mile away. Through my binoculars I spotted the tiny form at her feet, and I raced to a vantage point where I could better see.

Unlike most elephants giving birth in the wild, Kagiso was alone. Her herd was not there, celebrating with a cacophony of trumpets and a pandemonium of touching, like a family reunion where all the elderly aunties rush to pinch the cheeks of a newborn. Kagiso wasn't celebrating, either. She was pushing at the still calf with her foot, trying to get it to stand. She reached down with her trunk and twined it with the baby's, which slipped limp out of her grasp.

I had seen births before where the calf was weak and shaky, where it took longer than the usual half hour to get it up on its feet and stumbling along beside its mom. I squinted, trying to see if there was

any rise and fall to the chest of the calf. But really all I needed to examine was the set of Kagiso's head, the sag of her mouth, the wilt of
her ears. Everything about her looked deflated. She knew already,
even if I didn't.

I had a sudden flash of Lorato, charging down the hill to protect
her grown son when he was shot.

If you are a mother, you must have someone to take care of.

If that someone is taken from you, whether it is a newborn or an
individual old enough to have offspring of its own, can you still call
yourself a mother?

Staring at Kagiso, I realized that she hadn't just lost her calf. She
had lost herself. And although I had studied elephant grief for a living,
although I had seen numerous deaths in the wild before and had recorded them dispassionately, the way an observer should—now, I
broke down and started to cry.

Nature is a cruel bitch. We researchers are not supposed to inter-
fere, because the animal kingdom works itself out without our inter-
vention. But I wondered if things might have been different had we
monitored Kagiso months earlier—even though I knew it was unlikely that we would have known further in advance that she was going
to have a baby.

On the other hand, I myself had no excuse.

I didn't notice that I'd skipped my period until my cargo shorts no
longer fit and I had to close them with a safety pin. After the death of
Kagiso's calf, after I spent five days recording her grief, I drove off the
reserve and into Polokwane to buy an over-the-counter pregnancy
test. I sat in the bathroom of a peri-peri chicken restaurant, staring at
the little pink line, and sobbed.

By the time I returned to camp, I had pulled myself together. I
talked to Grant and asked for a three-week leave of absence. Then I
left Thomas a voice mail, taking him up on his offer to visit the New
England Elephant Sanctuary. It took less than twenty minutes for

Thomas to call me back. He had a thousand questions: Would I mind bunking at the sanctuary? How long could I stay? Could he pick me up at Logan Airport? I gave him all the information he wanted, leaving out one very critical detail. Namely, that I was pregnant.

Was I right to keep this from him? No. Blame it on the fact that I immersed myself in a matriarchal society every day, or blame it on cowardice: I just wanted to take a careful, closer look at Thomas before I let him claim partial ownership of this child. I didn't know, at that point, if I would even keep the baby. And if I did, clearly I was going to raise it in Africa by myself. I simply didn't feel that one night under a baobab tree meant Thomas necessarily deserved a vote.

In Boston I stumbled off the airplane, rumpled and tired, stood in line at passport control, collected my luggage. When the doors belched me into the arrivals lounge, I saw Thomas immediately. He was standing behind the railing, sandwiched between two black-suited chauffeurs. In his fist, he was holding an uprooted plant upside down, like a witch's bouquet.

I wheeled my bag around the barrier. "Do you bring dead flowers to all the girls you pick up at airports?" I asked.

He shook the plant so that a little dirt rained down on the floor, over my sneakers. "It's the closest I could get to a baobab tree," Thomas said. "The florist was no help, so I had to improvise."

I tried not to let myself see this as a sign that he, too, was hoping we could pick up where we had left off, that what we'd had was more than a flirtation. In spite of the carbonation of hope inside me, I was determined to play dumb. "Why would you want to bring me a baobab?"

"Because an elephant wouldn't fit in the car," Thomas said, and he smiled at me.

Doctors will tell you that it wasn't medically possible, that it was too early in the pregnancy. But at that moment, I felt the butterfly flutter of our baby, as if the electricity between us was all she needed to combust into life.

. . .

On the long drive to New Hampshire, we talked about my research: how Mmaabo's herd was coping after her death; how heartbreaking it had been to see Kagiso mourning her dead calf. Thomas told me, with great excitement, that I would be there for the arrival of his seventh sanctuary elephant—an African named Maura.

We did not talk about what had happened between us under that baobab tree.

We also did not talk about how I had found myself missing Thomas at odd moments, such as when I saw two young bulls kicking around a dung ball as if they were soccer stars, and I wanted to share it with someone who would appreciate it. Or how I woke up sometimes with the feel of him on my skin, as if his fingerprints had left a scar.

In fact, with the exception of the plant he'd brought to the arrivals lounge, Thomas had made no mention of anything except our relationship as scientific colleagues. So much so that I was beginning to wonder if I had dreamed the night between us; if this baby was a figment of my imagination.

By the time we arrived at the sanctuary, it was night, and I could barely keep my eyes open. I sat in the car as Thomas opened an electronic gate and then a second, internal one. "The elephants are really good at showing us how strong they are. Half the time when we put up a fence, an elephant will take it down just to let us know that she *can*." He glanced at me. "We had a rash of phone calls when we first opened the sanctuary . . . neighbors saying that there was an elephant in the backyard."

"So what happens when they get out?"

"Well, we get them back in," Thomas said. "The whole point of living here is that they won't get beaten or hurt for escaping, like they would have been in a zoo or circus. It's like a toddler. Just because a kid pushes your buttons doesn't mean you don't love him."

The mention of a toddler made me cross my arms over my abdomen. "Do you ever think about that?" I asked. "Having a family?"

"I have one," Thomas replied. "Nevvie and Gideon and Grace. You'll meet them tomorrow."

I felt as if I'd been run through the chest with a spear. Had I never even *asked* Thomas if he was married? How could I have been so stupid?

"I couldn't run this place without them," Thomas continued, oblivious to the total internal breakdown happening in the passenger seat. "Nevvie worked for twenty years at a circus down South as an elephant trainer. Gideon was her apprentice. He's married to Grace."

Slowly, I began to puzzle out the relationships. And the fact that none of those three people seemed to be his wife or offspring.

"Do they have children?"

"No, thank God," Thomas said. "My insurance rates are already sky-high; I can't imagine the liability of having a kid wandering around."

That, of course, was the right response. It would have been ludicrous to raise a child on a game reserve, just as it would be crazy to raise one on the grounds of a sanctuary. By definition, the animals Thomas took in were "problem" elephants—ones that had killed trainers or acted out in some way that made the zoo or circus want to get rid of them. But his answer made me feel like he had failed an exam, one that he didn't even know was being administered.

It was too dark to see anything in the enclosures, but as we passed another high fence, I unrolled the window of the car so that I could smell that familiar dusty, sweetgrass scent of elephants. In the distance, I heard a low rumble that sounded like thunder. "That would be Syrah," Thomas said. "She's our welcome committee."

He pulled up to his cottage and took my luggage out of the car. His home was tiny—a living room, a kitchenette, a bedroom, an office no bigger than a closet. There was no guest room, but Thomas didn't put my battered suitcase in his bedroom, either. He stood awkwardly in the middle of his own house, pushing his glasses up the bridge of his nose. "Home sweet home," he said.

Suddenly I wondered what I was doing here. I barely knew Thomas Metcalf. He could have been a psychopath. He could have been a serial killer.

He could have been a lot of things, but he *was* the father of this baby.

"Well," I said, uncomfortable. "Long day. Would it be okay if I took a shower?"

Thomas's bathroom was, to my surprise, pathologically neat. His toothbrush was in a drawer, parallel to the tube of toothpaste. His vanity was scrubbed spotless. The pill bottles in his medicine cabinet were organized alphabetically. I ran the shower until the small room filled with steam, until I stood like a ghost in front of the mirror, trying to see into my future. I showered beneath the hottest water until my skin was pink and raw, until I had worked out the best way to cut my visit short, because clearly coming here had been a mistake. I don't know what I had been thinking: that Thomas had been eight thousand miles away, pining for me? That he had been secretly wishing I would travel halfway across the globe to pick up where we had left off? Clearly, the hormones swimming through my system were making me delusional.

When I stepped out in a towel, my hair combed through and my heels leaving damp footprints on the wooden floor, Thomas was fitting sheets and blankets on the couch. If I had needed any clearer proof that what had transpired in Africa had been a rogue mistake, rather than a beginning, here it was staring me in the face. "Oh," I said, as something broke inside me. "Thanks."

"This is for me," he said, averting his eyes. "You can take the bed."

I felt heat rising to my face. "If that's what you want."

You have to understand—there is a romance to Africa. You can see a sunset and believe you have witnessed the hand of God. You watch the slow lope of a lioness and forget to breathe. You marvel at the tripod of a giraffe bent to water. In Africa, there are iridescent blues on the wings of birds that you do not see anywhere else in nature. In Africa, in the midday heat, you can see blisters in the atmosphere. When you are in Africa, you feel primordial, rocked in the cradle of the world. Given that sort of setting, is it any wonder that recollections might be rose-colored?

"You're the guest," Thomas said politely. "It's whatever *you* want."

What did I want?

I could have taken the bedding and slept alone on the couch. Or I could have told Thomas about the baby. Instead, I walked toward him, and let the towel I was holding around me fall to the floor.

For a moment, Thomas just stared. He reached out one finger and traced the curve from my neck to my shoulder.

Once, as a college student, I had gone swimming at night in a bioluminescent bay in Puerto Rico. Every time I moved my arms or my legs, there was a fresh shower of iridescent sparks, as if I were creating falling stars. This is how it felt when Thomas touched me—as if I had swallowed light. We ricocheted against furniture and walls; we did not make it to the couch. Afterward, I lay in his arms on the rough wooden floor. "You told me *Syrah* was the welcome committee."

He laughed. "I can go get her if you want."

"That's okay. I'm good."

"Don't sell yourself short. You're fabulous."

I turned in his arms. "I didn't think you wanted to do this."

"I didn't think *you* wanted to do this," Thomas said. "I didn't want to make any assumptions, you know, that what had happened before would happen again." He tangled his hand in my hair. "Penny for your thoughts?"

Here's what I was thinking: that gorillas will lie to deflect blame from themselves. That chimps deceive. And monkeys will sit high in a tree and pretend there's danger, even when there isn't. But not elephants. An elephant will never pretend to be something she's not.

Here's what I said: "I was just wondering if we're ever going to get to do this in a bed."

A white lie. What was one more?

The land in South Africa often looks parched, its heels and elbows cracked with drought, its valleys baked red by the sun. This sanctuary, by comparison, was a lush Garden of Eden: verdant hills and damp fields, flowering, muscled oak trees with their arms bent in fourth position. And, of course, there were the elephants.

There were five Asian elephants, one African, and another African on the way. Unlike in the wild, the social bonds here were not formed by genetics. Herds were limited to two or three elephants, which had chosen to roam the property together of their own accord. There were some elephants, Thomas told me, who just did not get along; there were some who preferred to be on their own; there were others who didn't move four feet away from their chosen companion.

It surprised me, how much the philosophy of the sanctuary was like ours in the field. Just like we might want to rush in and save a gravely injured elephant, we wouldn't, because it would disrupt nature. We took our lead from the elephants, and considered ourselves lucky to be able to watch unobtrusively. Likewise, Thomas and his staff wanted to give his retired elephants as much freedom as possible, instead of micromanaging their existence. They might not be released into the wild in their dotage, but this would be the next best thing. The elephants here had spent most of their lives being hooked and chained and beaten to force behavior. Thomas believed in free contact—he and his staff still went into the enclosures to feed the elephants and to medically treat them if necessary—but behavior modification was done only with reward and positive reinforcement.

Thomas took me around the sanctuary on an ATV so that I could get my bearings. I rode behind him, my arms wrapped around his waist and my cheek pressed into the warmth of his back. The gates were designed with openings small enough for the vehicles to pass through, but too small for an elephant to escape. There were separate enclosures for the Asian elephants and the African elephants, and each had its own barn—although right now, Hester was the only African elephant in hers. The barns themselves were giant hangars, so clean that you could practically eat off the floors. Heaters ran through the concrete to keep the elephants' feet warm in the winter, and heavy straps hung on the doors, like the long fabric tongues of a car wash, so that heat could be retained in the winter but the elephants could choose to go in and out. There were automatic watering mechanisms in each stall. "It must cost a fortune to run this place," I murmured.

"A hundred and thirty-three thousand dollars," Thomas answered.

"Each year?"

"Each *elephant*," he told me, and laughed. "God, I wish it were per year. I sank everything into securing the land, when I saw the property advertised. And we let Syrah sell herself, by inviting all the neighbors and the press to come see what we were doing. We get donations, but that's a drop in the bucket. Produce alone costs about five thousand bucks per elephant."

My Tuli elephants had years of drought, where you could see the macramé knots of their spines and the grooves of their ribs beneath the skin; South Africa was different from Kenya and Tanzania, where the elephants always looked comparatively fat and happy to me. But at least my elephants had *some* food. The property of the sanctuary was vast and verdant, but there would never be enough brush and vegetation to support the elephants here; and they did not have the luxury of roaming hundreds of miles along elephant corridors to find more—nor did they have a matriarch to lead them there.

"What's that?" I asked, pointing to what looked like an olive barrel, strapped to the steel grid of the stall.

"A toy," Thomas explained. "There's a hole in the bottom, and inside is a ball that's stuffed with treats. Dionne has to put her trunk in and move the ball around if she wants to get the treats out."

As if he'd called her, at that moment an elephant swept through the whispering straps of the doors into the barn. She was small and speckled, with a dusting of hair on the top of her head. Her ears were tiny, compared to those of the African elephants I was used to, and ragged around the edges. The bony ridges over her eyes were pronounced, a hooded cliff. Those eyes were big and brown, so thickly lashed that they could have put a model to shame, and they were riveted on me—the stranger. I felt as if she was trying, intensely, to tell me a story, yet I was not fluent in her language. Suddenly, she shook her head, the same in-your-face warning behavior I was used to seeing at the game reserve when we inadvertently invaded the space of a herd. It made me smile, because her smaller ears didn't quite have the same intimidation factor. "Asian elephants do that, too?"

"No. But Dionne was raised in the Philadelphia Zoo with African elephants, so her attitude's a little bigger than those of most of the other Asian girls. Isn't that right, gorgeous?" Thomas said, sticking out his arm so that she could sniff at it with her trunk. From nowhere, he produced a banana, and she delicately took it from Thomas's hand and tucked it into the side of her mouth.

"I didn't know it was safe to keep African and Asian elephants together," I said.

"It isn't. She got hurt during a shoving match, and after that, the zoo staff kept her segregated. But they didn't have the space for that, so they decided to send her here to the sanctuary."

His cell phone started to ring. He took the call, turning away from Dionne and me. "Yes, it's Dr. Metcalf," he said. He covered the receiver, glancing back, mouthing: *The new elephant.*

I waved him away and then stepped closer to Dionne. In the field, even with the herds that were used to seeing me, I never forgot that these elephants were wild animals. Wary, I held out my hand, the way I might have approached a stray dog.

I knew Dionne could smell me from where she was, across the stall. Hell, she could probably smell me from outside the barn. Her trunk lifted in an S, its tip swiveling like a periscope. The fingers pinched together, then snaked through the bars of the stall. I stayed very still, letting her brush my shoulder, my arm, my face; reading me by touch. With each exhalation I smelled hay and banana. "Nice to meet you," I said softly, and she traced her way down my arm, until her trunk found the cup of my palm.

She blew a raspberry, and I burst out laughing.

"She likes you," said a voice.

I turned to find a young woman behind me, with a flaxen pixie haircut and pale skin, so delicate that my first thought was of a soap bubble destined to burst. My second thought was that this woman was too tiny to do the heavy lifting necessary to take care of elephants. She looked young, hand-blown, fragile.

"You must be Dr. Kingston," she said.

"Alice, please. And you're . . . Grace?"

Dionne began to rumble. "Oh yes, I'm not paying attention to you, am I?" Grace patted Dionne on her brow. "Breakfast will be ready shortly, Your Majesty."

Thomas walked back into the barn. "I'm sorry. I have to run up to the office. It's about Maura's transport—"

"Don't worry about me. Seriously, I am a big girl and I'm surrounded by elephants. I couldn't be happier." I glanced at Grace. "Maybe I can even help."

Grace shrugged. "Fine with me." If she saw Thomas give me a quick kiss before he left to jog up the hill, she didn't comment on it.

If I had believed Grace to be weak, however, she proved me wrong in the next hour, as she told me what her day was like: The elephants were fed twice, at 8:00 A.M. and then again at 4:00 P.M. Grace had to pick up the prȯduce and make the individual meals. She would sweep out manure, pressure-wash the stalls, water the trees. Her mother, Nevvie, restocked the grain for the elephants and picked up the food left behind in the fields, which was delivered to the compost field; she also tended the garden that grew produce for the elephants and their caregivers, and did office work for the sanctuary. Gideon took care of gate maintenance and landscaping; oversaw the boiler, the tools, and the four-wheelers; mowed the grass; stacked the hay; hauled boxes of produce; and did rudimentary elephant health care and maintenance. All three of them took turns doing training, and being the overnight caregiver. And that was just on an ordinary day—one on which nothing went wrong or when an elephant did not need some special attention.

As I helped Grace organize breakfast for the elephants in the barn kitchen, I thought—again—how much easier my job was at the game reserve. All I had to do was show up and take notes and analyze data;

and every now and then help a park ranger or vet dart an elephant or administer some sort of medication to one who was injured. I wasn't *running* the wild. And I certainly didn't have to fund it.

Grace told me that she never intended to live this far north. She had grown up in Georgia and couldn't stand the cold. But then Gideon had come to work for her mother, and when Thomas asked for their help starting this sanctuary, Grace went along as a silent partner. "So you weren't working at the circus?" I asked.

Grace dropped potatoes into individual buckets. "I was going to be a second-grade teacher," she said.

"They have schools in New Hampshire."

She looked at me. "Yes," she said. "I guess they do."

I got the feeling that there was a story there, one I didn't understand, much like my silent conversation with Dionne. Had Grace followed her mother here? Or her husband? She was good at her job, but lots of people were good at their jobs without actually enjoying what they were doing.

Grace worked with ridiculous speed and efficiency; I'm sure I was only slowing her down. There were greens and onions and sweet potatoes and cabbage, broccoli, carrots, grains. Some elephants needed vitamin E or Cosequin added to their diets; others needed supplement balls—apples hollowed out with medicine inside and peanut butter on the top. We hauled the buckets into the back of the four-wheeler, heading out to find the elephants, so that they could have breakfast.

We followed dung and broken branches and prints in mud puddles to track the elephants from the places they were last seen the night before. If it was colder in the morning, like it was now, they'd be more likely to have moved to a higher elevation.

The first elephants we located were Dionne, who'd left the barn when we went in to prepare the food, and her best friend, Olive. Olive was bigger, although Dionne was taller. Olive's ears draped in soft folds, like velvet curtains. They stood close enough to touch, and their trunks were entwined, like young girls holding hands.

I was holding my breath, and I didn't realize it, until I saw Grace looking at me. "You're like Gideon and my mother," she said. "It's in your blood."

The elephants must have been used to the vehicle, but it was still amazing for me to be this close while Grace hefted the first two buckets and dumped them out about twenty feet apart. Dionne immediately picked up a Blue Hubbard squash and crunched the entire thing in her mouth at once. Olive alternated food choices, following each bite of vegetable with a palate cleanser of straw.

We continued this, going on a treasure hunt for the other elephants. I met them all by name, taking note of which elephant had a cut in one ear, which had an odd gait from previous injuries, which ones were skittish, which ones were friendly. They congregated in twos and threes, reminding me of the Red Hat ladies I saw once in Johannesburg, celebrating the good fortune of old age.

It wasn't until we reached the African elephant enclosure that I realized Grace had slowed the ATV down and was idling outside the gate. "I don't like going in there," she admitted. "Gideon usually does it for me. Hester's a bully."

I could see why she felt that way. A moment later, Hester came charging out of the woods, her head shaking and her massive ears flapping. She trumpeted so loudly the hair stood up on my arms. Immediately, I felt myself smile. *This*, I knew. *This*, I was used to.

"I could do it," I suggested.

From the look on Grace's face you would have thought I'd suggested that I sacrifice a goat with my bare hands. "Dr. Metcalf would kill me."

"Trust me," I lied, "if you know one African elephant, you know them all."

Before she could stop me, I hopped off the ATV and lugged the bucket with Hester's food through the gap in the fencing. The elephant lifted her trunk and roared. Then she picked up a stick and whipped it at me.

"You missed," I said, my hands on my hips, and I walked back to the ATV to get the bale of hay.

Let's not even begin to make a list of all the reasons I should never have done this. I didn't know this elephant or how she reacted to strangers. I didn't have Thomas's permission. And I certainly shouldn't have been lifting heavy bales of hay, or putting myself in danger, if I had any thoughts of keeping this baby.

But I also knew never to show fear, so when Hester came at me as I was carrying the hay, her feet flying in the dust and creating a cloud around me, I stood my ground.

Suddenly I heard a loud bellow, and I was lifted off my feet and hauled outside the gap in the fencing. "Jesus," a man said. "Do you have a death wish?"

Hester lifted her head at the sound of the voice, then bent over her food, as if she hadn't been attempting to scare the hell out of me a moment before. I squirmed, trying to get out of the iron grip of this stranger, who was staring with confusion at Grace in the ATV even as he held me in a vise. "Who are you?" he asked.

"Alice," I said, my voice clipped. "Lovely to meet you. Can you put me down now?"

He dropped me on my feet. "Are you an idiot? That's an African elephant."

"Actually, I'm the opposite of an idiot. I'm a postdoc. And I *study* African elephants."

He was over six feet tall, with skin the color of coffee and eyes that were unsettling, so black I felt like I was losing my balance. "You haven't studied Hester," he said under his breath, so quietly that I knew I wasn't supposed to hear him.

He was at least ten years older than his wife, who I estimated to be in her early twenties. He strode toward the ATV, where Grace was standing. "Why didn't you radio me?"

"When you didn't come to get Hester's bucket I figured you were busy." She reached up on her tiptoes and wrapped her arms around Gideon's neck.

The whole time Gideon was embracing Grace, he stared at me over her shoulder as if he was still trying to decide if I was a moron. In his arms, Grace was lifted off her feet. It was nothing more than a height discrepancy, but it looked like Grace was dangling from the edge of a cliff.

By the time I wandered back to the main office, Thomas had disappeared, headed into town to make arrangements for the arrival of the tractor-trailer that would bring his newest elephant to the sanctuary. Me, I hardly noticed. I wandered the grounds as if I were doing field research, learning here what I couldn't learn in the wild.

I hadn't had much exposure to Asian elephants, so I sat and watched them for a while. There's an old joke: What's the difference between African and Asian elephants? Three thousand miles. But they *were* different—calmer than the African elephants I was used to, laid-back, less demonstrative. It made me think about the gross generalizations we made about humans from those two cultures, and how the elephants followed suit: In Asia, you were more likely to find someone averting his eyes to be polite. In Africa, the head would be defiantly lifted and the gaze met directly—not to show aggression but because that was acceptable for the culture.

Syrah had just waded into the pond; she was splashing around with her trunk, spraying her friends. A chorus of squeaking and chirping followed, as one of the other elephants delicately skidded down the slope into the water.

"Sounds like gossip, doesn't it?" a voice behind me said. "I've always hoped they're not talking about me."

The woman had one of those faces that is difficult to judge by age—her hair was blond and pulled back into a braid, yet her skin was smooth enough to make me jealous. She had broad shoulders and ropy muscles in her forearms. I remembered my mother telling me that if you wanted to know an actress's age, no matter how many face-lifts she had had, you should look at her hands. This woman's were wrinkled, coarse, and full of garbage.

"Let me help you," I said, taking some of the refuse from her: gourd shells and husks and half a rind from a watermelon. I followed her lead, dumping them into a bucket, and then wiped my hands on the bottom of my shirt. "You must be Nevvie," I said.

"And you must be Alice Kingston."

The elephants behind us were rolling in the water, playing. Their vocalizations seemed musical compared to those of the African elephants, which I knew by heart. "These three are busybodies," Nevvie said. "They're always talking. If Wanda wanders down a hill out of sight to graze and then walks up it again five minutes later, the other two greet her like she's been gone for years."

"Did you know that the sound of an African elephant was used in the movie *Jurassic Park* for the *T. rex*?" I said.

Nevvie shook her head. "And here I thought I was an expert."

"You are, aren't you?" I said. "You used to work at a circus?"

She nodded. "I like to say that when Thomas Metcalf rescued his first elephant, he also rescued me."

I wanted to hear more about Thomas. I wanted to know that he had a good heart, that he had saved someone on the brink, that I could depend on him. I wanted in him all the traits any female would want in the male she chose as the father for her offspring.

"The first elephant I ever saw was Wimpy. She was privately owned by a family circus that came every summer to the small town in Georgia where I grew up. Oh, she was wonderful. Smart as a whip, loved to play, loved people. Over the years, she had two babies, which also became part of that circus, and she treated them like they were her pride and joy."

None of this surprised me; I had long ago learned that elephant mothers put human ones to shame.

"Wimpy was the reason I wanted to work with animals. She was why I apprenticed at a zoo when I was a teenager, and why I got a job as a trainer when I finished high school. It was another family circus, this one in Tennessee. I worked my way up from the dogs to the ponies to their elephant, Ursula. I was with them for fifteen years." Nevvie folded her arms. "But the circus went bankrupt and got liquidated, and I got a job with the Bastion Brothers Traveling Show of Wonders. The circus had two elephants that had been labeled *dangerous.* I figured I'd make that judgment call myself, after I met them. So you can imagine how surprised I was when I was introduced to the animals and realized one was Wimpy, the same elephant I'd seen as a kid. At some point in her life, she must have been sold to the Bastion brothers."

Nevvie shook her head. "I never would have recognized her. She was chained up. Withdrawn. I wouldn't have identified her as the elephant I used to know even if I'd been watching her all day. The second elephant was Wimpy's calf. He was housed across the way from Wimpy's trailer, in an enclosure made of hot wire. On the ends of his tusks were little metal caps that I had never seen before. As it turned out, that calf wanted his mama, and kept tearing down the hot wire to try to get to her. So one of the Bastion brothers had come up with a solution: to put those caps on the calf's tusks, and wire them to a metal plate in his mouth. Every time he tried to tear down the hot wire with his tusks to get closer to his mother, he got an electric shock. Of course, every time he squealed in pain, Wimpy had to hear it, and see it." Nevvie looked up at me. "An elephant can't commit suicide. But I'm pretty sure Wimpy was trying her damnedest."

In the wild, a female elephant would not separate from her male calf until he was ten to thirteen years old. To be artificially separated, forced to see a baby in distress and unable to do anything about it . . . well, I thought of Lorato charging down the hill to stand over the body of Kenosi. I thought of grief in elephants, and how maybe a loss was not always synonymous with a death. Before I even realized what I was doing, I crossed my arms over my abdomen.

"I prayed for a miracle, and one day Thomas Metcalf arrived. The Bastard brothers wanted to get rid of Wimpy, because they figured she was close to dying anyway, and now that they had her calf, they didn't need her. Thomas sold his car to pay a rental trailer to transport Wimpy up north. She was the first elephant at this sanctuary."

"I thought it was Syrah."

"Well," Nevvie said, "that's true also. Because Wimpy passed two days after she got here. It was too late for her. I like to think that at least she knew, when she died, she was safe."

"What about her baby?"

"We didn't have the resources here to take on a male elephant."

"But surely you've tracked what happened to him?"

"That calf is an adult male now, somewhere," Nevvie said. "It's not a perfect system. But we do what we can."

I looked at Wanda, delicately dipping a toe into the water of the pond, while Syrah patiently blew bubbles under the water. As I watched, Wanda waded in, splashing at the surface with her trunk, sending up a fountain of spray.

"Thomas may know," Nevvie said, after a moment.

"About what?"

Her face was smooth, unreadable. "About that baby," she replied. Then she picked up the bucket of rinds and slop and headed up the hill to the garden, as if she had only been speaking of elephants.

The arrival of Maura, the new elephant, had been pushed up a week, throwing the entire sanctuary into a tornado of preparation. I pitched in where I could, trying to help get the African enclosure ready to host its second elephant. In the frenzy, the last thing I expected to find was Gideon, in the Asian barn, giving Wanda a pedicure.

He sat on a stool on the outside of the stall, the elephant's front right foot poking through an open trap in the steel grid, resting on a girder. Gideon hummed as he used an X-Acto knife on the pads on the bottom of her foot, shaving away the calluses and trimming the cuticles. For such a big man, I thought, he was surprisingly gentle.

"Please tell me she gets to pick a nail polish color," I said, coming up behind him, hoping I could start a conversation that would erase the unfortunate way we had met.

"Foot-related diseases kill half the elephants in captivity," Gideon said. "Joint pain, arthritis, osteomyelitis. Try standing on concrete for the next sixty years."

I crouched down. "So you do preventative care."

"We file down the cracks. Keep rocks from getting caught. Do foot soaks in apple cider for abscesses." He jerked his chin toward the stall, so that I would notice Wanda's left front foot, immersed in a big rubber tub. "One of our girls even had giant sandals made by Teva, with rubber bottoms, to help with the pain."

I would never have imagined this was a concern for elephants, but then again, the elephants I knew had the benefit of rough terrain to naturally condition their feet. They had limitless space to exercise stiff joints.

"She's so calm," I said. "It's like you've hypnotized her."

Gideon ignored the compliment. "She wasn't always like this. When she first came, she was full of beans. She'd drink up a trunk full of water, and when you got close enough to the stall, she'd spray the whole load at you. She threw sticks." He glanced at me. "Like Hester. But with less impressive aim."

I felt my cheeks redden. "Yes, I'm sorry about that."

"Grace should have told you. She knows better."

"It wasn't your wife's fault."

Something flickered across Gideon's features—regret? Annoyance? I did not know him well enough to read his expression. At that moment, Wanda pulled back her foot. She snaked her trunk through the bars of the stall and overturned the bowl of water sitting beside Gideon, soaking his lap. He sighed, righted the bowl, and said, "Foot here!" Wanda lifted her leg again for him to finish.

"She likes to test us," Gideon said. "I guess she's always been that kind of elephant. But where she came from, if she acted out like that, she'd get beaten. If she refused to move, she got pushed around by a Bobcat. When she first arrived, she'd bang on the bars, making a huge racket, like she was daring us to punish her. And we'd all cheer her on, and tell her to make even *more* noise." Gideon patted Wanda's foot, and she delicately pulled it back inside the stall. She stepped out of the cider bath, lifted the tub with her trunk, dumped the liquid down a drain, and handed it to Gideon.

Startled, I laughed. "I guess now she's a model of propriety."

"Not quite. She broke my leg a year ago. I was tending to her hind foot when I got stung by a hornet. I jerked my hand up, and something about the way I hit her on the bottom must have spooked her. She reached through the bars with her trunk and smacked me against them over and over, like she was having some kind of bad trip. Took Dr. Metcalf and my mother-in-law both to get Wanda to put me down so they could tend to me," he said. "Three clean breaks in my femur."

"You forgave her."

"Wasn't her fault," Gideon flatly replied. "She can't help what's been done to her. In fact, it's incredible that she lets anyone close enough to touch her, after all that." I watched him cue Wanda to turn, to present her other front foot. "It's amazing," Gideon said, "what they're willing to excuse."

I nodded, but I was thinking of Grace, who had wanted to be a teacher and wound up scraping elephant dung off the barn floors. I wondered if these elephants, which had become accustomed to a cage, could recall the person who had first put them into it.

I watched Gideon tap Wanda's foot, so that she pulled it away from the gap in the fencing and rocked the fat pad on the floor of the barn, testing his handiwork. And I thought—not for the first time— that forgiving and forgetting aren't mutually exclusive.

When Maura arrived, the trailer was parked inside the African enclosure. Hester was nowhere nearby. She had been grazing in the northernmost corner of the property; the trailer had been dropped along the southern edge. For four hours, Grace and Nevvie and Gideon had tried to coax Maura out, bribing her with watermelon, apples, and hay. They had played the tambourine, hoping that the noise would interest her. They had piped classical music through portable speakers and, when that failed, classic rock.

"Has this ever happened before?" I whispered as I stood next to Thomas.

He looked exhausted. There were circles beneath his eyes, and I don't think he'd actually managed to sit through an entire meal in the two days since he'd gotten word that Maura was en route. "We've had drama—when Olive was brought here by her circus trainer, she sauntered out of the trailer and walloped him twice before she went off into the woods. I have to tell you, though, the guy was a jerk. Olive just did what all of us were *thinking* of doing. But all the others—they were either too curious or too cramped to stay in the trailer for very long."

The night was coming violently, clouds screaming with crimson throats. It would get cold and dark soon; if we were going to stay and wait, we would need lanterns, floodlights, blankets. I had no doubt this was Thomas's plan; it was what I would have done—what I *had* done when I was observing transition in the wild—not from captivity to sanctuary, but at birth or death.

"Gideon," Thomas began, about to issue instructions, when there was a rustle at the tree line.

I had been surprised hundreds of times by elephants that traveled soundlessly and swiftly in the bush; I should not have been as startled as I was by the appearance of Hester. She moved almost too quickly for an animal of her size, light on her feet and excited by this big, foreign metal object in her enclosure. Thomas had told me that the elephants became animated if a bulldozer was brought in to do excavation or landscape work; they were curious about things bigger than themselves.

Hester began to cross back and forth in front of the trailer ramp. She rumbled, a hello. This went on for about ten seconds. When she didn't get a response, it evolved into a short roar.

From inside the trailer came a rumble.

I felt Thomas's hand reach for mine.

Maura gingerly walked down the ramp, her body in silhouette, pausing halfway. Hester stopped moving back and forth. Her rumbles escalated into a roar, a trumpet, and then a rumble—the same cacophonous joy I'd heard when elephants that had been separated from their herd were reunited.

Hester lifted her head and flapped her ears rapidly. Maura urinated and began to secrete from her temporal glands. She inched her trunk toward Hester but still would not come fully down that ramp. Both elephants continued to rumble as Hester put her front two feet onto the ramp and turned her head until her torn ear was close enough for Maura to touch. Then Hester lifted her front left foot, presented it to Maura. It was as if she was telling her life story. *Look at how I was hurt. Look at how I survived.*

Watching this, I started to cry. I felt Thomas's arm come around me as Hester finally curled her trunk around Maura's. She let go, backing off the ramp, as Maura tentatively followed. "Imagine being part of a traveling circus," Thomas said, his voice tight. "That's the last time she'll ever have to walk out of a trailer."

The two elephants swayed in tandem, moving toward the tree line. They were so close that they seemed to be one giant mythical creature, and as the night puckered close around them, I struggled to distinguish the elephants from the thicket where they vanished.

"Well, Maura," Nevvie murmured. "Welcome to your forever home."

There were a lot of explanations I could give for the decision I made at that moment: that the elephants in this sanctuary needed me more than the elephants in the wild did; that I was starting to think the work I had built my scholarship around was not limited by geographic borders; that the man holding my hand, like me, had been brought to tears by the arrival of a rescued elephant. But none of these were the reason.

When I first went to Botswana, I had been chasing knowledge, fame, a way to contribute to my field. But now, as my circumstances had changed, my reasons for being in that game reserve had, too. Lately my arms hadn't been outstretched to embrace my work. They'd been pushing away thoughts that scared the hell out of me. I wasn't running toward my future anymore. I was running *away* from everything else.

A forever home. I wanted that. I wanted that for my baby.

It was so dark now that—like the elephants—I couldn't see and had to find my way with my other senses. So I framed his face with my hands, breathed in the scent of him, touched my forehead to his. "Thomas," I whispered. "I have something to tell you."

VIRGIL

W hat tipped me off was that stupid pebble.

The minute Thomas Metcalf saw it, he went ballistic. Okay, granted, he wasn't exactly the gold standard for sanity, but the minute he focused on that necklace there was a clarity in his eyes that had not been there when we first walked into the room.

Rage often brings out the real person.

Now, sitting in my office, I pop yet another Tums into my mouth—I think this is my tenth, not that I'm really counting—because I can't seem to get rid of the fizzy pressure in my chest. I've chalked it up to heartburn from that crap we ate for lunch from the hot dog cart. But there's a tiny, fleeting thought that maybe this isn't a gastric issue at all. Maybe it's just pure, unadulterated intuition. A nervous hunch. Which I have not felt in a very, very long time.

My office is covered with evidence. In front of each box taken from the PD there are several paper bags tipped onto their sides, with the contents carefully arranged in a semicircle beneath them: a flow-chart of crime, a felonious family tree. I am careful where I step, making sure that I don't crush a brittle leaf with a black spot of blood on it or overlook a small paper packet with a fiber inside.

I'm thankful for my own inefficiency, at that moment. Our evidence room was full of material that could have or should have been returned to its owners but never was—either because the investigating officer never told the property officer the items could be destroyed or returned, or because the property officer wasn't involved in the investigations and wouldn't have known that information on his own. After Nevvie Ruehl's death was ruled accidental, my partner had retired and I had either forgotten or subconsciously decided not to tell Ralph to remove the boxes. Maybe on some level I wondered whether Gideon might file a civil suit against the sanctuary. Or maybe on some level I wondered about Gideon's role that night. Whatever the reason, I'd known that I'd need to comb through these boxes again.

It's true that, if you want to get technical, I've been fired from this case. Except that Jenna Metcalf is a thirteen-year-old kid who probably changed her mind six times this morning before she decided on a breakfast cereal. She threw words at me like handfuls of mud, and now that they've dried, I can brush them off.

It's true, too, that I'm not sure if the death of Nevvie Ruehl was caused by Thomas or his wife, Alice. I suppose Gideon can't be ruled out, either, now. If he was sleeping with Alice, his mother-in-law might not have been all too happy. I just don't believe the death was a trampling, even if I signed off on that ten years ago. But if I'm going to figure out who the murderer is, first I need proof that this was a murder.

Thanks to Tallulah and the lab, I know that Alice Metcalf's hair was found on the victim. But did she find Nevvie's body after the trampling and leave that hair behind before she ran? Or was she the reason there was a body in the first place? Could the hair transfer have been innocent, as Jenna wanted to believe—two women who brushed by each other in the office earlier that morning, neither one knowing that by the end of the day one of them would be dead?

Alice is, of course, the key. If I could find her, I'd have my answers. What I know about her is that she ran away. People who run away either have something they're trying to reach or something they're trying to avoid. I'm just not sure, in this case, which one it was. But either way—why not take her daughter with her?

I hate saying that Serenity might be right about anything, but it would be considerably easier if Nevvie Ruehl were around to tell me what happened that night. "Dead men don't talk," I mutter out loud.

"I beg your pardon?"

Abigail, my landlady, scares the shit out of me. All of a sudden she's standing in the doorway, frowning at the paraphernalia strewn around the office.

"Fuck, Abby, don't sneak up on me like that."

"Must you use that word?"

"Fuck?" I repeat. "I don't know what you've got against it. It can be a verb, an adjective, a noun—it's very versatile." I smile broadly at her.

She sniffs at the detritus on the floor. "I'll remind you that each tenant is responsible for his own refuse collection."

"This isn't trash. It's work."

Abigail's eyes narrow. "It looks like a crystal moth lab."

"First of all, it's *meth*—"

Her hands flutter at her throat. "I *knew* it . . ."

"No!" I say. "Just trust me, okay? This looks *nothing* like a crystal meth lab. This is all evidence, from a case."

Abigail puts her hands on her hips. "You've already used that excuse."

I blink at her. And then I remember—one time, when I'd been on a bender not long ago and had been wallowing in my own stink for a full week without leaving the office, Abigail had come to investigate. When she walked in, I was passed out cold on my desk, and the place looked like a bomb had gone off. I told her I'd been up working all night and must have dozed off. I told her that the litter on the floor was physical evidence collected by the major crimes unit.

Although, really, when was the last time you saw the MCU gather empty bags of microwave popcorn and old *Playboy*s?

"Have you been drinking, Victor?"

"No," I say, and with no small sense of wonder I realize that the thought has not even crossed my mind in the past two days. I don't want a drink. I don't *need* one. Jenna Metcalf hasn't just ignited a spark of purpose in me. She's managed to dry me out, cold turkey, the way three rehab centers couldn't.

Abigail takes a step forward, until she is balanced between the bags of evidence and only inches away from me. She leans up on her toes as if she's going in for a kiss, but she sniffs at my breath instead. "Well," she says. "Will wonders never cease." She retraces her careful steps until she is at the threshold again. "You're incorrect, you know. Dead men *can* talk. My late husband and I have a code, like that escape artist, the Jewish one—"

"Houdini?"

"That's right. He's going to leave me a message, which only I can interpret, if he finds a way back from the beyond."

"*You* believe in that crap, Abby? Never would have guessed." I look up at her. "How long's he been gone?"

"Twenty-two years."

"Let me guess. You two have discussions all the time."

She hesitates. "I would have evicted you years ago, if not for him."

"He told you to cut me a break?"

"Well, not exactly," Abigail replies. "But he was a Victor, too." She pulls the door shut behind her.

"Good thing she doesn't realize my name's Virgil," I mutter, and I crouch down beside one unopened paper bag.

Inside are the red polo shirt and cargo shorts that Nevvie Ruehl was wearing when she died. The same uniform that Gideon Cartwright had been wearing that night, and Thomas Metcalf.

Abby is right: Actually dead men—and *women*—can talk.

I pick up an old newspaper from a stack behind my desk and spread it out over the blotter. Then I carefully pull the red shirt and the shorts out of the bag and lay them down flat. There are stains on the fabric—blood and mud, I imagine. There are bits that are completely shredded, too, the result of the trampling. I take a magnifying glass from my desk drawer and start investigating each ragged rip. I look at the edges, trying to determine if there is any way to tell if the cut was made by a blade rather than by stretching and tearing. I do this for an hour, losing track of the holes that I have already examined.

It isn't until my third pass on the shirt that I see a tear I have not noticed before. Namely because it isn't the fabric that was rent in two. It is a gap along a seam, as if the stitching has just unraveled where the shoulder meets the left sleeve. It is only a few centimeters in diameter, the sort of rip made when something is caught, rather than torn.

Looped in the stitched hem is the crescent moon of a fingernail.

I flash through the image in my head: a struggle, someone grabbing on to the front of Nevvie's shirt.

The lab can tell us if this fingernail matched the mtDNA of Alice. And if it doesn't, we can get a sample from Thomas. And if it matches neither of them, maybe it belonged to Gideon Cartwright.

I place the fingernail in an envelope. Carefully I fold the clothing and put it back into the bag. It's then that I notice another envelope, this one with a smaller paper packet inside, as well as photos of a preserved fingerprint. The small piece of paper had been soaked with ninhydrin, leaving behind those telltale purple fingerprint ridges. These had been matched to Nevvie Ruehl's left thumbprint, as taken by the medical examiner in the morgue. No surprise there; a receipt found in her shorts pocket would likely have her fingerprints on it.

I take the small square paper out of the envelope. By now the chemical has faded, a light lavender. I can try to get the lab to process it again, to check for additional prints, but at this point they will probably be inconclusive.

It isn't until I slip the paper back inside the envelope that I realize what it is. GORDON'S WHOLESALE, it reads. And the date and time, the morning before Nevvie Ruehl died. I didn't know which caregiver had picked up the produce orders. But maybe the employees at the wholesale outfit would remember the employees from the sanctuary.

If Thomas was what Alice Metcalf had been running from, maybe all I need to do to find her is locate what she'd been running to.

Alice Metcalf had seemingly vanished off the face of the earth. Had Gideon Cartwright gone with her?

I didn't really *mean* to call Serenity. It just sort of happened.

One minute I was holding the phone, and the next, she was picking up on the other end. I swear, I don't even remember dialing, and I hadn't had a single drop to drink.

What I wanted to ask when I heard her voice was: *Have you heard from Jenna?*

I don't know why I was even concerned. I should have let her stomp off like a kid throwing a tantrum and said good riddance.

Instead, I couldn't sleep at all last night.

I think that's because the minute Jenna first stepped into my office, with that voice that haunted my dreams, she ripped off a Band-Aid so fast that I started to bleed again. Jenna may be right about one thing—this *is* my fault, because I was too stupid to stand up to Donny Boylan ten years ago when he wanted to bury an inconsistency in the evidence. But she's wrong about another—this isn't about her, finding her mother. It's about me, finding my way.

The thing is, I don't have a great track record with that.

So there I was, holding the phone, and before I knew it, I was asking Serenity Jones, the so-called lapsed psychic, to come with me on a fact-finding mission to Gordon's Wholesale Produce Market. It wasn't until after she agreed, with game-show-contestant enthusiasm, to pick me up and be my de facto partner that I understood why she was the one I'd reached out to. It wasn't that I thought she would actually be helpful in my investigation. It was because Serenity knew how it felt not to be able to live with yourself if you didn't right what you had done wrong.

Now, an hour later, we're in her little sardine can of a car, driving to the edge of Boone, where Gordon's Wholesale has been in existence for as long as I can remember. It is the kind of place that sells mangoes in the dead of winter, when the whole world is dying for a mango and the only place growing them is Chile or Paraguay. Their summertime strawberries are the size of a newborn's head.

I go to turn on the radio, just because I don't know what to say, and find a little paper elephant folded and tucked into the corner.

"She made that," Serenity says, and she doesn't have to say Jenna's name for me to understand.

The paper slips out of my fingers, like a Chinese football. It arcs in a perfect loop into Serenity's massive purple purse, which gapes open on the console between us like Mary Poppins's carpetbag. "You heard from her yet today?"

"No."

"Why do you think that is?"

"Because it's eight A.M. and she's a teenager."

I squirm in the passenger seat. "You don't think it was because I was an asshole yesterday?"

"After ten or eleven A.M., it will be. But right now I think it's because she's sleeping like any other kid during summer vacation."

Serenity flexes her hands on the steering wheel, and I find myself staring—not for the first time—at the furry cover she has stretched over it. It's blue, and has googly eyes and white fangs. It looks a little like the Cookie Monster, if the Cookie Monster had swallowed a steering wheel. "What the hell is that thing?" I ask.

"Bruce," Serenity answers, as if it's a stupid question.

"You named your steering wheel?"

"Honey, the longest relationship I've ever had is with this car. Given that *your* closest companion has the first name of Jack and the last name of Daniel's, I don't think you're in a position to judge." She smiles sunnily at me. "Damn, I've missed this."

"Bickering?"

"No, police work. It's like we're Cagney and Lacey, except you're better looking than Tyne Daly."

"I'm not touching that one," I mutter.

"You know, in spite of what you think, what you and I do isn't all that different."

I burst out laughing. "Yeah, except for that desire for measurable scientific evidence thing that I have."

She ignores me. "Think about it: We both know what questions to ask. We both know what questions *not* to ask. We are fluent in body language. We live and breathe intuition."

I shake my head. There's no way what I do could be compared to what she does. "There's nothing paranormal about my job. I don't get a vision, I focus on what's right in front of me. Detectives are observers. I see a person who can't look me in the eye and I try to figure out whether it's grief or shame. I pay attention to what makes someone cry. I listen, even when no one's speaking words," I say. "Did it ever occur to you that there is no such thing as clairvoyant? That maybe psychics are just really good at detective work?"

"Or maybe you've got that backward. Maybe the reason a good detective can read his subjects is because he's a little bit psychic."

She pulls into the Gordon's Wholesale parking lot. "This is a fishing expedition," I tell Serenity, quickly lighting a cigarette as I get out of the car and she hurries to catch up to me. "And we are going to reel in Gideon Cartwright."

"You don't know where he went after the sanctuary closed?"

"I know he stuck around long enough to help move the elephants to their new home. And after that . . . your guess is as good as mine," I say. "I assume that all the caregivers took turns coming here to pick up produce. If Gideon had been planning to run away with Alice, maybe he let something slip in conversation."

"You don't know if the same employees are around ten years later—"

"I don't know that they're not, either," I point out. "Fishing, remember? You never know what you're going to pull up when you reel in. Just go along with what I say."

I grind out my cigarette beneath my heel and walk into the produce stand. It's a glorified wooden shack staffed by lots of twenty-somethings who sport dreadlocks and Birkenstocks, but there's one old man who is stacking tomatoes into a giant pyramid. It's pretty damn impressive, and at the same time, there's a perverse part of me that wants to take the one from the very bottom corner of the pile and send them all tumbling.

One of the employees, a girl with a nose ring, smiles at Serenity as she hauls a big basket of sweet corn toward the cash register. "Let me know if you need any help," she says.

I've already figured that Gordon's Wholesale's decision to sell at cost to the New England Elephant Sanctuary had to have been sanctioned by whoever ran the business. And it may be ageist of me, but I'm going to assume that the old guy might know more than the dude with bloodshot eyes.

I pick up a peach and take a bite. "My God, Gideon was right," I say to Serenity.

"Excuse me," the man says. "You can't sample the merchandise without paying."

"Oh, I'll buy that peach. I'll buy the whole lot. My friend was right—your fruit is the best produce I've ever tasted. He said, *Marcus, if you are ever in Boone, New Hampshire, and you don't stop at Gordon's, you are doing yourself a grave disservice.*"

The man grins. "Well, I won't disagree with you." He holds out a hand. "I'm Gordon Gordon."

"Marcus Latoile," I reply. "And this is my . . . wife, Helga."

Serenity smiles at him. "We're on our way to a thimble convention," she says, "but Marcus *insisted* we stop when he saw your sign." Just then, there is a crash on the other side of a beaded curtain.

Gordon sighs. "Kids today, they're all about sustainability and living green. But they don't know their ass from their elbow. Excuse me just a sec?"

The minute he moves away, I round on Serenity. "A *thimble* convention?"

"*Helga?*" she counters. "Plus, it was the first thing I could come up with on the spot. I wasn't expecting you to *lie* to the man's face."

"I wasn't lying, I was doing detective work. You say what you have to say to get the confession, and people clam up around investigators because they think they're going to get into trouble, or get someone else in trouble."

"And you think *psychics* are charlatans?"

Gordon returns, an apology on his lips. "The bok choy came in with worms."

"Hate it when that happens," Serenity murmurs.

"Can I interest you in some melon?" Gordon says. "It's like pure sugar."

"I'll bet. Gideon said it was a crying shame your wares were wasted on the elephants," I tell him.

"The elephants," Gordon repeats. "You don't mean Gideon Cartwright?"

"You remember him?" I say, beaming. "I can't believe it. I just can't believe it. We were roommates in college, and I haven't seen him since then. Hey, does he still live around here? I'd love to catch up with him—"

"He left town a long time ago, after the elephant sanctuary closed," Gordon says.

"It *closed*?"

"It was a pity. One of the employees got trampled to death. Gideon's mother-in-law, in fact."

"Must have been quite a blow for him and his wife," I say, playing dumb.

"That's the only blessing, really," Gordon answers. "Grace died a month before it happened. She never knew."

I feel Serenity stiffen beside me. This is news to her, but I vaguely remember Gideon saying during the investigation that his wife was gone. Losing one family member is a tragedy. Losing two, back to back, seems like more than a coincidence.

Gideon Cartwright had been the very picture of anguish when his mother-in-law was killed. But maybe I should have looked more closely at him as a suspect.

"You have any idea where he went after the sanctuary closed?" I ask. "I'd love to reconnect with him. Offer my condolences."

"I know he was headed to Nashville. That's where the elephants were going, to a sanctuary nearby. It's where Grace was buried, too."

"Did you know his wife?"

"Sweet kid. She certainly didn't deserve to die young."

"Was she sick?" Serenity asks.

"I suppose she was, in a fashion," Gordon says. "She walked into the Connecticut River, with stones in her pockets. They didn't find her body for a week."

ALICE

Twenty-two months is a long time to be pregnant.

It is an enormous investment of time and energy for an elephant. Add to that the time and energy it takes to get a newborn calf to a point where it can survive on its own, and you can begin to understand what is at stake for an elephant mother. It does not matter who you are or what kind of personal relationship you've forged with an elephant: Come between her and her calf, and she will kill you.

Maura had been a circus elephant that was then brought to a zoo as the mate of a male African elephant. Sparks flew, but not the way the zookeepers had intended—and small wonder, since in the wild a female elephant would never have lived with a male in close proximity. Instead, Maura charged her paramour, destroyed the fencing of the enclosure, and pinned a keeper against the fence, crushing his spinal cord. When she came to us, she was labeled a killer. Like any animal coming to the sanctuary, she had dozens of veterinary tests, including one for tuberculosis. But a pregnancy test was not part of the protocol, and so we didn't know she was going to have a calf until very nearly before it happened.

When we figured it out—the swelling breasts and dropped belly—we quarantined Maura for those last couple months. It was just too risky to guess how Hester, the other African elephant in the enclosure, would react, since she had never had a baby of her own. We also didn't know how much practice Maura had had as a mother until Thomas was able to locate the circus she had traveled with and learned that she had given birth once before, to a male calf. It was one of a bevy of reasons that the circus had classified her as dangerous. Not wanting to risk the maternal aggression of a female elephant, they had chained her during birth so that they could take care of the newborn. But Maura had gone crazy, trumpeting, roaring, throwing her chains, trying to get to her baby. Once she was allowed to touch him, she was fine.

When the calf was two, they'd sold him to a zoo.

When Thomas told me this, I'd gone out to the enclosure where Maura was grazing and sat down with my own baby playing at my feet. "I won't let it happen again," I told her.

At the sanctuary, we were all excited for our own reasons. Thomas saw the moneymaking potential a calf would bring to the sanctuary— although unlike a zoo that saw ten thousand more visitors as a result of a newborn elephant addition, we would not be showing the calf off. People were just more likely to give funds to support a baby. There was nothing cuter than photos of a baby elephant, the comma of its trunk dangling like an afterthought, its head poking from between the columns of its mother's legs—and, we hoped, our fund-raising materials would be full of them. Grace had never seen a birth. Gideon and Nevvie, on the other hand, had seen two during their time at the circus, and were hoping for a happier outcome.

And me? Well, I felt a kinship with this giant. Maura had made the sanctuary her home at approximately the same time I had, and I had delivered my own daughter six months later. Over the past eighteen months, as I went out to watch Maura interacting, I would sometimes catch her eye. It's unscientific and anthropomorphic of me to say so, but off the record? I think we both felt lucky to be there.

I had a beautiful baby girl and a brilliant husband. I had been able to gather data using some of Thomas's audiotapes of elephant communication that I was cobbling together into an article about grief and cognition in elephants. I got to spend every day learning from these compassionate, intelligent animals. Given that, it was easy to concentrate on the positive rather than the negative: the nights I found Thomas poring over the books, wondering how we could keep the sanctuary open; the pills he had started to take so that he could sleep at all; the fact that I had not yet documented an actual death at the sanctuary and I had been there a year and a half; the guilt I felt over wishing for an animal to die, just so that I could further my research.

Then there were the arguments I got into with Nevvie, who thought she knew everything, because she had worked the longest with elephants. She discounted any contributions I had to make because she didn't believe the way elephants behaved in the wild could translate into sanctuary life.

Some of these conflicts were minuscule—I'd prepare food for the elephants and Nevvie would change the individual meals, because she felt that Syrah didn't like strawberries or because Olive's stomach was upset by honeydew (although I'd seen no evidence to support either claim). But sometimes she decided to pull rank and it affected me personally—like, for example, when I put Asian elephant bones into the African enclosure to measure the reaction of the elephants, and she moved them away because she felt it was disrespectful to the elephants that had died. Or when she was babysitting for Jenna and insisted it was all right to give her honey to help with teething, in spite of the fact that every parenting book I read said not to feed it to a child until age two. As soon as I brought up the issue with Thomas, he got upset. "Nevvie's been with me from the start," he said, by way of explanation. As if it did not matter that I was supposed to be with him till the end.

Since neither of us knew when Maura had become pregnant, her delivery date was an estimate—one on which Nevvie and I disagreed. Based on the development of Maura's breasts, I knew it wasn't going to be long. Nevvie insisted that births always happened at a full moon, which was three weeks away.

I had seen one birth in the wild, although you'd think, given the sheer number of babies in the herds, I would have had the opportunity to see more. It was an elephant named Botshelo, the Tswana word for "life." I happened to be tracking a different herd when I came upon hers beside a riverbed, behaving very strangely. They were typically a relaxed herd, but now they were bunched around Botshelo, facing out, protecting her. For about a half hour, there were some rumbles, and then a splash. They shifted enough for me to see Botshelo tearing at the birth sac and flipping it onto her head, as if it were a lampshade and she was the life of the party. In the grass beneath her was the tiniest little elephant, a female, surrounded by an explosion of sound: rumbling, trumpeting, chaos. The herd urinated, they secreted; and as they rolled the whites of their eyes at me, it was almost as if they were trying to get me to celebrate. The baby was touched from tip to toe by every member of the herd; Botshelo put her trunk around the calf and under the calf and in her calf's mouth: *Hello. Welcome.*

The calf was rolling on her side, discombobulated, her legs starfished in all directions. Botshelo used her feet and her trunk to lift the calf. The baby would manage to get her front end up, only to have it crash forward when her back end lifted, or vice versa, a tripod with the legs at odd lengths. Finally, Botshelo knelt, pressing her face against the head of the calf, and then stood, as if she was trying to show her baby how to do it. When the calf tried and slipped, Botshelo kicked up enough grass and dirt to give her more stable footing. After twenty minutes of Botshelo's intense ministrations, that little baby wobbled along at her mother's side, Botshelo's trunk pulling her up every time she tipped over. Eventually the baby took refuge beneath her mother, her floppy trunk pressed up against her mother's belly as she rooted to nurse. The whole process of birth was matter-of-fact, abbreviated, and also the most incredible experience I had ever witnessed.

One morning when I went out to check on Maura, as I had made it my habit to do, with Jenna strapped to my back like a papoose, I noticed a bulge at the elephant's bottom. I four-wheeled to the Asian barn, where Nevvie and Thomas were talking about a fungus that one of the elephants had developed on her toenails. "It's time," I said breathlessly.

Thomas acted like he had when I had told him my own water had broken. He started running around, excited, scattered, overwhelmed. He radioed Grace and asked her to come and take Jenna back to our cottage and sit with her while the rest of us went to the African enclosure. "There's no rush," Nevvie insisted. "I've never heard of an elephant giving birth during the day. It happens at night so that the baby's eyes can adjust."

If it took that long for Maura, I knew it meant that something would be wrong. Her body was already showing all the signs of advanced labor. "I think we have a half an hour, tops," I said.

I watched Thomas's face turn from Nevvie's to mine, and then he radioed Gideon. "Meet us at the African barn, ASAP," he said, and I turned away when I felt Nevvie's gaze on me.

The mood, at first, was celebrative. Thomas and Gideon argued over whether it would be better for the calf to be male or female; Nevvie talked about what it was like when she delivered Grace. They joked about whether an elephant could have drugs during the birth, and if it would be called a pachydural. Me, I focused on Maura. As she rumbled, suffering through contractions, an auditory current of sisterhood flew through the grounds of the sanctuary. Hester trumpeted back to Maura; then the Asian elephants, at a further distance, checked in.

A half hour had passed since I first told Thomas to come quickly, then an hour. After two hours of moving in circles, Maura had still not progressed. "Maybe we should call the vet," I suggested, but Nevvie waved me off.

"I told you," she said. "It'll happen after sunset."

I knew of plenty of rangers who'd seen elephants give birth at all times of the day, but I bit my tongue. I wished that Maura were in the wild, if only so that one of her herd could communicate that there was nothing to worry about, that everything was going to be all right.

Six hours later, though, I had my doubts.

By then, Gideon and Nevvie had both gone to prepare and distribute food for the Asian elephants and Hester. We may have been having a birth, but there were still six other elephants that needed care. "I think you should call the vet," I told Thomas as I watched Maura stumble, weary. "Something's wrong."

Thomas didn't hesitate. "I'll check on Jenna and make the call." He looked at me, troubled. "Will you stay with Maura?"

I nodded and sat down on the far side of the fence, my knees drawn up, to watch Maura suffer. I had not wanted to say this out loud, but all I could think of was Kagiso, the elephant I had found with a dead calf shortly before I left Africa. I did not even want to think of her, for superstitious fear that I might jinx this birth.

Not more than five minutes after Thomas left, Maura pivoted, presenting her hindquarters to me so that I could clearly see the amniotic balloon extending from between her legs. I scrambled to my feet, torn between wanting to get Thomas and knowing that I wouldn't have time. Before I could even equivocate, the entire amniotic sac slipped out in a gush and rush of fluid, and the calf landed on the grass, still caught in its white caul.

If Maura had sisters in a herd, they would be telling her what to do. They would encourage her to tear the sac, to help that baby stand. But Maura had no one but me. I cupped my hand over my mouth and tried to mimic the distress call, the SOS I had heard elephants make when a predator was in the area. I hoped I could shock Maura into action.

It took three tries, but finally, Maura used her trunk to tear at the sac. I knew, though, even as she did, that something was wrong. Unlike the jubilation of Botshelo and her herd, Maura's body was hunched. Her eyes were downcast; her mouth drooped. Her ears were low and flat against her body.

She looked like Kagiso, when Kagiso's calf was dead.

Maura tried to pull the small, stillborn male to his feet. She pushed at him with her front foot, but he did not move. She tried to curl her trunk around the body and lift him, but he slipped from her grasp. She pulled away the afterbirth and then rolled the body of the calf. She was still bleeding, streaks down her rear legs as dark and pronounced as the secretions from her temporal glands, but she continued to dust and shove the calf, which had not taken a single breath.

I was in tears by the time Thomas arrived again, Gideon in tow, with the news that the vet would arrive within the hour. The whole sanctuary had gone silent and still; the other elephants had stopped calling; even the wind had died. The sun had turned its face in to the shoulder of the landscape; and in the custom of mourning, the fabric of the night had been ripped, revealing a star at each tiny tear. Maura stood over the body of her son, her body an umbrella, shielding him.

"What happened?" Thomas said, and for the rest of my life, I would always think that he had been accusing me.

I shook my head. "Call back the vet," I said. "He doesn't need to be here yet." By now, the bleeding had stopped. There wasn't anything that could be done.

"He'll want to do a necropsy on the calf—"

"Not until she's done grieving," I said, and the word triggered my silent wish of just days ago: that one of these elephants would die, so that I could continue my postdoc research.

I felt as if I had subconsciously willed this. Maybe Thomas was right to accuse me. "I'm going to stay here," I announced.

Thomas stepped forward. "You don't have to—"

"This is what I *do*," I said tightly.

"What about Jenna?"

I saw Gideon take a step away as our voices escalated. "What about her?" I asked.

"You're her mother."

"And you're her father." For this one night in a year of Jenna's life, I could pass up putting my baby to bed so that I could watch Maura stand over hers. This was my job. Had I been a doctor, this would have been the equivalent of being paged for an emergency.

But Thomas wasn't paying attention. "I was counting on that calf," he murmured. "It was going to save us."

Gideon cleared his throat. "Thomas? How about I take you back to the cottage, and I'll have Grace bring a sweater to Alice?"

After they left, I took notes, marking the times Maura ran her trunk along the spine of the calf, and her listless toss of the amniotic sac. I wrote down the differences in her vocalizations—from a cooing rumble of reassurance to the call of a mother trying to get her calf to return to her side—but it was a one-sided conversation.

Grace returned with a sweater and a sleeping bag, and sat with me for a while in silence, just watching Maura and feeling her sadness. "It's heavier here," she remarked. "The air." Although I knew that the barometric pressure could not be affected by the death of an elephant, I understood what she meant. The quiet pushed in at the soft spot at the bottom of my throat, in my eardrums, threatening to suffocate us.

Nevvie came to pay her respects, too. She didn't say anything, just handed me a bottle of water and a sandwich and stood a distance away, seemingly shuffling through a deck of memories she didn't want to share.

Just as I was nodding off, at three in the morning, Maura finally stepped away from the calf. She scooped the baby up in her trunk, but it slipped out of her grasp twice. She tried to lift it by its neck and, failing that, its legs. After several aborted attempts, she managed to curl the body of the baby under her trunk, the way she might lift a bale of hay.

Carefully, slowly, Maura started to walk north. In the distance, I could hear a contact call from Hester. Maura responded softly, muted, as if she were worried about waking the calf.

Gideon and Nevvie had taken the four-wheelers when they left, so I had no choice but to travel on foot. I didn't know where Maura was headed, so I did exactly what I shouldn't have done—I ducked through the opening in the gate made for the vehicles and walked in the shadows behind her.

Luckily, Maura was either too lost in her own grief or too focused on her precious load to notice me, slinking along behind the trees as quietly as possible. We walked, twenty yards between us, past the pond and through the birch woods and across a meadow until Maura reached the spot where she liked to come at the hottest part of the day. Underneath a sprawling oak was a carpet of pine needles; Maura would lie on her side and nap in the shade.

Today, though, she placed the calf there and began to cover him with branches, breaking off pine boughs and kicking up fallen needles and tufts of moss, until the corpse was partially covered. Then she stood over him again, making a pillared temple of her body.

And I worshiped. I prayed.

. . .

Twenty-four hours after Maura had delivered the calf, I had still not slept, and neither had she. More critically, she had not had any sustenance. Although I knew she could go without food for a little while, she had to have water. So when Gideon found me, safely on the far side of the fencing again, I asked him for a favor.

I needed him to bring back one of the shallow tubs we used for foot soaks in the barns, and five half-gallon jugs of water.

When I heard the ATV approach behind me, I looked at Maura to see if she'd react. Usually the African elephants were curious when it was feeding time. But Maura didn't even turn her head in the direction of Gideon's approach. As he idled to a stop on the path, I said, "Get off."

What I was doing would have been strictly forbidden in the game reserve, because I was planning to adjust the ecosystem. It was also reckless, because I was encroaching on the personal space of a grieving elephant mother. And I didn't give a flying fuck.

"No," Gideon said, figuring out exactly what I was up to. "You climb on."

So I did, wrapping my arms around him as we drove through the small opening in the fencing, into the enclosure with the elephant. Maura charged, flying toward us with her ears spread and her heavy feet thundering on the ground. I felt Gideon throw the ATV in reverse, but I put my hand on his arm. "Don't," I said. "Turn it off."

He looked over his shoulder at me, wild-eyed, caught between obeying his boss's wife and his own instincts for self-preservation.

The vehicle shuddered to a stop.

So did Maura.

Very slowly, I got off the ATV and pulled the heavy rubber tub from the flatbed on the back. I set this about ten feet away from the vehicle and then poured several gallons of water inside. Then I climbed behind Gideon again. "Reverse," I whispered. "*Now.*"

He backed up as Maura's trunk twitched in our direction. She stepped closer and drank the whole tub of water at once.

She angled herself, so that her tusks were only inches away from my skin, close enough for me to see the nicks and scars on them from years of use, close enough for her to look me in the eye.

Maura reached out with her trunk and stroked my shoulder. Then she lumbered back to the body of her calf and resumed her position sheltering him.

I felt Gideon's hand on my back. It was partly comfort, partly reverence. "Breathe," he instructed.

After thirty-six hours, the vultures came. They circled overhead like witches on their brooms. Every time they swooped, Maura would flap her ears and bellow, scaring them off. That night, it was the fisher cats. Their eyes flashed neon green as they crept closer to the calf's body. Maura, coming out of her trance as if a switch had been flipped, ran at them with her tusks to the ground.

Thomas had given up asking me to come home. *Everyone* had given up asking me. I would not leave until Maura was ready to leave. I would be her herd, and remind her that she still had to live, even if her calf couldn't.

The irony did not escape me: I was playing the role of the elephant, while Maura was acting rather human by refusing to stop grieving her dead son. One of the most amazing things about elephants mourning in the wild is their ability to grieve hard, but then truly, unequivocally, let go. Humans can't seem to do that. I've always thought it's because of religion. We expect to see our loved ones again in the next life, whatever that might be. Elephants don't have that hope, only the memories of *this* life. Maybe that's why it is easier for them to move on.

Seventy-two hours postdelivery, I tried to imitate the "let's go" rumble I'd heard a thousand times in the wild and to point myself in that direction, like an elephant would. Maura ignored me. By now, I could barely stand, and my vision was blurred. I hallucinated a bull elephant breaking through the fence, only to realize that it was an ATV approaching. On it rode Nevvie and Gideon. Nevvie looked at me and shook her head. "You're right, she's a mess," Nevvie said to

Gideon. And then to me: "You're going back home. Your girl needs you. If you don't want to leave Maura alone, I'll stay with her."

Because Gideon didn't trust me to hang on to him without falling asleep, I did not climb behind him on the ATV. I sat in the circle of his arms, the way a child might have done, and nodded off until he parked in front of our cottage. Embarrassed, I leaped off the vehicle, thanked him quickly, and walked inside.

To my surprise, Grace was asleep on the couch beside Jenna's crib—which was in the middle of the living room, since we didn't have space for a nursery. I woke her and told her to go home with Gideon, and then I went down the hall to Thomas's office.

Like me, he was wearing the clothes he'd been wearing three days ago. He was bent over a ledger, so engrossed in what he was studying that he didn't notice I was there. A bottle of prescription medicine was spilled on its side on the desk, and a depleted bottle of whiskey sat sentinel beside him. I thought he might have fallen asleep working, but when I got closer I saw that his eyes were wide open, glassy, sightless.

"Thomas," I said softly, "let's go to sleep."

"Can't you see I'm busy?" he said, so loud that, in the other room, the baby started to cry. "Shut the fuck up!" he yelled, and he lifted his book and threw it at the wall behind me. I ducked, then bent down to retrieve it. The pages fell open before me.

Whatever had engrossed Thomas so deeply . . . it wasn't this book. This was an empty journal, one blank page following the next.

I understood now why Grace had not felt comfortable leaving the baby alone with him.

It was not until after we'd had our wedding ceremony in the Boone Town Hall that I found bottles of pills, lined up like foot soldiers in Thomas's dresser. Depression, he'd told me when I asked. After his father—his last surviving parent—had died, he could not muster the strength to get out of bed. I had nodded, trying to be compassionate. I was less unnerved by the news of his clinical despair than I was about the fact that I had entered into marriage with someone so quickly I did not even know his parents were both deceased.

Thomas hadn't had another depressive episode since then that he'd told me about, but to be honest, I hadn't asked, either. I wasn't sure I wanted to know the answer.

Shaking, I backed out of the room and closed the door. I picked up Jenna, who quieted immediately, and carried her to the bed I shared with a stranger, who happened to be the father of my child. Against all odds, I fell immediately into a deep, velvet sleep, my daughter's tiny hand caught like a fallen star in my own.

When I woke up, the sun was a scalpel, and a fly was buzzing in my ear. I brushed at my temple, willing it to go away, only to realize it wasn't a fly, and I couldn't get rid of it. It was the distant sound of construction equipment, the backhoe we used to do landscaping work in the sanctuary.

"Thomas," I called, but he didn't answer. I scooped up Jenna, who was awake and smiling now, and carried her into his office. Thomas was at his desk, his face pressed to the blotter, completely unconscious. I watched his back rise and fall twice to make sure he was alive, then bundled Jenna into a sling on my back, the way I had learned from the African women who cooked at the camp in the reserve. I left the cottage, climbed on an ATV, and headed toward the northern edge of the sanctuary, where I had left Maura last night.

The first thing I noticed was the hot wire. Maura paced back and forth in front of it, trumpeting and raging, jerking her head and tusking at the ground, coming as close to that wire as she could without it shocking her. Through all of these aggressive gestures, she never took her eye off her calf.

Which was chained onto a large wooden pallet beside Nevvie—who was directing Gideon where to dig a grave.

I drove the ATV through the gate, past Maura, and skidded to a stop a foot away from Nevvie. "What the hell do you think you're doing?"

She glanced at me, and at the baby on my back, and with one look let me know what she thought of my mothering skills. "What we always do when an elephant dies. The necropsy samples were already taken this morning by the vet."

Blood roared in my ears. "You separated a grieving mother from her calf?"

"It's been three days," Nevvie said. "This is for her own good. I've been with mothers who see their calves suffer, and it breaks them. It happened to Wimpy, and it will happen again, if we don't do something about it. Is that what you want for Maura?"

"What I want for Maura is for her to make the decision when it's time to let go," I shouted. "I thought that was the whole philosophy of this sanctuary." I turned my face to Gideon, who had stopped digging with the construction equipment and was standing awkwardly to the side. "Did you even *ask* Thomas?"

"Yes," Nevvie said, lifting her chin. "He said he trusted me to know what to do."

"You don't know anything about how a mother grieves for her calf," I said. "This isn't mercy. It's cruelty."

"What's done is done," Nevvie argued. "The sooner Maura doesn't have to see that calf, the sooner she'll forget what happened."

"She will *never* forget what happened," I promised. "And neither will I."

Not much later, Thomas woke up subdued, his old self. He gave Nevvie a dressing-down for taking matters into her own hands, neatly erasing his own responsibility in the situation for giving her permission when he was not in a sound mental state to do so. He wept, apologizing to me, and to Jenna, for letting the demons in. Nevvie, miffed, disappeared for the rest of the afternoon. Gideon and I removed the straps and the chains from the calf's body, although we did not attempt to slide him off the pallet. The moment I turned off the electricity on the hot wire, Maura tore it away as if it were made of straw and rushed toward her son. She stroked him with her trunk, backed up to him with her hind legs. She stood beside him for another forty-five minutes, and then slowly lumbered into the birch forest, away from the calf.

I waited ten minutes, listening for her return, but it didn't happen. "Okay," I said.

Gideon climbed onto the backhoe and bit into the earth beneath the oak tree where Maura liked to rest. I strapped the calf's body onto the pallet again, so that he could be lowered into the grave when it was deep enough. I took a shovel Gideon had brought and began to cover the body with dirt, a tiny gesture to add to the fill that Gideon was scooping with the excavator.

By the time I patted down the overturned earth on top of the grave, rich as coffee grounds, my hair had fallen from its ponytail and perspiration ringed my underarms and soaked my back. I was sore and exhausted, and the emotion I'd pushed away for the past five hours suddenly rushed over me, knocking me off my feet. I fell to my knees, sobbing.

All of a sudden Gideon was there, his arms around me. He was a big man, taller and broader than Thomas; I leaned into him the way you press your cheek to solid ground after falling a great distance. "It's okay," he said, although it wasn't. I couldn't bring Maura's baby back. "You were right. We never should have separated her from the calf."

I pulled back. "Then why did you?"

He looked me in the eye. "Because sometimes when I think for myself, I get into trouble."

I could feel his hands on my shoulders. I could smell the salt of his sweat. I looked at his skin, dark against mine.

"Thought you might need this," Grace said. She was holding a jug of iced tea.

I did not know when Grace had come walking up; I did not know what she thought, to find her husband comforting me. It was nothing more than that, yet we still jumped apart, as if we had something to hide. I wiped my eyes with the hem of my shirt as Gideon reached out for the jug.

Even when Gideon left, his hand in Grace's, I could feel the heat of his palms on me. It made me think of Maura standing over her calf, trying to be a haven when, clearly, it was already too late.

JENNA

When you're a kid, most people actively go out of their way to not notice you. Businessmen and businesswomen don't look because they're wrapped up in their phone calls or texts or sending emails to their bosses. Mothers turn away because you're a glimpse into the future, when their sweet little porker of a baby will become another antisocial teenager, plugged into music and incapable of holding a conversation beyond grunts. The only folks who actually look me in the eye are lonely old ladies or little kids who want attention. For this reason, it's incredibly easy to hop on a Greyhound without ever buying a ticket, which is pretty awesome, because who has $190 lying around? I just hang out near the ragged edges of a family that can't keep itself together—there's a shrieking baby and a boy who's about five with his thumb jammed in his mouth, and a teenager texting so fast that I think her Galaxy is going to burst into flames. When the boarding call to Boston is made, and the frazzled parents try to count the luggage *and* their offspring, I follow their older daughter onto the bus like I belong with them.

No one stops me.

I know the driver is going to count heads before he pulls out of the station, so I immediately go to the bathroom and lock myself inside. I stay there until I can feel the wheels rolling, until Boone, NH, is an afterthought. Then I slip into the rear seat of the bus, the one no one ever wants because it smells like the urinal cake, and pretend to be fast asleep.

Let's talk for just a second about the fact that my grandmother is going to ground me until I'm, oh, sixty. I left her a note, but I've purposely turned off my phone because I don't really want to hear her reaction when she finds it. If she thinks that my Internet searches for my mom are ruining my life, she's not going to be thrilled to hear that I'm stowing away on a bus, bound for Tennessee, so that I can track her in person.

I'm a little pissed at myself, actually, for not thinking to do this before. Maybe it was my father's anger—totally out of character for a guy who spends most of his time virtually catatonic—that jogged my memory. Whatever it was, something fell into place so that I would remember Gideon, and how important he was to me and my mother. The way my father had reacted to the pebble necklace was like a jolt of electricity, lighting up neurons that had simmered quietly for years, so that banners waved and neon signs flashed in my mind: *Pay attention*. It's true that even if I *had* remembered Gideon before now, I still wouldn't have been able to figure out where he had gone ten years ago. But I do know somewhere he stopped along the way.

When my mother disappeared and my father's business was revealed to be bankrupt, the elephants were sent to The Elephant Sanctuary in Hohenwald, Tennessee. All you have to do is a quick Google search to read about how their board of directors—hearing about the New England sanctuary's plight—had scrambled to find space to house the homeless animals. Accompanying the elephants was the only employee who'd been left behind: Gideon.

I didn't know if the sanctuary had hired him to continue caring for our animals or if he had dropped the elephants off and moved on. If he had reunited with my mother. If they still held hands when they thought no one was looking.

See, that's the other thing about people who think kids are invisible: They forget to be careful around you.

I know it's stupid, but there was a big part of me that was hoping Gideon was there and had no idea where my mom was, in spite of the fact that this was the reason I was currently wedged on a bus with my sweatshirt hood drawn tight so no one would try to make eye contact with me, just so I could find this out. I couldn't really handle the thought that my mother had spent the past ten years happy. I didn't wish her dead and I didn't wish her life to be miserable. But, I mean, shouldn't *I* have been part of that equation?

Anyway, I had run through the possible scenarios in my head:

1. Gideon was working at the sanctuary and was living with my mother, who'd taken on an alias, like Mata Hari or Euphonia Lalique or something equally mysterious, so that she could remain hidden. (Note: I didn't really want to think about what she would be hiding *from*. My father, the law, me—none of those were options I felt like exploring.) Gideon would recognize me at first glance, of course, and take me to my mother, who would dissolve in an implosion of joy and beg forgiveness and tell me she'd never stopped thinking of me.

2. Gideon was no longer working at the sanctuary, but given that the elephant community is a pretty small one, there was still some contact information for him in the files. I would show up on his doorstep, and my mother would answer the door, and then you can fill in the rest from scenario 1.

3. I finally found Gideon, wherever he was, but he told me he was sorry—that he had no idea what had happened to my mother. That yes, he had loved her. That yes, she had wanted to run away from my father with him. Maybe even that the death of Nevvie was somehow tied to this star-crossed love affair. But that in the long years I had spent growing up, it simply had not worked out between them, and she had left him the same way she left me.

That, of course, was the worst scenario of all. There was only one that was even more grim; it was so dark that I had let my imagination peek through a crack in its door, only to slam it shut before it spilled into every corner of my mind:

4. Through Gideon, I locate my mother. But there is no joy, no reunion, no wonder. There's just resignation, as she sighs and says, *I wish you hadn't found me.*

Like I said, I'm not even going to think about that possibility, just in case—as Serenity says—the energy sent out into the universe by a random thought can actually bring about an outcome.

I don't think that it will take Virgil long to figure out where I've gone, or to come to the same conclusion I have—that Gideon is the connection to my mother, maybe the reason she ran away, maybe even the link to the accidental death that may not be an accident. And I feel a little bad about not telling Serenity where I'm headed. But then, she reads people for a living; I hope she can figure out that I have every intention of coming back.

Just not alone.

There are connections to be made in Boston, New York, and Cleveland. At each stop, I get off the bus holding my breath, certain that this is the one where I will find a cop waiting to take me home. But that would require my grandmother to report me missing, and let's face it, she doesn't have a great track record for that.

I keep my phone turned off because I don't want her calling, or Virgil, or Serenity. I follow the same pattern at each bus terminal, looking for a family that might not notice me dangling from its fringe. I sleep, on and off, and play games with myself: If I see three consecutive red cars on I-95, it means my mother will be happy to see me. If I see a VW Beetle before I finish counting to 100, it means she ran away because she didn't have a choice. If I see a hearse, it means she's dead, and that's why she never came back to me.

I don't see any hearses, just in case you're wondering.

One day, three hours, and forty-eight minutes after I leave Boone,

New Hampshire, I find myself at the bus station in Nashville, Tennessee, stepping into a wave of heat that hits me like a knockout punch.

The terminal is in the middle of the city, and I'm surprised by the amount of activity and noise. It's like walking into a headache. There are men wearing bolo ties and tourists nursing bottles of water and people playing the guitar for coins in front of storefronts. Everyone seems to be wearing cowboy boots.

Immediately I fade back into the air-conditioned terminal and find a map of Tennessee. Hohenwald—where the sanctuary is located—is southwest of the city, about an hour and a half away. I'm guessing it's not a big tourist destination, so there's no public transport out there. And I'm not stupid enough to hitchhike. Is it possible that getting this last eighty miles will be harder than the thousand before it?

For a little while, I stand in front of the giant map of Tennessee that is on the wall, wondering why American kids never study geography, because if they did maybe I'd have a working knowledge of this state. I take a deep breath and walk out of the bus station, downtown, wandering in and out of stores selling western attire and restaurants with live music. There are also cars and trucks parked along the streets. I look at the license plates—a lot are probably rentals. But some have baby car seats inside, or CDs scattered on the floor—the detritus of an owner.

Then I start reading bumper stickers. There are some I expect (AMERICAN BY BIRTH, SOUTHERN BY THE GRACE OF GOD) and some that make me feel sick to my stomach (SAVE A DEER, SHOOT A QUEER). But I am looking for hints, clues, the way Virgil might have looked. Something that will tell me more about the family who owns that vehicle.

Finally, on one pickup truck, I find a sticker that says PROUD OF MY COLUMBIA HONOR STUDENT! This is a jackpot on two counts: There is a flatbed I can hide in, and Columbia—according to the map at the Greyhound terminal—is en route to Hohenwald. I put my foot on the rear bumper, ready to hoist myself into the flatbed and lie down when no one is looking.

"What are you doing?"

I've been so busy canvassing the people on the street to see if they are paying attention, I don't see the little boy sneak up behind me. He is probably about seven years old, and he is missing so many of his teeth that the remaining ones look like headstones in a graveyard.

I crouch down, thinking of all the babysitting I've done over the years. "I'm playing hide-and-seek. Wanna help?"

He nods.

"Cool. But that means you have to keep a secret. Can you do that? Can you not tell your mom or dad that I'm hiding here?"

The boy jerks his chin up and down, emphatic. "Then do I get to have a turn?"

"Totally," I promise, and I hike myself into the flatbed.

"Brian!" a woman calls, huffing as she runs around the corner, a teenage girl sulking behind her with her arms crossed. "Get over here!"

The metal bed is as hot as the surface of the sun. I can literally feel the blisters forming on my palms and the backs of my legs. I poke my head up the tiniest bit, so that I can make eye contact with him, and I put my finger to my pursed lips, the universal sign for *Sssh*.

His mother is closing in on us, so I lie down and cross my arms and hold my breath.

"My turn next," Brian says.

"Who are you talking to?" his mother demands.

"My new friend."

"I thought we talked about lying," she says, and she unlocks the cab door.

I feel bad for Brian, not just because his mother doesn't believe him, but because I have no plans to give him a turn at hide-and-seek. I'll be long gone by then.

Someone inside slides open the back window of the truck cab for ventilation. Through it, I can hear the radio as Brian and his sister and his mom head down the interstate toward, I hope, Columbia, Tennessee. I close my eyes as the sun bakes me and pretend I am on a beach, not a slab of metal.

The songs that come on are about driving trucks like this one, or about girls with hearts of gold who've been done wrong. They all sound the same to me. My mother had an aversion to banjos so strong it bordered on allergy. I remember her turning off the radio every time a singer had the slightest twang in her voice. Could a woman who hated country-western music have chosen to make a new home within striking distance of the Grand Ole Opry? Or had she used that dislike as a smoke screen, figuring that anyone who knew her would never expect her to settle down in the heart of country-westernland?

As I bob along in the flatbed, I think:

1. Banjos actually are kind of cool.
2. Maybe people change.

ALICE

It's really not a stretch to say that, for elephants, mating is a song and dance.

As in all communication for those animals, vocalizations are paired with gestures. On an ordinary day, for example, a matriarch might make a "let's go" rumble, but at the same time she will position her body in the direction she wants to take the herd.

The sounds of mating are more complicated, however. In the wild we hear the pulsing, guttural musth rumbles of males—deep and low, puttering, what you might imagine if you drew a bow made of hormones against an instrument of anger. Males might produce a musth rumble when they are challenged by another male, when they're surprised by an approaching vehicle, when they are searching for mates. The sounds differ from elephant to elephant and are accompanied by ear waves and frequent urine dribbling.

When a musth male is vocalizing, the whole herd of females will start to chorus. Those sounds attract not just the male who started the conversation but all the eligible bachelors, so that the females in estrus now have the chance to choose the most attractive mate—and by this I don't mean the one with the best comb-over but rather the male who is most likely to survive—a healthy, older elephant. A female that doesn't like a particular male might run away from him, even if he has already mounted her, to find someone better. But, of course, that presumes there's someone better to be found.

For this reason, several days before she comes into estrus, a female gives an estrus roar—a powerful call that brings even more boys to the yard, and thus a greater range of mates from which to select. Finally, when she allows herself to be mated, she sings an estrus song. Unlike the musth rumbles of males, these songs are lyrical and repetitive, throaty purrs that rise quickly and then trail off. The female flaps her ears loudly and secretes from her temporal glands. After the mating, the other females in her family join in, a symphony of roars and rumbles and trumpets like those they'd make at any other socially exciting moment—a birth, or a reunion.

We know that when male whales sing, those who have the most complex songs are the ones who get the females. On the contrary, in the elephant world, a musth male will mate with anyone he can; it's the female who sings, and it's out of biological necessity. A female elephant is in estrus for only six days, and the only available males may be miles away. Pheromones don't work at those distances, so she has to do something else to attract potential mates.

It has been proven that whale songs are passed down from generation to generation, that they exist in all the oceans of the world. I have always wondered if the same holds true for elephants. If the calves of elephants learn the estrus song from their older female relatives during mating season, so that when it's their own turn, they know how to sing to attract the strongest, fiercest males. If, by doing this, the daughters learn from their mothers' mistakes.

SERENITY

Here's what I haven't told you: Once before, in my heyday as a psychic, I lost the ability to communicate with spirits.

I was doing a reading for a young college girl who wanted me to reach out to her deceased dad. She brought along her mother, and they had their own tape recorders, so that each could replay whatever happened at our session. For an hour and a half, I put his name out there; I struggled to connect. And the only thought that came into my head was that this man had killed himself with a gun.

Other than that: silence.

Exactly like what I get now, when I try to connect with the dead.

Anyway, I felt horrible. I was charging these women for ninety minutes of nothing. And although I didn't offer a money-back guarantee, I had never in my life as a psychic come up so dry before. So I apologized.

Upset about the outcome, the girl burst into tears and asked to use the restroom. As soon as she left, her mother—who had been largely silent during this entire experience—told me about her husband, and the secret she had not confided to her daughter.

He had indeed committed suicide, using a shotgun. He'd been a very well-known college basketball coach in North Carolina who'd had an affair with one of the boys on his team. When his wife discovered this, she told him she wanted a divorce, and that she would ruin his professional career unless he paid her to keep quiet. He refused and said he truly cared about the boy. So she told her husband he could have his new paramour, but she would sue him for every cent he had, and would still go public with what he'd done to her. That was the cost of love, she said.

He walked downstairs into their basement and blew his brains out.

At his funeral, as she was saying her last good-bye in private, she said, *You son of a bitch. Don't think I'll forgive you now that you're dead. Good riddance.*

Two days later the daughter called me to say that the strangest thing had happened. The recording she had made was completely blank. Although there had been dialogue between us during the session, all you could hear on the playback was a hissing sound. And even stranger: The same thing was true of the recording that had been made by her mother.

It was clear to me that the dead husband had heard his wife loud and clear at the funeral, and had taken her at her word. She didn't want anything to do with him, and so he stayed away from us all. Permanently.

Talking to spirits is a dialogue. It takes two. If you're trying hard and coming up empty, it's either because of a spirit who *won't* communicate or because of a medium who *can't*.

"It does not work like a faucet," I snap, trying to put some distance between myself and Virgil. "I can't turn it on and off."

We are in the parking lot outside of Gordon's Wholesale, processing the information we just received about Grace Cartwright's suicide. I have to admit, it wasn't what I was expecting to hear, but Virgil is convinced that this is an integral piece of the puzzle. "Let me get this straight," he says soberly. "I'm saying to you that I'm willing to actually admit that psychic powers aren't a load of bullshit. I'm saying to you that I'm willing to give your . . . talent . . . a chance. And you won't even try?"

"Fine," I say, frustrated. I lean against the front bumper of my car, shaking out my shoulders and arms the way a swimmer does at the starting block. Then I close my eyes.

"You can do it here?" Virgil interrupts.

I crack open my left eye. "Isn't that what you had in mind?"

His face reddens. "I guess I thought you'd need . . . I don't know. A tent or something."

"I can manage without my crystal ball and tea leaves, too," I say drily.

I haven't admitted to either Jenna or Virgil that I can no longer communicate with spirits. I've let them believe that the acts of stumbling over Alice's wallet and necklace on the grounds of the old elephant sanctuary were not flukes but actual psychic moments.

I may have even convinced myself of that. So I close my eyes and think, *Grace. Grace, come talk to me.*

That's how I used to do it.

But I'm getting nothing. It's as empty and static as the time I tried to contact that North Carolina basketball coach who'd killed himself.

I glance at Virgil. "You get anything?" I ask. He's typing away on his phone, searching for Gideon Cartwright in Tennessee.

"Nope," he admits. "But if I were him I'd be using an alias."

"Well, I'm not getting anything, either," I tell Virgil, and this is, for once, the truth.

"Maybe you should do it . . . louder."

I put my hand on my hip. "Do I tell you how to do your job?" I say. "It's sometimes like this, for suicides."

"Like what?"

"Like they're embarrassed by what they've done." Suicides, almost by definition, are all ghosts—stuck earthbound because they are desperate to apologize to their loved ones or because they are so ashamed of themselves.

It gets me thinking about Alice Metcalf again. Maybe the reason I haven't been able to communicate with her is that, like Grace, she killed herself.

Immediately I push that thought away. I've let Virgil's expectations go to my head; the reason I haven't been able to contact Alice—or any other potential spirit, for that matter—has a hell of a lot more to do with me than it does with them.

"I'll try again later," I lie. "What is it you want from Grace, anyway?"

"I want to know what made her kill herself," he says. "Why would a happily married woman with a steady job and a family, put stones in her pockets, and walk into a pond?"

"Because she wasn't a happily married woman," I reply.

"And we have a winner," Virgil says. "You find out your husband is sleeping with someone else. What do you do?"

"Take a blessed moment and glory in the fact that at least I walked down the aisle at some point?"

Virgil sighs. "No. You confront him, or you run away."

I unravel that thought. "What if Gideon wanted a divorce and Grace said no? What if he killed her and tried to make it look like a suicide?"

"The medical examiner would have figured out right away during the autopsy if it was a homicide rather than a suicide."

"Really? Because I was under the impression that law enforcement doesn't always make the most legitimate rulings when it comes to cause of death."

Virgil ignores my jab. "What if Gideon was planning to run away with Alice and Thomas found out about it?"

"You had Thomas signed into the psychiatric ward before Alice disappeared from the hospital."

"But he very well could have been fighting with her earlier that night, so that she ran into the enclosures. Maybe Nevvie Ruehl was in the wrong place at the wrong time. She tried to stop Thomas, and instead, he stopped *her*. Meanwhile Alice ran, knocked her head into a branch, and passed out a mile away from them. Gideon met her at the hospital and they worked out a plan—one that took her far away from her angry husband. We know that Gideon accompanied the elephants to their new home. Maybe Alice slipped away and met him there."

I fold my arms, impressed. "That's brilliant."

"Unless," Virgil muses, "it went down another way. Say Gideon told Grace he wanted a divorce so he could run off with Alice. Grace, devastated, committed suicide. The guilt over Grace's death made Alice rethink their plan—but Gideon wasn't willing to let her desert him. Not alive, anyway."

I think about that for a moment. Gideon could have come to the hospital and convinced Alice that her baby was in trouble—or told her any lie that would have made her leave abruptly with him. I'm not stupid—I watch *Law & Order*. So many murders happen because the victim trusts the guy who comes to the door, or asks for help, or offers a ride. "Then how did Nevvie die?"

"Gideon killed her, too."

"Why would he kill his own mother-in-law?" I ask.

"You're kidding, right?" Virgil says. "Isn't that every guy's fantasy? If Nevvie heard that Gideon and Alice were sleeping together, she probably was the one who started the fight."

"Or maybe she never touched Gideon. Maybe she went after Alice in the enclosure. And Alice ran away to save herself, and passed out." I glance at him. "Which is what Jenna has been saying all along."

"Don't look at me like that," Virgil says and scowls.

"You should call her. She might remember something about Gideon and her mother."

"We don't need Jenna's help. We just have to get to Nashville . . ."

"She doesn't deserve to be left behind."

For a moment Virgil looks like he's going to argue. Then he reaches for his phone and stares down at it. "Do you have her number?"

I called her once, but it was from home, not my cell. I don't have her number with me. Unlike Virgil, however, I know where to look for it.

We drive to my apartment. He glances with longing at the bar that we have to walk past to access the staircase. "How do you resist?" he murmurs. "It's like living above a Chinese restaurant."

Virgil stands in the doorway as I rummage through the stack of mail on my dining room table to find the ledger that I make my clients sign. Jenna, of course, was the most recent acquisition. "You can come in, you know," I say.

It takes me another moment to locate the phone, which is hiding underneath a kitchen towel on the counter. I pick it up and punch Jenna's number in, but the phone doesn't seem to have a dial tone.

Virgil is looking at the photograph on my mantel—me sandwiched between George and Barbara Bush. "Nice of you to go slumming with the likes of Jenna and me," he says.

"I was a different person back then," I reply. "Besides, celebrity isn't what it's cracked up to be. You can't see it in the photo, but the president's hand is on my ass."

"Could've been worse," Virgil murmurs. "Could've been Barbara's."

I try Jenna's number again, but nothing happens. "Weird. There's something wrong with my line," I tell Virgil, who pulls his cell phone from his pocket.

"Let me try," he suggests.

"Forget it. I can't get cell service here unless I'm wearing tinfoil on my head and hanging from the fire escape. The joys of country living."

"We could use the phone at the bar," Virgil offers.

"The hell with that," I say, imagining myself trying to pry him away from a whiskey. "You used to be a beat cop before you were a detective, right?"

"Yeah."

I stuff the ledger into my purse. "Then you can direct us to Greenleaf Street."

The neighborhood where Jenna lives is like a hundred other neighborhoods: lawns trimmed neatly in patchwork squares, houses dressed in red and black shutters, dogs yapping behind invisible fences. Little kids ride their bikes up and down the sidewalk as I pull the car to the curb.

Virgil glances at Jenna's front yard. "You can tell a lot about a person from their house," he muses.

"Like what?"

"Oh, you know. A flag often means they're conservative. If they drive a Prius, they're going to be more liberal. Half the time it's bullshit, but it's an interesting science."

"Sounds a lot like a cold reading. And I'm pretty sure it's about as accurate."

"Well, for what it's worth—I guess I didn't expect Jenna to grow up so . . . white bread. If you know what I mean."

I do. The cul-de-sac, the meticulous houses, the recycling bins stacked at the curb, the 2.4 children in each yard—it feels so Stepford. There's something unsettled about Jenna, something ragged at the edges, that does not belong here.

"What's her grandmother's name?" I ask Virgil.

"How the fuck would I know?" he says. "But it doesn't matter; she works during the day."

"Then you should stay here," I suggest to Virgil.

"Why?"

"Because I have less of a chance of Jenna slamming the door in my face if you're not with me," I say.

Virgil may be a pain in the butt, but he isn't stupid. He slouches in the passenger seat. "Whatever."

So I walk solo up the cobblestone pathway to the front door. It's mauve, and there's a little wooden heart nailed to the front of it, painted with the words WELCOME FRIENDS. I ring the doorbell, and a moment later it swings open by itself.

At least that's what I think, until I realize that there's a tiny kid standing in front of me, sucking his thumb. He's maybe three, and I am not all that good with small humans. They make me think of rodents, chewing your good leather shoes and leaving crumbs and droppings behind. I'm so stunned by the thought that Jenna has a sibling—one that was apparently born after she moved in with her grandmother—that I can't even find the words to say hello.

The kid's thumb comes out of his mouth, like the plug from a dike, and not surprisingly, the waterworks start.

Immediately a young woman comes running and scoops him into

her arms. "I'm sorry," she says. "I didn't hear the doorbell. Can I help you?"

She is screaming this, of course, because the kid is wailing even louder. And she's already glaring at me, as if I actually did physical harm to her kid. Meanwhile, I'm trying to figure out who this woman is and what she is doing in Jenna's home.

I offer my prettiest television smile. "I guess I came at a bad time," I say. Loudly. "I'm looking for Jenna?"

"Jenna?"

"Metcalf?" I say.

The woman jostles her kid on her hip. "I think you have the wrong address."

She starts to close the door, but I wedge my foot inside it, digging in my purse for that ledger. It opens easily to the back page, where Jenna has written, in her loopy teenager handwriting, 145 Greenleaf Street, Boone.

"One forty-five Greenleaf Street?" I ask.

"You've got the right place," she answers, "but there's no one here by that name."

She shuts the door in my face, and I stare down at the ledger in my hand. Stunned, I walk back to the car and slip inside, toss the ledger at Virgil. "She played me," I tell him. "She gave me a fake address."

"Why would she do that?"

I shake my head. "I don't know. Maybe she didn't want me to send junk mail."

"Or maybe she didn't trust you," Virgil suggested. "She doesn't trust either of us. And you know what that means." He waits until I glance up at him. "She's a step ahead of us."

"What do you mean?"

"She's smart enough to have figured out why her dad reacted the way he did. She must already know about her mother and Gideon; and she's doing exactly what we should have done an hour ago." He reaches over and turns the key in the ignition. "We're going to Tennessee," Virgil says, "because a hundred bucks says Jenna's already there."

ALICE

Dying of grief is the ultimate sacrifice, but it is not evolutionarily feasible. If grief were that overwhelming, a species would simply be erased. That's not to say there haven't been cases in the animal kingdom. I knew of a horse that had died suddenly, and its long-term stablemate followed shortly after. There was a pair of dolphins that had worked in tandem at a theme park; when the female passed away, the male swam in circles with his eyes closed for weeks.

After Maura's baby died, her pain was written all over her face and in the way she moved her body gingerly, as if the friction of the air against it was excruciating. She isolated herself in the vicinity of the grave; she wouldn't come into the barn at night. She didn't have the solace of her family around her, to bring her back to the world of the living.

I was determined not to let her be a casualty of her own sorrow.

Gideon affixed to the fence a giant bristled brush that had been a gift from the public works department when it purchased a new street sweeper, an enrichment tool that Maura would have previously loved to rub up against. But Maura didn't even glance in the direction of the hammering when he was installing it. Grace tried to cheer Maura up by giving her red grapes and watermelon, her favorite foods—but Maura stopped eating. The vacancy of her stare, the way she seemed to take up less material space than she had before—it made me think of Thomas, staring down at the blank book in his office three nights after the calf's death. Physically present, but mentally somewhere else.

Nevvie thought we should let Hester into the enclosure to see if she could console Maura, but I didn't think it was the right time yet. I had seen matriarchs charge elephants in their own herd—close relatives—if they got too close to a calf that was alive. Who knew what Maura, in her grief, would do to protect a calf that was dead? "Not yet," I told Nevvie. "As soon as I see that she's ready to move on."

It was academically interesting, recording how a lone elephant would rebound from loss, without a herd to support her. It was also heartbreaking. I spent hours cataloging Maura's behavior, because that was my job. I would take Jenna with me whenever Grace couldn't keep an eye on her, because Thomas was so busy himself.

Whereas the rest of us were still moving in slow motion, trapped by the viscous sadness that surrounded Maura, Thomas had snapped back into a model of efficiency. He was so focused and energized that I wondered if I'd just hallucinated the image of him catatonic at his desk the night after the calf died. The money he'd been counting on from donors who were excited about a baby elephant's arrival would no longer materialize, but he had a new idea to sustain funding, and that consumed him.

If I was going to be honest, I didn't mind picking up the slack of running the sanctuary while Thomas was busy. Anything was better than the shock of seeing him the way he'd been—broken and unreachable. *That* Thomas—the one who had apparently existed before I knew him—was one I didn't ever want to see again. I hoped that maybe I was the necessary ingredient in that equation, that my presence was enough to keep his depression from returning in the future. And because I was unwilling to be the trigger that might set Thomas off, I was willing to do whatever he wanted or needed. I was going to be his biggest cheerleader.

Two weeks after the calf died—which is how I'd started marking time—I drove to Gordon's Wholesale to pick up our weekly order. But when I went to pay with our credit card, it was declined.

"Run it again," I suggested, but it didn't make a difference.

Embarrassed—it wasn't a state secret that the sanctuary was always low on funding—I told Gordon I'd just drive to an ATM and pay him in cash.

When I tried, however, the machine wouldn't spit out any money. ACCOUNT CLOSED, the screen read. I ducked inside the bank and asked to speak to a manager. Surely there was a mistake.

"Your husband withdrew the money in that account," the woman told me.

"When?" I asked, dumbfounded.

She checked her computer. "Last Thursday," she told me. "The same day he applied for a second mortgage."

My face burned. I was Thomas's wife. How could he make decisions like this without talking to me about them? We had seven elephants whose diet was going to be seriously depleted without this week's produce delivery. We had three employees who expected to be paid on Friday. And as far as I could tell, we no longer had any money.

I didn't go back to Gordon's Wholesale. Instead, I drove home, snapping Jenna out of her car seat so fast that she started to cry. I burst through the door of the cottage, calling for Thomas, who didn't answer. I found Grace cutting up squash in the Asian barn, and Nevvie pruning wild grapevines, but neither of them had seen Thomas.

By the time I walked back home, Gideon was waiting. "You know anything about a nursery shipment?" he asked.

"Nursery?" I repeated, thinking of babies. Of Maura.

"Yeah, like plants."

"Don't accept the delivery," I said. "Stall them." Just then Thomas walked past us, waving the truck through the gates.

I handed Gideon the baby and grabbed Thomas by the arm. "Do you have a minute?"

"Actually," he said, "I don't."

"I think you do," I countered, and I dragged him inside to his office, closing the door for privacy. "What's on that truck?"

"Orchids," Thomas said. "Can't you picture it? A field of purple orchids stretching out to the Asian barn?" He grinned. "I dreamed about it."

He'd bought a truckload of exotic flowers that we didn't need, because of a dream? Orchids would not grow in this soil. And they were not cheap. That delivery was money thrown away.

"You bought *flowers* . . . when our credit card's been shut off and our bank account has been drained?"

To my shock, Thomas's face glowed. "I didn't just buy flowers. I invested in the future. I don't know why I haven't thought of it before, Alice," he said. "The storage space above the African barn? I'm going to make it an observation deck." He was talking so fast that his words tangled, like yarn rolling out of his lap. "You can see everything from up there. The whole property. I feel like I'm king of the world when I look out the window. Imagine *ten* windows. A wall of glass. And big donors coming to watch the elephants from that deck. Or renting out the space for functions—"

It wasn't a bad idea. But it was an ill-timed one. We didn't have any extra funds to allocate to a renovation project. We barely had enough to cover operating expenses for the month. "Thomas. We can't afford that."

"We can if we don't hire anyone to do the building."

"Gideon doesn't have time to—"

"Gideon?" He laughed. "I don't need Gideon. I can do it myself."

"How?" I asked. "You don't know anything about construction."

He turned on me, feral. "You don't know anything about me."

As I watched him walk out the office door, I thought that might just be true.

I told Gideon that there had been a mistake, that the orchids needed to be returned. I am still not sure how he managed this miracle, but he came back with the refunded money in hand, which went directly to Gordon's Wholesale for our crates of cabbage and thick-necked squash and overripe melons. Thomas didn't even seem to realize that his orchids were gone; he was too busy hammering and sawing in the old attic space above the African barn from dawn to dusk. And yet every time I asked to see his progress, he snapped at me.

Maybe, I thought scientifically, this was Thomas's reaction to grief. Maybe he was throwing himself into a project so that he wouldn't think about what we'd lost. To that end, I decided the best way to snap him out of his folly was to help him remember what he still *had*. So I cooked elaborate meals, even though I'd never really mastered more than macaroni and cheese. I packed picnics and brought Jenna to the African barn, and enticed Thomas to join us for lunch. One afternoon, I asked him about his project. "Let me peek," I begged. "I won't tell anyone anything until it's done."

But Thomas shook his head. "It'll be worth the wait," he promised.

"I could help you. I'm good at painting . . ."

"You're good at a lot of things," Thomas said, and he kissed me.

We had been having a lot of sex. After Jenna went to sleep, Thomas would come back from the African barn and shower, then slip into bed beside me. Our lovemaking was almost desperate—if I was trying to escape the memory of Maura's calf, Thomas seemed to be trying to keep himself tethered to something. It was almost as if I didn't matter, as if any body beneath him would have done the job— but I couldn't place blame, since I was using Thomas, too, to forget. I'd fall asleep, exhausted, and in the middle of the night, when my hand inched across the sheets to find him, he would be gone again.

At first, on the picnic, I kissed him back. But then his hand slid under my shirt, fumbling with the clasp of my bra. "*Thomas*," I whispered. "We're in *public*."

Not only were we sitting in the shadow of the African barn, where any of the employees might pass by, but Jenna was staring at us. She pulled herself to her feet and stumbled toward us, a tiny zombie.

I gasped. "Thomas! She's walking!"

His face was buried in the curve of my neck. His hand covered my breast.

"Thomas," I said, shoving him away. *"Look."*

He backed off, annoyed. His eyes were nearly black behind his glasses, and even though he didn't say anything, I could hear him clearly: *How dare you?* But then Jenna tumbled into his lap, and he scooped her up and kissed her forehead and each cheek. "What a big girl," he said, as Jenna babbled against his shoulder. He set her down on the ground, pointing her in my direction. "Was it a fluke or a new skill?" he asked. "Should we run the experiment again?"

I laughed. "This girl is doomed, having two scientists as parents." I held out my arms. "Come back to me," I coaxed.

I was speaking to my daughter. But I might as well have been pleading to Thomas as well.

A few days later, when I was helping Grace prepare meals for the Asian elephants, I asked her if she ever argued with Gideon.

"Why?" she said, suddenly guarded.

"It just seems like you get along so well," I replied. "It's a little daunting."

Grace relaxed. "He doesn't put the toilet seat down. Drives me crazy."

"If that's his only flaw, I'd say you're incredibly lucky." I raised a cleaver, chopping a melon in half, focusing my attention on the juice that bled out of it. "Does he ever keep secrets from you?"

"Like what he's getting me for my birthday?" She shrugged. "Sure."

"I don't mean those kinds of secrets. I mean the kind that make you think he's hiding something." I put down the knife and looked her in the eye. "The night the calf died . . . you saw Thomas in his office, didn't you?"

We had never talked about it. But I knew Grace must have seen him, rocking back and forth in his chair, his eyes empty, his hands shaking. I knew that was why she had refused to leave Jenna alone with him.

Grace's gaze slid away from mine. "Everyone's got their demons," she murmured.

I knew, from the way she said it, that this was not the first time she had seen Thomas that way. "It's happened before?"

"He always bounces back."

Was I the only person at the sanctuary who didn't know? "He told me it was just once—after his parents died," I said, my face hot. "I thought marriage was a partnership, you know? For better or for worse. In sickness and in health. Why would he lie to me?"

"Keeping a secret isn't always lying. Sometimes it's the only way to protect the person you love."

I scoffed. "You only say that because you haven't been on the receiving end."

"No," Grace said softly. "But I've been the one who keeps the secret." She began to shovel peanut butter into the empty bellies of the halved melons, her hands quick and practiced. "I love taking care of your daughter," she added, a non sequitur.

"I know. I'm grateful."

"I love taking care of your daughter," Grace repeated, "because I'm never going to have one of my own."

I looked at her, and in that moment, she reminded me of Maura—there was a shadow in her eyes that I'd noticed before, that I'd chalked up to youth and insecurity, but that actually may have been the loss of something she never really had. "You're still young," I said.

Grace shook her head. "I have PCOS," she clarified. "It's a hormone thing."

"You could get a surrogate. You could adopt. Have you talked to Gideon about the alternatives?" She just stared at me, and I understood: *Gideon didn't know*. This was the secret she had been keeping from him.

Suddenly Grace grabbed my arm, so tightly that it hurt. "You won't tell?"

"No," I promised.

She settled, picking up her knife again to start cutting. We worked in silence for a few moments, and then Grace spoke again. "It's not that he doesn't love you enough to tell you the truth," she said. "It's that he loves you too much to risk it."

That night, after Thomas slipped into the cottage after midnight, I pretended to be asleep when he poked his head into the bedroom. I waited until I heard the shower running, and then I got out of bed and walked out of the cottage, careful not to wake Jenna. In the dark, as my eyes adjusted, I ran past Grace and Gideon's cottage, where the lights were off. I thought of them twined together in bed, with an infinitesimal space between them at every point they touched.

The spiral staircase was painted black, and I banged my shin against it before I realized I had already reached the far edge of the African barn. Moving silently—I didn't want to wake the elephants and have them send out an inadvertent alert—I crept up the stairs, biting my lip against the pain. At the top, the door was locked, but one master key opened everything at the sanctuary, so I knew I'd be able to get inside.

The first thing I noticed was that, as Thomas had said, the moon-lit view was remarkable. Although Thomas hadn't installed the plate-glass windows, he had cut out rough openings and covered them with a sheet of clear plastic. Through them, I could see every acre of the sanctuary, illuminated by the grace of the full moon. I could easily imagine a viewing platform, an observatory, a way for the public to see the amazing animals we sheltered without us having to disturb their natural habitat or make them part of a display, like they'd been in zoos and circuses.

Maybe I was overreacting. Maybe Thomas was just trying to do what he'd said: save his business. I turned, feeling along the wall until I could locate the light switch. The room flooded, so bright that for a moment I couldn't see.

The space was empty. There was no furniture, no boxes, no tools, not even a stick of wood. The walls had been painted a blinding white, along with the ceiling and the floor. But scrawled on every inch were letters and numbers, written over and over in a looping code.

C14H19NO4C18H16N6S2C16H21NO2C3H6N2O2C189H 285N55O57S.

It was like walking into a church and finding occult symbols written in blood on the walls. My breath caught in my throat. The room was closing in on me, the numbers shimmering and blending into each other. I realized, as I sank down onto the floor, this was because I was crying.

Thomas was sick.

Thomas needed help.

And although I was not a psychiatrist, although I didn't have experience with any of this, it did not look like depression to me.

It just looked . . . crazy.

I stood up and backed out of the room, keeping the door unlocked. I didn't have much time. But instead of going to our cottage, I went to the one shared by Gideon and Grace and knocked on the door. Grace answered wearing a man's T-shirt, her hair tousled. "Alice?" she said. "What's wrong?"

My husband is mentally ill. This sanctuary is dying. Maura lost her calf. You pick.

"Is Gideon here?" I asked, when I knew that he was. Not everyone had a husband who sneaked off in the middle of the night to write gibberish on the ceiling and floor and walls of an empty room.

He came to the door in a pair of shorts, his torso bare, a shirt in hand. "I need your help," I said.

"One of the elephants? Is something wrong?"

I didn't answer, just turned on my heel and started to walk toward the African barn again. Gideon fell into step beside me, pulling the T-shirt over his head. "Which girl is it?"

"The elephants are fine," I said, my voice shaking. We had reached the base of the spiral staircase. "I need you to do something, and I need you to not ask me any questions. Can you handle that?"

Gideon took one look at my face and nodded.

I climbed as if I were headed to my own execution. In retrospect, maybe I was. Maybe this was the first step to a long and fatal fall. I opened the door so that Gideon could see the interior.

"Holy shit," he breathed. "What *is* this?"

"I don't know. But you have to paint over it before morning." Just like that, the threads of self-restraint snapped, and I doubled over, unable to breathe, unable to stem the tears anymore. Gideon immediately reached for me, but I backed away. "Hurry," I choked out, and I ran down the stairs, back to my cottage, where I found Thomas just opening the door of the bathroom, a cloud of steam haloing his body.

"Did I wake you?" he asked, and he smiled, that crooked smile that had made me hang on his words in Africa, that I saw whenever I closed my eyes.

If I had any chance of saving Thomas from himself, then I had to make him believe I wasn't the enemy. I had to make him believe that I believed in him. So I pasted what I hoped was a similar smile on my face. "I thought I heard Jenna cry."

"Is she all right?"

"Fast asleep," I told Thomas, swallowing around the wishbone of truth caught in my throat. "It must have been a nightmare."

I had lied to Gideon when he asked what was written on the wall. I *did* know.

It wasn't a random string of letters and numbers. It was chemical formulas for drugs: anisomycin, U0126, propanolol, D-cycloserine, and neuropeptide Y. I had written about them in an earlier paper, when I was trying to find links between elephant memory and cognition. These were compounds that—if given quickly after a trauma—interacted with the amygdala to keep a memory from being coded as painful or upsetting. Using rats, scientists had successfully been able to eliminate the stress and fear caused by certain memories.

You can imagine the implications for that—and recently, some medical professionals *had*. Controversies had sprung up around hospitals that wanted to administer drugs like this to rape victims. Beyond the practical issue of whether or not the blocked memory actually would stay blocked forever, there was a moral issue: Could a traumatized victim actually give permission to be given the drug, if by definition she was traumatized and unable to think clearly?

What had Thomas been doing with my paper, and how did it tie in to plans to raise money for the sanctuary? But then, maybe it didn't. If Thomas truly had snapped, he might see relevance in the clues of a crossword puzzle; he might see meaning in the weatherman's forecast. He would be constructing a reality full of causal links that were, to the rest of us, unrelated.

It had been a long time, but the conclusion of my paper was that there was a reason the brain had evolved in a way that allowed a memory to be red-flagged. If memories protected us from future dangerous situations, was it in our best interests to chemically forget them?

Would I ever unsee that room, looped with the graffiti of chemical formulas? No, not even after Gideon had painted it white again. And maybe that was for the best, because it reminded me that the man I thought I had fallen in love with was not the one who came into the kitchen this morning, whistling.

I had plans. I wanted to get Thomas help. But no sooner had he left for the observation deck than Nevvie showed up with Grace. "I need your help moving Hester," Nevvie said, and I remembered that I'd promised her we could try to put the two African elephants together today.

I could have postponed it, but then Nevvie would have asked why. And I didn't feel like talking about last night.

Grace held out her arms for Jenna, and I thought about our conversation yesterday. "Did Gideon—" I began.

"He finished," she said, and that was all I needed to know.

I followed Nevvie out to the African enclosures, peeking at the upstairs level of the barn, with its sheet of plastic and the overpowering smell of fresh paint. Was Thomas in there, even now? Was he angry, to find his handiwork destroyed? Devastated? Indifferent?

Did he suspect me of doing it?

"Where *are* you today?" Nevvie asked. "I asked you a question."

"Sorry. I didn't sleep well last night."

"Do you want to take down the fence or drive her forward?"

"I'll get the gate," I said.

We had built a hot-wire fence to separate Hester from Maura when we realized Maura was pregnant. To tell the truth, if either elephant had wanted to get to the other side, she could have easily torn it down. But these two had not been together long enough to bond before they were separated. They were acquaintances, not friends. They had no great affection for each other yet. Which is why I didn't think Nevvie's idea was going to work.

In Tswana, there is a saying: *Go o ra motho, ga go lelwe.* Where there is support, there is no grief. You see this in the wild, when elephants mourn the death of a herd member. After a while, a few elephants will peel off to go to a watering hole. Others will investigate the brush for sustenance. It comes down to one or two elephants left behind—usually the daughters or young sons of the fallen elephant—who are reluctant to resume their daily lives. But the herd always comes back for them. It may be en masse, it may be just an emissary or two. They vocalize with "let's go" rumbles and angle their bodies to encourage the mourning elephants to join them. Eventually, they all do. But Hester was not Maura's cousin or sister. She was just another elephant. Maura had no incentive to listen to her, no more than I might have followed a complete stranger who walked up to me and suggested we go to lunch.

While Nevvie drove off in the ATV in search of Hester, I disconnected the fence controller and unwound the wire, creating an open gate. I waited until I heard the engine revving and spotted the elephant following Nevvie placidly. She was a sucker for watermelon, and there was a whole one on the ATV for her that would be placed closer to Maura.

I hopped on the vehicle as we drove to the site of the calf's grave, where Maura still stood, her shoulders sloped and her trunk dragging on the ground. Nevvie cut the engine, and I hopped off, setting the food for Hester a distance away from Maura. We had brought a treat for Maura, too, but unlike Hester, she did not touch hers.

Hester speared the watermelon on her tusk and let the juice drip into her mouth. Then she curled her trunk around the melon, plucked it from the ivory skewer, and crushed it between her jaws.

Maura didn't acknowledge her presence, but I could see her spine stiffen at the sound made by Hester's crunching. "Nevvie," I said quietly, climbing onto the ATV again. "Turn on the engine."

Lightning fast, Maura pivoted and thundered toward Hester, her head shaking and her ears flapping. Dirt chuffed, a cloud of intimidation. Hester squealed and threw back her trunk, just as willing to stand her ground.

"*Go,*" I said, and Nevvie angled the ATV so that Hester was headed off before she could get close to Maura. Maura didn't even turn toward us as we shepherded Hester away, to the other side of the hot-wire fence. She faced the raw, dark grave of the calf, which stretched like a yawn across the earth.

Sweating, my heart still pounding from the confrontation, I let Nevvie lead Hester deeper into the African enclosure while I reaffixed the wire joints, crimped them closed, and reattached the battery clamps. Nevvie drove up again a few minutes later, as I was finishing.

"Well," I said. "I told you so."

I took advantage of the fact that Grace was still watching Jenna and stopped off at the African barn to talk to Thomas. Climbing the spiral staircase, I heard no sound from inside the space. It made me wonder if Thomas had found the whitewashed walls and if that had been enough to snap him back to equilibrium. But when I reached the door, the knob turned in my hand and I stepped into the room to find one wall entirely covered with the same symbols I'd seen last night, and another wall half finished. Thomas stood on a chair, writing so furiously I thought the plaster might burst into flame. I felt as if my skeleton had turned to stone. "Thomas," I said. "I think we need to talk."

He glanced over his shoulder, so absorbed in his work that he hadn't even heard me come in. He didn't seem embarrassed, or surprised. Just disappointed. "It was going to be a surprise," he said. "I was doing it for you."

"Doing what?"

He stepped off the chair. "It's called molecular consolidation theory. It's been proven that memories stay in an elastic state before they are chemically encoded by the brain. Disturb that process, and you can alter the way the memory is recalled. To date, the only scientific successes have occurred when the inhibitors are given immediately after the trauma. But let's say the trauma's already past. What if we could regress the mind back to that moment, and give the drug. Would the trauma be forgotten?"

I stared at him, completely lost. "That's not possible."

"It is if you can go back in time."

"*What?*"

He rolled his eyes. "I'm not building a TARDIS, a time machine," Thomas said. "That would be insane."

"Insane," I repeated, the word breaking on the jetty of a sob.

"It's not literal bending of the fourth dimension. But you can alter perception for an *individual*, so that time is effectively reversed. You take them back to the stress, through an altered consciousness, and have them reexperience the emotional trauma long enough for the drug to do its job. And here's the part that's a surprise for you. Maura, she's going to be the subject."

At the sound of the elephant's name, my gaze snapped to his. "You aren't touching Maura."

"Not even if I can fix her? If I can make her forget her calf's death?"

I shook my head. "It doesn't work that way, Thomas—"

"But what if it did? What if there were implications for humans? Imagine the work that could be done with veterans who suffer from PTSD. Imagine if the sanctuary cemented its name as a critical research facility. We could get seed money from the Center for Neural Science at NYU. And if they agree to partner with me, the media attention could bring in investors to offset the loss of revenue the calf had been projected to bring in. I could win a *Nobel*."

I swallowed. "What makes you think you can regress a mind?"

"I was told I could."

"By *whom*?"

He reached into his back pocket and took out a piece of paper with the letterhead of the sanctuary at the top. Written on it was a phone number I recognized. I had called it last week, when my credit card was declined at Gordon's.

Welcome to Citibank MasterCard.

Beneath the customer service hotline number was a list of anagrams for the words *Account Balance*:

Cabal cannot cue; banal ceca count, accentual bacon, cabala once cunt, canal beacon cut, cab unclean coat, lacuna ant bocce, nebula coca cant, a cab nuance clot, a cab cannot clue, a cable can count, a conceal can but, cabal can't cue on, anal acne cub cot, ban ocean lac cut, cabal act once nu, *actual can be con.*

The last words were circled so deeply that the paper had begun to disintegrate. "You see? It's in code. *Actual can be con.*" Thomas's eyes burned into mine as if he were explaining the meaning of life. "What you see is not what you believe."

I stepped toward him, until we were standing only inches apart. "Thomas," I whispered, holding my palm up to his cheek. "Baby. You're sick."

He grasped my hand, a lifeline. Until then I hadn't realized how hard I was trembling. "Damn right I'm sick," he muttered, squeezing so hard that I twisted in pain. "I'm sick of you *doubting* me." He leaned so close that I could see the ring of orange around his pupils, and the pulse in his temple. "I am doing this for *you*," he said, biting off each word, spitting them in my face.

"I'm doing this for you, too," I cried, and I ran out of the airless room and down the spiral stairs.

Dartmouth College was sixty-five miles south. They had a state-of-the-art hospital there. And it happened to have the closest inpatient psychiatric facility to Boone. I don't know what made the psychiatrist agree to see me, considering I did not have an appointment and there was a waiting room full of people with equally pressing issues. All I could think, as I clutched Jenna against me and sat across from Dr. Thibodeau, was that the receptionist must have taken one look at me and thought I was feeding her a line. *Husband, my ass,* she probably thought, staring at my wrinkled uniform, my unwashed hair, my crying baby. She's *the one who's in crisis.*

I had spent a half hour telling the doctor what I knew of Thomas's history, and what I had seen last night. "I think the pressure's broken him," I said. Out loud, the words swelled like garish balloons. They took up all the space in the room.

"It's possible that what you're describing are symptoms of mania," the doctor said. "It's part of bipolar illness—which we used to call manic-depressive disorder." He smiled at me. "Being bipolar is like being forced to take LSD. It means your sensations and emotions and creativity are at their peak, but also that the highs are higher and the lows are lower. You know what they say—if a manic does something bizarre and it turns out to be right, he's brilliant. If it turns out to be wrong, he's crazy." Dr. Thibodeau smiled at Jenna, who was gumming one of his paperweights. "The good news is, if that's what's actually going on with your husband, it's treatable. The medications we put people on to control these mood swings bring them back to center. When Thomas realizes that he's living not a reality but just a manic episode, he's going to swing in the other direction and get very depressed, because he isn't the man he thought he was."

That makes two of us, I thought.

"Has your husband harmed you?"

I thought of the moment he grabbed my hand, how I heard the crunch of bones and cried out. "No," I said. I had betrayed Thomas enough; I would not do this, too.

"Do you think he might?"

I stared down at Jenna. "I don't know."

"He needs to be evaluated by a psychiatrist. If it is bipolar disorder, he may need time in the hospital to be stabilized."

Hopeful, I glanced at the doctor. "So you can bring him here?"

"No," Dr. Thibodeau said. "Institutionalizing someone is a stripping of personal rights; we can't take him by force unless he's hurt you."

"Then what am I supposed to do?" I asked.

The doctor met my gaze. "You're going to have to convince him to come in voluntarily."

He gave me his card and told me to call him when I felt Thomas was ready to become an inpatient. During the drive back to Boone, I thought about what I could possibly say to convince Thomas to go to the hospital in Lebanon. I could tell him Jenna was sick, but then why wouldn't we go to her pediatrician one town over? Even if I said I'd found him a donor or a neuroscientist interested in his experiment, it would only get him in the door. The minute we checked in at the psychiatric reception desk, he'd know what I was actually doing.

I came to the conclusion that the only way to get Thomas to voluntarily check in to a psychiatric ward was to make him see, simply and honestly, that this was best for him. That I still loved him. That we were in this together.

Fortified, I drove into the sanctuary, parked at the cottage, and carried a sleepy Jenna inside. I settled her on the couch and then went back to close the door I'd left ajar.

When Thomas grabbed me from behind, I screamed. "You scared me," I said, turning in his arms, trying to read his expression.

"I thought you left me. I thought you took Jenna, and that you weren't coming back."

I ran my hand through his hair. "No," I swore. "I would never."

When he kissed me, it was with the desperation of a man who is trying to save himself. When he kissed me, I believed that Thomas was going to be fine. I believed that maybe I would never have to call Dr. Thibodeau, that this was the beginning of Thomas's sway to center. I told myself that I could believe all of this, no matter how unfounded or unlikely, without realizing how much that made me like Thomas.

There is something else about memory, something Thomas hadn't brought up. It's not a video recording. It's subjective. It's a culturally relevant account of what happened. It doesn't matter if it's accurate; it matters if it's important in some way to *you*. If it teaches you something you need to learn.

For a few months, it seemed as if life at the sanctuary was settling back to normal. Maura took extended walks away from her calf's grave before returning to settle down there each night. Thomas began to work in his home office again, instead of constructing the observation deck. We left it locked and boarded up, like a ghost village. A grant he'd written for funding months ago came in unexpectedly, giving us a little breathing room for supplies and salaries.

I began to compare my notes about Maura and her grief to those about the other elephant mothers I'd seen lose calves. I spent hours walking with Jenna, at a toddler's pace; I pointed to wildflowers by color, to teach her new words. Thomas and I argued about whether it was safe for her, in the enclosures. I loved those arguments, for their simplicity. Their sanity.

One lazy afternoon, when Grace was sitting for Jenna in the stagnant heat, I was doing a trunk wash in the Asian barn with Dionne. We trained the elephants in this behavior, so that we could test for TB: We'd fill a syringe with saline, flush it into a nostril, and get the elephant to lift her trunk as high as possible. Then we'd hold a gallon-size Ziploc bag over the trunk as she lowered it and the fluid drained out. The sample was collected in a container and sent off to the lab. Some elephants hated the process; Dionne was one of the easier ones. So perhaps my guard was down, and that's why I didn't notice Thomas suddenly striding into the barn. He grabbed me by the neck, dragging me away from the elephant so that she couldn't reach us through the metal bars.

"Who's Thibodeau?" Thomas yelled, smacking my head against the steel so hard that my vision blurred.

I honestly didn't know what he was talking about.

"Thi ... bo ... deau," Thomas repeated. "You must know. His card was in *your* wallet." His hand was a vise around my throat. My lungs felt like they were on fire. I clawed at his fingers, at his wrists. He pressed a small white rectangle close to my face. "Ring a bell?"

I could barely see anything but stars at the edges of my vision. Still, somehow, I was able to make out the logo for the Dartmouth-Hitchcock hospital. The psychiatrist I'd seen, the one who had given me his card. "You want to lock me away," Thomas accused. "You're trying to steal my research. You've probably already called NYU to take credit, but the joke's on you, Alice, because you don't have the code to dial in to the colloquium's private conference line, and not *knowing* that flags you as an impostor—"

Dionne was bellowing, crashing against the reinforced bars of the barn. I tried to explain; I tried to speak. Thomas slammed me harder against the steel, and my eyes rolled upward.

Suddenly there was air, and light, and I was falling to the cement floor, gasping as my chest filled with fire. I rolled to my side to see Gideon punching Thomas so hard that his head arced backward and blood bloomed from his nose and mouth.

I scrambled to my feet and ran out of the barn. I did not get very far before my legs gave out beneath me, but to my surprise I didn't fall. I wound up caught in Gideon's arms. He stared at my throat, touched a finger to the red necklace made by Thomas's hands. He was so gentle, like silk over a scar, that something inside me snapped.

I shoved at him. "I didn't ask for your help!"

He let go of me, surprised. I staggered away from him, avoiding the spot where I knew Grace had taken Jenna swimming, and made my way to the cottage. I went right to Thomas's office, where he had been spending his time keeping the books and updating the files of the individual elephants. On his desk was a ledger we used to record all our income and expenses. I sat down and flipped through the first few pages, marking the deliveries of hay and the payments for veterinary care, the lab bills and the produce contract. Then I skipped to the end.

$C_{14}H_{19}NO_4C_{18}H_{16}N_6S_2C_{16}H_{21}NO_2C_3H_6N_2O_2C_{189}H_{285}N_{55}O_{57}S.C_{14}H_{19}NO_4C_{18}H_{16}N_6S_2C_{16}H_{21}NO_2C_3H_6N_2$

$O_2C_{189}H_{285}N_{55}O_{57}S$. $C_{14}H_{19}NO_4C_{18}H_{16}N_6S_2C_{16}H_{21}NO_2$
$C_3H_6N_2O_2C_{189}H_{285}N_{55}O_{57}S$.

I put my head down on the desk and cried.

I wrapped a gauzy blue scarf around my neck and went to sit with Maura near the calf's grave. I had been there for maybe an hour when Thomas approached, on foot. He stood on the other side of the fence, hands in his pockets. "I just wanted to tell you I'm going away for a while," he said. "It's somewhere I've been before. They can help me."

I didn't look at him. "I think that's a good idea."

"I left the contact information on the kitchen counter. But they won't let you talk to me. It's . . . part of the way they do things."

I did not think I'd need Thomas while he was gone. We had been running this sanctuary in his absence even when he had been on the premises.

"Tell Jenna . . ." He shook his head. "Well. Don't tell Jenna anything, except that I love her." Thomas took a step forward. "I know it's not worth much, but I'm sorry. I'm not . . . I'm not *me* right now. That's not an excuse. But it's all I have."

I didn't watch him leave. I sat with my arms wrapped tight around my legs. Twenty feet away, Maura picked up a fallen branch with a paintbrush of pine needles at the end and began to sweep the ground in front of her.

She did this for several minutes and then started to walk away from the grave. After moving a few yards, she turned and looked at me. Then she walked a bit, and paused, waiting.

I got to my feet and followed.

It was humid; my clothes stuck to my skin. I couldn't speak; my throat hurt that bad. The ends of the scarf I wore moved like butterflies on my shoulders in the hot breath of the breeze. Maura moved slowly and deliberately, until she reached the hot-wire fence. In the distance on the far side, she stared longingly at the pond.

I didn't have tools or gloves. I didn't have anything I needed to disable the electric fence. But I pried the box open with my fingernails and disengaged the batteries. I used all my strength to untie the makeshift gate I'd wired weeks before, even though the wire bit into my fingers and my hands grew slick with blood. Then I dragged the fence open, so that Maura could walk through.

She did, but paused at the edge of the pond.

We didn't come all this way for nothing. "Let's go," I rasped, and I kicked off my shoes and waded into the water.

It was cold and clear, deliciously fresh. My shirt and scarf stuck to my skin, and my shorts ballooned around my thighs. I ducked underwater, letting my hair fall out of its ponytail, and resurfaced, kicking to stay afloat. Then I flicked a handful of water at Maura.

She took two steps back and then reached her trunk into the pond and sprayed a stream over my head like a rain shower.

Her movement was so calculated, so unexpected—and so *playful*, after weeks of despair, that I laughed out loud. It didn't sound like my voice. It was stripped and ragged, but it was joy.

Maura gingerly waded into the pool, rolling to her left side and then to her right, tossing a spray of water over her back and then over me again. It reminded me of the herd I had taken Thomas to watch in the water hole in Botswana, back when I thought my life would be different than it had turned out to be. I watched Maura splash and roll, buoyed by the water, lighter than she'd been in a long time, and very slowly I let myself float, too.

"She's playing," Gideon said, from the far bank. "That means she's letting go."

I had not realized he was here; I had not known we were being watched. I owed Gideon an apology. I had not asked to be rescued, true, but that did not mean I didn't need saving.

I felt silly, unprofessional. Swimming across the pool, I left Maura to her own devices and emerged dripping, unsure of what to say. "I'm sorry," I offered. "I shouldn't have said what I said to you."

"How are you?" Gideon asked, concerned.

"I'm . . ." I paused, because I didn't know the answer. Relieved? Nervous? Scared? Then I smiled a little. "Wet."

Gideon grinned, taking my cue. He held out his empty hands. "I don't have a towel."

"I didn't know I would be swimming. Maura seemed to need a little encouragement."

He held my gaze. "Maybe she just needed to know someone was there for her."

I stared at him, until Maura sprayed us both with a fine mist. Gideon jumped away from the stream of cold water. But to me, it felt like a baptism. Like starting over.

That night I called a staff meeting. I told Nevvie and Grace and Gideon that Thomas would be visiting investors abroad for a while and that we would have to run the sanctuary without him. I could tell none of them believed me, but they pitied me enough to pretend. I gave Jenna ice cream for dinner, just because, and put her to sleep in my bed.

Then I went to the bathroom and unwound the scarf from my neck, where it had dried in wrinkles after my swim with Maura. There was a string of fingerprints, dark as South Sea pearls, ringing my throat.

A bruise is how the body remembers it's been wronged.

Padding down the hall in the dark, I found the Post-it note that Thomas had left in the kitchen. MORGAN HOUSE, he had printed, in his linear, architectural handwriting. STOWE, VT. 802-555-6868.

I picked up the phone and dialed. I didn't need to talk to him, but I did want to know that he'd gotten there safely. That he was going to be all right.

The number you have dialed is no longer in service. Please check the number and dial again.

So I did. And then I went to the computer in Thomas's office and looked up Morgan House on the Internet, only to find it listed as the name of a professional poker player in Vegas, and a halfway home for pregnant teens in Utah. There was no inpatient facility anywhere by that name.

VIRGIL

W e're going to miss the goddamned flight.

Serenity booked the tickets by phone. They cost as much as my rent. (When I told her that there was no way I could afford to pay her right now, Serenity just waved away my embarrassed concern. *Sugar*, she said, *that is why God created credit cards*.) Then we drove eighty-five miles per hour down the highway to the airport, because the flight to Tennessee left in an hour. Since we didn't have luggage, we raced to the automatic ticket machines, hoping to avoid the line of people checking baggage. Serenity's ticket spit out, no problem, with a free drink coupon. When I entered my confirmation code, though, I got a flashing message: SEE TICKET AGENT.

"Are you shitting me?" I mutter, looking at the line. On the loud-speaker, I hear flight 5660 to Nashville being announced, leaving from Gate 12.

Serenity looks at the escalator that leads to the TSA checkpoint. "There'll be another flight eventually," she says.

But by then, who knows where Jenna will be, and if she'll have gotten to Gideon first. And if Jenna's come to the same conclusion I have—that Gideon could have been responsible for her mother's dis-appearance, and possible death—who knows what he'll do to keep her from telling the rest of the world what he did.

"Get on that flight," I say. "Even if I don't make it. It's going to be just as important to find Jenna as it is to find Gideon, because if she finds him first, it could be bad."

Serenity must hear the urgency in my voice, because she nearly flies up the escalator and is swallowed by the queue of sullen travelers removing their shoes and belts and laptops.

The line for the ticket counter is not getting any shorter. I shift from foot to foot, impatient. I check my watch. Then I tear away from the pack like a tiger that's been unleashed and cut to the front of the line. "Excuse me," I say. "I'm about to miss my flight."

I'm expecting outrage, shock, swearing. I even have a ready excuse about my wife being in labor. But before anyone can complain, an airline employee intercepts me. "You can't do that, sir."

"I'm sorry," I tell her. "But my flight's leaving *right now*—"

She looks like she's well past the age for mandatory retirement, and sure enough, she says, "I've been working here since probably before you were born. So I can tell you unequivocally: Rules are rules."

"Please. It's an emergency."

She looks me in the eye. "You don't belong here."

Beside me, the next guy in line is summoned to an agent. I consider tackling him and taking his place. But instead, I look at the old woman, the lie about my pregnant wife caught between my teeth. Yet I hear myself say, "You're right. I don't. But I'm trying like hell to get there because someone I care about is in trouble."

I realize that, of all the years of cop work I did, and all the private investigations, this might be my first true confession.

The agent sighs, walking toward an empty computer terminal behind the counter, gesturing for me to follow. She takes the confirmation number I hand her, keying in letters so slowly I could invent entire alphabets between the touches of her fingers. "I've been here for forty years," she tells me. "Don't come across a lot of guys like you."

This woman is helping me; she's a bona fide human willing to work her magic instead of leaving me at the mercy of a glitched computer terminal—so I bite my tongue. After an eternity, she hands me a boarding pass. "Just remember, no matter what happens, you'll get there eventually."

I grab the boarding pass and start to run for the gate. I take the escalator steps two at a time. To be totally honest, I can't even remember getting through security, I just know that I am racing down the hall to Gate 12 as I hear the loudspeaker announcing the final call for travelers headed to Nashville, like a narrator broadcasting my fate. I sprint toward the gate agent as she is about to close the door and fling the boarding pass in her direction.

I step onto the plane, so winded I can't even speak, and immediately see Serenity in a seat about five rows back. I collapse beside her as the flight attendant begins her spiel for departure.

"You made it," she says, nearly as amazed as I am. She turns to the guy in the window seat to her left. "Guess I got all worked up for nothing."

The man smiles at her stiffly, then buries his nose in the in-flight magazine as if he has been waiting all his life to read about the best golf courses in Hawaii. From his attitude, I'm pretty sure Serenity has been talking his ear off. I almost want to apologize.

Instead, I pat Serenity's hand where it sits on the armrest between us. "Oh ye of little faith," I say.

Our flight is not exactly uneventful.

After being grounded in Baltimore due to thunderstorms, we sleep upright in chairs at the gate, waiting for clearance to fly again. It comes shortly after 6:00 A.M., and by 8:00, we are in Nashville, rumpled and exhausted. Serenity rents a car with the same credit card she used to get our plane tickets. She asks the rental agent if he knows how to get to Hohenwald, Tennessee, and while he is digging for a map I sit down and try to stay awake. A coffee table sports a *Sports Illustrated* magazine and a dog-eared copy of the white pages from 2010.

The Elephant Sanctuary isn't listed in the white pages, which makes sense, since it is a business, even though I check under both *Elephant* and *Sanctuary*. But there is a Cartwright, G., in Brentwood.

Suddenly, I am alert again. It is almost, as Serenity says, like the universe is trying to tell me something.

What are the odds that G. Cartwright may be the same Gideon Cartwright we had been hoping to find? It is almost too easy, and yet how can we come this far without checking? Especially if Jenna is trying to find him, too?

There is no phone number listed, just the address. And so instead of driving to Hohenwald, Tennessee, to blindly search for Gideon Cartwright, we wind up driving to a place called Brentwood, just outside of Nashville, and the residence that might belong to him.

The street is a dead end, which seems fitting. Serenity pulls the car up to the curb, and for a moment we both just stare at the house on the hill, which looks as though it has not been inhabited for some time. The shutters upstairs are hanging at odd, broken angles; the whole exterior needs a good scraping and a coat of paint. Weeds grow knee-high in what once must have been a tended lawn and garden.

"Gideon Cartwright is a slob," Serenity says.

"No argument there," I murmur.

"I can't imagine Alice Metcalf living here."

"I can't imagine *anyone* living here." I get out of the car and navigate the uneven stones of the front walkway. On the porch is a potted spider plant, now brown and brittle, and a tacked sign from the town of Brentwood that has been faded by rain and sun: THIS PROPERTY IS CONDEMNED.

The screen falls off when I open it to knock on the front door. I prop it against the house. "Clearly if Gideon lived here, it was past tense," Serenity says. "As in, *Moved out ages ago.*"

I don't disagree with her. But I also don't tell her what I'm thinking: that if Gideon turns out to be the joint at the crux of Nevvie Ruehl's death and Thomas Metcalf's anger and Alice's disappearance, then he has a lot to lose if a kid like Jenna starts asking the wrong questions. And if he wants to get rid of her, this is exactly the sort of place no one would ever look twice.

I knock again, harder. "Let me do the talking," I say.

I don't know which of us is more surprised when we hear footsteps approaching the door. It swings open, and standing before me is a disheveled woman. Her gray hair is tangled in a messy braid; her blouse is stained. On her feet are two different shoes. "Can I help you?" she asks, but she does not look me in the eye.

"Sorry to disturb you, ma'am. We're looking for Gideon Cartwright."

My investigator's brain is buzzing. My gaze is taking in everything behind her: the cavernous parlor, without a stick of furniture. The cobwebs lacing the corners of each doorway. The moth-eaten carpets and the scatter of newspapers and mail on the floor.

"Gideon?" she says, and she shakes her head. "I haven't seen him for years." She laughs, then raps her cane against the doorframe. For the first time I notice its white tip. "Then again, I haven't seen *anyone* for years."

She's blind.

She would be an awfully convenient roommate, if Gideon was living there and had something to hide. More than ever, I want to get into this house and make sure Jenna isn't trapped in some room in the basement or in a concrete cell in the gated backyard.

"But this *is* Gideon Cartwright's home?" I press for the answer, so that before I officially break the law by trespassing without a warrant, it's for good reason.

"No," the woman says. "It belongs to my daughter, Grace."

Cartwright, G.

Serenity's eyes fly to mine. I grab her hand and squeeze it before she can open her mouth.

"Who did you say you were again?" the woman asks, her brow furrowed.

"I didn't," I admit. "But I'm surprised you didn't recognize me by my voice." I reach for the old woman's hand. "It's me, Nevvie. Thomas Metcalf."

From the look on Serenity's face, I think she might have swallowed her tongue. Which wouldn't necessarily be a disaster. "Thomas," the woman gasps. "It's been a very long time."

Serenity elbows me. *What are you* doing*!* she mouths silently.

The answer is: I have no idea. I'm having a conversation with a woman I saw zipped into a body bag, who now apparently lives with her daughter—a girl who allegedly committed suicide. And I'm pretending to be her former boss, who may have gone crazy ten years ago and attacked her.

Nevvie reaches up until her searching hand finds my face. Using her fingers, she traces my nose, my lips, my cheekbones. "I knew you'd come for us one day."

I pull away, before she can figure out that I'm not who I said I was. "Of course," I lie. "We're a family."

"You must come inside. Grace will be back soon, and we can visit in the meantime . . ."

"I'd like that," I say.

Serenity and I follow Nevvie inside. Not a single window in the house is open, and there is no air circulation. "I wonder if I could trouble you for a glass of water?" I ask.

"No trouble at all," Nevvie says. She leads me into a living room, a big space with a vaulted ceiling and several couches and tables covered with white sheets. One couch has had its protective cover removed. Serenity sits on it while I peek under the sheets, trying to find a desk, a filing cabinet, any sort of information to explain this turn of events.

"What the holy hell is happening?" Serenity hisses at me as soon as Nevvie shuffles into the kitchen. "Grace will be back soon? I thought she was *dead*. I thought Nevvie was *trampled*."

"I thought that, too," I admit. "I saw a body, that's for sure."

"Was it *hers*?"

But that I can't answer. When I had reached the scene, Gideon was cradling the victim in his lap. I remember the skull split like a melon, the hair shampooed with blood. But I don't know if I ever actually got close enough to see the face. Even if I had, I wouldn't have been able to say it was Nevvie Ruehl, since I'd never even seen a picture of her; I trusted Thomas when he named the victim, because he would have recognized his own employee.

"Who called the police that night?" Serenity asks.

"Thomas."

"So maybe he was the one who wanted you to believe Nevvie was dead."

But I shake my head. "If Thomas had been the one to go after her in the enclosure, she'd be a lot more nervous than she is right now, and she certainly wouldn't have invited us into her house."

"Unless she's planning to poison us."

"Then don't drink the water," I suggest. "Gideon was the one who found the body. So either he made a mistake—which I don't buy—or he wanted people to think it was Nevvie."

"Well, she didn't just get up from the autopsy table," Serenity says.

I meet her gaze. And I don't have to say anything else.

One victim had been taken away that night in a body bag. One victim had been found unconscious, with a blow to the head that maybe could even have resulted in latent blindness, and had been taken to the hospital.

Just then, Nevvie comes into the room, carrying a tray with a pitcher of water and two glasses. "Let me help," I say, taking them from her hands and setting them down on top of a covered coffee table. I pick up the pitcher and pour a glass for each of us.

There is a clock somewhere; I can hear the ticking even if I cannot see it. It's probably rotting away underneath one of the sheets. It's like the whole room is filled with the ghosts of former furniture.

"How long have you lived here?" I ask her.

"I've lost track now. Grace was the one who took care of me, you know, after the accident. I don't know what I would have done without her."

"Accident?"

"You know. That night at the sanctuary. The one where I lost my sight. I suppose after hitting my head like that, it could have been much worse. I'm lucky. Or so they say." She sinks down, oblivious to the sheet that covers the wing chair. "I don't remember any of it, which is probably a blessing. When Grace gets here, she can explain everything." She glances in my direction. "I never blamed you or Maura, Thomas. I hope you know that."

"Who's Maura?" Serenity pipes up.

Until this moment, she hasn't spoken in Nevvie's presence. Nevvie turns, a hesitant smile playing over her lips. "How rude of me. I didn't realize you brought a guest."

I look at Serenity, panicked. I have to introduce her in a way that follows the fiction I've created, where I am impersonating Thomas Metcalf. "No, I'm the one who's been rude," I say. "You remember my wife, Alice?"

The glass slides out of Nevvie's hand, shattering on the floor. I kneel to mop up the water, using one of the sheets covering the furniture.

But I am not mopping fast enough. The water soaks through the sheet, and the puddle widens. The knees of my jeans are drenched and the spill has swelled into a pool. It covers Nevvie's feet, in her mismatched shoes.

Serenity cranes her neck to look around the room. "Sweet Jesus . . ."

The wallpaper is weeping. Water trickles from the ceiling. I glance at Nevvie and find her leaning back in her chair, her hands gripping the armrests, her face wet with her own tears and the sobs of this house.

I can't move. I can't explain what the hell is happening. Overhead, I watch a crack form in the center of the ceiling and spread as if it is only a matter of time before the plaster gives way.

Serenity grabs my arm. "Run," she shouts, and I follow her out of the house. My shoes splash in puddles that have pooled on the hardwood floors. We don't stop until we are back at the curb, panting. "I think I lost my goddamn weave," Serenity says, patting the back of her head. Her pink hair, soaked, makes me think of the bloody skull of the victim at the elephant sanctuary.

I lean down, still gasping for air. The house on the hill looks just as ramshackle and uninviting as it did when we first arrived; the only evidence of our visit is the damp, frantic trail of footprints on the path—tracks that are rapidly vanishing in the heat, as if we were never there at all.

ALICE

Two months is a long time to be gone. A lot can happen in two months.

I didn't know where Thomas was, and I wasn't sure I wanted to find out. I didn't know if he was coming back. But he hadn't just left Jenna and me, he had left seven elephants and a sanctuary staff. Which meant that someone needed to take over the business.

In two months, you can start to feel confident again.

In two months, you might discover that, in addition to being a scientist, you are also a very good businesswoman.

In two months, a child can start talking up a storm, cobbled sentences and twisted syllables, naming the world that looks just as new to her as it does to you.

In two months, you can start over.

Gideon had become my right-hand man. Although we talked about hiring a new employee, we didn't have the money for it. We could do this, he assured me. If I could balance my research with the more cerebral financial work, he could be the brawn. Because of this, he was often working an eighteen-hour day. One evening after dinner, I picked up Jenna and wandered out to the point on the property where he was trying to mend a fence. I reached for a pair of pliers and went to work beside him. "You don't have to do that," he told me.

"Neither do you," I said.

It became a routine: After six o'clock, we would work in tandem at whatever was still left on the endless to-do list. We took Jenna with us, and she would collect flowers and chase the wild rabbits that ran through the tall grass.

Somehow, we fell into that habit.

Somehow, we fell.

Maura and Hester were together again in the African enclosure. They had begun to bond, and were rarely seen apart. Maura was definitely in charge; when she challenged Hester, the younger elephant would turn around, presenting her bottom, a sign of subordinance. I had witnessed Maura returning to the grave site of her calf only once since our evening in the swimming pond. She had managed to compartmentalize her grief, to move on.

I took Jenna with me every day to observe the elephants, even though I knew Thomas thought it was dangerous. He was not here; he no longer got a vote. My toddler was a natural scientist. She would move around the enclosures collecting rocks and grasses and wildflowers, and would sort them into piles. Most of these afternoons, Gideon found some work in our vicinity, so that he could sit down and rest with us for a little while. I started to bring an extra snack for him, more iced tea.

Gideon and I talked about Botswana, about the elephants I had known there and how they were so different from the animals here. We talked about the stories he'd heard from the keepers who traveled with the elephants when they arrived at the sanctuary, of animals being beaten or stuffed into a chute while being trained. One day, he was telling me about Lilly, the elephant whose leg had never set properly after breaking. "She was in a different circus before that," Gideon said. "The ship she was traveling on was docked in Nova Scotia, when it caught on fire. It sank; some of the animals on it were killed. Lilly made it out alive, but with second-degree burns on her back and her legs."

Lilly, who I'd been taking care of now for nearly two years, had been hurt even more than I'd imagined. "It's amazing," I said. "How they don't blame us for what other people did to them."

"I think they forgive." Gideon looked at Maura, his mouth turning down at the corners. "I *hope* they forgive. Do you think she remembers me taking the baby away?"

"Yes," I said bluntly. "But she doesn't hold it against you anymore."

Gideon looked like he was about to respond. But suddenly his face froze, and he leaped up and started running.

Jenna, who knew better than to stray close to the elephants—who had never tested her limits before—was standing two feet away from Maura, staring up at her in a trance. She looked at me, smiling. "Elephant!" she announced.

Maura reached out her trunk, huffing over Jenna's fairy-fine pigtails.

It was a moment of magic, and of supreme danger. Children, and elephants, are unpredictable. One sudden move and Jenna could have been trampled.

I rose, my mouth dry. Gideon was already there, moving slowly so as not to startle Maura into action. He scooped Jenna into his arms, as if this were a game. "Let's get you back to your mama," he said, and he looked over his shoulder at Maura.

That's when Jenna started to scream. "Elephant," she yelled. "I want!" She kicked against Gideon's abdomen and squirmed like a fish on the line.

It was a full-blown tantrum. The noise startled Maura, who bolted into the woods, trumpeting. "Jenna," I snapped. "You don't go near the animals! You know better than that!" But the fear in my voice only made her cry harder.

Gideon grunted as one of her little sneakers connected with his groin. "I'm so sorry—" I said, reaching for her, but Gideon turned away. He kept rocking Jenna, bouncing her in his arms, until her screams thinned and her sobs became hiccups. She grabbed the collar of his red uniform shirt in her fist and started to rub the corner of it against her cheek, the way she did with her blanket when she was falling asleep.

A few minutes later, he laid my dozing child down at my feet. Jenna's cheeks were flushed, her lips parted. I crouched beside her. She might have been made of porcelain, of moonlight.

"She was overtired," I said.

"She was terrified," Gideon corrected, sitting down beside me again. "After the fact."

"Well." I looked up at him. "Thank you."

He stared off into the trees, where Maura had vanished. "Did she run off?"

I nodded. "She was terrified after the fact, too," I said. "Do you know that in all the years I've been doing research I've never seen an elephant mother lose her temper with a baby? No matter how annoying or whiny or difficult the baby's being?" I reached out to pull a ribbon out of Jenna's hair, which was trailing like an afterthought in the wake of her outburst. "Unfortunately, I don't seem to have the same skill set in my parenting."

"Jenna's lucky to have you."

I smirked. "Considering I'm all she's got."

"No," Gideon said. "I watch you, when you're with her. You're a good mother."

I shrugged, waiting for the self-deprecating joke to come, but the words—the validation—meant too much to me. Instead, I heard myself say, "You'd be a good father, too."

He picked up one of the dandelions Jenna had yanked out of the ground and stockpiled before she wandered over toward Maura. He carved a slit in its stem with his thumb and threaded a second through the first. "I sort of thought I would be one, by now."

I pressed my lips together, because Grace's secret wasn't mine to give.

Gideon continued to string the weeds together. "Do you ever wonder if you fall for a person . . . or just the idea of her?"

What I think is that there is no perspective in grief, or in love.

How *can* there be, when one person becomes the center of the universe—either because he has been lost or because he has been found?

Gideon took the crown of daisies and slipped it over Jenna's head. It tipped sideways on the knob of one pigtail, falling over her brow. In her sleep, she stirred.

"Sometimes I think there's no such thing as falling in love. It's just the fear of losing someone."

There was a breeze, carrying the scent of wild apples and timothy grass; the earthy smell of elephant hide and manure; the juice of the peach that Jenna had eaten earlier, and that had dripped onto her sundress. "Do you worry?" Gideon asked. "About what will happen if he doesn't come back?"

It was the first time, really, that we had talked about Thomas leaving. Although we had shared stories of how we met our spouses, that was where the conversation had stayed: at the highest peak of potential, at the moment in those relationships when everything still seemed possible.

Lifting my chin, I looked squarely at Gideon. "I worry about what will happen if he *does*," I said.

It was colic. It was not uncommon in elephants, especially ones who had been given bad hay, or whose diet had been radically and quickly changed. Neither of those was the case for Syrah, but still she lay on her side, drowsy, bloated. She wouldn't eat or drink. Her stomach growled. Gertie, the dog who was her constant companion, sat at her side and howled.

Grace was at my cottage, babysitting for Jenna. She'd stay there all night, so that we could watch over the elephant. Gideon had volunteered, but I was in charge now. There was no way I couldn't be there, too.

We stood in the barn with our arms crossed, watching the vet examine the elephant. "He's just going to tell us what we already know," Gideon whispered to me.

"Yeah, and then he's going to give her drugs to make her better."
He shook his head. "What do you plan to pawn to pay his bill?"

Gideon was right about that. Money was so tight right now that we had to borrow from our operating expenses if we were going to cover the cost of emergencies, like this one. "I'll figure it out," I said, scowling.

We watched the vet give Syrah an anti-inflammatory—flunixin—and a muscle relaxant. Gertie curled up beside her in the hay, whimpering. "All we can really do is wait and hope she starts passing boluses," he said. "In the meantime, get her to drink some water."

But Syrah didn't want to drink. Every time we came near her with a bucket, whether it was heated or cooled, she huffed and tried to turn her head away. After several hours of this, Gideon and I were both emotionally wrecked. Whatever the vet had administered did not seem to be working.

It is a pitiful thing, seeing such a strong and majestic animal laid low. It made me think of the elephants in the bush I'd seen who had been shot by villagers, or injured by snares. I knew, too, that colic wasn't something to be taken lightly. It could lead to impaction, and that could lead to death. I knelt beside Syrah, palpating her, feeling the tightness of her abdomen. "Has this happened before?"

"Not to Syrah," he said. "But it's not the first time I've seen it." He seemed to be chewing on a thought, equivocating. Then he looked at me. "Do you use baby oil on Jenna's skin?"

"I used to put it in the bath," I said. "Why?"

"Where is it?"

"If I still have any, it would be under the sink in the bathroom—"

He stood up and walked out of the barn. "Where are you going?" I called, but I couldn't follow him. I wouldn't leave Syrah.

Ten minutes later, Gideon returned. He was holding two bottles of baby oil and a Sara Lee pound cake I recognized from my own refrigerator. I followed him into the kitchen of the Asian barn, where we prepared meals for the elephants. He started to unwrap the cake's packaging. "I'm not hungry," I told him.

"This isn't for you." Gideon set the cake on the counter and began to stab it with a knife, repeatedly.

"I think it's dead," I said.

He opened a bottle of baby oil and poured it over the cake. The fluid began to sink into the sponge, settling into the puncture marks he'd made. "At the circus, the elephants colicked sometimes. The vet used to tell us to get them to drink oil. I guess it gets things moving."

"The vet didn't say—"

"Alice." Gideon hesitated, his hands stilling over the cake. "Do you trust me?"

I looked at this man, who had worked by my side for weeks now to create the illusion that this sanctuary could survive. Who had saved me once. And my daughter.

I read once, in a silly women's magazine at the dentist, that when we like someone, our pupils dilate. And that we tend to like people whose pupils are dilated when they look at us. It's an endless cycle: We want the people who want us. Gideon's irises were nearly the same color as his pupils, which created an optical illusion: a black hole, an endless fall. I wondered what mine looked like, in response. "Yes," I said.

He instructed me to get a bucket of water, and I followed him into the stall where Syrah still lay on her side, her belly rising and falling with effort. Gertie sat up, suddenly alert. "Hey, beautiful," Gideon said, kneeling in front of the elephant. He held out the cake. "Syrah, she's got a real sweet tooth," he told me.

She sniffed the cake with her trunk. She touched it gingerly. Gideon broke off a small piece and tossed it into Syrah's mouth while Gertie sniffed at his fingers.

A moment later Syrah took the entire cake and swallowed it whole.

"Water," Gideon said.

I settled the bucket where Syrah could reach and watched her siphon out a trunkful. Gideon leaned in, his strong hands stroking her flank, telling her what a good girl she was.

I wished he would touch me like that.

The thought came so fast that I fell back on my heels. "I have to—I have to go check on Jenna," I stammered.

Gideon glanced up. "I'm sure she and Grace are both asleep."

"I have to . . ." My voice trailed off. My face was hot; I pressed my palms against my cheeks. Turning, I hurried out of the barn.

Gideon was right; when I reached the cottage, Grace and Jenna were curled together on the couch. Jenna's hand was caught in Grace's. It made me feel sick, to know that while Grace had been taking care of someone I loved, I had been wishing I could do the same with someone *she* loved.

She stirred, careful to sit up without waking Jenna. "Is it Syrah? What happened?"

I gathered Jenna into my arms. She woke up briefly before her eyes drifted shut again. I didn't want to disturb her, but it was more important, in that moment, to remember who I was. What I was.

A mother. A wife.

"You should tell him," I said to Grace. "About not being able to have a baby."

She narrowed her eyes. We had not discussed this since first broaching the topic weeks ago. I knew she was worried that maybe I had already said something to Gideon, but that wasn't it at all. I wanted them to have that conversation so Gideon would know Grace trusted him, wholly. I wanted them to have that conversation so they could make plans for a future that included surrogacy or adoption. I wanted the bond between them to be so strong that I could not, even accidentally, find a chink in the wall of their marriage through which I could peek.

"You should tell him," I repeated. "Because he deserves to know."

The next morning, two wonderful things happened. Syrah got up, seemingly over her colic, and wandered with a bouncing Gertie into the Asian enclosure. And the fire department dropped off a gift: a used fire hose that they wanted to donate, since they'd recently upgraded their equipment.

Gideon, who had gotten even less sleep than I had, seemed to be in a terrific mood. If Grace had taken my advice and spoken to him about her secret, he either had taken it well or was too happy about Syrah's recovery to let the news affect him. At any rate, he certainly didn't seem to be thinking twice about my awkward exit the night before. He hefted the hose over his shoulder. "The girls are going to love this," he said, grinning. "Let's test it out."

"I have a million things to do," I replied. "And so do you."

I was being a bitch. But if that created a wall between us, that was safer.

The vet returned to examine Syrah and gave her a clean bill of health. I buried myself in the office, checking accounts, trying to figure out where I could borrow from Peter to pay Paul, so that the vet's bill would be covered. Jenna sat at my feet, coloring the photos in old newspapers with her crayons. Nevvie had taken one of the trucks into town for a tune-up, and Grace was cleaning out the African barn.

It wasn't until Jenna tugged on my shorts and told me she was hungry that I realized hours had passed. I made her peanut butter and jelly, cutting the sandwich into squares just the right size for her hands. I took off the crusts, saving them in my pocket for Maura. And then I heard the sound of someone dying.

Grabbing Jenna, I started to run toward the African barn—where the sounds were coming from. I had a series of concussive, thunderous thoughts: *Maura and Hester are fighting. Maura is injured. One of the elephants has hurt Grace.*

One of the elephants has hurt Gideon.

I threw open the barn door to find Hester and Maura in their stalls, with the retractable bars that separated the two wide open. In this big expanse, they were frolicking, dancing, chortling in the artificial rain of the fire hose. As Gideon sprayed them, they turned in circles and squealed.

They weren't dying. They were having the time of their lives.

"What are you *doing*?" I yelled, as Jenna kicked to get out of my arms. I set her on the ground, and she immediately began to jump in puddles on the cement.

Gideon grinned, waving the fire hose through the bars, back and forth. "Enrichment," he said. "Look at Maura. Have you ever seen her acting crazy like this?"

He was right; Maura seemed to have lost all vestiges of grief. She was shaking her head and stomping in the spray, throwing her trunk up every time she sang out.

"Is the furnace fixed?" I asked. "And the oil changed in the ATV? Have you taken down the fence in the African enclosure or stumped the northwest field? Did you regrade the slope of the pond in the Asian enclosure?" It was a laundry list of all the things we needed to do.

Gideon twisted the nozzle of the hose, so that the water slowed to a trickle. The elephants trumpeted and turned, waiting for more. Hoping.

"That's what I thought," I said. "Jenna, honey, come on." I started toward her, but she ran away from me, splashing in another puddle.

Gideon's mouth flattened. "Hey, boss," he said, and he waited for me to turn.

As soon as I did, he twisted the nozzle so that the spray hit me square in the chest.

It was frigid and shocking, so forceful that I staggered backward, pushing my sopping hair out of my face and looking down at my drenched clothing. Gideon angled the hose so that it struck the elephants instead. He grinned. "You need to chill out," he said.

I lunged for the hose. He was bigger than me, but I was faster. I turned the spray on Gideon until he held his hands up in front of his face. "Okay!" He laughed, choking on the stream. "Okay! I give up!"

"You started it," I reminded him, as his hands tried to wrestle the nozzle away from me. The hose wriggled like a snake between us, and we were faith healers, fighting for a moment of the divine. Slippery, soaked, Gideon finally managed to wrap his arms around me, trapping my hands between us so that the spray hit our feet and I couldn't hold the nozzle anymore. It fell to the ground, swiveling in a semicircle before it came to rest, spraying a fountain toward the elephants.

I was laughing so hard I was out of breath. "Okay, you win. Let me go," I gasped.

I was temporarily blinded; my hair was plastered to my face. Gideon pushed it away, so that I could see him smiling. His teeth, they were impossibly white. I couldn't take my eyes off his mouth. "I don't think so," he said, and he kissed me.

The shock was even more intense than that first blast of the hose. I froze, for only a heartbeat. And then my arms were around his waist, my palms hot against the damp skin of his back. I ran my hands over the landscape of his arms, the valleys where the muscles joined together. I drank from him like I'd never seen a well this deep.

"Wet," Jenna said. "Mama wet."

She stood beneath us, one hand patting each of our legs. Until that moment, I had completely forgotten about her.

As if I didn't have enough to be ashamed of.

For the second time, I ran away from Gideon as if my life were being threatened. Which, I guess, was the truth.

For the next two weeks I avoided Gideon, relaying messages instead through Grace or Nevvie, making sure I was not alone with him in a barn or enclosure at any time. I left him notes in the kitchens of the barns, lists of what needed to be done. Instead of meeting up with Gideon at the end of the day, I sat with Jenna on the floor of the cottage, playing with puzzles and blocks and stuffed animals.

One night, Gideon radioed from the hay barn. "Dr. Metcalf," he said. "We have a situation."

I could not remember the last time he had referred to me as Dr. Metcalf. Either this was a reaction to the coldness I'd been sending out in waves or there was a true and urgent problem. I settled Jenna between my legs on the ATV and drove past the Asian barn, where I knew Grace would be preparing the evening meals. "Can you watch her?" I asked. "Gideon said it was urgent."

Grace reached for a bucket, turning it over to make a step stool.

"Come on up here, pumpkin," she said. "See those apples? Can you hand them to me one at a time?" She glanced over her shoulder at me. "We're fine," she said.

I drove up to the hay barn to find Gideon in a standoff with Clyde, who supplied our bales. Clyde was a guy we trusted; too often farmers tried to unload their moldy hay on us because they figured it was just elephants, so what was the difference? He had his arms folded across his chest. Gideon stood with one foot braced on a hay bale. Only half the load had been moved into storage from Clyde's truck.

"What's the problem?" I asked.

"Clyde says that he won't take a check, because the last one bounced. But I can't seem to find any of the spare cash, and until I do, Clyde isn't inclined to let me unload the rest of the bales," Gideon said. "So maybe you've got a solution."

The reason the last check bounced was that we didn't have any money. The reason there was no spare cash was that I'd used it to pay for produce this week. If I wrote another check, this one would bounce, too—I had used the last of the funds in our account to pay the vet's bill.

I didn't know how I was going to pay for groceries for my daughter next week, much less hay for the elephants.

"Clyde," I said. "We're going through a rough patch."

"So's the whole country."

"But we have a relationship," I replied. "You and my husband have been in business together for years, right?"

"Yeah, and he always managed to pay me." He frowned. "I can't let you have the hay for nothing."

"I know. And I can't let the elephants starve."

I felt like I was in quicksand. Slowly, but surely, I was bound to drown. What I needed to do was fund-raise, but I barely had time for it. My research had been long forgotten; I hadn't touched it in weeks. I could barely stay ahead of operations without trying to gauge the interest of new donors.

Interest.

I looked at Clyde. "I'll pay you ten percent more if you give me the hay now and let me settle with you next month."

"Why would I do that?"

"Because whether or not you want to admit it, Clyde, we have a history, and you owe us the benefit of the doubt."

He didn't owe us anything. But I was hoping the guilt of being the straw that broke the sanctuary's back would be enough to make him pretend otherwise.

"Twenty percent," Clyde bargained.

I shook his hand. Then I climbed into the truck and began to haul the hay bales.

An hour later, Clyde drove away, and I sat down on the edge of a bale. Gideon was still working, his back flexing as he stacked the bales for more efficient storage, lifting them higher than I physically could manage.

"So," I said. "You're just going to pretend I'm not here?"

Gideon didn't turn around. "Guess I learned from a master."

"What was I supposed to do, Gideon? Do you have the answer? Because believe me, I want to hear it."

He faced me, his hands resting lightly on his hips. He was sweating; bits of chaff and straw were caught on his forearms. "I'm sick of being your fall guy. Return the orchids. Get hay for free. Turn fucking water into wine. What's next, Alice?"

"Should I not have paid the vet, then, when Syrah was sick?"

"I don't know," he said brusquely. "I don't care."

He pushed past me as I stood up. "Yes, you do," I called, running after him, wiping my hand across my eyes. "I didn't ask for any of this, you know. I didn't want to run a sanctuary. I didn't want to worry about sick animals and paying salaries and going bankrupt."

Gideon stopped in the doorway. His silhouette was framed by the light as he turned. "So what *do* you want, Alice?"

When was the last time anyone asked me that?

"I want to be a scientist," I said. "I want to make people see how much elephants can think, and can feel."

He walked forward, filling my field of vision. "And?"

"I want Jenna to be happy."

Gideon took one more step. He was so close now that his question drew across the bow of my neck, making my skin sing. "And?"

I had stood my ground before a charging elephant. I had risked my scientific credibility to follow my gut instinct. I had packed up my life and started over. But looking into Gideon's face and telling the truth was the most courageous thing I had ever done. "I want to be happy, too," I whispered.

Then we were tumbling, over the uneven steps of the hay bales, into a nest of straw on the floor of the barn. Gideon's hands were in my hair and under my clothes; my gasp became his next breath. Our bodies were landscapes, maps burned into our palms where we touched. When he moved in me, I knew why: Now, we would always find our way back home.

Afterward, with hay scratching my back and my clothes tangled around my limbs, I started to speak.

"Don't," Gideon said, touching his fingers to my lips. "Just don't." He rolled onto his back. My head lay pillowed on his arm at a pulse point. I could feel every beat of his heart.

"When I was little," he told me, "my uncle got me a Star Wars figurine. It was signed by George Lucas, still in the box. I was, I don't know, maybe six or seven. My uncle told me not to take it out of the packaging. That way, one day, it would be worth something."

I tilted my chin so I could look at him. "Did you take it out of the packaging?"

"Shit, yeah."

I burst out laughing. "I thought you were going to tell me you had it on a shelf somewhere. And that you were willing to use it to pay for the hay."

"Sorry. I was a kid. What kid plays with a toy in a box?" His smile faded a little. "So I slipped it out of the box in a way that no one would notice, if they didn't look too closely. I played with that Luke Skywalker figure every day. I mean, it went to school with me. Into the bathtub. It slept next to me. I loved that thing. And yeah, it might not have been as valuable that way, but it meant the world to me."

I knew what he was saying: that the untouched collector's item might have been worth something, but all those stolen moments were priceless.

Gideon grinned. "I'm really glad I took you off the shelf, Alice."

I punched him in the arm. "You make me sound like a wallflower."

"If the shoe fits . . ."

I rolled on top of him. "Stop talking."

He kissed me. "I thought you'd never ask," he said, and his arms closed around me again.

The stars squinted at us by the time we walked out of the barn. There was still straw in my hair and dirt on my legs. Gideon didn't look much better. He climbed on the ATV, and I sat behind him, my cheek pressed against his back. I could smell myself on his skin.

"What do we say?" I asked.

He looked over his shoulder. "We don't," he replied, and he started the engine.

Gideon stopped at his cottage first, getting off the ATV. The lights were out; Grace was still with Jenna. He did not risk touching me there, out in the open, but he stared at me. "Tomorrow?" he asked.

That could have meant anything. We could have been arranging a time to move the elephants, to clean the barn, to change the spark plugs on the truck. But what he was really asking was if I would go back to avoiding him, the way I did before. If this would happen again.

"Tomorrow," I repeated.

A minute later, I reached my own cottage. I parked the ATV and climbed off, trying to straighten the nest of my hair and to brush off my clothes. Grace knew I had been up at the hay barn, but I didn't just look like I'd been unloading bales. I looked like I'd been through a war. I rubbed my hand over my mouth, wiping away Gideon's kiss, leaving only excuses.

When I opened the door, Grace was in the living room. So was Jenna. And holding her, with a smile on his face that could light up a galaxy, was Thomas. Spying me, he passed our daughter to Grace and reached for a package on the coffee table. Then he came closer, his eyes wide and clear. He handed me an overturned plant with its gnarled roots serving as blooms, just as he had done two years ago when I first arrived at the Boston airport. "Surprise," he said.

JENNA

The Elephant Sanctuary in Tennessee has a nice little downtown storefront with big pictures on the walls of all their animals, plus plaques that give the history of each elephant. It's weird, seeing the names of the elephants that used to be at the New England Sanctuary. I pause the longest at the picture of Maura, the elephant my mother liked the most. I stare at it so hard that the image starts to blur.

There is a table full of books you can buy, and Christmas ornaments, and bookmarks. There's a basket full of stuffed elephants. There is a looping video of a bunch of Asian elephants making sounds like a New Orleans swing band, and another of two elephants playing in a fire hose, just like city kids when the hydrants get turned on in the summer. Another, smaller video player explains protected contact. Instead of using bull hooks or negative reinforcement, which is pretty much how the elephants had lived most of their lives, the sanctuary caregivers use positive reinforcement for training. There is always a barrier between the caregiver and the elephants—not just to give the caregiver safety but to relax the animal, who can always walk away if she doesn't want to participate. It's been that way since 2010, and it's really helped, the video says, with elephants that have serious trust issues with humans as a result of free contact.

Free contact. So that's what it's called when you can go right into an enclosure, like my mother and our caregivers used to do. I wonder if the death at our sanctuary, and the debacle that followed, led to the change.

Only two other visitors are in the welcome center with me—both wearing fanny packs and Tevas with socks. "We don't actually offer tours of the facility," an employee explains. "Our whole philosophy is to let the elephants live out their lives being elephants, instead of being on display." The tourists nod, because it's the politically correct thing to do, but I can tell they're disappointed.

Me, I'm on the prowl for a map. Downtown Hohenwald is no more than a single block, and there is no hint of the twenty-seven hundred acres of sweeping elephant vista anywhere nearby. Unless the animals are all shopping at the dollar store, I don't know where they're hiding out.

I slip out the front door before the tourists do and wander around back to the small employee parking lot. There are three cars and two pickup trucks. None have any logos on the doors for The Elephant Sanctuary; they could belong to just anyone. But I lean close to the passenger-side windows of each car and peek inside to see if there's anything to identify the vehicles' owners.

One belongs to a mom; there are sippy cups and Cheerios all over the floor.

Two are owned by dudes: fuzzy dice, hunting catalogs.

At the first pickup truck, though, I hit pay dirt. Flapping out of the driver's visor is a sheaf of papers, with the logo of The Elephant Sanctuary at the top.

There's a messy cloud of hay in the back of the pickup, which is a good thing, because it's so damn hot that bare metal would have practically branded me. I stow away in the flatbed, which is quickly becoming my favored mode of transport.

Less than an hour later, I'm bouncing down a road to a high metal gate with an electronic opening mechanism. The driver—a woman—punches in a code so that the gate opens. We drive about a hundred feet before we hit a second gate, at which she does the same thing.

As she drives, I try to get the lay of the land. The sanctuary is enclosed by a normal chain-link fence, but the interior corral is made of steel pipes and cable. I can't remember what our facility was like, but this one is pristine and orderly. Land stretches out forever—hills and forests, ponds and grasslands, punctuated by several big barns. Everything is so green it makes my eyes hurt.

When the truck pulls up to one of the barns, I flatten myself, hoping that I will not be seen as the driver gets out. I hear the door slam, and footsteps, and then the happy trumpet of an elephant as this caregiver walks into the barn.

I'm out of that truck like a rocket. I duck along the far wall of the barn, following the heavy cabled fence until I see my first elephant.

It's African. I may not be an expert like my mom, but I know that much. I can't tell if it's a male or a female from this position, but it's freaking *huge*. Although maybe that's redundant, when you're talking about elephants and you're only separated by three feet and some steel.

Speaking of steel—there's metal on the elephant's tusks. Sort of like they were dipped in gold at the tips.

Suddenly the elephant shakes its head, flapping its ears and releasing a cloud of reddish dust between us. It's loud and unexpected; I fall back, coughing.

"Who let you in?" a voice accuses.

I turn around to find a man towering over me. His hair is nearly shaved to his scalp; his skin is mahogany. His teeth are, by contrast, almost electroluminescent. I think he's going to grab me by my collar and drag me physically out of the sanctuary, or call the guards or whoever else keeps trespassers out of this place, but instead, his eyes get wide and he stares at me as if I just apparated before him. "You look just like her," he whispers.

I had not expected it to be so easy to find Gideon. But then again, maybe after traveling a thousand miles to get here, I deserved a cosmic break.

"I'm Jenna—"

"I know," Gideon says, looking around me. "Where is she? Alice?"

Hope is a balloon, always just a breath away from being deflated. "I was hoping she was *here*."

"You mean she didn't come with you?" The disappointment on his face—well, it is like I am looking into a mirror.

"Then you don't know where she is?" I say. My knees feel weak. I can't believe I've come all this way, and have found him, and it's all for nothing.

"I tried to cover for her, when the police came. I didn't know what happened out there, but Nevvie was dead, and Alice was missing . . . so I told the cops I assumed she had taken you and run off," he says. "That was her plan all along."

All of a sudden, my body is infused with light. *She wanted me; she wanted me; she wanted me.* But somewhere between plotting her future and executing it, things had gone horribly wrong for my mother. Gideon, who was supposed to be the key to the lock, the antidote that would reveal the secret message, is just as clueless as I am. "Weren't *you* part of that plan?"

He looks at me, trying to gauge how much I know about his relationship with my mother. "I thought I was, but she never tried to contact me. She disappeared. Turned out, I was a means to an end," Gideon admits. "She loved me. But she loved you so much more."

I have forgotten where I am until that moment, when the elephant in front of us lifts its trunk and trumpets. The sun is beating down on my scalp. I am dizzy, like I've been drifting in the ocean for days and just sent off my last flare, only to realize that the rescue boat I was so sure I saw was a trick of the light. The elephant, with its fancy plated tusks, makes me think of a merry-go-round horse I had been scared of as a child. I don't even know when or where my parents might have taken me to a carnival, but those terrifying wooden stallions, with their frozen manes and their gnashing teeth, had made me cry.

I feel like doing that now, too.

Gideon keeps staring at me, and it's weird, like he is trying to see underneath my skin or riffle through the folds of my brain. "I think there's someone you should meet," he says, and he starts walking the fence line.

Maybe this has been a test. Maybe he needed to see that I was truly devastated before he would take me to my mother. I don't let myself hope, but as I follow him I move faster and faster. *What if, what if, what if.*

We walk for what feels like thirty miles in the ridiculous heat. My shirt is soaked through with sweat by the time we climb the hill and I see, at its crest, another elephant. He doesn't have to tell me it's Maura. When she places her trunk delicately along the top edge of the fencing, the fingers opening and closing gently like the head of a rose, I know she remembers me the same way I remember her—at some internal, visceral level.

My mother is really, truly not here.

The elephant's eyes are dark and hooded, her ears translucent in the sun, so that I can see the highway maps of veins running through them. Heat radiates from her skin. She looks leathery, primitive, cretaceous. The accordion folds of her trunk roll upward like a wave to reach over the fence toward me. She blows in my face, and it smells like summer and straw.

"This is why I stayed," Gideon says. "I thought one day Alice would come to check on Maura." The elephant reaches out and curls her trunk around his forearm. "She had a really hard time, when she first got here. Wouldn't leave the barn. She stayed in her stall, her face pressed into the corner."

I thought of the long entries in my mother's journals. "You think she felt guilty about the trampling?"

"Maybe," Gideon says. "Maybe it was fear of punishment. Or maybe she missed your mother, too."

The elephant rumbles, like a car running its engine. The air around me vibrates.

Maura picks up a pine log that is lying on its side. She scrapes her tusk along the edge of it, then lifts it with her trunk and presses it against the heavy steel fence. She scratches at the bark again, dropping the tree and rolling it beneath her foot. "What is she doing?"

"Playing. We cut down trees for her, so that she can strip off the bark."

After about ten minutes, Maura lifts the log as if it is a toothpick and raises it as high as the fence. "Jenna," Gideon cries. "Move!"

He shoves me, landing on top of me, a few feet away from where the log has crashed down, exactly in the spot where I was standing.

His hands are warm on my shoulders. "You all right?" he asks, helping me to my feet, and then he smiles. "The last time I held you, you were only two feet tall."

But I pull away from him to crouch down and stare at this gift I've been given. It's about three feet long by ten inches wide, a hefty club. Maura's tusks have created patterns—lines that cross and grooves that intersect without rhyme or reason.

Unless, that is, you're looking carefully.

With my finger I trace the lines.

With a little imagination, I can make out a *U* and an *S*. That knot waves the wood grain like a *W.* On the other side of the log, a semi-circle is caught in between two long scrapes: *I-D-I.*

Sweetheart, in Xhosa.

Gideon may not think my mother ever came back, but I'm beginning to believe she's all around me.

Just then, my stomach grumbles so loud I sound like Maura. "You're starving," Gideon says.

"I'm okay."

"I'm getting you something to eat," he insists. "I know that's what Alice would have wanted me to do."

"Okay," I say, and we walk back to the barn I had first seen when I arrived in the pickup truck. His car is a big black van, and he has to move a box of tools from the passenger seat before I can sit down.

As we are driving, I can feel Gideon still sneaking glances at me. It's like he's trying to memorize my face or something. That's when I realize that he's wearing the red shirt and cargo shorts that were the uniform at the New England Elephant Sanctuary. Everyone at The Elephant Sanctuary here in Hohenwald wears straight khaki.

It doesn't make sense. "How long did you say you've worked here?"

"Oh," he says. "Years."

What are the odds that, in a sanctuary twenty-seven hundred acres large, I would run into Gideon first, instead of any other person?

Unless, of course, he made sure I did.

What if I hadn't found Gideon Cartwright? What if he'd found *me*?

I am thinking like Virgil, but that isn't necessarily a bad thing, in terms of self-preservation. Sure, I'd set out all determined to find Gideon. But now that I have, I am wondering if it was such a great idea. I can taste fear, like a penny on my tongue. For the first time, it occurs to me that maybe Gideon had something to do with my mother's disappearance.

"Do you remember that night?" he asks. It's like he pulled the thread out of my mind.

I picture Gideon driving my mother away from the hospital, pulling over, and wrapping his hands around her throat. I picture him doing the same thing to me.

I force myself to keep my voice steady. I think of how Virgil would do this, if he were trying to get information from a suspect. "No. I was a baby; I guess I slept through most of it." I stare at him. "Do *you*?"

"Unfortunately, yes. I wish I could forget."

We are almost in town by now. The ribbon of residences whizzing by starts to give way to box stores and gas stations.

"Why?" I blurt out. "Because you were the one who killed her?"

Gideon swerves, braking. He looks like I've slapped him across the face. "Jenna . . . I loved your mother," he swears. "I was trying to protect her. I wanted to marry her. I wanted to take care of you. And the baby."

All the air in the car is gone, just like that. It's like a seal of plastic has been placed over my nose and mouth.

Maybe I've heard him wrong. Maybe he said he would have taken care of *me, the baby*. Except he didn't.

Gideon slows the car to a stop and looks into his lap. "You didn't know," he murmurs.

In one move, I press down on my seat belt latch and open the passenger door. I start to run.

I can hear the door slam behind me—it's Gideon, coming after me.

I enter the first building I can find, a diner, and run past the hostess to the back, where the restrooms usually are. In the ladies' room I lock the door, climb onto the sink, and slide open the narrow window cut into the wall beside it. I can hear voices outside the ladies' room, Gideon begging someone to come in and get me. I shimmy through the window, drop down on the lid of the closed Dumpster in the alley behind the diner, and bolt.

I race through the woods. I don't stop until I am on the outskirts of town. Then, for the first time in a day and a half, I turn on my cell phone.

I have a signal, three bars. I have forty-three messages from my grandmother. But I ignore them and dial Serenity's number.

She picks up on the third ring, and I'm so grateful, I burst into tears. "Please," I say. "I need help."

ALICE

Sitting in the attic of the African barn, I wondered—not for the first time—if *I* was the one who was crazy.

By then, Thomas had been home for five months. Gideon had painted over the walls again. There were drop cloths on the floor, and cans of paint lining the edges, but otherwise, the space was empty. No evidence remained of the break from reality that had swallowed my husband whole. At times, I was able to convince myself that I had imagined the entire episode.

It was pouring today. Jenna had been so excited to leave for school in her new rubber boots, which were fashioned to look like ladybugs. They had been a gift from Grace and Gideon for her second birthday. Because of the weather, the elephants had chosen to stay in their barns. Nevvie and Grace were folding and stuffing envelopes for a fund-raising campaign. Thomas was on his way home from New York City, where he'd been meeting with officials from Tusk.

Thomas never told me where he'd gone for treatment, just that it wasn't in this state, and he had driven there when he realized that the first center he'd planned on checking into was now closed. I didn't know whether or not to believe him, but he seemed like himself again, and if I had doubts, I kept them quiet. I did not ask to see the books, or to second-guess him. The last time I had done that, I'd nearly been strangled.

He had come back from his recuperation with new medication, and with checks from three private investors. (Had they been inpatients, too? I wondered, but I didn't really care, as long as their checks didn't bounce.) He took over the reins of running the sanctuary as if he'd never left. But if that transition was flawless, his reintegration into our marriage was not. Although he hadn't had a manic or a depressive episode for months, I still could not trust him, and he knew it. We were circles in a Venn diagram, Jenna caught at our overlap. Now, when he spent long hours in his office, I couldn't help but wonder if he was hiding gibberish like he'd written before. When I asked him if he felt stable, he accused me of turning on him and started locking the door. It was a vicious cycle.

I dreamed about leaving. Taking Jenna and running away. I would pick her up at preschool—and just keep driving. Sometimes I was even brave enough to say it out loud, when Gideon and I found time to be together.

I didn't do it, though, because I suspected Thomas knew I was sleeping with Gideon. And I didn't know which a court would find better equipped to parent: the father with a mental illness or the mother who had betrayed him.

It had been months since Thomas and I had slept together. I would pour my glass of wine at 7:30, just after Jenna had been put to bed, and would read on the couch until I fell asleep. My interactions with him were limited to polite conversation in front of Jenna when she was awake and heated arguments while she slept. I still took Jenna into the enclosures with me—after her close call as a baby, she had learned her lesson; and how could a child grow up in an elephant sanctuary without feeling comfortable around elephants? Thomas still thought this was an accident waiting to happen, when, in reality, I was more afraid of my daughter being left alone with *him*. One night, after I'd taken Jenna with me inside the fences again, he grabbed my arms so hard that bruises formed. "What judge would think of *you* as a fit mother?" he hissed.

Suddenly I realized he wasn't just talking about Jenna in the enclosures. And that I wasn't the only one thinking of sole custody.

It was Grace who suggested that maybe it was time for Jenna to go to a preschool program. She was nearly two and a half now, and the only social interaction she had came from adults and elephants. I seized on the idea, because it would give me three hours a day when I didn't have to worry about Jenna being left with Thomas.

If you had asked me who I was then, I could not have told you. The mother who dropped Jenna off in town with a lunch box full of carrots and sliced apples? The researcher who submitted her paper on Maura's grief to academic journals, praying over each file before pushing the Send button? The wife in a little black dress who stood beside Thomas at a Boston cocktail party, clapping enthusiastically when he took the microphone to talk about elephant conservation? The woman who bloomed in the arms of a lover, as if he were the only sunlight left in the world to feed her?

Three-quarters of my life, I felt like I was playing a role, like I could walk offstage and stop pretending. And the minute I was out of the public eye, I wanted to be with Gideon.

I was a liar. I was hurting people who did not even know they were being hurt. And I still was not strong enough to stop myself.

But an elephant sanctuary is a very busy place, with very little privacy. Particularly when you are having an affair and both of your spouses work there, too. There were a few frantic couplings in the outdoors, and one so sudden behind the door of the Asian barn that we'd played Russian roulette, forgoing protection for the mercy of each other's bodies. So perhaps it wasn't irony—just desperation—that led me to find a secure, secluded place for our trysts—a spot that Thomas would never venture, and that Nevvie and Grace would never think to look.

The door opened, and like always, my breath caught just in case. Gideon stood in a downpour, twisting an umbrella so that it pinched shut. He left it propped against the metal railing of the spiral staircase and stepped into the room.

I had spread a drop cloth on the floor while I was waiting for him. "It's a monsoon out there," Gideon huffed.

I stood up and began to unbutton his shirt. "Then we ought to get you out of these wet clothes," I said.

"How long?" he asked.

"Twenty minutes," I said. It was as long as I thought I could disappear and not be missed. To his credit, Gideon never complained and never tried to keep me. We moved inside the parameters of our fences. Even a little freedom was better than none.

I pressed up against him, resting my head on his chest. I closed my eyes as he kissed me, lifting me so that I could wrap my legs around him. Over his shoulder, through the sheer plastic that had never been replaced, I watched the rain stream down in sheets, a cleansing.

I don't really know how long Grace was standing in the doorway at the top of the stairs, watching us, holding her umbrella down so that it did no good at all to shield her from the storm.

The phone call had come from Jenna's school. She was running a fever; she'd thrown up. Could someone come get her?

Grace would have gone herself. But she thought I'd want to know. She could not find me in the African barn, which was where I'd told her I was headed. She saw Gideon's red umbrella. Maybe, she thought, he'd know where I was.

I sobbed. I apologized. I begged her to forgive Gideon, not to tell Thomas.

I gave Gideon back.

And I retreated into my research again, because I could not work with any of them. Nevvie would not speak to me. Grace couldn't, without dissolving into tears. And Gideon knew better. I held my breath, expecting them to give Thomas their notice, any day. And then I realized they wouldn't. Where else would the three of them find jobs taking care of elephants together? This was their home, maybe more than it ever had been mine.

I began to plan my escape. I'd read stories about parents who kidnapped their own children. Who dyed their hair and spirited them across borders with fake IDs and new names. Jenna was young enough to grow up with only the faintest memories of this life. And I, well, I could find something else to do.

I would never publish again. I couldn't without risking being found by Thomas, who would then take Jenna away from me. But if anonymity kept us safe, wasn't it worth it?

I went so far as to pack a duffel with Jenna's clothing and mine, and to hold back a few dollars here and there, until I had a couple hundred tucked into the lining of my computer sleeve. That, I hoped, was enough to buy us a start on a new life.

On the morning that I intended to make our escape, I had run through the steps in my mind a thousand times.

I would dress Jenna in her favorite overalls, and her pink sneakers. I would feed her a waffle, her favorite, cut into sticks so that she could dip it in maple syrup. I would let her pick one stuffed animal to take in the car with her to school, like usual.

But we would not go to school. We would just pass the building and get on the highway, and be long gone before anyone thought to question it.

I had run through the steps in my mind a thousand times, but that was before Gideon burst into the cottage clutching a note in his hand, asking me if I'd seen Grace, his eyes begging for the answer to be yes.

She had written it by hand. She said by the time he found this, it would be too late. The note, I later found out, was waiting in the bathroom on the counter when Gideon woke up. It was weighed down with a cairn of stones, a small and perfect pyramid, maybe even the same kind that Grace had stuffed in her pockets before she lay herself down on the bottom of the Connecticut River, not two miles from the spot where her husband was fast asleep.

SERENITY

*P*olter*geist* is one of those German words, like *zeitgeist* or *schaden-freude*, that everyone thinks they know but no one really understands. The translation is "noisy ghost," and it's legitimate; they are the loud bullies of the psychic world. They have a tendency to attach themselves to teenage girls who dabble in the occult or who have wild mood swings, both of which attract angry energy. I used to tell my clients that poltergeists are just plain pissed off. They're often the ghosts of women who were wronged or men who were betrayed, people who never got a chance to fight back. That frustration manifests itself in biting or pinching the inhabitants of a house, cupboards banging or doors slamming, dishes whizzing across a room, and shutters opening and closing. In some cases, too, there is a connection to one of the elements: spontaneous winds that blow paintings off walls. Fires that break out on the carpets.

Or a deluge of water.

Virgil wipes his eyes with the tail of his shirt, trying to take this all in. "So you think we were just chased out of that house by a ghost."

"A poltergeist," I say. "But why split hairs?"

"And you think it's Grace."

"It makes sense. She drowned herself because her husband was cheating on her. If anyone's going to come back and haunt as a water poltergeist, it would be her."

Virgil nods, considering that. "Nevvie seemed to think her daughter was still alive."

"Actually," I point out, "Nevvie said her daughter would be *back soon*. She didn't specify in what *form*."

"Even if I wasn't completely wiped out from pulling an all-nighter, this would be hard for me to wrap my head around," Virgil admits. "I'm used to hard evidence."

I reach over and grasp the edge of his shirt, wring it out on the ground. "Yeah," I say sarcastically. "I guess this doesn't count as hard evidence."

"So Gideon fakes Nevvie's death, and she winds up in Tennessee in a house that belonged to her daughter at some point." He shakes his head. "Why?"

I can't answer that. But I don't have to, because my phone starts to ring.

I rummage in my purse and finally locate it. I know that number.

"Please," Jenna says. "I need help."

"Slow down," Virgil says, for the fifth time.

She swallows, but her eyes are red from crying and her nose is still running. I rummage in my bag for a tissue and can find only a lens cloth for cleaning sunglasses. I offer her that instead.

The directions she gave us were a teenager's directions: *You pass a Walmart, and somewhere there's a left. And a Waffle House, I'm pretty sure the turn is after the Waffle House.* Honestly, it's a miracle that we managed to find her at all. When we did, she was behind a service station's chain-link fence and Dumpster, halfway up a tree.

Jenna, goddammit, where are you? Virgil yelled, and only after she heard his voice did her face poke through the branches and the leaves, a small moon in a green field of stars. She climbed gingerly down the trunk, until she lost her footing and fell into Virgil's arms. *I've got you,* he told her; he hasn't let go of her yet.

"I found Gideon," Jenna says, her voice hitched and uneven.

"Where?"

"At the sanctuary."

She starts crying again. "At first I started to think that maybe he hurt my mom," she says, and I see Virgil's finger's flex on her shoulders.

"Did he touch you?" Virgil asks. I am thoroughly convinced that, if Jenna gives a positive response, Virgil would kill Gideon with his bare hands.

She shakes her head. "It was just . . . a feeling."

"Good thing you listened to your gut, sugar," I say.

"But he said he never saw my mother, after the night she was taken to the hospital."

Virgil presses his lips together. "He could be lying through his teeth."

Jenna's eyes fill again. It makes me think of Nevvie, and the room that would not stop weeping. "He said my mom was having a baby. *His* baby."

"I know my psychic powers are a little off," I murmur, "but I did *not* see that coming."

Virgil lets go of Jenna and starts pacing. "That's motive." He starts muttering, working through a time line in his head. I watch him tick off points on his fingers, shake his head, start over, and finally, grimly, turn to her. "There's something you need to know. While you were with Gideon in the sanctuary, Serenity and I were with Nevvie Ruehl."

Her head snaps up. "Nevvie Ruehl's dead."

"No," Virgil corrects. "Someone wanted us to *think* Nevvie Ruehl was dead."

"My father?"

"Your dad wasn't the one who found the trampled body. That was Gideon. He was sitting with her when the medical examiner and the cops arrived."

She wipes her eyes. "But there was *still* a body."

I look down at the ground, waiting for Jenna to connect the dots.

When she does, the arrow points in a different direction than I expect. "Gideon didn't do it," she insists. "I thought that, too, at first. But she was pregnant."

Virgil takes a step forward. "Exactly," he says. "That's why Gideon wasn't the one to kill her."

Before we leave, Virgil goes to use the restroom at the service station, and Jenna and I are left alone. Her eyes are still bloodshot. "If my mom *is* . . . dead . . ." She lets her voice trail off. "Could she wait for me?"

People like to think that they can reunite with a loved one who's passed. But there are so many layers to the afterlife; it's like saying that you're bound to run into someone because you both live on planet Earth.

However, I think Jenna's had enough bad news for one day. "Sugar, she might be here with you right now."

"I don't get it."

"The spirit world is modeled on the real world, and the real things we've seen. You might go into your grandmother's kitchen and she'll be down there making coffee. You may be making your bed and she walks by the open door. But every now and then, the edges will blur, because you're inhabiting the same space. You're like oil and vinegar in the same container."

"So," she says, her voice cracking. "I don't ever really get her back."

I could lie to her. I could tell her what everyone wants to hear, but I won't. "No," I tell Jenna. "You don't."

"And what happens to my dad?"

I can't answer that for her. I don't know if Virgil will try to prove that Thomas was the one who killed his wife that night. Or if it would even stick, given the poor man's mental state.

Jenna sits on the picnic table and draws her knees up to her chest. "I had this friend once, Chatham, who always talked about Paris like it was practically Heaven. She wanted to go to the Sorbonne for college. She was going to stroll down the Champs-Élysées; she was going to sit at a café and watch skinny French women walking down the street, all that stuff. Her aunt surprised her by taking her there on a business trip when she was twelve. When Chatham came home, I asked her if it was all it was cracked up to be, and you know what she said? 'It was kind of like any other city.'" Jenna shrugs. "I didn't think it would feel like this, when I got here."

"To Tennessee?"

"No. To . . . the end, I guess." She looks up at me, her eyes brimming with tears. "Just because I know now that she didn't want to leave me behind doesn't make it easier, you know? Nothing's changed. She's not here. I *am*. And I still feel empty."

I slide an arm around her. "It's no small feat, finishing a journey," I tell her. "But no one ever mentions that once you get there, you still have to turn around and head all the way home."

Jenna dashes her hand across her eyes. "If it turns out Virgil is right, I want to see my dad before he goes to jail."

"We don't know that he'll—"

"It wasn't his fault. He didn't know what he was doing."

She says this with such conviction that I realize it isn't necessarily what she believes. Just what she *needs* to.

I pull her closer and let her cry for a little while against my shoulder. "Serenity," Jenna asks, her voice muffled against my shirt. "Will you let me talk to her whenever I need to?"

There's a reason people are dead. Back when I *could* be a medium, I'd only do two spirit communications at most for a client. I wanted to help people through their grief, not be 1-800-Dial-the-Dead.

When I was good at this, when I had Lucinda and Desmond to protect me from the spirits that needed me to do their bidding, I knew how to put up walls. That's what kept me from being awakened in the middle of the night by a conga line of spirits who needed to get a message to the living. It let me use my Gift on my terms instead of theirs.

Now, though, I would trade my privacy if it meant that I could connect with spirits again. I would never do a fake reading for Jenna— she deserves better than that—so there's no way I could possibly give her what she wants.

But all the same, I look her in the eye and say, "Of course."

. . .

Suffice it to say that the trip home is long, hellish, and silent. We wouldn't be able to get on a plane without permission from Jenna's guardian, because she's a minor, and so we wind up driving through the night. I listen to the radio to keep myself awake, and then Virgil starts talking, somewhere around the Maryland border. He glances back first, to make sure Jenna is still fast asleep.

"Say she's dead," Virgil says. "What do I do?"

It's a surprise conversation starter. "You mean Alice?"

"Yeah."

I hesitate. "I guess you figure out for sure who did it, and you go after them."

"I'm not a cop, Serenity. And now it turns out that I probably never *should* have been." He shakes his head. "All this time I thought it was Donny who fucked up. But it turns out it was me."

I glance at him.

"I mean, it was a clusterfuck at the sanctuary that day. No one knew how to secure a crime scene when there were wild animals roaming around. Thomas Metcalf was off his gourd, although we didn't know it at first. There were missing people who hadn't been reported as missing. One of them was an adult female. That's all I was looking for. So I made an assumption, when I found an unconscious body that was dirty and covered with blood. I told the paramedics that it was Alice, and they took her off to the hospital and admitted her under that name." He turns, looking out the window, so that his profile is traced by the passing headlights of other cars. "She didn't have ID. I should have followed up. Why can't I remember what she looked like when I saw her? Was the hair blond or red? Why didn't I pay attention?"

"Because you were focused on getting her medical attention," I say. "Don't beat yourself up. You didn't *try* to mislead anyone," I point out, thinking of my own recent career as a swamp witch.

"That," he says, "is where you're wrong." He turns to me. "I buried evidence. That red hair that was found on Nevvie's body? When I saw it in the ME's report, I didn't know it belonged to Alice—but I *did* know it meant the case was more than an accidental death. Still, I let my partner convince me that the public just wanted to feel safe, that a trampling was bad enough, but a murder would be even worse. So I made that page of the ME's report disappear, and just like Donny had said—I became a hero. I was the youngest guy to get promoted to detective, did you know that?" He shakes his head.

"What did you do with the page?"

"I put it in my pocket the morning of my detective ceremony. And then I got into my car and drove over a cliff."

I jam on the brakes. "You did *what*?"

"First responders thought I was a goner. I guess I flatlined, but apparently I managed to fuck that up, too. Because I woke up in rehab, with a shitload of OxyContin in my veins, and enough pain to kill ten men who were way stronger than me. Needless to say, I didn't go back to the job. IA doesn't look too kindly on guys who have a death wish." He looks at me. "So now you know who I really am. I couldn't stand the thought of pretending to be the good guy for the next twenty years, when I knew I wasn't one. At least now when I tell people I'm an alcoholic loser, I'm not lying to them."

I think of Jenna, hiring a fraud of a psychic and an investigator with secrets of his own. I think of all the mounting evidence that Alice Metcalf is the body that was recovered from the sanctuary ten years ago, and how not once was I able to sense that.

"I have to tell you something, too," I confess. "Remember how you kept asking me if I could communicate with Alice Metcalf's spirit? And I said no, which probably meant she wasn't dead?"

"Yeah. Guess your Gift might need recalibrating."

"It needs more than that. I haven't had a syllable of psychic communication since I gave Senator McCoy the wrong information about his son. I am used up. Done. Dry. This stick shift has more paranormal talent than I do."

Virgil starts to laugh. "You're telling me you *are* a hack?"

"It's worse. Because I wasn't always." I look at him. There is a green mask around his eyes, a reflection from the mirror, as if he is some kind of superman. But he isn't. He's flawed, and scarred, and battle-weary, just like me. Just like all of us.

Jenna lost her mother. I lost my credibility. Virgil lost his faith. We've all got missing pieces. But for a little while, I believed that, together, we might be whole.

We cross into Delaware. "I don't think she could have picked two worse people to help her if she tried." I sigh.

"That's all the more reason," Virgil says, "to make it right."

ALICE

I did not go to Georgia for Grace's funeral.

She was buried in a family plot beside her father. Gideon went, and Nevvie, of course—but the reality of running an animal sanctuary meant someone had to stay behind to take care of the animals, no matter how pressing the reason to leave. In the horrible week that it had taken for Grace's body to wash ashore—a week when Gideon and Nevvie still held out hope that she was alive somewhere—we had all been pitching in to cover for her. Thomas would interview for a new caregiver, but that wasn't a hire that could be made quickly. And now, with our staff below half capacity, it meant that Thomas and I were working round the clock.

When Thomas told me that Gideon had come back to the sanctuary after the funeral, I was not presumptuous enough to believe that he had returned because of me. I did not know, really, what to expect. We'd had a year of secrets, a year of bliss. What had happened to Grace was the punishment, the payment due.

Except nothing had *happened* to Grace. Grace had been the one to make it happen.

I did not want to think about that, so instead I buried myself in cleaning the barns until the floors were sparkling, in creating new enrichment toys for the Asian elephants. I cut back the brush that had begun to overgrow the fence at the north end of the African enclosure. That would have been Gideon's job, I thought, even as I wielded the hedge trimmers. I kept myself moving, so that I could not think about anything except the task in front of me.

I did not see Gideon until the next morning, when he was driving an ATV with a load of hay into the same barn where I was making medicine balls out of apples for that day's feeding. I dropped the knife and ran to the doorway, my hand raised to call him closer, but at the last minute I stepped back into the shadows.

Really, what could I possibly say to him?

I watched for a few minutes as he unloaded the hay, his arms flexing as he stacked the bales into a pyramid. Finally, gathering my courage, I stepped out into the sunshine.

He paused, then set down the bale he had been holding. "Syrah's limping again," I said. "If you get a chance, can you take a look?"

He nodded, not meeting my gaze. "What else do you need me to do?"

"The air conditioner in the office is broken. But it's not a priority." I crossed my arms tightly. "I'm so sorry, Gideon."

Gideon kicked the hay, creating a haze of dust between us. He looked at me for the first time since I'd approached. His eyes were so bloodshot that it looked as if something had burst inside him. I thought maybe it was shame.

I reached out, but he ducked so that my fingers only grazed him. Then he turned his back on me and grabbed another bale of hay.

I blinked at the sun in my eyes as I returned to the kitchen in the barn. To my shock, Nevvie stood in the spot I'd been minutes before, using a spoon to scoop peanut butter into the apples I had cored.

Neither Thomas nor I had expected Nevvie to return anytime soon. After all, she had just buried her child. "Nevvie . . . you're back?"

She did not look up at me as she worked. "Where else would I be?" she said.

• • •

A few days later, I lost my own daughter.

We were in the cottage, and Jenna was crying because she did not want to lie down and rest. Lately, she had been afraid to fall asleep. Instead of a nap, Jenna called it the Leaving Time. She was certain that if she closed her eyes, I would not be here again when she opened them, and no matter what I did or said to convince her otherwise, she sobbed and fought her exhaustion until her body triumphed over her will.

I tried singing to her, rocking her. I folded dollar bills into origami elephants, which usually distracted her enough to stop the crying. She finally drifted off the only way she could these days—with my body curled around hers like a snail's shell, a protective home. I had just extricated myself from that position when Gideon knocked at the door. He needed help erecting a hot-wire fence so that he could regrade parts of the African enclosure. The elephants liked to dig for fresh water, but the holes they created were dangerous to the elephants themselves and to us on our ATVs and on foot. You could fall into one and snap your leg or strike your head; you could break an axle on your vehicle.

Hot wire was a two-person job, particularly with the African elephants. One of us would have to string the fence while the other pushed the animals back with a vehicle. I was reluctant to go with him for two reasons: I didn't want Jenna to wake up and have her worst fear—that I was indeed gone—realized, and I didn't know where my relationship with Gideon stood right now. "Get Thomas," I suggested.

"He went into town," Gideon said. "And Nevvie's doing a trunk wash on Syrah."

I looked at my daughter, fast asleep on the couch. I could have awakened her and taken her with me, but it had taken so long to get her to sleep, and Thomas—if he found out—would have been furious, as usual. Or I could have given Gideon twenty minutes of my time, tops, and returned before Jenna roused.

I chose the latter, and it took only fifteen minutes—that's how fast and how smoothly we worked in tandem. Our synchronicity made my heart hurt; I had so much I wanted to say to him.

"Gideon," I said, as we finished. "What can I do?"

His gaze slid away. "Do you miss her?"

"Yes," I whispered. "Of course I do."

His nostrils flared, and his jaw seemed made of stone. "That's why we can't do this anymore," he muttered.

I could not breathe. "Because I'm sorry Grace is gone?"

His shook his head. "No," he said. "Because I'm not."

His mouth contorted, twisted around a sob, and he fell to his knees. He buried his face against my stomach.

I kissed the crown of Gideon's head and wrapped my arms around him. I held him so tightly that he could not fall apart.

Ten minutes later, I raced back to the cottage on the ATV to find the front door was open. Maybe I had forgotten to close it, in my haste. That's what I was thinking, anyway, when I walked inside and realized Jenna was gone.

"Thomas," I yelled, racing outside again. "Thomas!"

He had to have her; he had to have her. This was my prayer, my litany. I thought about the moment she had awakened and found me missing. Had she cried? Panicked? Gone to find me?

I had been so sure I'd taught her about safety, that she was capable of learning, that Thomas was wrong about her getting hurt. But now I looked at the enclosures, at the gaps in the railing that a toddler could so easily crawl through. Jenna was three now. She knew her way. What if she'd wandered out the door and through the fencing?

I radioed for Gideon, who came immediately when he heard the terror in my voice. "Check the barns," I begged. "Check the enclosures."

I knew that these elephants had worked with humans in zoos and circuses, but that didn't mean they wouldn't charge someone who invaded their domain. I also knew that elephants preferred the lower voices of males—I always tried to make my voice huskier when I spoke to them. Since high-pitched voices are nervous voices, elephants associate female pitches with anxiety. And a child's voice would fall into that category.

I knew a man once who owned property high up in the game reserve, who had gone bushwhacking with his two little girls and found himself surrounded by a wild elephant herd. He told his daughters to roll themselves up in a ball and be as small as possible. *No matter what happens*, he said, *do not lift your head.* Two large females came forward to smell the girls and pushed against them a little bit, but they did not injure a hair on the head of either child.

But I would not be there to tell Jenna to get into a tiny ball. And she would be fearless, because she'd seen me interact with the elephants.

I drove the ATV into the closest enclosure, the African one, because I did not think Jenna could have gotten too far. I raced past the barn and the pond and the high spot where the elephants sometimes went in the cool mornings. I stood at the top of the highest ridge and took out my binoculars and tried to spot movement as far as my eye could see.

I spent twenty minutes driving around, tears in my eyes, wondering how I would explain to Thomas that our daughter was missing—and then Gideon's voice crackled on the radio. "I've got her," he said.

He told me to meet him at the cottage, and there I found my baby on Nevvie's lap, sucking on a Popsicle, all sticky palms and cherry lips. "Mama," Jenna said, holding it out to me. "*I scream.*"

But I couldn't look at her. I was too busy focusing on Nevvie, who seemed oblivious to the fact that I was so angry I was shaking. Nevvie's hand rested on my daughter's head like a blessing. "Someone woke up crying," she said. "Looking for *you.*"

It was not an excuse. It was an explanation. If anything, *I* was the one to blame, because I had left my baby alone.

Suddenly I knew I wouldn't yell, and I wouldn't reprimand Nevvie for taking my daughter away without asking me first.

Jenna had needed a mother, and I hadn't been there. Nevvie had needed a child, so that she could still parent someone.

At the time, it seemed a match made in Heaven.

The strangest behavior I have ever witnessed among elephants happened in the Tuli Block, on the bank of a dry riverbed during a prolonged drought, in an area where many different animals passed. The night before, lions had been sighted. That morning, there was a leopard on the bank above. But the predators had gone, and an elephant named Marea had given birth.

It was a normal birth—the herd protected her during labor by facing outward; they trumpeted in ecstasy when the calf arrived; and Marea managed to get him up on his feet by balancing him against her leg. She dusted him and introduced him to the herd, each family member touching the baby and checking in.

All of a sudden an elephant named Thato began to walk up the length of the dry riverbed. Now, she was an acquaintance of this herd, but not a member of it. I have no idea what she was doing alone, away from the rest of her own family. As she came by the newborn calf, she wrapped her trunk around his neck and began to lift him.

We see all the time how a mother might try to lift her newborn to get him moving, by sliding her trunk beneath his belly or between his legs. But it is not normal to pick a calf up by the neck. No mother would do that intentionally. The little calf was slipping out of the grasp of Thato's trunk as she walked away. The more he slipped, the higher she lifted, trying to keep that baby in her grip. Finally he fell, slamming hard to the ground.

That was the catalyst that spurred the herd to action. There was rumbling and trumpeting and chaos, and the family members touched the newborn to make sure he was all right, to prove that in fact he had not been hurt. Marea gathered him close and pulled him between her legs.

There was so much about this situation I did not understand. I'd seen elephants pick up babies when they were in the water, to keep them from drowning. I'd seen elephants lift babies that were lying down to get them to stand on their feet. But I had never seen an elephant try to carry off a calf, like a lioness with a cub.

I didn't know what made Thato think she could get away with kidnapping another's calf. I didn't know if that was her intent, or if she scented the lion and the leopard and felt he was in danger.

I didn't know why the herd did not react when Thato tried to take the calf. She was older than Marea, for sure, but she was not a member of the family.

We named that baby Molatlhegi. In Tswana, it means, "the lost one."

The night after I almost lost Jenna, I had a nightmare. In my dream, I was sitting near the spot where Molatlhegi had nearly been taken by Thato. As I watched, the elephants moved to higher ground, and water began to trickle down the dry throat of the riverbed. The water gurgled, running deeper and faster, until it splashed over my feet. On the far side of the river I saw Grace Cartwright. She stepped into the water fully clothed. She reached down to the riverbed, picked up a smooth stone, and tucked it into her shirt. She did this over and over, filling her pants, her coat pockets, until she could barely bend and stand again.

Then she began to walk deeper into the river's current.

I knew how deep the water got, and how quickly that could happen. I tried to yell to Grace, but I couldn't make a sound. When I opened my mouth, a thousand stones poured out.

And then suddenly *I* was the one in the water, weighted down. I felt the current pull my hair free from its braid; I struggled for air. But with every breath I was swallowing pebbles—agate and spiky calcite, basalt and slate and obsidian. I looked up at the watercolor sun as I sank.

I woke up, panicking, Gideon's hand pressed against my mouth. Fighting him, I kicked and rolled, until he was at one side of the bed and I was at the other and there was a barricade between us of the words we should have said but didn't.

"You were screaming," he said. "You were going to wake the whole camp."

I realized that the first bloody streaks of dawn were in the sky. That I had fallen asleep, when I only meant to steal a few moments.

When Thomas woke, an hour later, I was back in the living room of the cottage, sleeping on the couch, my arm flung over Jenna's tiny body as if nothing could possibly get past me to take her away, as if there was no way I would ever let her wake up and find me absent. He glanced at me, seemingly unconscious, and stumbled into the kitchen in search of coffee.

Except I wasn't actually asleep when he passed by. I was thinking about how my nights had been dark and dreamless my whole life, except for one notable exception, when my imagination kicked into overdrive and every midnight hour was a pantomime of my greatest fears.

The last time that happened, I'd been pregnant.

JENNA

My grandmother stares at me as if she's seeing a ghost. She grabs me tight, running her hands over my shoulders and my hair as if she needs to do an inventory. But there's a viciousness in her touch, too, as if she is trying to hurt me just as badly as I've hurt her. "Jenna, my God, where have you *been*?"

I kind of wish I'd taken Serenity or Virgil up on their offer to drive me home, to smooth the path between my grandmother and me. Right now, it's like Mount Kilimanjaro has sprung up between us.

"I'm sorry," I mutter. "I had to do some . . . stuff." I use Gertie as an excuse to break away from her. My dog starts licking my legs like there's no tomorrow, and when she jumps up on me, I bury my face in the ruff at her neck.

"I thought you had run away," my grandmother says. "I thought maybe you were doing drugs. Drinking. There are stories on the news all the time about girls who get kidnapped, good girls who make the mistake of telling a stranger what time it is when they ask. I was so worried, Jenna."

My grandmother is still wearing her meter maid uniform, but I can see that her eyes are red and her skin is too pale, like she hasn't slept. "I called everyone. Mr. Allen—who told me that you *haven't* been babysitting for his son, because his wife and baby are visiting her mother in California . . . the school . . . your friends—"

Horrified, I stare at her. Who the hell did she call? Short of Chatham, who doesn't even live here anymore, there's no one I hang around with. Which means my grandmother contacting a random kid to find out if I'm at her house having a sleepover is even *more* humiliating.

I don't think I can go back to school in the fall. I don't know if I can go back in the next twenty years. I'm mortified, and I'm mad at her, because it's hard enough to be a loser whose mother's dead and whose father killed her in a fit of crazy without becoming the laughingstock of the eighth grade.

I push Gertie away from me. "Did you call the police, too?" I ask. "Or is that still a sticking point for you?"

My grandmother's hand comes up as if she's going to hit me. I cringe; this would be the second time this week I've been hit by someone who is supposed to love me.

But my grandmother never touches me. She has raised her hand to point upstairs. "Go to your room," she tells me. "And don't come out until I say you can."

Because it's been two and a half days since I last showered, the bathroom is my first stop. I run the water in the tub so hot that a curtain of steam fills the tiny room, and the mirrors fog up, so that I don't have to look at myself as I strip off my clothes. Then I sit in the tub, my knees pulled up to my chest, and let the water keep running until it is almost level with the edge.

Taking a huge breath, I slide down the slope of the tub so that I am lying on the very bottom. I cross my arms, coffin-style, and open my eyes as wide as I can.

The shower curtain—pink with white flowers—looks like a kaleidoscope. There are bubbles that escape from my nose periodically, like little kamikaze warriors. My hair fans around my face like seaweed.

And this is how I found her, I imagine my grandmother saying. *Like she'd just fallen asleep underneath the water.*

I picture Serenity sitting with Virgil at my funeral, saying that I look so peaceful. I figure Virgil might even go home afterward and tip a glass—or six—in my honor.

It's getting harder to not burst upright. The pressure on my chest is so strong I have a quick flash of my ribs snapping, my chest caving in. My eyes have stars dancing in front of them, underwater fireworks.

In the minutes before it happened, was this how my mother felt?

I know she did not drown, but her chest was crushed; I've read the autopsy report. Her skull was cracked; was she struck in the head before that? Did she see the blow coming? Did time slow down and sound move in waves of color; could she feel the motion of blood cells at the thin skin of her wrists?

I just want, once, to share something she felt.

Even if it's the last thing I feel.

When I am certain that I am going to implode; that it is time to let the water rush into my nostrils and fill me so I sink like a stricken ship, my hands grab the lip of the tub and haul the rest of me into the air.

I gasp, and then I cough so violently that there is blood in the water. My hair mats my face, and my shoulders convulse. I lean over the side of the tub, chest pressed against the porcelain, and I vomit into the trash can.

Suddenly I remember being in a tub when I was tiny, when I could barely sit up by myself without toppling over like an egg. My mother would sit behind me, propping me in the V of her body. She would soap herself and then soap me. I slipped like a minnow through her hands.

Sometimes she sang. Sometimes she read journal articles. I sat in the circle of her legs, playing with rubber cups in a rainbow of colors—filling them, dumping them over my head and her knees.

I realize then that I've already felt something my mother felt.

Loved.

• • •

What do you think it was like for Captain Ahab, in the seconds before that harpoon line wrenched him out of the boat? Did he say to himself, *Well, bummer, but that damn whale was worth it?*

When Javert finally realized that Valjean had something he himself didn't—mercy—did he shrug and find a new obsession, like knitting or *Game of Thrones?* No. Because without Valjean to hate, he didn't know who he was anymore.

I've spent years looking for my mom. And now, all signs are starting to point to the fact that I couldn't have found her if I'd crawled every inch of this earth. Because she left it, ten years ago.

Dead is so *final*. So *done*.

But I'm not crying, like I thought I would, not anymore. And there's the tiniest green shoot of relief breaking through the wasteland of my thoughts: *She did not willingly leave me behind.*

Then there's the fact that the person who killed her is most likely my own father. I don't know why this is less of a shock to me. Maybe because I don't remember my father at all. He was already gone when I knew him, living in a world his own brain had created. And since I'd already lost him once, I don't feel like I'm losing him again.

My mom, though, that's different. I had *wanted*. I had *hoped*.

Virgil is all about crossing the t's and dotting the i's, because so much has been screwed up in this investigation already. He said that tomorrow he'll figure out a way to test the DNA of the body that everyone thought was Nevvie's. Because then we will all *know*.

The funny thing is that now that this moment is here—the one I've pegged as my high-water mark for years—does it matter? Here's the thing: I may finally have the truth. I may have *closure*, which is what the school counselor was always talking about with me when she corralled me in her stupid office. But here's something I don't have: my mother.

I start to reread my mother's journals, but I can't; it makes it hard to breathe. So I take out my stash of money, which is literally down to six individual dollar bills, and fold each of them into a tiny elephant. I have a herd marching across my desk.

Then I turn on my computer. I log on to the NamUs website and click on the new cases.

There's an eighteen-year-old boy who disappeared after dropping his mom off at work in Westminster, North Carolina. He drove a green Dodge Dart with the license plate 58U-7334. He had shoulder-length blond hair and fingernails filed into points.

A seventy-two-year-old female from West Hartford, Connecticut, who takes medicine for paranoid schizophrenia and who walked away from a group home after telling the staff she was going to audition for Cirque du Soleil. She had been wearing blue jeans and a sweatshirt with a picture of a cat on it.

A twenty-two-year-old girl from Ellendale, North Dakota, who left her house with an older unidentified male and never came back home.

I could click on these links all day long. And by the time I was done, there would be hundreds more. There are an endless number of people who have left a love-shaped hole in the heart of someone else. Eventually someone brave and stupid will come along and try to fill that hole. But it never works, and so instead, that selfless soul winds up with a gap in *his* heart, too. And so on. It's a miracle that anyone survives, when so much of us is missing.

For just a moment, I let myself imagine what my life might have been like: my mother and my baby sister and I, cuddled under a blanket on the couch on a rainy Sunday, her arms around us, one on each side, as we watched a chick flick. My mother yelling at me to pick up my sweatshirt, because the living room is not my hamper. My mother doing my hair for my junior prom, while my sister pretends to put on mascara in the bathroom mirror. My mother taking too many pictures as I pin the boutonniere on my date, and me pretending to be annoyed but, in reality, being psyched that for her this moment is nearly as monumental as it is for me. My mother rubbing my back when that same boy breaks up with me a month later, telling me he was an idiot, because who couldn't love a girl like me?

The door to my room opens, and my grandmother walks in. She sits on the bed. "I thought at first you didn't realize how worried I could possibly have been, when you didn't come home that first night. Or even try to get in touch with me."

I look down at my lap, my face hot.

"But then I realized I was wrong. You could understand it perfectly, better than anyone else, because you know what it's like to have someone disappear."

"I went to Tennessee," I confess.

"You went *where?*" she says. "*How?*"

"Bus," I tell her. "I went to the sanctuary where all our elephants were sent."

My grandmother's hand flutters at her throat. "You traveled a thousand miles to go to a zoo?"

"It's not a zoo, it's like the anti-zoo," I correct. "And yeah. I went because I was trying to find someone who knew my mother. I thought Gideon might be able to tell me what happened to her."

"Gideon," she repeats.

"They worked together," I say. I do not say: *They were having an affair.*

"And?" my grandmother asks.

I nod, slowly pulling the scarf from around my neck. It's so light that I imagine it would not even register on a scale: a cloud, a breath, a memory. "Grandma," I whisper. "I think she's dead."

Until now, I hadn't realized that words have sharp edges; that they can cut your tongue. I don't think I could utter another sentence right now if I tried.

My grandmother reaches for the scarf, wrapping it around her hand like a bandage. "Yes," she says. "I think so, too."

Then she rips the scarf in half.

I cry out, I'm that shocked. "What are you *doing?*"

My grandmother scoops up the stack of my mother's journals that are piled on my desk, too. "It's for your own good, Jenna."

Tears spring to my eyes. "Those are *not* yours."

It hurts, seeing her with all that I have left of my mom. She's ripping away my skin, and now I'm raw and exposed.

"They're not *yours*, either," my grandmother says. "This is not your research, and it's not your history. Tennessee? This has gone too far. You need to start living your *own* life, instead of *hers*."

"I hate you!" I scream.

But my grandmother is already on her way out the door. She pauses at the threshold. "You keep looking for your family, Jenna. But it's always been right under your nose."

When she leaves, I pick up the stapler on my desk and throw it at the door. Then I sit down, wiping my nose with the back of my hand. I start plotting how I will find that scarf, and sew it together. How I will steal back those journals.

But the truth is, I don't have my mother. I never will. I don't get to rewrite my story; I just have to stumble to the end of it.

The case of my mother's disappearance glows on the laptop screen in front of me, full of details that don't matter anymore.

I click on the settings of the NamUs profile and, with a single keystroke, delete it.

One of the first things my grandmother taught me when I was little was how to get out of the house during a fire. Each of our bedrooms had a special emergency ladder stacked underneath the window, just in case. If I smelled smoke, if I felt the door and found heat, I was supposed to throw open the sash, hook the ladder into place, and rappel my way down the side of the house to safety.

Never mind that as a three-year-old I couldn't lift that ladder, much less pry open the window. I knew what the protocol was, and that was supposed to be enough to ward off the possibility of any harm coming to me.

The superstition worked, I guess, because we've never had a fire in this house. But that dusty old ladder is still underneath my bedroom window, having served as a shelf for my books, a rack for my shoes, a table for my knapsack—but never as a means of escape. Until now.

This time, though, I leave a note for my grandmother. *I will stop,*

I promise. *But you have to give me one last chance to say good-bye. I promise I'll be back in time for dinner tomorrow.*

I open the window and hook the ladder into place. It doesn't seem sturdy enough to hold my weight, and I think about how ridiculous it would be if you were trying to survive a house fire but wound up killing yourself instead in a fall.

The ladder gets me only to the sloped roof over the garage, which really isn't a help at all. But by now I'm quite the escape artist, so I inch myself over the edge and hook my fingers into the rain gutter. From there, it's only a drop of about five feet to the ground.

My bike is where I left it, balanced against the front porch railing. I hop on and start pedaling.

Riding is different, in the middle of the night. I move like the wind; I feel invisible. The streets are damp because it's been raining, and the pavement shines everywhere but the trail left by my bike tires. The zooming taillights of cars remind me of sparklers I used to play with on the Fourth of July: how the glow hung in the darkness, how you could wave your arms and paint an alphabet of light. I navigate by feel, because I can't read the signs, and before I know it, I'm in downtown Boone at the bar beneath Serenity's apartment.

It's hopping. Instead of a token few drunks, there are girls squeezed into Spandex dresses, hanging on the biceps of bikers; there are skinny dudes leaning against the brick wall to have a smoke between shots. The noise from the jukebox spills into the street, and I hear someone urging *Chug! Chug! Chug!* "Hey, baby," a guy slurs. "Can I buy you a drink?"

"I'm *thirteen*," I say.

"I'm Raoul."

I duck my head and push past him, dragging my bike into the entryway to Serenity's house. I lug it up the stairs and into her foyer again, careful not to upset the table this time. But before I can knock on the door softly—I mean, it's 2:00 A.M.—it opens.

"You couldn't sleep, either, sugar?" Serenity says.

"How did you know I was here?"

"You don't exactly float up the stairs like a fairy when you're dragging that damn thing around." She falls back so that I can step into her apartment. It looks the way I remember it from the first time I came here. When I still believed that finding my mother was what I wanted most in the world.

"I'm surprised your grandmother let you come here this late," Serenity says.

"I didn't give her a choice." I sink down on the couch, and she sits beside me. "This so sucks," I say.

She doesn't pretend to misunderstand me. "Well, don't jump to conclusions just yet. Virgil says—"

"Fuck Virgil," I interrupt. "Whatever Virgil says won't bring her back to life. Do the math. If you tell your husband you're pregnant with another guy's kid, he isn't going to throw you a baby shower."

I've tried, believe me, but I can't summon up hate for my father— only pity, really, a dull ache. If my dad was the one who killed my mom, I don't think he'll wind up going to trial. He's institutionalized already; no prison is going to be more punishing than the confines of his own mind. It just means exactly what my grandmother said—she's the only family I really have left.

I know it's my fault. I know I'm the one who asked Serenity to help me find my mother; who got Virgil on board. This is what curiosity gets you. You might live on top of the biggest toxic waste dump on the planet, but if you never dig, then all you ever know is that your grass is green and your garden is lush.

"People don't realize how hard it is," she says. "When my clients used to come to me, asking to talk to Uncle Sol or their beloved grandma, all they were focusing on was the hello, the chance to say what they didn't say when the person was alive. But when you open a door, you have to close it behind you. You might say hello, but you also wind up saying good-bye."

I face her. "I wasn't asleep. When you and Virgil were talking, in the car? I heard everything you said."

Serenity freezes. "Well, then," she says. "I guess you know I'm a fraud."

"You aren't, though. You found that necklace. And the wallet."

She shakes her head. "I just happened to be in the right place at the right time."

I think about this for a moment. "But isn't that what being psychic *is*?"

I can tell that she never thought about it that way. One man's coincidence is another's connection. Does it matter if it's gut feeling, like Virgil says, or psychic intuition, if you still get what you're searching for?

She pulls a blanket up from the floor to cover her feet, and casts it wide so it will cover me, too. "Maybe," she concedes. "Still, it's nothing like what it used to be. Other people's thoughts—they just were suddenly *there* in my head. Sometimes the connection was crystal clear, and sometimes it was like being on a cell phone in the mountains, where you only catch every third word. But it was more than stumbling over something shiny in the grass."

We are cuddled under a blanket that smells like Tide and Indian food, and rain is striking the windows from outside. I realize this is very close to the image I'd conjured earlier, of what my life would have been like if my mother had survived.

I glance at Serenity. "Do you miss it? Hearing from people who are gone?"

"Yes," she admits.

I lean my head on her shoulder. "Me, too," I say.

ALICE

Gideon's arms were the safest place in the world. When I was with him, I forgot: how Thomas's highs and his lows scared the hell out of me; how every morning started with an argument and every night ended with my husband locked in his office with his secrets and the shadows of his mind. When I was with Gideon I could pretend that the three of us were the family I had hoped to be.

Then I found out we would be four.

"It's going to be okay," he'd promised when I told him the news, although I did not believe him. He couldn't tell the future. He could just, I hoped, be mine.

"Don't you see?" Gideon had said, lit from within. "We were meant to be together."

Maybe we were, but what a price to pay. His marriage. Mine. Grace's life.

Still, we dreamed out loud in Technicolor. I wanted to take Gideon back to Africa with me, so he could see these incredible animals before they had been broken by humans. Gideon wanted to move south, where he'd come from. I resurrected my dream of running away with Jenna, but this time, I imagined that he would come with us. We pretended to be racing forward, but we didn't move an inch, because of the trapdoors that threatened to swallow us: He had to tell his mother-in-law; I had to tell my husband.

But we had a deadline, because it was getting very hard to hide the changes to my body.

One day, Gideon found me working at the Asian barn. "I told Nevvie about the baby," he said.

I froze. "What did she say?"

"She told me I should have everything I deserve. Then she walked away from me."

Just like that, this wasn't a fantasy anymore. It was real, and it meant that if he had been brave enough to confront Nevvie, I had to be brave enough to confront Thomas.

I did not see Nevvie all day, or Gideon, either, for that matter. I tracked Thomas's whereabouts and followed him around from enclosure to enclosure; I cooked him dinner. I asked him to help me do a foot soak on Lilly, when normally I would have asked Gideon or Nevvie for assistance. Instead of avoiding him, as I'd been doing for months, I talked to him about the applications he'd received for a new caregiver and asked him if he'd made a decision yet to hire anyone. I lay down with Jenna until she fell asleep and then went to his office and started to read an abstract, as if it was normal for us to share the space.

I thought he might tell me to get lost, but Thomas smiled at me, an olive branch. "I forgot how nice it used to be," he said. "You and me working side by side."

Resolve is like porcelain, isn't it? You can have the best intentions, but the moment there's a hairline crack, it is only a matter of time before you go to pieces. Thomas poured himself a tumbler of scotch, and another one for me. I left mine sitting on the desk.

"I'm in love with Gideon," I said bluntly.

His hands went still on the decanter. Then he picked up his glass and finished the shot. "You think I'm blind?"

"We're leaving," I told him. "I'm pregnant."

Thomas sat down. He buried his face in his hands and started to weep.

I stared for a moment, torn between comforting him and hating myself for being the one to reduce him to this, a broken man with a failing sanctuary, a cheating wife, and a mental illness.

"Thomas," I begged. "Say something."

His voice hitched. "What did I do wrong?"

I knelt in front of him. I saw, in that instant, the man whose glasses had fogged in the steamy heat of Botswana, the man who had met me at the airport clutching the roots of a plant. The man who had a dream and had invited me to take part in it. I had not seen that man for a very long time. But was it because he'd disappeared? Or because I'd stopped looking?

"You did nothing," I replied. "It was me."

He reached out, grasping my shoulder with one hand. With the other, he smacked me so hard across the face that I tasted blood.

"Whore," he said.

Clutching my cheek, I fell backward. I backed away from him as he advanced toward me, scrambling to get out of the room.

Jenna was still asleep on the couch. I raced toward her, determined to take her with me as I walked out the door this last time. I could buy clothes and toys and anything else she needed later. But Thomas grabbed my wrist, wrenching it behind me, so that I fell again and he reached our child first. He picked up her small body, and she curled into him. "Daddy?" she sighed, still caught in the web between dreams and truth.

He wrapped his arms around her, turning so that Jenna was no longer facing me. "You want to go?" Thomas said. "Be my guest. But you want to take my daughter with you? Over my dead body."

He smiled at me then, a terrible, terrible smile. "Or better yet," he said. "Over yours."

She would wake up, and I would be gone. Her worst fear, come true. *I'm sorry, baby*, I said silently to Jenna. Then I ran for help, leaving her behind.

VIRGIL

Even if I'd been able to find the body that was buried ten years ago, I wouldn't have been able to get a court order. I don't know what I was thinking I'd resort to, shy of sneaking into a graveyard, Frankenstein-style, to dig up a corpse that I had assumed was Nevvie Ruehl. But before a body is released to a funeral home, the medical examiner does the autopsy. And the autopsy would have had a DNA sample taken by the state lab, stored somewhere in FTA card files for posterity.

No way in hell am I going to be able to get the state lab to cough up evidence to me, now that I'm a civilian. Which means I have to find someone they *would* give it to. So a half hour later, I'm leaning on the ledge of the evidence room at the Boone PD, sweet-talking Ralph again. "You're back?" He sighs.

"What can I say? I missed you desperately. You haunt my dreams."

"I already took a chance letting you in last time, Virgil. I'm not risking my job for you."

"Ralph, you and I both know that the chief wouldn't give this job to anyone else. You're like the Hobbit guarding the ring, man."

"What?"

"You're the Dee Brown of the department. Without him, nobody would have even known the Celtics *existed* in the nineties, right?"

Ralph's wrinkles deepen as he grins. "Well, now you're talking," he says. "It's true. These young guys don't know their ass from their elbow. I come down here every morning and someone's moved crap around, trying to classify it some newfangled computerized way, and you know what happens? Shit gets lost. So I move it back where it belongs. You know what I say—if it ain't broke . . ."

I nod like I'm hanging on his every word. "This is what I'm talking about. You're the central nervous system of this outfit, Ralph. Without you, everything would fall apart. That's why I knew you were the right guy to turn to for help."

He shrugs, trying to look humble. I wonder if he realizes I'm good-copping him, buttering him up so that I can get something out of him in return. Up in the break room, officers are probably still talking about how he's senile and so slow-moving that he could drop dead in the evidence room and no one would notice for a week.

"You remember how I was reviewing an old case, right?" I say, leaning closer, so that he's in on the secret. "I'm trying to get a DNA sample from the blood that was taken by the state lab. Any chance you could place a few calls, make that happen?"

"I would if I could, Virgil. But the state lab's pipes burst five years ago. They lost eight whole years' worth of evidence when the FTA cards were destroyed. It's like 1999 through 2007 never happened."

The smile on my face stiffens. "Thanks anyway," I tell him, and I slip out of the PD before anyone can see me.

I'm still trying to figure out how I'm going to break this news to Jenna when I pull up to my office building and see Serenity's VW Bug parked out front. As soon as I get out of my truck, Jenna is in my face, peppering me with questions. "What did you find out? Is there a way to figure out who was buried? What about the fact that it's been ten years, is that going to be a problem?"

I glance at her. "Did you bring me coffee?"

"What?" she says. "No."

"Then get me some and come back. It's too early for the third degree."

I climb the stairs to my office, aware that Jenna and Serenity are trailing behind. I unlock the door, stepping over the hills of evidence to get to my desk chair, where I collapse. "It's going to be more challenging than I thought to find a DNA sample from whoever we identified as Nevvie Ruehl ten years ago."

Serenity looks around the office, which is marginally more disarrayed than a bomb site. "It's a wonder you can find anything at *all* in here, sugar."

"I wasn't looking *here*," I argue, wondering why I am even bothering to explain the flowchart of police evidence preservation to someone who probably believes in magic, and then my eye falls on the small envelope tossed on top of the other detritus on my desk.

Inside is the fingernail I'd found in the seam of the victim's uniform shirt.

The same uniform shirt that had freaked Jenna out, because it was stiff with blood.

Tallulah takes one look at Serenity and throws her arms around me. "Victor, this is so sweet of you. We never get to hear how the stuff we do in the lab plays out in the real world." She beams at Jenna. "You must be so happy to have your mom back."

"Oh, I'm not—" Serenity says, at the same time Jenna goes, "Um, not quite."

"Actually," I explain, "we haven't found Jenna's mother yet. Serenity's helping me out with the case. She's a . . . psychic."

Tallulah makes a beeline for Serenity. "I had this aunt? She told me her whole life she was going to leave me her diamond earrings. But she dropped dead without a will, and wouldn't you know it, those earrings never turned up. I'd love to know which one of my sleazy cousins stole them."

"I'll let you know if I hear anything," Serenity murmurs.

I lift up the paper bag I have brought to the lab. "I need another favor, Lulu."

She raises a brow. "By my count you haven't paid me back for the last one."

I flash my dimples. "I promise. As soon as this case is solved."

"Is that a bribe to push your test to the front of the line?"

"Depends," I flirt. "Do you like bribes?"

"You know what I like . . . ," Tallulah breathes.

It takes me a moment to untangle myself from her and shake the contents of the paper bag onto a sterile table. "What *I'd* like is for you to take a look at this." The shirt is dirty, shredded, nearly black.

Tallulah takes a swab from a cabinet, moistens it, and rubs it over the shirt. The cotton tip comes away pinkish brown.

"It's ten years old," I tell her. "I don't know how badly it's been compromised. But I'm hoping like hell you can tell me if it looks at all like the mtDNA you took from Jenna." From my pocket, I pull the envelope with the fingernail inside. "And this one, too. If my hunch is right, one is going to be a match, and one isn't."

Jenna stands on the other side of the metal table. The fingers of one hand just graze the edge of the shirt fabric. The fingers of the other hand are pressed into her own carotid artery, feeling the pulse. "I'm going to throw up," she mutters, and she bolts from the room.

"I'll go," Serenity says.

"No," I tell her. "Let me."

I find Jenna at the brick wall behind the building where we laughed ourselves silly once. Except now she's dry-heaving, her hair in her face and her cheeks flushed. I put my hand on the small of her back.

She wipes her mouth on her sleeve. "Did you ever get the flu when you were my age?"

"I guess. Yeah."

"Me, too. I stayed home from school. But my grandma, she had to go to work. So there was no one to pull my hair out of my face or to hand me a washcloth or get me ginger ale or anything." She looks at me. "It would have been nice, you know? But instead I get a mom who's probably dead and a father who killed her."

She collapses against the wall, and I sit down beside her. "I don't know about that," I admit.

Jenna turns to me. "What do you mean?"

"You were the one who first said that your mom wasn't a murderer. That the hair on the body proved that she had some contact with Nevvie at the site where she was trampled."

"But you said you saw Nevvie in Tennessee."

"I did. And I do think that there was a mix-up, and that the body identified as Nevvie Ruehl wasn't Nevvie Ruehl. But that doesn't mean Nevvie wasn't involved in some way. That's why I asked Lulu to test the fingernail. Say the blood comes back matching your mom's and the fingernail doesn't—that tells me someone was fighting with her before she died. Maybe that fight got out of control," I explain.

"Why would Nevvie want to hurt my mom?"

"Because," I say, "your dad isn't the only one who would have been upset to hear she was having Gideon's baby."

"It is a fact universally acknowledged," Serenity says, "there is no greater force on earth than a mother's revenge."

The waitress who comes to refill her coffee cup gives her a strange look.

"You should embroider that on a pillow," I tell Serenity.

We are at the diner down the street from my office. I didn't think Jenna would want to eat after being sick, but to my surprise, she is ravenous. She's consumed an entire plate of pancakes, and half of mine.

"How long will it take the lab to get the results?" Serenity asks.

"I don't know. Lulu knows I want it done yesterday."

"I still don't get why Gideon would have lied about the body," Serenity says. "He must have known it was Alice when he found her."

"That's easy. He's a suspect if the body is Alice's. He's a victim if the body is Nevvie's. And when *she* wakes up in the hospital, and remembers what went down, she bolts because she's afraid she's going to be arrested for murder."

Serenity shakes her head. "You know, if you get tired of being an investigator, you'd make a fantastic swamp witch. You could make a fortune doing cold readings."

By now other people in the diner are giving us strange looks. I guess it's legitimate to talk about the weather and the Red Sox, but not murder investigations, or the paranormal.

The same waitress walks over. "If you're nearly done, we could use the table."

This is bullshit, because the diner is half empty. I start to argue, but Serenity waves her hand. "The hell with them," she says. She takes a twenty-dollar bill out of her pocket—enough to cover the bill with a three-cent tip—and slaps it on the table before hoisting herself out of the booth and walking outside.

"Serenity?"

Jenna's been so quiet that I've almost forgotten about her. "What you said about Virgil being a good swamp witch. What about me?"

Serenity smiles. "Honey, I've told you before that you probably have more actual psychic talent than you think. You've got an old soul."

"Can you teach me?"

Serenity looks at me, and then back at Jenna. "Teach you what?"

"How to be psychic?"

"Sugar, it doesn't work that way—"

"Well, how *does* it work?" Jenna presses. "You don't actually know, do you? You haven't had it work, in fact, for a really long time. So maybe trying something different isn't a bad idea."

She faces me. "I know you're all about facts and figures and evidence you can touch. But you're the one who said that sometimes when you look at the same thing a dozen times, it takes try number thirteen before what you're looking for jumps out at you. The wallet, and the necklace, and even the shirt with the blood on it—all that stuff's been waiting for a decade, and no one managed to find it." Then she turns to Serenity. "You know I said last night that you were in the right place at the right time whenever we found those things? Well, I was there, too. What if those signs weren't meant for you, but for me? What if the reason you can't hear my mom is because *I'm* the one she wants to talk to?"

"Jenna," Serenity says softly, "it would be the blind leading the blind."

"What have you got to lose?"

She barks a frustrated little laugh. "Oh, let's see. My self-respect? My peace of mind?"

"My trust?" Jenna says.

Serenity meets my gaze over the kid's head. *Help me*, she seems to be saying.

I understand why Jenna needs this: Otherwise, it's not a complete circle, it's a line, and lines unravel and send you off in directions you never intended to go. Endings are critical. It's why, when you're a cop and you tell parents their kid was just found in a car crash, they want to know exactly what happened—if there was ice on the road; if the car swerved to avoid the tractor-trailer. They need the details of those last few moments, because it is all they will have for the rest of their lives. It's why I should have told Lulu I did not want to go out with her ever again, because until I do, there will still be a sliver of hope in the door that she can wedge herself into. And it's why Alice Metcalf has haunted me for a decade.

I'm the guy who will never turn off a DVD, no matter how crappy the movie. I cheat and read the last chapter of a book first, in case I drop dead before I finish it. I don't want to be left hanging, wondering what will happen for eternity.

Which is kind of interesting, because it means that I—Virgil Stanhope, the master of practicality and the Grand Poobah of proof—must believe at least a tiny bit in some of the metaphysical fluff Serenity Jones peddles.

I shrug. "Maybe," I say to Serenity, "she has a point."

ALICE

One reason infants can't remember events when they are very small is that they don't have the language to describe them. Their vocal cords simply aren't equipped, until a certain age, which means instead they use their larynxes for emergency situations only. In fact, there is a direct projection that goes from the amygdala of an infant to his voice box, which can make that baby cry very quickly in a situation of extreme distress. It's such a universal sound that studies have been done showing that just about every other human—even college-age boys who have no experience with babies—will try to provide assistance.

As the child grows, the larynx matures and is capable of speech. The sound of crying changes as babies turn two or three, and as it does, people not only become less likely to want to help them but actually respond to the sound with feelings of annoyance. For this reason, children learn to "use their words"—because that's the only way they can get attention.

But what happens to that original projection, the nerve that runs from the amygdala to the larynx? Well . . . nothing. Even as vocal cords grow up around it like heliotrope, it stays where it was, and is very rarely used. Until, that is, someone leaps out from beneath your bed at right at sleepaway camp. Or you turn a corner in a dark alley and a raccoon jumps into your path. Or any other moment of complete and abject terror. When that happens, the "alarm" sounds. In fact, the noise you'll make is one you probably could not replicate voluntarily if you tried.

SERENITY

Back when I was good at this kind of thing, if I wanted to contact someone in particular who had passed, I'd rely on Desmond and Lucinda, my spirit guides. I imagined them as telephone operators connecting to a direct office line, because it was so much more efficient than having an open house and sorting through the hordes to find the individual I was hoping to speak to.

That's called open channeling: You put out your shingle, open for business, and brace yourself. It's a little like a news conference, with everyone shouting out questions at once. It's hell for the medium, incidentally. But I suppose it's no worse than putting out feelers and having no one show up.

I ask Jenna to find me a place that she thinks was special to her mother, and so the three of us trek back to the elephant sanctuary grounds, hiking to a spot where a giant oak with arms like a titan presides over a patch of purple mushrooms. "I come here sometimes to hang out," Jenna said. "My mom used to bring me."

It's almost ethereal, the way the mushrooms create a little magic carpet. "How come these don't grow everywhere?" I ask.

Jenna shakes her head. "I don't know. According to my mom's journals, it's where Maura's calf was buried."

"Maybe it's nature's way of remembering," I guess.

"More like it's the extra nitrates in the soil," Virgil mutters.

I shoot him a sharp glance. "No negativity. Spirits can feel that."

Virgil looks like he's about to have a root canal. "Should I just go over there or something?" He points off into the distance.

"No, we need you. This is about energy," I say. "That's how spirits manifest."

So we all sit down, Jenna nervous, Virgil reluctant, and me—well—desperate. I close my eyes and wing a little prayer to the powers that be: *I will never ask for my Gift again, if you let me do this one thing for her.*

Maybe Jenna is right; maybe her mother has been trying to communicate with her all along, but until now, she was unwilling to accept the fact that Alice was dead. Maybe she's finally ready to listen.

"So," Jenna whispers. "Should we hold hands?"

I used to have clients who would ask how they could tell their loved ones that they missed them. *You just did*, I would say. It really *is* that easy. So this is what I tell Jenna to do. "Tell her why you want to talk to her."

"Isn't that obvious?"

"To me, maybe not to her."

"Well." Jenna swallows. "I don't know if you can miss someone you can barely remember, but that's how I feel. I used to make up stories about why you hadn't been able to come back to me. You were captured by pirates, and you had to sail around the Caribbean looking for gold, but every night you looked at the stars and thought, *At least Jenna's seeing them, too.* Or you had amnesia, and you lived every day trying to find clues about your past, like all these tiny arrows that would point you back to me. Or you were on a secret mission for the country, and you couldn't reveal who you were without blowing your cover, and when you finally came home and flags were waving and crowds were cheering I'd get to see you as a hero. My English teachers said I had the most amazing imagination, but they didn't understand, it wasn't make-believe to me. It was so real that sometimes it hurt, like a stitch in your side when you run too hard, or the ache in your legs when you have growing pains. But I guess it turns out that maybe you *couldn't* come to me. So I'm trying to get to *you*."

I look at her. "Anything?"

Jenna takes a deep breath. "No."

What would make Alice Metcalf, wherever she is, stop and listen?

Sometimes the universe gives you a gift. You see a girl, terrified that her mother is gone forever, and you finally understand what needs to be done.

"Jenna." I gasp. "Can you see her?"

She jerks her head around. "Where?"

I point. "Right there."

"I don't see anything," she says, near tears.

"You have to focus . . ."

Even Virgil is leaning forward now, squinting.

"I can't . . ."

"Then you're not trying hard enough," I snap. "She's getting brighter, Jenna—that light, it's swallowing her. She's leaving this world. This is your last chance."

What would make a mother pay attention?

Her child's cry.

"*Mom!*" Jenna shrieks until her voice is hoarse, until she's bent forward in the field of violet mushrooms. "She's gone?" Jenna sobs, frantic. "She's really gone?"

I crawl forward to put my arm around her, wondering how to explain that I never really saw Alice at all, that I lied to get Jenna to pour her heart into that one desperate word. Virgil gets to his feet, scowling. "It's all crap, anyway," he mutters.

"What's this?" I ask.

I reach for the sharp object that has poked into my calf, making me wince. It's buried under the heads of the mushrooms, invisible, until I dig through their roots and find a tooth.

ALICE

All this time, I've said that elephants have an uncanny ability to compartmentalize death, without letting grief cripple them permanently.

But there is an exception.

In Zambia, a calf that had been orphaned by poaching began to hang around with a bunch of young bulls. Just as teenage males will walk up to each other and punch each other on the shoulder to say hello while girls hug, the behavior of these male elephants was very different from what a young female elephant might have experienced otherwise. They tolerated her hanging around because they could mate with her—like Anybodys in *West Side Story*—but they didn't really want her there. She calved when she was only ten years old, and since she had no mother to guide her and no practice being an allomother in a breeding herd, she treated that baby the way she had been treated by the bulls. When the baby fell asleep beside her, she would get up and walk away. The calf would wake up and start bellowing for its mother, but she would ignore the cries. By contrast, in a breeding herd, if a baby squeals, at least three females rush to touch it all over and see if it is okay.

In the wild, a young female is an allomother long before she bears her own offspring. She has fifteen years to practice being a big sister to the calves that are born to the herd. I'd seen calves approach young female elephants to suckle for comfort, even though the juveniles did not have breasts or milk yet. But the young female would put her foot forward, the way her mother and aunties did, and proudly pretend. She could act like a mother without having any of the real responsibility until she was ready. But when there is no family to teach a young female to raise her own calf, things can go horribly awry.

When I was working in Pilanesberg, this story repeated itself. There, young bulls that had been translocated began to charge vehicles. They killed a tourist. More than forty white rhino were found dead in the reserve before we realized that these subadult males were the ones who'd attacked them—highly aggressive behavior that was far from normal.

What is the common denominator for the odd behavior of the young female elephant that didn't care about her own calf and the belligerent pack of teenage bulls? Certainly there was a lack of parental guidance. But was that the only issue at play? All those elephants had seen their families killed in front of them, as a result of culling.

The grief that I have studied in the wild, where a herd loses an old matriarch, for example, must be contrasted to the grief that comes from observing the violent death of a family member—because the long-term effects are so markedly different. After a natural death, the herd encourages the grieving individual to eventually move on. After a mass killing by humans, there is—by definition—no herd left for support.

To date, the animal research community has been reluctant to believe that elephant behavior might be affected by the trauma of watching one's family being killed. I think this isn't scientific objection as much as it is political shame—after all, we humans have been the perpetrators of this violence.

At the very least, it is crucial when studying the grief of elephants to remember that death is a natural occurrence. Murder is not.

JENNA

"It's from Maura's calf," I tell Virgil, as we wait in the same room where we met Tallulah two hours ago. That's what I keep telling myself. Because it's really too hard to think about the alternative.

Virgil turns the tooth over in his hand. It makes me think of the descriptions of elephants rubbing their feet over tiny bits of ivory in my mother's journals, the ones my grandmother took from me. "It's too small to be from an elephant," he says.

"There are other animals around, too, you know. Fisher cats. Raccoons. Deer."

"I still think we should take it to the police," Serenity says.

I can't look her in the eye. She's explained her little trick, that my mother had never appeared (as far as she knew, anyway). But for some reason this only makes me feel worse.

"We will," Virgil agrees. "Eventually."

The door opens, and an air-conditioned breeze slices between us. Tallulah enters, looking pissed. "This is getting ridiculous. I don't work for you exclusively, Vic. I'm doing you a favor—"

He holds out the tooth. "I swear to God, Lu, if you do this I will never ask for anything again. We may have found the remains of Alice Metcalf. Forget the blood in the shirt. If you can find DNA in *this*—"

"I don't need to," Tallulah says. "This tooth doesn't belong to Alice Metcalf."

"I told you it came from an animal," I mutter.

"No, it's human. I worked in a dental office for six years, remember? It's a second molar, I could tell you that in my sleep. But it's a deciduous tooth."

"What's that?" Virgil asks.

Tallulah hands it back to him. "It belonged to a kid. Probably one under the age of five."

The pain that erupts in my mouth is like nothing I've ever felt. It's a cavern with lava inside. It's stars, exploding where my eyes were. It's a raw, shimmering nerve.

It's what happened.

When I wake up, my mother is gone, just like I knew would happen all along.

It is why I don't like to close my eyes, because when you do, people disappear. And if people disappear, you don't know for sure that they are ever coming back.

I can't see my mother. I can't see my father. I start to cry, and then someone else, someone different, picks me up. Don't cry, *she whispers.* Look. I have ice cream.

She shows me: It is the chocolate kind on a stick that I cannot eat fast enough, so it melts all over my hands and turns them the same color as Gideon's. I like when that happens, because then we match. She puts on my jacket, and my shoes. She tells me we are going on an adventure.

Outside, the world seems too big, like the way it feels when I close my eyes to go to sleep and worry that no one will ever find me again in all the darkness. That's when I start to cry, and my mother always comes. She lies down with me on the couch, until I stop thinking about how the night has swallowed us, and by the time I remember to start thinking about it again the sun is back.

But tonight my mother doesn't come. I know where we are going. It's the

place where I run in the grass sometimes, and where we go to watch the ele-
phants. But I'm not supposed to be in here anymore. My father shouts about
it. A cry swells in my throat, and I think it's going to come out, but she
bounces me on her hip and says, Now, Jenna, you and I, we're just going
to play a game. You love games, don't you?

And I do. I love games.

I can see the elephant in the trees, playing hide-and-seek. I think maybe
that is the game we are going to play. It's funny to think of Maura being It.
I giggle, wondering if she will tag us with her trunk.

That's better, *she says.* That's my good girl. That's my happy girl.

But I am not her good girl or her happy girl. I belong to my mother.

Lie down, *she tells me.* Lie on your back and look up at the stars.
Let's see if you can find the elephant in the spaces between them.

I like games, so I try. But all I see is the night, like a bowl knocked upside
down, and the moon falling out. What if the bowl drops and traps me? What
if I'm hidden, and my mother can't find me?

I start to cry.

Ssh, *she says.*

Her hand comes over my mouth and pushes down. I try to get away,
because I do not like this game. In her other hand she holds a big rock.

For a while I am asleep, I think. I dream my mother's voice. All I can
see are the trees leaning together, like they are trying to tell secrets, as
Maura bursts through them.

And then I am somewhere else, outside, above, around, watching
a picture of myself like when my mother puts on movies of me as a
baby and I see myself on TV, even though I am still here. I am being
carried, and there's a bounce to it, and we go a long way. When Maura
puts me down she rubs me with her back foot, and I think she would
have been so good at hide-and-seek after all, because she is so gentle.
When she pats me with her trunk, it is the way my mother taught me
to touch the baby bird that fell out of its nest this spring, like I am
pretending to be the wind.

Everything is soft: the secret of her breath on my cheek, the paintbrush branches she covers me with, like a blanket to keep me warm.

One minute Serenity is standing in front of me, and the next she's gone. "Jenna?" I hear her say, and then she's black-and-white, dappled like static.

I'm not in the lab. I'm not anywhere.

Sometimes the connection was crystal clear, and sometimes it was like being on a cell phone in the mountains, where you only catch every third word, Serenity had said.

I try to listen, but I'm only getting bits and pieces, and then the line goes dead.

ALICE

They never found her body.

I had seen it with my own eyes, and yet by the time the police got there, Jenna was gone. I read it in the newspapers. I couldn't tell them that I had seen her, lying there on the ground in the enclosure. I couldn't contact the police at all, of course, because then they would come for me.

So I scrutinized Boone from eight thousand miles away. I stopped journaling, because every day was another day I didn't have my child. I worried that by the time I reached the end of the book, the canyon between who I used to be and who I was now would be so broad that I wouldn't be able to see the far side. I saw a therapist for a while, lying about the circumstances of my sadness (a car accident) and using a fake name (Hannah, a palindrome, a word that means the same thing even if you turn it inside out). I asked him if it was normal after the disappearance of a child to still hear her crying in the night, and to wake up to that imaginary sound. I asked him if it was normal to wake up and, for a few glorious seconds, to believe she was on the other side of the wall, still sleeping. He said, *It is normal for* you, and that's when I stopped seeing him. What he *should* have said is: *Nothing will ever be normal again.*

. . .

In 1999, on the day I first learned of the cancer bleaching the life out of my mother, I'd driven blindly through the bush trying to outrun the news. To my shock, I'd found five elephant carcasses with their trunks cut away—and one very devastated, very frightened calf.

Her trunk was limp, her ears translucent. She could not have been more than three weeks old. But I had not known how to care for her, and her story did not end happily.

Neither did my mother's. I took a six-month leave of absence from my postdoctoral research to be with her until she passed away. When I returned to Botswana, I was all alone in the world, and threw myself into my work to avoid my grief—only to realize that these great, gracious elephants treated death so matter-of-factly. They did not find themselves thinking in circles: wondering why I had not called home on Mother's Day; questioning why I had always argued with my mother, instead of telling her how much I modeled myself on her self-sufficiency; proclaiming I was too busy with my work or too broke to fly home for Thanksgiving, Christmas, New Year's, my birthday. Those spiraling thoughts were killing me, each turn of the screw sinking me into a quicksand of guilt. Almost by accident, I began to study the grief of elephants. I told myself all sorts of excuses about why this was of visceral academic importance. But really, all I wanted to do was learn from the animals, which made it look so easy.

When I came back to Africa to heal from the second loss of my life, it was during a time when poaching was on the rise. The killers had gotten smarter. Where they used to shoot the oldest matriarchs and bulls with the biggest tusks, they now randomly targeted a young-ster, knowing that would make the herd bunch together in defense, which of course made it easier for poachers to kill en masse. For a long time no one wanted to admit that the elephants in South Africa were at risk again, but they were. Elephants in bordering Mozam-bique were being poached heavily, and the orphaned calves ran terri-fied back into the Kruger.

It was one of those calves that I found while I was hiding in South Africa. Her mother, a victim of poaching, had been shot in the shoul-der and collapsed with a festering wound. The calf, which refused to leave her mother's side, was surviving by drinking her urine. I knew as soon as I found them in the bush that the mother would have to be euthanized. I knew, too, this would lead to the death of her daughter.

I wasn't about to let that happen again.

I set up my rescue center in Phalaborwa, South Africa, modeling it on Dame Daphne Sheldrick's elephant orphanage in Nairobi. The philosophy is very basic, actually: When an elephant calf loses its family, you must provide a new one. Human keepers stay with the babies around the clock, offering bottles and affection and love, sleeping next to them at night. The keepers are rotated, so that no elephant becomes too attached to one person. I learned the hard way that if a calf forms too tight an attachment to one human, it can sink into depression if that caregiver takes even a day or two of vacation; the grief of that loss can even lead to death.

The caregivers never strike their charges, not even if they are acting out. A reprimand is usually enough; these babies so badly want to please their caregivers. Elephants remember everything, though, so it is important to always provide a little extra warmth later, lest the elephant think that it has been punished not for being naughty but because it is unlovable.

We feed the babies specially formulated milk, but also cooked oatmeal after five months—much like you'd introduce a human baby to solids. We supplement coconut oil to provide the fat content they would have had from their mothers' breast milk. We measure their progress by looking at their cheeks, which—like those of human infants—should be chubby. By age two, they are transferred to a new facility, one with slightly older elephants. Some of the caregivers will have rotated through the nursery, so that the newly transferred elephants recognize them. They recognize, too, their former companions who have already graduated from the nursery. The caregivers now sleep apart from the elephants, but within hearing range of the barn. Every day they lead the elephants out into the Kruger to be introduced to natural herds. The older elephants in the facility jostle to see who should act as matriarch. They take the new babies under their wings, with each female adopting her own calf to pretend-mother. The babies march out first, followed by the slightly older elephants. Eventually, they will integrate with a wild herd.

On a few occasions, we have even had elephants that are now wild return for help—once, when a young mother's milk dried up and she was in danger of losing her baby; and again when a nine-year-old bull got its leg caught in snare wire. They do not trust all humans indiscriminately, because they know firsthand the devastation people can cause. But they apparently don't judge all of us by those few, either.

The locals started to call me Ms. Ali—short for Miss Alice. And eventually, that became the name of the facility: *If an elephant calf is found, bring it to Msali.* If I do my job right, then these orphaned elephants eventually walk away, happily connected to a wild herd in the Kruger, where they belong. After all, we raise our own children to live without us, one day.

It's when they leave us too soon that nothing makes sense.

VIRGIL

Do you remember when you were a kid and you thought that clouds must feel like cotton, and then one day you learned that they are actually made up of droplets of water? That if you tried to stretch out on one and take a nap, you—you would just hurtle through it and smash on the ground?

First, I drop the tooth.

Except I don't, really. Because dropping it would suggest that I had been holding on to it, and it's more like there's no resistance to my hand anymore, so that the tooth just sinks through and pings on the floor. I look up, completely freaked out, and grab for the closest thing to me, which happens to be Tallulah.

My hand swipes right through her, and her body dissipates and curls as if it is made of smoke.

The same thing is happening to Jenna. She flickers in and out, her face twisted in fear. I try to call out her name, but it sounds like I'm at the bottom of a well.

Out of nowhere, I remember the long line of people at the airport who didn't react when I cut ahead, the ticket agent who took me aside and said, *You don't belong here.*

I remember the half dozen waitresses at the diner who walked obliviously past me and Jenna, until finally one bothered to notice. Was it just that the others couldn't see us?

I think of Abby, my landlady, dressed like she's stepped out of a Prohibition rally, which I now realize she probably *did*. I think of Ralph in the evidence room, who was old enough to be a fossil back when I was on the job. Tallulah, the waitress, the ticket agent, Abby, Ralph—all of these people, they were like me. *In* this world, but not *of* it.

And I remember the crash. The tears that were on my face, and the Eric Clapton song on the radio, and the way I pushed my foot down on the accelerator as I rounded the tight curve. I had stiffened my arms so that I wouldn't be a coward and jerk the car to safety, and at the last minute, I reached down and unbuckled my seat belt. The moment of impact was still a shock, even though I was expecting it— glass from the windshield raining over my face, the steering wheel column boring into my chest, my body being thrown. For one glorious, silent second, I flew.

On the long ride home from Tennessee, I had asked Serenity what she thought it felt like to die.

She thought for a second. *How do you fall asleep?*

What do you mean? I said. *It just happens.*

Right. You're awake, and then you drift for a moment, and then you're out like a light. Physically, you relax. Your mouth goes slack. Your heart rate slows down. You detach from the third dimension. There's some level of awareness, but for the most part, it's like you're in another zone. Suspended animation.

Now, I have something to add to that. When you're asleep, you think there's a whole other world that feels completely real while you are dreaming it.

Serenity.

I struggle to turn around so that I can see her. But I am suddenly so light and weightless that I don't even have to move, I just think and I'm where I need to be. I blink, and I can see her.

Unlike me, unlike Tallulah, unlike Jenna, her body has not dissipated or flickered. She is rock solid.

Serenity, I think, and her head turns.

"Virgil?" she whispers.

The last thought I have before I am gone completely is that in spite of what Serenity's said—in spite of what I had *believed*—she's not a lousy psychic. She's a fucking great one.

ALICE

I lost two babies, you know. One whom I knew and loved, and one I never met. I knew before I ran from the hospital that I had miscarried.

Now I have more than a hundred babies who consume every waking moment of my life. I have become one of those brittle, busy people who emerge from suffering like a tornado, turning so fast that we do not even realize how much self-destruction we're causing.

The worst part of my day is when it is over. If I could, I would be a caretaker, sleeping in the nursery with the calves. But someone needs to be the public face of Msali.

People here know I used to do research in the Tuli Block. And that I lived, for a brief while, in the States. But most people don't connect the academic I used to be to the activist I am now. I have not been Alice Metcalf for a long time.

As far as I'm concerned, she is dead, too.

When I wake up, I am screaming.

I do not like to sleep, and if I must, I want it to be thick and dreamless. For this reason I usually work myself to the bone, and pass out for two or three hours each night. I think about Jenna every day, every moment, but I have not thought about Thomas or Gideon for a long time. Thomas, I know, is still living in an institution. And a drunken Google search one night during the rainy season revealed that Gideon joined the army, and died in Iraq when an IED went off in a crowded public square. I printed out the newspaper article that talked about the posthumous Medal of Honor he had been awarded. He was buried at Arlington. I thought if I ever went back to the States, I might visit to pay my respects.

I lie in bed and stare at the ceiling, letting myself come back to this world slowly. Reality is frigid; I have to dip one toe at a time and grow accustomed to the shock before wading in further.

My gaze falls on the one remnant of my past life that I have with me in South Africa. It is a club roughly two and a half feet long, maybe eight inches wide. Made from a length of a young tree; the bark has been stripped away in random swirls and stripes. It's quite beautiful, like a native totem, but if you stare at it long enough, you would swear that there's a message to be decoded.

The Elephant Sanctuary in Tennessee, which became the home for our animals, had a website that let me track their progress, and also raised awareness of the work they were doing with elephants that had suffered in captivity. About five years ago, they held a Christmas auction to raise money. An elephant who had recently died had loved to pass the time by stripping trees of their bark in the most unlikely, delicate patterns; pieces of her "artwork" were being sold as donations.

I knew right away that this was Maura. I had watched her do this very thing dozens of times, pinning the logs we gave her for playtime against the bars of the barn stall, dragging her tusks to peel away the silver birch, the crusted pine.

It wasn't odd for the Msali Elephant Orphanage in South Africa to want to support the sanctuary's cause. They never knew I was the woman behind the check that was mailed; or that, when I received the item along with a picture of the elephant I had known so well—*R.I.P. Maura* written delicately across the top—I had cried for an hour.

For the past five years, that cylinder of wood has been hanging on the wall across from my bed. But as I watch now, it falls off the wall, hits the floor, and breaks into two clean halves.

At that moment, my phone rings.

"I'm looking for Alice Metcalf," a man says.

My hands turn to ice. "Who's calling?"

"Detective Mills from the Boone Police Department."

So this is it. So now everything has caught up with me. "This is Alice Metcalf," I murmur.

"Well, ma'am, with all due respect, you are one tough person to find."

I close my eyes, waiting to be blamed.

"Ms. Metcalf," the detective says, "we've found the body of your daughter."

SERENITY

One minute I am standing in a room at a private laboratory with three other people, and the next, I'm alone in that same room, on my hands and knees looking for a tooth that has fallen.

"Can I help you?"

I jam the tooth into my pocket and turn to find a bearded man in a white coat. I approach him hesitantly, tap him hard on the shoulder. "You're really *here*."

He recoils, rubbing his collarbone, looking at me like I'm crazy. Maybe I am. "Yes, but why are *you?* Who let you in?"

I am not about to tell him my suspicion: that the "person" who had let me in was an earthbound spirit, a ghost. "I'm looking for an employee named Tallulah," I say.

His features soften. "Were you a personal friend?"

Were. I shake my head. "An acquaintance."

"Tallulah passed away about three months ago. I guess it was a heart condition that wasn't diagnosed? She was in the middle of training for her first half marathon." He puts his hands in the pockets of his lab coat. "I'm really sorry to have to break the news to you."

I stumble out of the lab, passing the secretary at the front desk and a security guard and a girl sitting on the concrete wall outside making a phone call. I can't tell who is alive and who isn't, so I look down at the ground, refusing to make eye contact.

In my car I turn the air-conditioning on full blast and close my eyes. Virgil had been sitting right here. Jenna had been in the back-seat. I had talked to them, touched them, heard them clear as a bell.

Clear as a bell. I take my cell phone out and start scrolling until I get to the list of recent calls. Jenna's number should be there, from when she rang me in Tennessee, scared and alone. But then again, spirits manipulate energy all the time. The doorbell rings when no one is there; a printer goes on the fritz; lights flicker when there's no storm.

I hit Redial, and get a recording. The number is out of service.

This just can't be what I think it is. It can't, I realize, because plenty of people saw me in public with Virgil and Jenna.

I turn the ignition and scream out of the parking lot, driving back to the diner where the rude waitress had serviced our table this morn-ing. When I walk into the building, a bell jangles overhead; on the jukebox, Chrissie Hynde is singing about brass in her pocket. I crane my neck over the high red leather booths, looking for the woman who had taken our order this morning.

"Hey," I say, interrupting her as she is serving a table full of kids in soccer uniforms. "Do you remember me?"

"I never forget a three-cent tip," she mutters.

"How many people were at my table?"

I follow her to the cash register. "Is this a trick question? You were by yourself. Even though you ordered enough to feed half the kids in Africa."

I open up my mouth to point out that Jenna and Virgil ordered their own meals, but that's not true. They had told me what they wanted to eat, and had each gone to the restroom.

"I was with a man in his thirties—his hair was buzzed short, and he was wearing a flannel shirt even in this heat . . . and a teenage girl, who had a messy red braid . . ."

"Look, lady," the waitress says, reaching beneath the till to hand me a business card. "There are places you can go for help. But this isn't one of them."

I glance down: GRAFTON COUNTY MENTAL HEALTH SERVICES.

. . .

At the Boone Town Office, I sit down with a Red Bull and a stack of records from 2004: births, deaths, marriages.

I read Nevvie Ruehl's death certificate so many times I think I might have memorized it.

IMMEDIATE CAUSE OF DEATH: (A) Blunt force trauma
(B) DUE TO: Trampling by elephant
Manner of death: Accidental
PLACE OF INJURY: New England Elephant Sanctuary,
Boone, NH
DESCRIBE HOW INJURY OCCURRED: Unknown

Virgil's death certificate is the one I find next. He died in early December.

IMMEDIATE CAUSE OF DEATH: (A) Penetrating trauma to
the chest
(B) DUE TO: Motor vehicle accident
Manner of death: Suicidal

Jenna Metcalf does not have a death certificate, of course, because her body was never found.

Until that tooth.

There was no mistake in the medical examiner's report. Nevvie Ruehl was indeed the person who died at the sanctuary that night, and Alice Metcalf was the unconscious woman Virgil had brought to the hospital, who subsequently disappeared.

Following this logic, I finally know for sure why Alice Metcalf would not have communicated with me—or even Jenna, for that matter. Alice Metcalf, most likely, is still alive.

The last death certificate I look up belongs to Chad Allen, the teacher whose unattractive baby Jenna told me she'd been babysitting. "Did you know him?" the clerk says, looking over my shoulder.

"Not really," I murmur.

"It was a real shame. Carbon monoxide poisoning. The whole family died. I was in his calculus class the year it happened." She glances at the pile of papers on the table. "Do you need copies of these?"

I shake my head. I just needed to see them with my own eyes.

I thank her and walk back to my car again. I start driving aimlessly, because really, I have no idea where I go from here.

I think about the airline passenger en route to Tennessee, who buried his nose in his magazine when I started to have a conversation with Virgil. Which, to him, would have sounded like a crazy lady ranting.

I consider the time we all visited Thomas at Hartwick House—how the patients could easily see Jenna and Virgil, but the nurses and orderlies had spoken only to me.

I remember the very first day I met Jenna, when my client Mrs. Langham bolted. What was it she'd overheard me saying to Jenna? That if she didn't leave immediately, I was going to call the cops. But of course, Mrs. Langham couldn't see Jenna, plain as day, in my foyer. She would have thought my words had been directed at *her.*

I realize I have pulled into a familiar neighborhood. Virgil's office building is across the street.

I park and get out of the Bug. It's so hot today that the asphalt is swimming beneath my feet. It's so hot that the dandelions in the cracks of the sidewalk have collapsed.

The air in the building smells different. Mustier, older. The pane of glass in the door is cracked, but I never noticed before. I walk up to the second floor, to Virgil's office. It is locked, dark. Posted on the door is a sign: FOR RENT. CALL HYACINTH PROPERTIES, 603-555-2390.

My head buzzes. It's like the beginning of a migraine, but I think it is actually the sound of everything I know, everything I believed, being challenged.

I'd always thought there was a great divide between a spirit and a ghost—the former had made it smoothly to the next plane of existence; the latter had something anchoring it to this world. The ghosts I had met before were stubborn. Sometimes they did not realize they were dead. They'd hear the noises of people living in "their" houses, and assume *they* were the ones being haunted. They had agendas and disappointments and anger. They were trapped, and so I took it upon myself to help them get free.

But that was when I had the ability to recognize them for what they were.

I'd always thought there was a great divide between a spirit and a ghost—I just didn't realize how small the gap was between the dead and the living.

From my purse, I take the ledger that Jenna had signed when she first came to my apartment. There's her name, the adolescent cursive round as a string of bubbles. There is the address, 145 Greenleaf.

The residential neighborhood is exactly as it was three days ago, when Virgil and I had come to talk to Jenna, only to find that she didn't live at this address. Now I realize that it's entirely possible she *did*. It's just that the current owners wouldn't know that.

The same mother I spoke with before answers the doorbell. Her little boy still clings like a barnacle to her leg. "You again?" she says. "I already told you, I don't know that girl."

"I know. I'm sorry to bother you again. But I've had some . . . bad news recently about her. And I'm trying to make sense of some things." I rub my temples with my hands. "Can you just tell me when you bought your house?"

Behind me is the soundtrack of summer: children screaming as they squeal down a Slip'n Slide next door, a dog howling behind a fence, the drone of a ride-on lawn mower. In the distance is the calliope song of the ice cream truck. This street, it's teeming with life.

The woman looks like she's about to shut the door in my face, but something in my voice must stop her and make her reconsider. "Two thousand," she says. "My husband and I weren't married yet. The woman who lived here had D-I-E-D." She glances down at her son. "We don't like to talk about that sort of thing in front of him, if you know what I mean. He has an overactive imagination, and sometimes it keeps him up at night."

People are always afraid of things they don't understand, so they dress them up in ways that are understandable. An overactive imagination. A fear of the dark. Maybe even mental illness.

I crouch down so that I am face-to-face with her son. "Who do you see?" I ask.

"A grandma," he whispers. "And a girl."

"They're not going to hurt you," I tell him. "And they're real, no matter what anyone says. They just want to share your house, like when other kids at school want to share your toys."

His mother yanks him away. "I'm calling 911," she huffs.

"If your son had been born with blue hair, even though there had never been blue hair in your family tree, and even though you didn't understand how any baby could have blue hair because you'd never come across it in your life . . . would you still love him?"

She starts to close the door, but I put my hand on it, pressing back to keep it open. "Would you?"

"Of course," she says tightly.

"This isn't any different," I tell her.

Back in my car, I pull the ledger out of my purse and flip to the last page. Very slowly, like stitches being pulled, Jenna's entry disappears.

As soon as I tell the desk sergeant that I've found human remains, I am ushered into a back room. I give the detective—a kid named Mills, who looks like he has to shave only twice a week, tops—as much information as I can. "If you look in your files, you'll find a case from 2004 that involved a death there, back when it was an elephant sanctuary. I think this might be a second fatality."

He looks at me curiously. "And you know this . . . why?"

If I tell him I am a psychic, I'm going to wind up in a room next to Thomas at the mental institution. Either that or he'll slap handcuffs on me, sure I am a crackpot ready to confess to committing a homicide.

But Jenna and Virgil had seemed completely real to me. I had believed everything they said, when they spoke to me.

Goodness, child, isn't that what a psychic is supposed to do?

The voice in my head is faint but familiar. That southern drawl, the way the sentence rises and falls like music. I would know Lucinda anywhere.

An hour later, I am escorted to the nature preserve by two officers. *Escorted* is a fancy word for stuffed in the back of a cop car because no one trusts you. I hike through the tall grass, off the beaten path, the way Jenna used to do. The policemen carry shovels and sifter screens. We pass the pond where we found Alice's necklace, and after doubling back on a loop, I find the spot where the purple mushrooms have erupted beneath the oak tree.

"Here," I say. "This is where I found the tooth."

The cops have brought along a forensic expert. I don't know what he does—soil analysis, maybe, or bones, or both—but he plucks the head off one of the mushrooms. "*Laccaria amethystina,*" he pronounces. "It's an ammonia fungus. It grows on soil that has a high concentration of nitrogen."

Goddamn Virgil, I think. He was right. "It only grows here," I tell the expert. "Nowhere else in the preserve."

"That's consistent with a shallow grave."

"An elephant calf was also buried here," I say.

Detective Mills raises his brows. "You're just a font of information, aren't you?" The forensic expert directs two of the other officers, the ones who drove me here, to start digging systematically.

They begin on the other side of the tree, across from where Jenna and Virgil and I were yesterday, heaps of dirt shaking through the sifters to catch whatever decomposed fragments they might be lucky enough to unearth. I sit in the shade of the tree, watching the pile of soil rise higher. The policemen roll up their sleeves; one has to jump into the hole to toss the dirt out.

Detective Mills sits down beside me. "So," he says. "Tell me again what you were doing here when you found the tooth?"

"Having a picnic," I lie.

"By yourself?"

No. "Yes."

"And the elephant calf? You know about that because . . . ?"

"I'm an old friend of the family," I say. "It's why I also know that the Metcalfs' child was never found. I think that girl deserves a burial, don't you?"

"Detective?" One of the policemen waves Mills toward the pit that he's been digging. There is a gash of white in the dark soil. "It's too heavy to move," he says.

"Then dig around it."

I stand at the edge of the pit as the policemen swipe the dirt away from the bone by hand, like children making a sand castle when the water keeps rushing in to destroy their work. Finally, a shape emerges. The eye sockets. The holes where the tusks would have grown. The honeycomb skull, chipped off at the top. The symmetry, like a Rorschach blot. *What do you see?*

"I told you so," I say.

After that, no one doubts my word. The dig systematically moves in quadrants, counterclockwise. In Quadrant 2, they find only a piece of rusted cutlery. In Quadrant 3, I am listening to the rhythmic pull and swish of soil being lifted and tossed when suddenly the noise stops.

I look up and see one of the policemen holding the small fan of a broken rib cage.

"Jenna," I murmur, but all I hear in response is the wind.

For days, I try to find her on the other side. I imagine her upset and confused, and worst of all, alone. I beg Desmond and Lucinda to reach out to Jenna, too. Desmond tells me that Jenna will find me when she is ready. That she has a lot to process. Lucinda reminds me that the reason my spirit guides had been silent for seven years was because part of my journey was to believe in myself again.

If that's true, I ask her, then how come now I can't talk to the one damn spirit I want to?

Be patient, Desmond says. *You have to find what's lost.*

I have forgotten how Desmond is always full of New Age crypto-quotes like that. But instead of being annoyed by it, I just thank him for the advice, and wait.

I call Mrs. Langham and offer her a free reading to compensate for my rudeness. She's reluctant, but she is the kind of woman who walks through Costco just to eat the samples in lieu of paying for lunch out, so I know she will not turn me down. When she comes, for the first time I actually manage to talk to her husband, Bert, instead of faking it. And it turns out he's just as much of a jerk in the afterlife as he was when he was living. *What does she want from me now?* he gripes. *Always bitching. For Christ's sake, I thought she'd leave me alone when I finally died.*

"Your husband," I tell her, "is a selfish, unappreciative ass who would prefer that you stop hounding him." I repeat, verbatim, what he said.

Mrs. Langham is quiet for a moment. And then she replies, "That sounds exactly like Bert."

"Mm-hmm."

"But I loved him," she says.

"He doesn't deserve it," I tell her.

When she comes back a few days later, to get advice on finances and important decisions—she brings a friend. That friend calls her sister. Before I know it, I have clients again, more than I can squeeze into my calendar.

But I make time for a lunch break every afternoon, and I spend it at Virgil's grave. It wasn't all that hard to find, since there is only a single cemetery in Boone. I bring him things I think he'd like: egg rolls, *Sports Illustrated*, even Jack Daniel's. I pour the last over the grave. It will probably kill the weeds, at least.

I talk to him. I tell him about how the newspapers all credited me for helping the police locate Jenna's remains. How the story of the sanctuary's demise was splayed across the front pages like Boone's own version of *Peyton Place*. I tell him that I was a person of interest until Detective Mills proved that I was in Hollywood, taping one of my shows, the night that Nevvie Ruehl died.

"Do you talk to her?" I ask him, one afternoon when the sky is swollen with rain clouds. "Have you found her yet? I'm worried about her."

Virgil hasn't responded to me, either. When I ask Desmond and Lucinda about it, they say that if Virgil's crossed over, he may not yet understand how to visit the third dimension again. It takes a great deal of energy and focus. There's a learning curve.

"I miss you," I say to Virgil, and I mean it. I've had colleagues who pretend they like me but are really just jealous; I've had acquaintances who wanted to hang out with me because I was invited to Hollywood shindigs; but I have never really had many true friends. Certainly not one who was such a skeptic yet still accepted me unconditionally.

Most of the time I'm in the cemetery alone, except for the caretaker, who walks around with a weed whacker and a pair of Beats headphones. Today, though, there's something going on near the fence line. I see a small gathering of people. A funeral, maybe.

I realize that I know one of the men at the grave site. Detective Mills.

He recognizes me immediately. It's one of the perks of having pink hair. "Ms. Jones," he says. "Good to see you again."

I smile at him. "You, too." Glancing around, I realize there are not as many people here as I first thought. A woman in black, two more cops, and the caregiver, who is patting down the freshly turned earth on a tiny wooden casket.

"It's nice of you to come today," he says. "I'm sure Dr. Metcalf appreciates the support."

At the sound of her name, the woman turns around. Her pale, pinched face is framed by a lion's mane of red hair. It is like seeing Jenna again, in the flesh—a bit older, with a few more emotional scars.

She holds out her hand, this woman I tried so desperately to locate, who has literally landed in my path. "I'm Serenity Jones," I say. "I'm the one who found your daughter."

ALICE

There is not very much left of my baby.

I know, as a scientist, that a body in a shallow grave is more likely to decompose. That predators will scavenge away bits and pieces of the skeleton. That the remains of a child are porous, with more collagen, and more likely to decay in acidic soil. Still, I am not prepared for what I see when I view the tangle of narrow bones, like a parlor game of pickup sticks. A spine. A skull. One femur. Six phalanges.

The rest is gone.

I will be honest: I almost did not come back. There was a part of me waiting for the other shoe to drop; a niggling feeling that this was a trap to walk into, that I would be handcuffed when I stepped off the plane. But this was my baby. This was the closure I'd been waiting for, for years. How could I *not* go?

Detective Mills took care of all the arrangements, and I flew in from Johannesburg. I watch Jenna's coffin being lowered into the screaming mouth of the earth, and I think, *This is still not my daughter.*

After the brief interment, Detective Mills asks if he can get me something to eat. I shake my head. "I'm exhausted," I say. "I'm going to get some rest." But instead of heading back to the motel, I take the rental car to Hartwick House, where Thomas has lived for ten years now.

"I'm here to visit Thomas Metcalf," I tell the front desk nurse.

"And you are?"

"His wife," I say.

She looks at me, astonished.

"Is there a problem?" I ask.

"No." She recovers. "It's just that he rarely has visitors. He's down the hall, third room on the left."

There is a sticker on Thomas's door, a smiley face. I push the door open to see a man sitting by the window, his hands curled around a book in his lap. At first I am sure there has been a mistake—this is not Thomas. Thomas doesn't have white hair; Thomas isn't hunched over, with narrow shoulders and a sunken chest. But then he turns around, and a smile transforms him, so that the features of the man I remember ripple just beneath this new surface.

"Alice," he says. "Where on earth have you *been*?"

It is such a direct question, and such a ludicrous one given all that has passed, that I laugh a little. "Oh," I say. "Here and there."

"There's so much to tell you. I don't even know where to start."

Before he can begin, however, the door opens again and an orderly walks in. "I hear you've got a visitor, Thomas. Would you like to go down to the community room?"

"Hello," I say, introducing myself. "I'm Alice."

"I told you she'd come," Thomas adds, smug.

The orderly shakes his head. "I'll be damned. I have heard a *lot* about you, ma'am."

"I think Alice and I would prefer to talk in private," Thomas says, and I feel a knot in the pit of my stomach. I had hoped that a decade might dull the sharp edges of the conversation we need to have, but I had been naïve.

"No problem," the orderly says, winking at me as he backs out of the room.

This is the moment when Thomas will ask me what happened that night at the sanctuary. When we will pick up from the awful, electric spot where we left off. "Thomas," I say, falling on my sword. "I am so, so sorry."

"You should be," he replies. "You're second author on the paper. I know your work is important to you, and far be it from me to curb that, but you should understand better than anyone the need to be the first to publish before someone else steals your hypothesis."

I blink at him. "What?"

He hands me the book he's holding. "For God's sake, be careful. There are spies all over the place."

The book is by Dr. Seuss. *Green Eggs and Ham.*

"This is your article?" I ask.

"It's encoded," Thomas whispers.

I had come here hoping to find someone else who was a survivor, someone who might be able to take the worst night of my life and help me shoulder the memory. Instead, I found Thomas so trapped by the past that he can't accept the future.

Maybe that is healthier.

"Do you know what Jenna did today?" Thomas says.

Tears spring to my eyes. "Tell me."

"She took all the vegetables she doesn't like to eat out of the re-frigerator and said she was going to give them to the elephants. When I told her they were good for her, she said this was just an experiment and the elephants were her control group." He grins at me. "If she's this smart at three, what will she be like at twenty-three?"

There was a moment, before everything went wrong, before the sanctuary had failed and Thomas had gotten sick, when we had been happy together. He had held our newborn in his arms, speechless. He had loved me, and he had loved her.

"She'll be amazing," Thomas says, answering his own rhetorical question.

"Yes," I say, my voice thick. "She will."

At the motel, I take off my shoes and my jacket and pull the shades tight. I sit down on the swivel chair at the desk and stare into the mirror. This is not the face of someone at peace. In fact, I do not at all feel the way I thought I would if I ever received a call that my daughter

had been found. This was supposed to be what I needed to stop strad-
dling the distance between *reality* and *what-if.* But I still feel rooted.
Stuck.

The blank face of the television mocks me. I do not want to turn
it on. I don't want to listen to newscasters telling me of some new hor-
ror in the world, of the limitless supply of tragedy.

When there is a knock on the door, I startle. I don't know anyone
in this town. It could only be one thing.

They've come for me, after all, because they know what I did.

I take a deep breath, resolved. It's all right, really. I was expecting
this. And no matter what happens, I know where Jenna is now. The
babies in South Africa are under the care of people who know how to
raise them. Really, I am ready to go.

But when I open the door, the woman with pink hair is standing
on the threshold.

Cotton candy, that's what it looks like. I used to feed it to Jenna,
who had such a sweet tooth. In Afrikaans, it's called *spook asem.* Ghost
breath.

"Hello," she says.

Her name. It's something like Tranquility . . . Sincerity . . .

"I'm Serenity. I met you earlier today."

The woman who had found Jenna's remains. I stare at her, wondering what she could possibly want. A reward, maybe?

"I know I said I found your daughter," she begins, her voice shaking. "But I lied."

"Detective Mills said you brought him a tooth—"

"I did. But the thing is, Jenna found *me* first. A little over a week
ago." She hesitates. "I'm a psychic."

Maybe it is the stress of having seen my daughter's bones interred;
maybe it is realizing that Thomas has the good fortune to be trapped
in a place where none of this ever happened; maybe it is the twenty-
two hours of flying and the jet lag I'm still battling. For all of these
reasons, rage rises in me like a geyser. I plant my hands on Serenity's
arms and shove her. "How *dare* you?" I say. "How dare you make light
of the fact that my daughter's dead?"

She topples back, caught off guard by my physical attack. Her giant purse spills onto the floor between us.

She falls to her knees, sweeping the contents back inside. "That's the *last* thing I'd ever do," she says. "I came to tell you how much Jenna loved you. She didn't realize she was dead, Alice. She thought you'd left her behind."

What this hack is doing is deadly, dangerous. I'm a scientist, and what she's saying is not possible, but it can still wreak havoc with my heart.

"What did you come here for?" I say, bitter. "Money?"

"I could see her," the woman insists. "I could talk to her, and touch her. I didn't know Jenna was a spirit; I thought she was a teenage girl. I watched her eat and laugh and ride a bike and check the voice mail on her cell phone. She looked and sounded as real to me as you do, right now."

"Why *you*?" I hear myself ask. "Why would she have come to *you*?"

"Because I was one of the few who noticed her, I guess. Ghosts are all around us, talking to each other and checking into hotels and eating at McDonald's and doing what you and I would ordinarily do—but the only people who see them are the ones who can suspend disbelief. Like little children. Mentally ill folks. And psychics." She hesitates. "I think she *came* to me because I could hear her. But I think she *stayed* because she knew—even if I didn't—that I could help her find you."

I am crying now. I cannot see clearly. "Go away. Just go away."

She gets to her feet, about to say something, and then on second thought just inclines her head and starts walking down the hall.

Glancing at the floor, I see it. A small piece of paper, something that fell from her purse that she accidentally left behind.

I should close the door. I should go inside. But instead I crouch down and pick it up: this tiny, origami elephant.

"Where did you get this?" I whisper.

Serenity stops moving. She turns, so that she can see what I am holding. "From your daughter."

Ninety-eight percent of science is quantifiable. You can do research until you are exhausted; you can count repetitive or self-isolating or aggressive behaviors until your vision blurs, you can cross-reference those behaviors as indicators of trauma. But you will never be able to explain what makes an elephant leave a beloved tire behind on the grave of its best friend; or what finally makes a mother step away from her dead calf. That is the 2 percent of science that can't be measured or explained. And yet that does not mean it doesn't exist.

"What else did Jenna say?" I ask.

Slowly, Serenity takes a step toward me. "Lots of things. How you worked in Botswana. How you had sneakers that matched hers. How you took her into the elephant enclosures, and how angry it made her father. How she never stopped looking for you."

"I see," I say, closing my eyes. "And did she also tell you I'm a murderer?"

By the time Gideon and I reached the cottage, the front door was wide open, and Jenna was gone. I could not breathe; I could not think.

I ran into Thomas's office, thinking maybe he had the baby in there. But Thomas was alone, his head pillowed on his arms, a confetti of spilled pills and a half-empty bottle of whiskey on the desk beside him.

My relief at seeing him passed out without my daughter nearby faded as I realized I still had no idea where Jenna was. Just like before: She had awakened, and found me missing. Her worst nightmare, now morphing into mine.

Gideon was the one who had a plan; I could not think clearly. He radioed Nevvie, who was making the night rounds, and when she didn't answer we split up to search. He headed for the Asian barn; I ran into the African enclosure. This was a déjà vu, so similar to the last time Jenna went missing that I was not surprised when I saw Nevvie standing just inside the African fence. Do you have the baby? *I cried.*

It was pitch black, and the clouds moved across the moon, so that the little I could make out was silvered and erratic, like an old movie whose frames don't quite fit together. But I noticed the way she froze when I said the word baby. *The way her mouth curved into a smile as sharp as a blade.* How does it feel, *she asked*, to lose your daughter?

I looked around wildly, but it was too dark to see more than a few feet in front of me. Jenna! *I screamed, but there was no answer.*

I grabbed Nevvie. Tell me what you did with her. *I tried to shake the answers out of her. And the whole time, she just smiled and smiled.*

Nevvie was strong, but I finally got my hands around her throat. Tell me, *I shouted at her. She gasped, twisted. If it was dangerous to walk in the enclosures in the day, because of the holes the elephants dug for water, then it was an absolute minefield at night—but I didn't care. All I wanted were answers.*

We stumbled forward; we stumbled back. And then I tripped.

Lying on the ground was Jenna's small, bloody body.

The sound that a heart makes, when it is breaking, is raw and ugly. And anguish, it's a waterfall.

How does it feel to lose your daughter?

Rage poured through me, coursed through my body, lifting me as I lunged for Nevvie. You did this to her, *I yelled, even as, silently, I thought:* No. I did.

Nevvie was stronger than me, fighting for her life. I was fighting for my child's death. And then I was falling into an old water hole. I tried to grab on to Nevvie, to anything, before the world went black.

The next part, I can't remember. Although God knows I have tried every day for the past ten years.

When I came to, it was still dark out, and my head was throbbing. Blood ran down my face and the back of my neck. I crawled out of the water hole I had pitched into, too dizzy to stand, getting my bearings on my hands and knees.

Nevvie stared up at me, the top of her skull cracked open.

And the body of my child, it was missing.

I cried, backing away, shaking my head, trying to unsee the empty spot where Jenna had been. I scrambled to my feet and ran. I ran because I had lost my daughter, two times over. I ran because I could not remember if I had killed Nevvie Ruehl. I ran until the entire world turned upside down, and I woke up in the hospital.

• • •

"The nurse was the one who told me Nevvie was dead—and that Jenna was missing," I say to Serenity, who is sitting on the swiveling desk chair while I perch on the edge of the bed. "I didn't know what to do. I had seen my daughter's body, but I couldn't tell anyone that I'd seen it, because then they would have known I had killed Nevvie, and they would have arrested me. I thought maybe Gideon had found Jenna and moved her, but then he also would have seen that I'd killed Nevvie—and I didn't know if he'd already called the police."

"But you didn't kill her," Serenity tells me. "The body was trampled."

"After."

"She could have fallen, like you did, and struck her head. And even if you'd been the one to make that happen, the police would have understood."

"Until they found out that I was sleeping with Gideon. And if I lied about that, I could be lying about everything." I look down at my lap. "I panicked. It was stupid to run, but I did. I just wanted to clear my head, to think through what I should do. All I could see was how selfish I'd been, and what it had cost me: the baby. Gideon. Thomas. The sanctuary. Jenna."

Mom?

I am staring past the face of Serenity Jones into the mirror behind the motel desk. But instead of seeing her pink updo, the hazy reflection is a messy auburn French braid.

It's me, she says.

I draw in my breath. "Jenna?"

Her voice leaps, triumphant. *I knew it. I knew you were alive.*

That's all it takes to make me admit what I ran from a decade ago, what made it possible to run in the first place. "I knew you *weren't*," I whisper.

Why did you leave?

Tears fill my eyes. "That night, on the ground, I saw your . . . I knew you were gone. I would never have left otherwise. I would have spent forever trying to find you. But it was too late. I couldn't save you, so I tried to save myself."

I thought you didn't love me.

"I loved you." I gasp. "So, so much. But not very well."

In the mirror behind the motel desk, behind the chair where Serenity is sitting, the image crystallizes. I see a tank top. The tiny gold hoops in her ears.

I swivel the desk chair so that Serenity is facing the mirror.

Her forehead is broad and her chin is pointed, like Thomas's. She has the freckles that were the bane of my existence at Vassar. Her eyes are exactly the same shape as mine.

She has grown up beautiful.

Mom, she says. *You loved me perfectly. You kept me here long enough to find you.*

Could it be as simple as that? Could love be not grand gestures or empty vows, not promises meant to be broken, but instead a paper trail of forgiveness? A line of crumbs made of memories, to lead you back to the person who was waiting?

It wasn't your fault.

That is when I break down. I don't think, until she speaks the words, that I knew how badly I needed to hear them.

I can wait for you, my girl says.

I meet her gaze in the mirror. "No," I say. "You waited long enough. I love you, Jenna. I always have and I always will. Just because you leave someone doesn't mean you ever let them go. Even when you couldn't see me, you knew deep down I was still there. And even when I can't see you," I say, my voice breaking, "I'll know that, too."

The minute I say this, I no longer see her face—just Serenity's reflection, next to mine. She seems shocked, empty.

But Serenity isn't looking at me. She's gazing at a vanishing point in the mirror, where Jenna is now walking, lanky and angular, all elbows and knees that she will never grow into. As she gets smaller and smaller, I realize that she's not heading away from me but moving toward someone.

I don't recognize the man who is waiting for her. He has close-cropped hair and wears a blue flannel shirt. It's not Gideon; I've never met this person before. But when he holds up a hand in greeting, Jenna waves back, excited.

I do recognize the elephant standing beside him, however. Jenna stops in front of Maura, who wraps her trunk around my baby, giving her the embrace I can't, before they all turn and walk away.

I watch. I keep my eyes wide open, until I cannot see her anymore.

JENNA

Sometimes, I go back and visit her.

I go during the in-between time, when it's not night and it's not morning. She always wakes up when I come. She tells me about the orphans who have arrived at the nursery. She talks about the speech she gave to the wildlife service last week. She tells me about a calf that has adopted a little dog as a friend, just like Syrah did with Gertie.

I think of these as the bedtime stories I missed.

My favorite is a true tale about a man from South Africa who was called the Elephant Whisperer. His real name was Lawrence Anthony, and, like my mother, he did not believe in giving up on elephants. When two particularly wild herds were going to be shot for the destruction they'd caused, he saved them and brought them to his game reserve to be rehabilitated.

When Lawrence Anthony died, the two herds traveled through the Zululand bush for more than half a day and stood outside the wall that bordered his property. They had not been near the house in over a year. The elephants stayed for two days, silent, bearing witness.

No one can explain how the elephants knew that Anthony had died.

I know the answer.

If you think about someone you've loved and lost, you are already with them.

The rest is just details.

AUTHOR'S NOTE

Although this book is fiction, the plight of elephants worldwide is, sadly, not. Poaching for the commercial ivory trade has been increasing, due to widespread poverty in Africa and the growing market for ivory in Asia. There are documented cases in Kenya, Cameroon, and Zimbabwe; in the Central African Republic; in Botswana and Tanzania; and in the Sudan. There's a rumor that Joseph Kony funded his Ugandan resistance army with the illegal sale of ivory poached from the Democratic Republic of Congo. Most illegal shipments are sent across badly regulated borders to ports in Kenya and Nigeria, and shipped to Asian countries like Taiwan and Thailand and China. Although Chinese officials say that they have banned the trade of ivory products, Hong Kong authorities recently seized two shipments of illegal ivory from Tanzania whose value totaled more than $2 million. Not long before this writing, forty-one elephants were killed in Zimbabwe by poisoning their water hole with cyanide, netting $120,000 worth of ivory.

You can tell that an elephant society is being poached when the population dynamic becomes skewed. At the age of fifty, the tusk of a male elephant will weigh more than seven times that of a female, so males are always the first targets. Then poachers come for the females. The matriarch is the largest, often with the heaviest tusks—and when matriarchs are killed, they are not the only casualties. You have to figure in the number of calves that are left behind. Joyce Poole and Iain Douglas-Hamilton are among the experts who have worked with elephants in the wild and who have dedicated themselves to stopping poaching and spreading awareness of the effects of the illegal ivory trade, including the disintegration of elephant society. Current estimates are that 38,000 elephants are being slaughtered each year in Africa. At this rate, elephants on that continent will all be gone in less than twenty years.

Yet poaching is not the only threat to elephants. They are captured for sale to elephant-back safaris, zoos, and circuses. Back in the 1990s in South Africa, when the elephant population grew too high, there was systematic culling. Entire families were darted from helicopters with scoline, which paralyzed them but did not render them unconscious. So they were fully aware as humans landed on the ground and moved systematically through the herd, shooting each elephant behind the ear. Eventually the hunters realized that the calves would not leave their mothers' bodies, so they were staked to the corpses while the hunters got them ready for translocation. Some were sold abroad to circuses and zoos.

It is those elephants that are sometimes lucky enough to end their lives of captivity at places like The Elephant Sanctuary in Hohenwald, Tennessee. Although Thomas Metcalf's New England Elephant Sanctuary is a fictional one, The Elephant Sanctuary in Tennessee is, fortunately, real. Moreover, the fictional elephants I created were all based on the true, heartbreaking stories of elephants from the Tennessee sanctuary. Like Syrah in this book, Tarra the elephant had a constant canine companion. Wanda's real-life counterpart—Sissy—survived a flood. Lilly was based on Shirley, who endured a ship fire and an attack that left her with a badly broken hind leg, due to which she still moves awkwardly. Olive and Dionne, seen together throughout the book, are pseudonyms for the inseparable Misty and Dulary. Hester, the African elephant with an attitude, is based on Flora, who was orphaned in Zimbabwe as a result of mass culling. These ladies are the lucky ones—residents of only a handful of sanctuaries in the world dedicated to allowing elephants who have lived and worked in captivity to retire in peace. Their stories are only a tiny sample of those of countless elephants who are still being mistreated by circuses or kept in adverse conditions at zoos.

I'd urge any animal lover to consider visiting www.elephants.com— the website for The Elephant Sanctuary in Hohenwald, Tennessee. In addition to watching live elecams (be careful, you will lose hours of valuable work time), you can "adopt" an elephant, or make a donation in memory of an animal lover, or feed all the elephants for one day— no amount is too small, and all are so greatly appreciated. Please also visit the Global Sanctuary for Elephants (www.globalelephants.org), which is helping establish holistic, natural elephant sanctuaries world-wide.

For those who would like to learn more about poaching and/or elephants in the wild, or to contribute to those fighting to get inter-national restrictions in place to prevent poaching, please visit: www.elephantvoices.org, www.tusk.org, www.savetheelephants.org.

Finally, I'd like to list the materials that were instrumental to me during the writing of this novel. Much of Alice's research was borrowed from the remarkable real-life studies and insights of these men and women.

Anthony, Lawrence. *The Elephant Whisperer.* Thomas Dunne Books, 2009.

Bradshaw, G. A. *Elephants on the Edge.* Yale University Press, 2009.

Coffey, Chip. *Growing Up Psychic.* Three Rivers Press, 2012.

Douglas-Hamilton, Iain, and Oria Douglas-Hamilton. *Among the Elephants.* Viking Press, 1975.

King, Barbara J. *How Animals Grieve.* University of Chicago Press, 2013.

Moss, Cynthia. *Elephant Memories.* William Morrow, 1988.

Moss, Cynthia J., Harvey Croze, and Phyllis C. Lee, eds. *The Amboseli Elephants.* University of Chicago Press, 2011.

Masson, Jeffrey Moussaieff, and Susan McCarthy. *When Elephants Weep.* Delacorte Press, 1995.

O'Connell, Caitlin. *The Elephant's Secret Sense*. Free Press, 2007.

Poole, Joyce. *Coming of Age with Elephants*. Hyperion, 1996.

Sheldrick, Daphne. *Love, Life, and Elephants*. Farrar, Straus & Giroux, 2012.

And dozens of academic papers written by researchers who continue to study elephants and elephant society.

There were many moments during the writing of this book when I thought that elephants may be even more evolved than humans—when I studied their grieving habits, and their mothering skills, and their memories. If you take away anything from this novel, I hope it is an awareness of the cognitive and emotional intelligence of these beautiful animals—and the understanding that it is up to all of us to protect them.

JODI PICOULT, *September 2013*

ACKNOWLEDGMENTS

It takes an entire herd to raise an elephant calf. Likewise, it takes many people to bring a book to fruition. I am indebted to all these "allomothers" who helped shepherd my book toward publication.

Thanks to Milli Knudsen and to Manhattan Assistant District Attorney Martha Bashford for information on cold cases; to Detective Sergeant John Grassel of the Rhode Island State Police for his extensive tutorial in detective work and for always answering my frantic questions. Thanks to Ellen Wilber for the sports trivia and to Betty Martin for knowing about (among other things) mushrooms. Jason Hawes of *Ghost Hunters*, who was my friend long before he was a TV star, introduced me to Chip Coffey—a remarkable, talented psychic who wowed me with his insight, who shared his own experiences, and who made me understand how Serenity's mind would work. Any of you nonbelievers out there—an hour in Chip's presence will change your mind.

The Elephant Sanctuary is a real place in Hohenwald, Tennessee—twenty-seven hundred acres of refuge for African and Asian elephants who have spent their lives either performing or in captivity. I am so grateful to them for allowing me into their facility to see the astounding work they do to heal these animals physically and psychologically. I spoke with people who either are still working at or were associated with the sanctuary: Jill Moore, Angela Spivey, Scott Blais, and a dozen current caregivers. Thank you for grounding my fiction in reality, but, more important, thank you for the work you do every day.

Thanks to Anika Ebrahim, my South African publicist at the time, who didn't bat an eye when I told her I needed an elephant expert. Thanks to Jeanetta Selier, senior scientist at the Applied Biodiversity Research Division at the South African National Biodiversity Institute, for being that storehouse of wild elephant knowledge, for personally introducing me to the herds in the Tuli Block of Botswana, and for vetting the accuracy of this book. I am grateful to Meredith Ogilvie-Thompson of Tusk for introducing me to Joyce Poole, who is as close as you can get to a rock star in the world of elephant research and conservation. Being able to speak firsthand to someone who has written some of the most seminal literature on elephant behavior is still mind-blowing to me.

I need to thank Abigail Baird, associate professor of psychology at Vassar College, for being my "research bitch," for explaining cognition and memory and academic articles to me in a way that I could understand them, and for rocking a black fleece in 110-degree weather like no one else: There is no one with whom I'd rather piece together an elephant skeleton. Also part of the Botswana Brigade: my daughter, Samantha van Leer, the "bitchlet"—thanks for taking orders, for documenting the research with more than a thousand photographs, for naming her furry blue steering wheel cover Bruce, and for always having exactly what I needed hidden somewhere in her voluminous pants. In the wild, an elephant mother and daughter stay in close proximity their whole lives; I hope I am that lucky.

This book marks the beginning of a new home for me at Ballantine Books/Random House. I am so honored to be part of this incredible crew, who have been working behind the scenes for a year with explosive excitement about this novel. Thanks to Gina Centrello, Libby McGuire, Kim Hovey, Debbie Aroff, Sanyu Dillon, Rachel Kind, Denise Cronin, Scott Shannon, Matthew Schwartz, Joey McGarvey, Abbey Cory, Theresa Zoro, Paolo Pepe, and the dozens of other foot soldiers in their invincible army. Your enthusiasm and your creativity blow me away every single day; not all authors are this lucky. Thanks to the dream team of PR: Camille McDuffie, Kathleen Zrelak, and Susan Corcoran: Best. Cheerleaders. Ever.

Working with a new editor is a little like an old-world Orthodox wedding: You trust people to pick your partner, but until you lift that veil, you don't really know what you're getting. Well, Jennifer Hershey is—by those standards—a stunner of an editor. Her insight, her grace, and her intelligence shine through every comment and suggestion. I think Jen's heart bleeds as much across every page of this novel as mine does.

To Laura Gross—what can I say, except that my life would not be what it is without your support and your tenacity. I adore you.

To Jane Picoult, my mother—who was my first reader forty years ago and is still my first reader today. It's because of the relationship and love between us that I could write Jenna in the first place.

Finally, to the rest of my family—Kyle, Jake, Sammy (again), and Tim—this is a book about keeping the people we love close to us; you guys are the reason I know why that's the most important thing on earth.

ABOUT THE AUTHOR

Jodi Picoult is the author of twenty-two novels, including the #1 *New York Times* bestsellers *Lone Wolf, Between the Lines, Sing You Home, House Rules, Handle with Care, Change of Heart, Nineteen Minutes,* and *My Sister's Keeper.* She lives with her husband and three children.

DATE DUE